BOOK

3

WARLORD

OF THE BROKEN LAND

DOC SPEARS

WARGATE

An imprint of Galaxy's Edge Press
PO BOX 534
Puyallup, Washington 98371
Copyright © 2022 by Doc Spears
All rights reserved.

Paperback ISBN: 978-1-949731-87-3
Hardcover ISBN: 978-1-949731-88-0

www.wargatebooks.com

✤ ✤ ✤

Benjamin Colt has been close to death many times. As a Green Beret on an alien world—the victorious Warlord of Mihdradahl—he was used to it. What he was not accustomed to was having no deadly threat facing him on all sides. With the very real possibility of peace at hand, he was more than ready for a relatively pleasant cold war with the Yellow kingdom of Annameria and the prospect of plenty of time to consider his impending fatherhood.

It's when the most complete victory is at hand that the greatest upsets happen. And in the span of a single morning, his world is thrown into turmoil.

A new enemy presents and with them, they bring the end of Benjamin Colt's peace, his purpose for living, and his entire future.

The Warlord wages battle as no other. But against an enemy that undermines the faith of a people, how is he to fight? What weapon can be wielded to prevent a civil war among the citizens of Queen Talis Darmon's kingdom? And in the chaos of their division, will the enemy to their south see it as the perfect time to invade?

Benjamin Colt draws on every source of wisdom and experience he has to battle enemies known and disguised. Because he must also learn the way to fight an invisible foe that tears at the fabric of Talis Darmon's mind, one driving her into a slow madness of forlorn that can only end in oblivion.

✤ ✤ ✤

01

"BENJAMIN COLT, BEFORE YOU DEPART ON TODAY'S ADVENTURE, SHALL we wish our awaited a good morning?"

"I wouldn't have it any other way, Talis Darmon." It was our ritual that every morning and nightfall we joined to lay hands on the egg. The incubator had a place of honor next to our bedroom, as it did in most expecting Vistaran homes. Inside the creche, a red and blue speckled egg lay nestled on a pillow. By day, the sun bathed our child's egg with the view of grand Shansara. By night, the soothing glow of the towers, spires, and floating sky bridges called, inspiring mystery and wonder for the growing child within to come explore what would someday be the seat of the kingdom for its future king or queen.

Shansara still inspired me that way. Its perfection was a constant reminder that in the great balance of things, wherever there was such beauty, somewhere existed forces offended and jealous. And my mission was to fight them, in whatever form they appeared.

It'd been three months since our return from battling the Karnak and the ultimate source of their evil. At first sight, the thumb-sized egg intimidated me. Me. Who'd battled armies of four-armed warriors on the sands, and living nightmares in a hell below. The egg was just too small, too frail appearing. How could it to hold the child I would someday hold against my skin? But each morning since, we marveled to find that while we'd slept, the egg had grown. It was now so big I could fully embrace the warmth of the rounded perfection beneath my spread fingers, hers beside mine as we caressed and coaxed our child.

1

Did it freak me out that our baby would hatch from an egg? No more than having a Tarn for an adopted sister. Or her even more menacing father as one of my closest friends. Or that I was a virtual superman. With an eight-legged dog. That I was a Warlord in service to my wife, the queen. Or any number of things. But, as I felt the first stirrings within the growing egg, it was like everything else on Mars. As real as real could be. And if it wasn't? If it was all some delusion? Then leave me in the nuthouse.

"Someone's anxious to stretch their legs," I said.

"Our child dreams of a father who will teach her to ride, to fight, to know duty and bravery."

"I'll teach her more than that, Talis Darmon. But are you so sure it's a girl?"

"Not at all. I could touch the essence of our awaited and know, but we agreed it should be a surprise. Yet I cannot speak of our child as 'it.'"

Boy or girl, it didn't matter to me. What mattered was that the Mars I'd been thrust upon was a place of desolate wonder, mystery, and danger. A brutal and violent world. One made even more so by my A-Team's arrival. But, maybe, after all that my friends and I had done to right the wrongs of the renegade members of my old team, our child would inherit a Vistara different from the one I'd fought on, both above and below.

I slipped my arms around my wife. "And you'll teach her the ways of beauty and grace, my princess. But if the poor kid inherits any of my looks, we'd better hope it's a boy in there."

"You are beautiful, my husband. Have no doubt that our child will be, too." She put her lips close to the egg. "Good morning, awaited. You are loved and eagerly anticipated. Dream well today." Talis Darmon returned the clear cover over the cradle.

The egg would grow for another year before the celebration of the birth day and the revelation of the face we could only imagine. But what lay here in the safety of our home was more than a gift for just us. Inside was a new life, growing in step with a resurrected world, one rising from a long sleep to realize its greatness returned. Our child would be a symbol of all that Vistara could become.

"Are you off then, Benjamin Colt?"

I no longer needed my decipher to understand Mihdra. And it was through newfound appreciation of the nuances in her tone that she made her true inquiry known to me.

What are you and your idiot friends up to today?

I may be Warlord. Charged with absolute authority in all matters existential to her kingdom. But she was the queen. And my wife. The high-wire act I constantly fought to pull off with the one who wore both crowns—balancing what was the appropriate amount of detail about what I was up to and how I did things—it was a struggle. What I'd learned was, if I was light on specifics to my queen, my wife worried. If I told my wife too much, my queen sometimes bristled that she was left out of the action.

Though she was the perfect combination of scholar, warrior, and almost every other thing, Talis Darmon was no different from any other member of my team. If it was a choice between action and a day locked in the administration of a kingdom—action won out.

It's not that I hesitated telling my queen the truth about the day's activities because I thought it would tempt her to join us. It was because the last time I'd told my wife about a similar activity, the contemplation of what I'd be doing caused her to lose her lunch. But anytime I'd ever thought I was sparing her worry by omitting the details and the danger—you know what happened. The queen would eventually hear from someone else what I'd been up to, and a royal ass-chewing followed.

I was the only one alive who could write the book on how to be a Warlord. How to be a good husband? All I'd really figured out was—I'd never be one of the Flying Wallendas. I couldn't balance a teacup using both hands.

"Me and the guys are testing another one of Karlo's new toys today, sweetie." I told her the nuts and bolts of what we had planned, unsure if I was being cruel or kind with my honesty.

"Ugh. Benjamin Colt, is it really necessary? And must *you* be the one to test such a thing?"

At least this time, she wasn't overcome by nausea at the thought. I let it alone and made my move to break contact by throwing a smoke grenade to obscure my escape.

"Always my full name. Sweetheart, we're alone. Call me Benjamin. Or Ben. It's cumbersome and unnecessary to always use my full name. Try it." Thank God, I hadn't introduced myself to her that first time as Sergeant Colt. I might have heard that for the rest of my life.

"Ben." She made a sour face. "So short and abrupt. It holds the same sound as a visceral function. It is not fitting."

"My name sounds like passing gas to you?"

She rolled her eyes, an interplanetary cultural phenomenon. "I married a vulgar soldier. I compared the sound of your contracted name to that of clearing one's throat. I see I should have specified so as to remove the means for your base humor."

"Your name doesn't sound anything but perfect. Talis." Suddenly, it struck my ear as odd. I tried again. "Talis Darmon. Dang it. Now it sounds weird to me to use only your first name." Damned if my brain hadn't somehow full-on converted to the Mihdradahl convention. Vistara might've become my world in every way now, but I still wouldn't be running around dressed like a cosplay gladiator.

"You mature, my husband. At long last."

"I always was a slow learner. Better late than never, baby." I kissed her. "I'll be home for supper. You have more of the same today?"

"Yes, Warlord. Your queen sits in minor council today. I anticipate nothing save more reports from the machinery of our progress. The optimism and renewed purpose that sprouts in continued growth across the kingdom has made these meetings veritably pleasant. No more must we handle the many crises. Instead, coordinating demands by the many sectors of development has become the challenge. I feel certain I will have wonderful things to share with you over dinner."

We were still on a cold war footing, trying to build our army to unquestionable superiority as a deterrence to the Yellow Kingdom.

Firsthand experience in Annameria made me a believer that our best strategy against their paranoid society was to be paranoid ourselves. There'd been no stirrings from them in the longest time. Whether they were busy building themselves up to invade or they'd become distracted by internal matters, it mattered not. Either way, I wasn't about to stop our efforts to build the biggest, baddest army that ever was. I gave my wife another quick kiss.

"See you tonight."

I was almost out the door when she called after me.

"Benjamin Colt. Don't land on your head."

✳ ✳ ✳

Karlo had been dismissive of the viability of Tarn paratroopers. "It's a dead concept. Who the heck needs to parachute a battalion of troops onto the battlefield anymore? Especially on Mars. We don't have airfields to seize. Flitters are nearly silent and boringly dependable. The next gen I've got cooking up will reach hypersonic speeds, too. Airborne ops are the stuff of anachronistic thinking."

"Blasphemer," I said. "Jumpin' Jim Gavin's rolling over in his grave." As a private in the 82nd, I'd been taught to venerate the prodigy airborne general as a god. But Karlo was mostly right. Still, no capability was disabling. I'd certainly hate to be on the receiving end of a platoon of raging Tarns dropping from the skies to break up my backyard barbecue like Russkies dropping on the schoolyard in *Red Dawn*. If we could get even a small number trained in static line and freefall parachuting, there was no telling how they might come in handy.

Double-K had insisted we teach him first. "As commanding general, I cannot ask of my troops something I myself would not do." After a few successful static line jumps, he pushed us to take him to the next level. A tandem jump or two was always the way to break into learning to freefall. With a novice jumper clipped to a jumpmaster, the student could practice their body position and learn to fall stable. The jumpmaster was in control, countering any problems with his own body position, and even deployed the parachute for them both.

Doug was the biggest of us, but with the Tarn hooked to the front of him, he was little more than a toddler glued between the shoulder blades of an NFL lineman. Dave busted out laughing first.

"Yo, Dougie, say it for me. Just once. 'Master Blaster runs Barter Town.' Say it, brah!"

Doug unhooked. "No shit. That's about exactly what we look like in tandem. This isn't going to work. He's too damn big. I'd never be able to bring us out of a spin."

"And I ain't gonna be the one to explain to your three widows that you were sky surfing on a Tarn's back when you frapped, brah."

Yes, Doug's living arrangement with his three Thorian girlfriends continued.

"They'd understand if I died having fun," he said, "'cept I wouldn't be. They know the story of how I almost bought it on that night jump when my rucksack came loose and spun me round like a test tube in a centrifuge. No thanks. Well, Double-K, this is your lucky day. You wanna freefall? We're going to AFF you."

Khraal Kahlees frowned. "Even though my decipher fails to translate, I understand enough Thulian to know it is yet another of your acronyms you so commonly pervert into verbs. What does this violation of the rules for a civilized language mean for my immediate future?"

Accelerated Freefall meant he'd fly alone, but with the three of us in the air around him, holding on to him like little nipping dogs that wouldn't let go. We felt confident we could get him stable and safely under canopy. So, after some more ground school, Dave, Doug, and I took him up.

It worked. Sort of.

With Doug grabbing one side of him, Dave on the other, and me in front to coach him, it was still too much to ask of a Tarn—maybe any Vistaran—to relax enough to fall correctly. We almost couldn't bring him out of his spin, and when we did, Dave had to pull his chute for him. Then he blew the landing. Instead of flaring the ram air canopy as he sensed the ground rush, he collided with Mother Vistara at full flight, digging himself a trench nearly as deep as the Furrow itself.

Freefall was a different critter in most every way than static line, and he let it be known it was not one he wanted to tame.

"Most unpleasant in every way. David Masamuni, you said, and I quote, 'It is better than sex.' You are either a liar or you perform the mating act much differently than I do."

"It's an acquired taste, brah."

Dougie reached up to hammer-fist the broad green chest. "I'm sure some Tarn has fallen out of a flitter before, but this makes you the first Vistaran to freefall and live. Means you buy tonight. It'll be better this next time. Let's get you right back up on the arkall that threw you."

The massive Tarn brushed the last of the red earth off his body. "No. As commanding general, I have done what is proper and experienced it for myself. Of all the means and methods you have introduced to improve our lethality—many I at first thought ill of but came to see the error of my bias—but freefall? Experience has proven to my satisfaction that I am correct to side mostly with Karlo Columbo—it is a frivolous thing. If ever the need presented, it is adequate that you Thulians have the ability. Static line jump school for the army, this we can discuss."

Karlo helped us pack up. "I'm already making more chutes for just that, Double-K. But I've got a much better idea to try out. Give me another week, and I'll have the prototype ready."

Now, here we were. The morning sun was higher than when I left Talis Darmon and our egg. Apache's face was in the wind, drool streaming from flapping tongue. It was a few hours' flight to reach the Furrow of the Creator's Hand, the giant canyon that separated us from the Yellow Kingdom of Annameria, two days south across the chasm.

I chose to try out Karlo's new gizmo over the big ditch. We'd tested the gadget with dead weight, it worked perfectly, and now it was time for a live run. To have the altitude I wanted for safety, I'd need to jump from so high that anywhere in Mihradahl, I'd need an oxygen tank.

So instead, the barren canyon seemed like the best test grounds. The atmosphere wasn't particularly thick anywhere on Vistara, but it was densest in the bottom of the canyon. Plus, it was far from any prying eyes. An exit jump over the chasm, then either the rays harnessed by the new device would arrest my fall to a gentle landing below, or I'd have plenty of time to open my chute to take the ride down. It was practically fail-safe.

Khraal Kahlees wasn't convinced.

"Falling such a distance I found intolerable. It was as though I was at the mercy of too many forces at once, all out of my ability to control. I eagerly anticipated being beneath the canopy again. I think this device and all freefall unnecessary."

I pulled back the gate on the gunwale of our open-deck flitter.

"You would've been a natural in Division. No shame in you staying a static line parachutist, Double-K. But if you want to know, the secret to freefall is… you gotta let yourself take pride that what you do, fills others with fear. See you on the ground." I did a reverse exit, saluted him in midair, and dropped away.

It was a beautiful day over the Furrow. But with almost no discernible changes in season, every day on Mars was a beautiful day. The nearby canyon wall gave me the sensation of falling that I suppose gives the rush that drives base jumpers to dive off buildings. I tried it once, found it ridiculously dangerous, and was satisfied to never do it again. A little wind shear and you'd kiss the building and your ass goodbye along with it. The two-way shooting range of combat was safer.

It was time to test the new harness I wore beneath the parachute. I crossed hands in balanced unison in front of me so as not to disrupt the flat attitude of my fall, stroked the band on my wrist, and waited. The rush of air in my face dwindled. Checking the cliffs, they no longer hurtled past me. The approach of the ground all but stopped. I was sinking down at the rate of a feather.

I touched the wristlet on my other hand. "Karlo, it works. I'm floating, dude."

"Of course it does," he said. "It's not powerful enough to provide lift, but the next iteration we test will have horizontal vectoring. It'll let us do anything we could have done under a canopy."

"I really will be Superman if I can glide, Karlo."

From over his shoulder I heard, "Then don't do it, Karlo. His head's already too big, brah."

It was twelve thousand feet to the ground. "At this rate, I won't touch down for a week. I'm dropping back to freefall. I'll bring the ray belt on line again when I'm at about two grand. See you downstairs." I cut out the device and resumed my fall. I fell for another two minutes, terminal velocity on Mars being much slower in the lower gravity than it would be on Earth. Finally, as the swell of the undulating sands below closed in, I double-checked against my altimeter that I was about two thousand feet above the ground, and stroked the band. It was time to float again.

I was still falling.

I gave it one more try.

Nothing.

Why wasn't it coming on?

Prototypes, I complained to myself. I pulled out the pilot chute and let it go. The deployment sequence seemed strange. I did a shoulder check, and above me was a tangle of garbage. The invisibly thin suspension lines and mystery material of Karlo's canopy were so much twine around a ball of rags. I hit the cutaway to get rid of the useless trash and clear the way for my reserve. Then, the inexplicable happened. The hot mess of the streamer trailing from my back wrapped loops around my body like a cowboy's lasso roping a steer.

The ground was seconds below me. This was going to hurt. I always thought I'd close my eyes if I was going to burn in, but instead, I locked on to the spot where I would dig my own grave.

In midair, I came to a stop like a motorcycle running head-on into a bridge abutment. My innards slammed into the wall of my chest and abdomen. My eyeballs strained like grape skins ready to burst into wine. I was at a frozen hover. The belt cut out, and I slammed the last three feet to the ground.

I came to, fuzzy and spitting dirt, the exasperated curses of the only Hawaiian on Vistara my summons to consciousness.

"Crazy haole! Why'd you wait so long to hit the antigravity switch?"

Doug's knife was out, cutting at the suspension lines still wrapped around me. "Dude, what the hell happened?"

I tested a tooth with my tongue. It was loose. I'd kissed a rock. The ground sucked up my red-tinged spit like a sponge. "Pfft. Friggin' thing didn't come on."

"Well, it must've, brah, or you'd be a greasy spot."

Karlo was there, examining my mouth. "Lemme see, Ben. Looks okay. A little healing ray and it should be fine."

Dave poked Karlo. "Brah, Ben says da kine switch on your gadget no good." Dave only broke into full pidgin when very stressed or very relaxed. He didn't seem to be in chill mode. "If it no work, what da point?"

Everything hurt. I brushed myself off. "Well, it kinda works, or I'd be as flat as a run-over dog turd! The gizmo fired up on command just fine the first time! What gives, Karlo?" I tossed the harness at him. Karlo squinted closely as he examined it.

"What I think happened is that the automatic activation program took priority over a second manual activation. Coding things into the crystals is still tricky. I didn't have Cynar around to double-check it. I'll have him go over it with me. Sorry, Ben. But we for sure know the fail-safe is working."

Double-K grunted. "Frivolous. All frivolous. An arkall has never failed to deliver me into battle. And if it stumbles, I do not die. More Thulian madness."

My wristlet vibrated. I let the full cloud appear and resolve into the face of Kleeve Hartus. He was the palest shade of Red Vistaran I had yet seen.

I pictured a sky full of flitters from Annameria strafing the towers of Shansara. A band of Mydreen raiders on arkall-back, ravaging through the city center. He was too flustered for it to be anything as simple as one of those.

"First Shield, what is it?"

"Warlord, where are you? You must return at once. The gravest of all things has occurred. I cannot adequately explain. Please, return immediately."

Kleeve Hartus was the most capable person I knew. As unflappable as Dave. As analytical as Karlo. As fierce as Doug and Double-K. What could have him so perturbed?

"Get your shit together and report!" I'd never spoken to him in such a way, and while I regretted my outburst, my words had the right effect.

"Warlord, it is a thing only written of. A vessel from the north appeared this morning and descended onto Shansara. There was fear as the city has never experienced. It was a massive thing, eclipsing the sun. And with its arrival above us, all instrumentality in the city ceased. The craft settled onto the palace grounds, and *they* appeared.

"From Temple Farnest, they came to say that we had fallen away from our faith, and summoned the queen to answer the charge. The White lord of the underworld said if we did not repent, the next visit will usher in the end of all days."

Not Red. Not Yellow. Not Green. But White. Even I knew what Kleeve Hartus meant by "the north." I'd once been mistaken for one of the mythical overlords of the underworld, and the mystique conferred by the mistaken identity had saved my life. I tried to force into reality what I wanted to have happened, knowing it hadn't.

"What did the queen say once the Guard arrested the Whites?"

His story was succinct, clipped, and told with pained anxiety.

"They took her to join her ancestors. She is gone to the under-world, Warlord."

02

THE STREETS WERE EMPTY, SOMETHING I HADN'T SEEN IN SHANSARA since the war. On the main loop of a sky bridge was the only foot traffic, a stream of people stacked to exit on the descending tributary that lead to the tiny borough where the sole temple resided. If this involved the Whites and the hoodoo of the Vistaran underworld, then I wanted a priest to question. But it was to the council chambers that I'd go first.

Kleeve Hartus bounded down the palace steps as I settled the flitter. "Warlord, I have reconvened the council in anticipation of your arrival. I had to send my Guards to retrieve most of them. Like the rest of the city, all had fled to their homes."

"I see a lot of people heading for the temple."

"Naturally, Warlord. They seek further guidance from the priest."

Dave trotted up the stairs beside us. "There were a lot of white robes outside the temple, First Shield. Isn't that how folks dress when they're taking the pilgrim's route north?"

"It is, David Masamuni. No doubt this has sparked many to travel the River Blix to Farnest."

The council chamber buzzed. Only resentment at a loss of stature ever agitated anyone in this group. But the normally aloof and reserved functionaries were a nest of fire ants. They railed against the Tarn soldiers who held them there awaiting my arrival.

The queen's chair sat empty.

"I want to know exactly what happened. Who can tell me?"

Like flustered children, a dozen council members started in at once, and I immediately regretted my mistake. I should've selected one individual to speak. Were they soldiers, my question would've been answered by the ranking individual. Here, they all thought of themselves as generals.

"Only a Thulian would need clarification. The White Lords have left the Underworld to make our faults known," one said.

"Our place is with our families!"

"It is to the temple we should be going."

Then Karlo cut in, his voice a vibrant force like a deep brass section. "Perrin Halser, I trust you will lend clarity to the Warlord's request."

Karlo's most trusted subordinate in charge of the Golden Hub—our center of innovation and manufacturing—was thoughtful and precise, much like Karlo. Unlike the other members of the council, who primarily created nothing but more bureaucracy, Perrin Halser was an engineer before he was made an administrator. I'd learned by observing Karlo that inherent in the kind of person who made the abstract into reality—the artists who turned ideas into functioning mechanisms—resided a rationality they seemed to apply to all things. The unremarkable appearing man with remarkable common sense bowed.

"I witnessed all, Warlord. Perhaps we should take seats and calm ourselves before I give my report?"

"I concur." I took my normal place next to the conspicuously empty seat at our head. What had happened to my Talis Darmon?

Perrin Halser waited, the grumbles settled, and he began.

"I was giving a report to the queen when the projection extinguished from our midst. The lights faded and outside, the sky grew dark. The hum of some great engine focusing the second ray of the repelling force drowned all other sounds. She was first to the terrace, and I followed. Above the courtyard was a craft as large as the grand esplanade itself.

"It was unlike any craft ever seen over Vistara. It was a sphere, from which dozens of sharp spikes projected, pulsing in as many colors. They struck me as parts of a mechanism that collected, focused, and transmitted many different rays beyond that for powering flight. It seemed a reasonable association that the interruption of all our instrumentalities, even simple mechanisms such as the amber stones, was caused by the operators of the encroaching craft."

"Out of my way! Let pass the scientist supreme, oafs." It was Cynar's vigor and not his pencil-thin arms that plowed the path through the forest of giant Tarns guarding the door.

"Cynar!" I cried. "Where have you been?" If anyone could add understanding to what had happened, it would be the former hermit.

"Apologies, Benjamin Colt! The effect that took hold trapped me within my workshop."

"You weren't in the council meeting when this happened?"

"You well know that I do not attend minor councils! I was doing important work, much of it lost as a result of this disruption." He held a slate up. "I have been searching for remnant signatures of whatever caused this phenomenon."

"And?"

"I have nothing useful to report yet, Warlord, but I have just commenced my investigation."

"Then take a seat and let Perrin Halser continue."

"I would welcome the chance to confer with our supreme scientist later," the chief engineer said as he dipped his head to Cynar, who returned the gesture. The crazy, long-bearded wizard had become almost pleasant in his interchanges as of late—at least, to any he deemed worthy of his courtesy. That honor applied to very few on the council, but Perrin Halser was one of those. The engineer continued.

"A ramp descended from the craft, and with it three beings of human Vistaran form, dressed in silver robes, their skin so gray as to be almost white."

"How can you even doubt they were White Lords?" asked the minister of works, her voice shrill with disbelief.

The director of the Golden Hub remained the grim professional. "The Warlord demands an objective report, Hallis Sifer. I will not taint it with my prejudices. He requires empirical observations." The woman huffed but didn't argue further.

"The voice of their spokesman was magnified by resonance through the craft behind them, and could be heard clearly at even this distance. He said, 'I, Zan-Sha, King and Exalted Protector, leave Temple Farnest to bring you a message. Your ancestors in the eternal underworld cry to you. Their call has been ignored, and the Blix remains unfettered by the journeys of those from this land. Vistarans have hardened their hearts and shut their ears, deafened by the carnal world with all its distractions and false rewards. For this reason, you are judged to be faithless. It is the responsibility of the steward of this land to inspire fidelity and devotion to the way. Where is the ruler of Mihdradahl? Where is the one who bears the blame for your falling away?'

"The queen answered, 'I am Talis Darmon Sylah, queen and regent of Mihdradahl. How is it that you name my people faithless, King Zan-Sha?'

"Their spokesman raised his staff to single her out on the terrace. 'Your people are named faithless because they have forgotten the way. And it is you who have clouded their minds away from their purpose and eternal reward. Present yourself to me for instruction.'

"Those of us not paralyzed by fear accompanied the queen and her bodyguard to where the White Lords summoned. We followed her to fall on knees and receive his words.

"'Talis Darmon Sylah, as ruler, you bear the responsibility for having led your people on a false path. But your example will set right again the way. In your heart remains the faith. It is time for you to join your waiting ancestors in the underworld. From the beginning of your line, to your parents, and to your child unborn in a dead egg, all await you. Today you travel to be joined with them for all time. Come, good servant. Your great reward is at hand.'"

How did some charlatan from beneath the north pole know about my wife's stillborn child? Such a deeply personal and painful thing thrown at her—had that convinced her they were the supernatural angels they claimed to be? There was no one for me to ask.

"Without looking back, she ascended. Before they departed, the one spoke a last time. 'Repent, all of Mihdradahl. When the call comes

15

to your heart, it must be answered. When your time above Vistara is complete, when the weariness of existence comes, no more should you toil and strive at vain tasks. Heed the call of your hearts. For if you sacrifice the oneness of life eternal with your ancestors in order to prolong the dream of the world above, then we must bring the end of all days.'

"They left, and when they did, the instruments and energies of all rays returned."

I turned on the queen's bodyguards, furious. "Your job is to protect the queen by all means and against any threat. You let her be taken!"

I'd never seen Korundi cower before. Massive foreheads fell, tusked jaws went slack. "Warlord—how can you ask such a thing of us? She was called to Farnest by the White Lords. To have done other would have been impossible."

Doug was moving. "Ben, I'm on it." I knew what he was doing, and there was no one I trusted more to get us ready.

We were going to get Talis Darmon back.

"Go."

Between us, we were one mind. Because that's what a teammate was. An extension of yourself. No more needed to be said.

There was another who understood what these few words meant. Khraal Kahlees drew a sharp breath and blurted, "Benjamin Colt! Cease your derangement. It is not a thing of sorrow. It is her reward. You think to interfere. You cannot. And if you also travel the Blix, you will not return. It will be to the underworld that you go. The warrior knows the pain of loss most of all. Do not allow temporary forlorn to call you there. Persevere and remain where your works are needed."

The room likewise erupted, their epiphany dawning like a rising sun exposing the profanity of what I intended.

"Heresy!"

"What madness could drive you?"

"Thulians desecrating the underworld! They must be stopped."

Kleeve Hartus was beside me, speaking so only I could hear. "Benjamin Colt, I too beg of you. Listen to Khraal Kahlees. It is done. Talis Darmon is gone. She joins her ancestors. It is natural and right.

16

Though you have risked all for your adopted world, I know you are not truly of Vistara. I have tried to be a brother to you, to aid you in learning the way. Abandon whatever false belief you cling to. A defiler can never enter Temple Farnest. If you attempt to do this thing, you will not reverse her course. Nor will you join her. All you will do is bring upon yourself oblivion. Such is the fate for any who would commit like blasphemy. Return to your senses, my friend, I plead."

His compassion, reason, and fortitude had made him one of three who Talis Darmon had entrusted with the protection of our egg when our deaths seemed inevitable by the barbed tentacles of nightmares made real. Now, those qualities seemed as though they were in the service of a zealot. A fanatic. A blind believer.

Like walking into a minefield, Dave and I'd discovered that Vistarans casual references to the afterlife were more than just metaphor. After nearly coming to blows, Kleeve Hartus had explained and even shown us the manner in which pilgrims traveled to the underworld. We'd been astonished to witness white-robed travelers enter a way station and ascend onto a conveyance that supposedly whisked them a hemisphere away to begin their transition to a life in another realm. Not one of the spirit, but a physical one, deep in the center of the planet.

We were told the train ride ended at a temple called Celest Hom, a place protected by the legendary gatekeepers to the underworld. I'd had a run-in with the Hortha—the deadly white apes of the north. Like the underground railroad, I could confirm by personal experience that the apes were real, not myth. Whether they were the rent-a-cops of the White Lords or not remained to be seen.

Once admitted by the Hortha, the pious were said to sail the underground waters of the River Blix for the last temple, Farnest. There the White Lords reviewed the pilgrim's history in the book of life and the sojourner at last entered the underworld to begin eternal life with all the departed of Vistara.

From the time we'd witnessed the carriage carrying white robed pilgrims depart, proving that at least some of this was more than metaphor, my pal Dave begged me to leave it alone. We'd been through a lot together. Whatever our predicament on Mars had thrown at him—even if it excited compound expletives of his own unique concoction—nothing interfered with his duty. With a heart full of hate, a mind calculating destruction, and hands directed to efficient carnage, he could transform from nonchalant beach bum to god of war with the flip of a switch.

But this one thing had been too fantastic for him.

"Let us never discuss this again," he'd told me. "My sanity can't handle it."

But curiosity had driven me to continue my investigations without him. Where had the people on that train car gone? And what could have happened to them when they got there?

I met with the priest who'd twice performed our wedding ceremony. His resolute assurance that the process was just as Kleeve Hartus had said made me seek a different source. The histories of my adopted world were as fractured and incomplete as most everything on Vistara. With the librarian's help, I learned the basics. While references to the Blix and Farnest were a part of common speech, the belief in the underworld was not universal. I shared with Talis Darmon my doubts about it all, and her training in metaphysics was apparent in her Socratic method.

"Thulia is a world of many faiths, is it not?"

I admitted it was.

"Do they all have proof of their beliefs?"

"I guess that's at odds with what faith is, isn't it?"

"Together we have seen that there are realms unexplainable, have we not, Benjamin Colt? I do not know what truly transpires at Temple Farnest, but for myself, knowing that the possibilities are infinite, our experiences have strengthened my faith. I do not believe it is a subject to spend much capital pondering over. The heart knows. Perhaps, someday, yours will as well. Whatever your belief, I am content. Because I know that whatever awaits, we will be there together."

I had my own theories about who the Whites were and what the underworld was. And it was time to test my hypothesis.

I looked my friend in the eye. "I know what you believe, Kleeve Hartus. Whatever happened to Talis Darmon, she's not on a supernatural journey. It's a con game. Whoever these Whites claim to be, they're no shepherds of an afterlife. There's something foul happening." I stood and spoke so the kidnappers flying north could hear me.

"I'm bringing Talis Darmon back."

The First Shield retreated a step, repulsed. "I never thought you capable of such evil. You who so nobly rose to a greatness not seen in all history. You who fought the Karnak at peril of your own soul. You were as a brother to me. No more." He turned and left.

Dave was at my side. "Karlo and Cynar ducked out. Let's get to the vault. If we wait any longer, we may have to fight our way there."

Khraal Kahlees dropped his head into all four hands. "You demolish a foundation that brings with it the downfall of this kingdom."

✳ ✳ ✳

Cursed outrages pelted us, but none moved to interfere. We bounded through the empty palace. The door to the vault room was cracked open and inside, Doug and Karlo had the arms room splayed out. Dougie was doling out full magazines by the dozen into piles by each kit.

"We're going old school, Ben. If these Whiteys can turn off all Vistaran tech, then we've got something their magic can't monkey with—a bullet to the brain." Satisfied we had enough ammunition, he busied himself pulling coils of strip charges off the shelf.

Beraal announced her entrance.

"It is I, Benjamin Colt, come at the behest of Khraal Kahlees." She paused to take in our work. She knew what preparing for war looked like. "I see it is as my father says. Please, do not do this thing, brother. At the first disruption heralding the appearance of the White

Lords, Talis Darmon sent me away to guard your egg and there I have remained. You bring shame to her to act in such a way as you have planned."

"You too, Beraal?" I moaned. "You can't buy into all this nonsense. Those weren't angels who came to town and kidnapped Talis Darmon. I don't know who those phonies were, but we're tracking them down and getting her back."

Dave had a map laid out and was asking Cynar questions. "Where're they headed? We don't want to chase them; we want to intercept them on their route and ambush 'em." Maps of Vistara were terrible. Most were of little use for navigation. We'd been successful in improving the representations of the kingdom to scale, but north of the near foothills of the Korund Range, the scroll was blank.

"The Sharpa Mountains lie at the northern pole. It is beneath them that the Temple Farnest and the entrance to the Vistaran underworld are said to be."

Where Talis Darmon was right now being taken.

"Where is Celeste Hom, Beraal?" I asked. "There's a path that must go through the Korund—the long way north to meet the Blix. Do you know where it is?"

"It does, Benjamin Colt. It is not traveled by Tarn, and rarely so even by human. I do not know its exact course, save it leads north."

"Do you know, Cynar?"

"I do not, Benjamin Colt. I have never concerned myself with the specifics of those Vistaran beliefs."

Doug paused his work. "You don't think there's some kind of eternal paradise full of people at the center of the planet, Cynar?"

"No, Douglas Knoblock. I may use the same vernacular as many, but I know of no convincing evidence that an eternal paradise exists beneath our feet. We who have been there know what we found in the deepest bowels of Vistara. A paradise, it was not."

"What do you think happens to all the people who go north?"

"Perhaps we will discover, then it will be known."

Dave gave a thumbs-up. "Glad you're going with us, brah. We need us some Cynar."

We hadn't yet discussed the team composition. I needed to clarify things ASAP.

"Cynar, it's not that I don't want you with us, but you have to stay."

He was indignant. "That is a remarkable thing for you to say to me, Benjamin Colt! It was I who brought us victory against the Karnak. Without my superior intellect, this world may well have fallen under the control of their ilk."

"And all your technology is based on the rays. Maybe you can figure out how to counter whatever they're using to disable everything. But there're more important things you're needed for here. The atmosphere works aren't close to returning on line yet."

The air wizard Tyreen Sorell was still at work in Maleska Mal, trying to extract the mysterious substance that made the factories produce atmosphere. It was our hope that Karlo could reverse engineer the process that made the material.

Then it occurred to me that there were four piles of gear being laid out.

"You too, Karlo. No matter what happens to us, those atmosphere works have to get running again. Without you two and Baby Blue, it can't happen."

Dave was quick to disagree. "If the locals go into Spanish Inquisition mode, they're just going to lump Karlo and Cynar in with us, brah. They won't be safe."

"I want to go with you, Ben." Karlo hung his head. "But what you're saying is true."

Karlo was always good at making rapid decisions from the facts at hand. He nodded, hating it, but forcing himself to admit I had the priorities of an entire world ordered correctly. "I'll stay back. I can take care of myself. If I have to denounce you all, play traitor, take an oath, I'll do whatever I have to so Baby Blue's protected and I get the chance to examine whatever mystery element Tyreen Sorell gives me."

"There's another thing, Karlo. You promised Talis Darmon you'd protect our child."

Karlo's moist eyes reassured me more than any words possibly could. "I haven't forgotten, Ben."

Cynar didn't even throw me shade, which told me just how dire the situation was. "There is wisdom in this, Benjamin Colt. It is worth the risk to be accused of heresy by the First Shield in order for us to achieve greater end. Perrin Halser will act as advocate for us. He holds much respect on the council, as does Karlo Columbo. As for me, they may hate me, but they know I am irreplaceable. We will remain and work to achieve what the air wizards have bungled and return abundant respiration to this world. I will gather for you what odds and ends from my genius may serve."

"Good. Then it's settled. Karlo and Cynar stay back. Getting the air works running is their first priority. And whatever you can do to help Beraal protect my child, do it."

Tarns didn't cry, but a tear streamed down Beraal's cheek. "I will protect your egg with my life, Benjamin Colt. But your child has already lost one parent. Do not make it an orphan. You know I speak from experience. Please reconsider."

Doug and Dave turned to the entrance, rifles raised toward the approaching footfalls.

With all hands held open, Khraal Kahlees stepped into the vault, his entrance cautious. "It is not with intent to stop your desecrations that I come. It is to tell you that I have made consultation with Chieftain Parkus Laan. He agrees. The oath of the Korund was made to Queen Talis Darmon. She has now passed to the underworld. With the Warlord's departure also at hand, it is clear—I can be general of Mihdradahl's army no more. Today, I and all Korundi return to our mountains."

He'd said what I was doing would bring the kingdom's downfall. Was this what he meant?

"Khraal Kahlees, if you take the army with you, as soon as the Yellows hear this, they'll invade."

"I regret that it cannot be helped, Benjamin Colt. Beraal Kahlees, my daughter, it is best that you come with me for the return to Califex. In our care should also travel the egg of Talis Darmon and my clansman, the Warlord.

"There will be no safety here for either of you."

03

Karlo directed us. "If this is going to work, we can't be seen helping you escape. Make for the Golden Hub and my workshop. I have the new flitter there."

"Another prototype, Karlo?" I said, the experience with one of his new gadgets fresh in my mind. "We can't afford any hiccups."

"It's solid, Ben. You have my word. Where will you go?"

"The one place we know for sure exists. The Hah Shur Valley."

Kleeve Hartus had taken both Dave and I there as a way to overcome our skepticism. We'd seen something happen there, but what, neither Dave nor I were really sure. It hadn't converted us to the belief that there was a place full of puffy clouds and harp music waiting for us all beneath Vistara.

I hefted my ruck. Jawn Kurz's sword at my side, more guns and ammo than I'd carried since we'd gone to conquer a realm of nightmares, it was time to go. "We'll be back. When Talis Darmon returns, she'll put everything right. You'll see." I was talking to Khraal Kahlees.

"You will not return, Benjamin Colt. I say farewell to you." He crossed all arms. "Warriors now walk with their glorious ancestors in the underworld." He used the honorific as if we'd already joined the dead.

Beraal laid sky hands on my shoulders and touched her forehead to mine. "Do not make the White Lords find you unworthy and send you to emptiness, brother. If you must, go as a pilgrim and join her there in happiness for all eternity. I will see you both when my duty to your child has been fulfilled. I live in hope of nothing less." She turned to follow her father and was gone.

Dave saddled up with his own massive ruck then blew out a deep breath. "Doug and I are with you, brah, no matter what. But even if we bring her back, do you think it's gonna wipe the slate clean? This is the last chance to reconsider and try to undo what's happened so far."

"Screw that, Davey-Dave." Doug closed the feed tray cover of his MK 46 over a full belt. "We've taken down bigger boogeymen than this. If we have to crush everyone's delusions, you know the saying—if it can be destroyed by the truth, then it deserves to be destroyed."

"And if we find out it's all true, Dougie?" I said.

"Spot conversion, dude, and eternal paradise. S'all good. Let's roll."

"We'll be in touch," I told Karlo. "Daily transmission by us at 0600 and 1800. Five-minute windows. If you're clear, answer."

"Roger, Ben."

Cynar folded his hands. "You will return, Warlord. And with the queen, reason will return also."

"Thank you, Cynar. Let's move it." A quick peek, and I led us out. The halls were still empty, and we poured it on. Even carrying a double load, we flew. To the livery, a flitter, a quick hop to Karlo's warehouse, then we'd be on our way. What we'd do at the Hah Shur Valley, I wasn't yet sure. We broke onto the open deck where a fleet of flitters were stabled.

"Halt, Benjamin Colt!"

Kleeve Hartus and a dozen of his Guards spread out from hiding behind the massive pillars supporting the promenade above. The first shield outstretched his hand like a cop, as if his palm held the power of all law. His men had us covered, guns leveled.

"Benjamin Colt, all thoroughfares are under blockade. No one wishes to harm you, but if you do not stand down, the Guard is sworn to stop you from this heresy." Doug and Dave had their own weapons on the first shield.

"You go down with us, brah," Dave said.

I met the first shield's eyes. "I never took you for a fanatic, Kleeve Hartus."

"A Guard is sworn to uphold the law unto death, Benjamin Colt. It is not fanaticism. It is fealty. I do not wish this as your end, my friend. Do not make us send you to your queen this way. But, perhaps, it is best for all. Guards—" he was about to order them to shoot when from above came a command.

"Drop those weapons, Red men! Or prepare to travel the Blix yourselves!"

From the observation deck above, a pair of Tarns aimed K-specs on the Guards' heads, stunned they'd been caught unaware as they'd just moments before thought to have the advantage of surprise over us. It was Sarkan Sell and Jodal Jark.

Shocked, Kleeve Hartus spun. "Korundi, I order you to stand down!"

The youthful Jodal Jark growled a laugh. "You do not command us, Red. Only the Warlord. Drop those weapons and flee for your lives. The Guard are not soldiers! You are all street sweepers and garbagemen with badges. City employees, not warriors. Twitch and see yourselves made cinders."

Sarkan Sell yelled, "Go, Warlord. We will await in the Korund for your return. Fear not, we will show these roamak the meaning of true fealty. If we could travel the road to war with you, we would. We serve you best by ensuring the launch of your rescue mission avoids preemption by traitors. Go quickly."

To a man, the Guards dropped weapons to the hard deck like they were millstones. They were not ready to ride the Blix today. The hum of a flitter came to life. Doug was behind the console and next to him, Dave's 203 was aimed at the first shield. "Better do as the Korundi say and beat feet, ladies, 'cause anyone left on this pad's gonna eat 40-mm shrapnel."

I leaped onto the flitter deck. Kleeve Hartus alone ignored Dave's advice, his eyes shooting lasers of hatred as we lifted, nosed around, and sped away. The barrage of fire I expected didn't come, and soon we were gone.

Doug grinned. "Good boys, those two. Always liked 'em."

I staggered and grabbed onto the rail as we banked to pass between two close-set spires. Buildings rushed by. Through panoramic windows, occupants flinched, recoiling in fear of a collision. The way Dougie flew us, their reaction was reasonable.

"It ain't surfin', brah. Don't kill us trying to pipeline."

The towers of the Golden Hub were ahead. We landed on the top of the warehouse Karlo called his lab and bounded to the stairs.

"I'll get the doors," Dave hollered as he bounced off. Like a toy store stocked to capacity, the enormous space was packed with Karlo's many creations. New versions of the tanks, the air defense rigs, and a dozen different innovations crowded the floor, teasing my imagination. I searched for something that looked like a flitter.

Doug pointed. "That's it. Gotta be. Pure sex."

It looked fast. Pointed like a bullet, hulled in smooth gleaming metal, it was the only covered air car in modern times in the kingdom. The hatch was open as though begging to be used for a quick getaway. Like a single engine Cessna or a 2+2 sports car, it was big enough for more than two, but it was going to be cramped. We tossed gear inside, then scrambled in after. Two reclined seats behind airplane yokes sat in front, a seamless transparent cabin around it. Doug leaped into a seat.

"This is more like it. Good old Karlo. I knew he was as Italian as his name. Thing's laid out like a Lamborghini. All it needs is a leather interior."

Daylight filled the cockpit as the warehouse doors opened to the outside world. We raised a few inches and eased forward. We crawled ahead at a hover as Doug spoke to himself, "Lift control. Power vector... I think I got it."

I reached out to catch Dave's thrown ruck, he dived in after, and I hit the lone crystal near the opening, hoping it sealed the portal. It slid down silently.

"On the deck, boys. We've got company."

The nose pitched up and we both slid to the rear, our rucks and weapons with us as Gs of acceleration pressed us hard into the rear wall. Bright flashes rocked the ship, ceased, and we leveled off. I massaged where the buttstock of Doug's loose MK 46 had flown back to kiss my cheek.

"I got us aimed north, Ben. Where to?"

My hip throbbed, and I removed my sword to massage where I'd landed on it. I took a bent walk forward and slid into the seat next to his. "We get hit with K-spec fire?"

"And it bounced right off, dude. This thing might be as easy to spot as a mirror at noon, but it deflects fizzle fire. And damn, does it go!"

I took the yoke and tried a few gentle maneuvers. The other controls on the panel were the same as an open-deck flitter. I slowed and put us in a gentle turn until I got my bearings. I dead reckoned to sight in on the tiny peaks that, on my first trip there, had grown into the strange formations ringing the Hah Shur depression. I gunned it.

"They're going to be hot on our trail. This rocket'll buy us time on the ground before they arrive."

"What's the plan, brah?"

In the bottom of the crater of the strange bowl of the Hah Shur peaks was a lone building, the Temple Transspellum. In it, Dave and I had witnessed Red pilgrims dressed in white ascend onto a carriage to take an underground rail that supposedly ended at the portal temple to the River Blix—Celeste Hom. Kleeve Hartus had reverently described the crystal ship that from there would carry a pious pilgrim on the Blix to arrive at the Temple Farnest. It was the final stop before the underworld, where Talis Darmon was en route in the company of her kidnappers.

"There's a priest. He's going to be our Google and get us an address and directions. Then we go like we're on fire. Once we're there, we kick the shit out of every White goon who had the bad sense to think they could touch her."

✳ ✳ ✳

"We're almost over the crater. Seize that building and strongpoint the entrance. Once I land, I'll be right behind you. Leave the third line gear here. If we need it, we'll bring it forward."

I slowed and eased us to a hover over the peaks. Through the transparent cabin beneath my feet sat the simple white cube that was the temple. The walls of the crater were steep, the trail from the tunnel entrance cut in winding switchbacks down to the floor. The hatch opened and Dave braced in the door, ready to leap first onto the roof.

I was dimming the crystal to start our descent when my stomach lurched like someone cut the cable to the elevator. It'd been me who clipped the strings. I made a panicked and too rapid correction and reversed direction, my stomach now headed down to my knees. This was a Ferrari and I'd been used to driving a Yugo. My mistake hadn't tossed my friends out, because they were both too busy questioning my parentage and mating habits.

"Sorry, I got it now," I told them. "Easing down."

"Slide right five meters, brah. Hold." With two "Geronimos" fading away to indicate they were out, I slid and turned to find a place to put down. In case these priests weren't the pacifists I assumed they were, I didn't want to set down directly in front of the only doors I absolutely knew to be located on this structure. We needed this ride to remain puncture-free if we were to get right back on the dusty trail and head the Whites off at the pass. Settled beside the building and out of sight of the main entrance, I powered down.

Doug startled me by dashing past the nose, headed for the hatch. I pushed back from the yoke to meet him for his sitrep. "Some little snowball stuck his head out, saw us, then sealed up tight. I'm gonna peel those doors open like a tin can."

I threw him his ruck, grabbed my rifle, and bounced after him. Dave was holding on the door. He handed me his pry bar to return to his back.

"No purchase. We tried it the easy way."

"This is the easy way, dude." Doug peeled the tape off the charge as he rolled it down the center. He walked backward around the corner of the building, feeding out shock tube as we covered his retreat.

"Big one coming. Fire in the hole."

A concussive explosion came at the speed of light and before it abated, we were moving, a cloud of dirt still in the air.

Dave yelled and tossed. "Bang out." The nine-banger was mid-dance as we entered. Through the smoke sat the sparkling gold carriage. Like a Hot Wheels track, a single flat strip ran along the ground before dropping abruptly into a dark tunnel. A white-robed, roly-poly man lay in the fetal position at the top of a staircase leading to a sub-level. Had he been standing in front of the portal when the charge blew, he'd be mush. I pulled him from the stairs and onto the landing. Even in Vistara's gravity, he was a heavy one.

"I'll take him; make sure we're good down there," I told the two, who disappeared down the stairs to look for any white robes playing hide and seek. The priest stirred as I regrasped between his shoulders and hefted him the rest of the way up to put my face an inch from the bald man's. "You know why I'm here." It wasn't a question.

He sputtered, "Violation! Violation! You to attack the temple? Why?" His rancid breath made me recoil. I let his feet touch down and stepped back. He coughed out the lingering fumes from the explosives.

"Coming up," Dave yelled from below. "Nothing down here but a small living area. No other exits."

Doug looked our prisoner over. "What's fat Doctor Evil got to say?"

The priest coughed violently then sucked a deep breath. "Evil? It is you who do great evil. Be gone from this sacred portal." Recognition dawned on his face. "You are the Thulians!"

"I am Warlord Benjamin Colt. Allow me to ask a question in a way that cannot be misunderstood, priest. Where is the queen?"

"The queen? I am alone. No pilgrim has arrived at Transspellum for months, certainly not her! I await a brother from the temple in Shansara to take my place so that I might learn why travel north has ceased. Have you caused some calamity in Mihdradahl that prevents the faithful from reaching the underworld? It is long suspected that you are naught but destroyers brought to Vistara!"

"I don't think he knows what's happened, Ben-dog," Doug said. "I didn't see any gizmos like the air wizards have. I don't think these priests have comms."

I fought myself calm. "Men claiming to be lords of the north appeared over Shansara this morning and took the queen. I want to know where they took her. Where's the Temple Farnest?"

A blast came from outside.

"Trouble," Doug said. Moving quickly to one side of the peeled back doors, he brought his gun up and fired a burst. Dave slid next to him and launched a grenade. "Make for the bird." Doug sent another burst then ran out, Dave after him.

"You're coming with us." I grabbed the scruff of his robe and pulled him to the portal. I let go of him to take a shot at a gold-cloaked Guard at the top of the corniche leading down the crater's wall. Several of them were down already, wounded and trying to crawl back to the tunnel for cover. The one I aimed at dropped, and the rest behind took the hint and backed up into the tunnel, leaving their wounded to continue to extricate themselves to cover. Smart. They'd get no medals for doing so, but neither would they be receiving posthumous commendations.

"COMING IN," Doug yelled. I stepped outside to send a few more well-directed shots into the tunnel to discourage a breakout, as Doug and Dave ran in behind me, arms loaded with our rucks and gear.

"The flitter's toast, Ben. The cockpit's ruined from a direct hit. It ain't going anywhere."

"Benjamin Colt," a voice echoed down at us, the walls of the tunnel functioning as a megaphone. "Release the priest and surrender. Admit your crimes and I will allow you to take the walk north and atone for your sins. Do it not and you will receive the oblivion you deserve."

"It's Kleeve Hartus," Dave said. "They got here quick."

"He knew where we were headed," I said. "He's the one who showed us this place. I shoulda figured."

"It was our best bet, brah."

Doug sent two short bursts into the tunnel mouth. "We're in a bad spot. Our only way out's an uphill assault to get to that tunnel. They got K-specs. They'll hammer us. We ain't getting out that way." He fired another burst. "But they ain't getting down here either."

"Time to take the train, brah," Dave said, thumbing at the carriage. He grabbed the priest by the collar, as if he were a toddler trying to escape after asked, "What's in your mouth?"

"You're not staying behind to stop the ride, you're coming with, fatty."

It was the choice of no choice. I tossed our rucks onto the conveyance, plush and outfitted with the comforts of a stretch limo, and followed in to drop my own overstuffed multicam leech. From the portal, Doug sent another burst of copper deterrence pills.

The priest sputtered, "It is not time for me to travel the Blix! I have not been called. And neither have you heretics! You will not be welcomed."

Dave jumped in, hefting the priest with him, and let go to deposit him like a dangling bag of dog poop onto a velvety bench. "Park it." He searched the interior. "How do you make this thing giddyap-go?"

As if commanded, the carriage eased ahead.

"Doug, we're going. Now," I yelled.

With the petulance of a boy told to stop poking his younger sibling, he sent one more burst, then sprang beside me. "Riding in style, I see."

"Duck," Dave said while pulling at Doug's closest sleeve. The conveyance floated silently into the tunnel, then dipped abruptly down and levelled off for a moment before the sensation of acceleration picked up again. If this was a roller coaster and not a train, then it looked to have few banks, turns, or loop-the-loops waiting us. A dot of dim amber light was far ahead and seemed to indicate an extremely long ride in a straight tunnel waited us. But, before it could light the way to the afterlife, the priest gave us his excommunication.

"You will suffer for your defilement, Thulians. The guardians of Celeste Hom await. They will find you impious and purge you from this world and the next.

"And I will not pray for your souls to find the path from your oblivion."

04

THE CARRIAGE PICKED UP MORE SPEED, SENDING US TOWARD THE EVER expanding spot of dim light, our acceleration accentuated by a tame but growing wind.

"I rode a bullet train like this one in Japan. Floats on magnets and whatnot. Hey tubby, how long 'til we reach the end of the line?" Dave picked up a flask from a niche in one of the padded armrests. "All these goodies make me think it could be awhile."

The priest rubbed a red mark on his face then brushed at the fine black soot covering his sleeves.

"I will not aid you. Abandon whatever scheme you have. Don't you desire redemption?"

Doug's scowl was the same one Mrs. Lincoln wore when asked if she liked the play. "Pfft. I'm way past that, Friar Tuck."

A cloud materialized overhead and in it, a pallor complexion resolved. His skin didn't suggest bloodlessness, it advised misplacement. The muscled and mostly ageless Reds and Yellows radiated a vigor. This man shared the shape and texture of their health, but his color was a parody of life. Not the silver scale of a fish, not the gray of an elephant, not the pale of sunless flesh, but a blend of all three. It was his silver slicked-back hair that made me take the cap off the pen with which I just signed his death warrant. This guy had the same stylist as someone else on my hit list.

To my eye, this character's color was closer to the Tester's metallic gray I spray-painted models with as a kid, rather than white, but our SME exclaimed differently.

"White Lord of Farnest!" The portly priest dropped and bowed deeply, his rounded abdomen preventing full supplication. He was a mouth breather and his excited gasps only made him seem more porcine. The floating head spoke.

"Faithful pilgrims, your journey to infinity begins."

I raged. "Return Talis Darmon at once and we won't destroy you."

The sallow metallic lips ignored me to continue spouting more flowered liturgy. I waved my hand through the cloud without the speaker's notice.

"It's a recorded message, brah. Hey! We'd like to speak to someone in customer service," Dave said to the silvered head. I'd missed some of the speech and tuned back in to hear if the announcer would give the game score.

"The Iridium Path brings you to Celeste Hom where you will embark on your voyage over the Blix, and at last meet the gates of the underworld. Reflect on your life and leave behind all thoughts of suffering and regret. Rejoice in joining your antecedent family. Meditate on the peace of the eternal reward that awaits. Welcome, pilgrims." The cloud dimmed.

Doug was unimpressed. "So, that was a White?" He kneed the priest. "You can get up, big boy. He didn't actually see you, dude."

The priest snapped up with a scowl. "They see your desecration."

Dave clicked on his weapon light and shined at the passing wall. "Doubtful. If they saw it was us coming and not the usual Kool-Aid drinkers, they'd have hit the breakers to this bad boy and shut us down already."

"Your derision reveals your ignorance of all that is sacred. We heard rumor that on your arrival from Thulia, you were mistaken for lords from the eternal underworld. Only a Tarn could be so easily bewildered. At the sight of such greatness, such resplendence, do you not feel shame to have permitted such deception for even a heartbeat?"

Doug snorted. "White? That guy's been huffing model paint. Or we got here in time for Mardi Gras. That color ain't natural."

The priest folded his arms into his sleeves and likewise turtled his head in between ample neck folds. "I cease my attempts to turn your hearts to piety."

A clear dome closed over us like a convertible roof to silence the growing wind. The tunnel walls suddenly flared into a kaleidoscope, pulsing in time with some ethereal instrument. The push of acceleration grew, as did the intensity of the colors and the amplitude of the meditative music.

The priest moaned, "For three hundred years have I committed myself to teaching the promises of the lessons. Always was I mindful that no matter how inspired, my words were crudely inadequate. I see now that they were more deficient than I could have imagined. It is even more beautiful than described. I come! I come! Ready to travel the Blix!" He relaxed back into the cushion.

I pulled fresh mags out of my ruck. A fuzz came over me. I missed twice as I tried to backfill my empty pouches. The light show and theremin music were having the same effect on me as too much cheap wine.

Doug swayed in his seat. "Whoa, dude. Some light show. When we were kids, we used to blow off school to do shrooms and ride Space Mountain. Anaheim had nothing on this."

Dave whipped on his Oakley's. "Dis da kine mind-screw." He rotated his hearing protection down and pressed the cups firm. I nudged Doug and pointed to Dave. He took the cue and joined me in doing the same. With our electronic ears turned off and dark glasses on, the effect lessened.

I brought the two close until our helmets bumped. "We gotta stay sharp. Anyone think they can sleep? We can stand one guy down and keep two of us on."

"Might be a long ride, brah," Dave yelled back. He pulled some earplugs out of his chest pouch. "I'm gonna double up and try."

Double plugged and feeling sharper, I faced forward and settled in with Doug, guns propped over the backrest of the front bench. Even through dark shades, the light show was mesmerizing. I got a tap on the shoulder.

"Check out fatso. He's tripped out."

The priest was locked in a trance, unblinking and under the spell of the experience.

"It's a mind-screw all right, Dougie. Meant to give a Valium sorta effect, getting us chill for what's coming next."

"Won't work on me," Dougie laughed. "I've trained for this. They'll know it when I show 'em what pure hate looks like." He patted the feed tray cover.

We traded off, and it was during our third rotation that the pulsing lights and eerie tones dimmed. We slowed. I gave a snoring Doug a shake behind us. "Get ready." Amber light returned. Deceleration pushed me aggressively into my rifle stock, loaded me on the balls of my feet, inadvertently readying me to spring. The dome retracted as the carriage broke out into a massive cavern. At once I was assaulted by too much to process. At least, anything much besides the jumbo-sized white apes.

The Hortha.

White furred arms in double pairs were raised in poses of welcome, tusks thrust to the ceiling, not intent on our murder, but in reverent hail of our arrival. From a commanding perch atop a column wrapped by spiral steps, a single decorated Hortha recovered from his pose beseeching the heavens, in time to see us glide to a stop.

For a second, the thick brow ridge and the white hair sprouting from the ears reminded me of a first sergeant I had in the 82nd. The Hortha in gold armor had the same expression of speechless amazement as that company first shirt did while he watched a new platoon leader clear a 1911. With his finger on the trigger, the butter bar racked the slide and sent a round right between his own feet. Just like then, the ape's forehead wrinkled, a furry hand shot out in accusation, and a howl I'd not heard since Fort Bragg filled the air.

My walk down memory lane ended with hell breaking loose.

From spots nestled in the cavern walls, apes beat fists on drums of bulging pectorals. A daisy chain of shrieking howls from sharp fanged mouths detonated all around us. From atop the alabaster column came not more animal noises, but a command in Mihdra.

"Punish all unclean offenders!"

Like the pistol report releasing sprinters from the starting line, they leaped. My red dot settled on the center of the closest furry white chest, and I punched the time clock to start the workday.

With every press of the trigger, tiny pink punctures appeared in the bare spot of pink skin the Hortha had over the sternum, the bullets making dimples like an index finger in Play-Doh. The white ape's charge continued, unperturbed as a frog hopping through Florida-sized raindrops. For a moment, the beast's undisturbed charge made doubt enter my heart, and I was apostate to my own faith.

I knew how to please the kill god better than this.

Without letting up, I drifted to the ridged skull and yellow eyes, and tried again. Chunks of thick skull tore loose and with them, brain. My steel core M855A1 worship was met with favor and I was once again a true apostle.

My eyes snapped to the next charging beast, but before I could break a shot, someone else's fire peppered the granite skull into red mist. There was a shriek in my ears and soft hands lacking the black nails of a Hortha pulled at me.

"Stop! You must not!"

I pivoted and drove my buttstock over my shoulder into the puffy priest's face, just as a white blur landed on the carriage tail. Four arms as thick as trees snatched the white-robed man, lifted him overhead as effortlessly as I could have, and then did what I could not. The beast stretched and the round body separated at the waist. The Hortha raged as the two halves dangled aside, just long enough for me to rotate the happy switch all the way back. I stitched him like a sewing machine. Puffs of red mist danced upward, until at last, I reached whatever computer sat at the center of the thick skull. The cranium snapped back, and heavy saliva flung from ivory yellow tusks to paint my glasses. My 60-round mag empty, I slapped in a 30-rounder, eyes driving my muzzle to the next furry albino gorilla.

From the reverse slope of the cavern came more Hortha, galloping out of their perches in their Grand Central Station to the underworld. Doug's MK 46 joined my own ballistic devotions to our rear. A wounded Hortha was a Hortha still in full charge, until the contents of their heads saw light. Together we met the last bull's charge on the tail of the carriage.

I spun back around. A sole ape dragged itself up a wide stone staircase, the marble floor streaked by a crimson path trailing back to the solitary column. It was the decorated ape perched on the central pedestal at our arrival, and the first of them yet to move in any direction except straight at us. A single precise shot puffed from Dave's carbine to punch the ape between its lower shoulder blades. A severed spinal cord clipped marioneted strings like diamond shears. Message received. The ape's chest plate clinked against the stone as it collapsed, the body too massive to resist even Mars's gravity as it became a bloody slinky, toppling down the stairs to rest in a limp pile.

Dim light filtered from the top of a landing, and the snorts of Hortha charging from outside raised my hackles. Dave and I blooped grenades into the passage. Two detonations crowded each other and stone fragments spalled from the rough walls of the corridor. A chunk sizeable enough to make me wince pinged off my helmet. The rude ringing filled my skull from eardrum to eardrum, but there was no button for me to press to prove I heard the tone of this hearing test. Around us, Hortha lay like red-stained rugs, the polished floor coated in slick red ooze, pooling slowly larger as the leaking went on.

"I'm good," I yelled.

"Up," said Dougie.

"Solid," Dave finished. "Is that our next ride?"

There'd been no chance earlier to admire the architecture, but our carriage had come to a halt in the center of a Greek temple, columns and smooth marble like someone's version of a mausoleum. A grand arch was bathed in a shimmering tapestry of lights, and through it sat a glittering crystal boat bobbing gently on a bed of mercury. The silver river disappeared into the marble face of yet another tunnel.

"Wanna bet we found the Blix?" I said. The sharp ringing in my ears had changed to the low whine of an idling aircraft engine. My own voice was all but inaudible to me. I pulled out the earplugs, pinched my nose, and swallowed hard. My eardrums popped. Better.

Moving as one, we sprang off the carriage. The talking Hortha wasn't dead. Spined, it used its upper arms to pull itself up the stairs. Its lower arms drooped like willow branches. The white coat was stained red. Its pelvis and legs twisted unnaturally, as if they wished to go in the opposite direction. All combined to make the Hortha a red-on-white spiral candy cane. Doug shouldered his gun.

"Hold up," I said. "Anyone else hear this one talk before the fight kicked off?" A silver metal cap domed its skull. What could only be the band of a decipher rested in the muscled valley between shoulder and bicep. In perfect Mihdra, it spoke.

"Kingdoms of the prideful, prince and slave, heavy from office and toils, all come to the portal of Celeste Hom to be found pious. What manner of false gods do you serve that dare attempt shake the pillars of the underworld? The White Lords of—"

A shot rang out, the gargantuan head snapped back, and the beast collapsed, its oration ceased.

Dave lowered his rifle. "Merry Christmas."

"Dammit, Dave," I cursed with real irritation. "We needed information."

"Sorry, Ben. Talking apes is where I draw the line, brah."

A blast of cold air raced from the top of the stairs, and a chill deeper than the night of the high Korund hit me. I pointed my rifle up. Icy air blew in on the pale rays of light from the world outside. It teased us closer, and I moved to take the invitation. I counted silently as we climbed, a reflex of my pace count habit—a tonic to silence my conscious mind. Twenty-five stairs put us at the top of the landing. Past the comforting carnage of two apes perforated by our 40-mm grenades, a long forgotten sight floated on the wings of a freezing wind.

Snow.

"Brainy was going for help," Doug said. "Could be more cavalry out there riding to the rescue."

We barreled through a curving tunneled passage, ready to kill. The outer doors were half open, and dregs of daylight filtered through. Standing in ankle-deep snow, we lowered our guns in wonder. White saw-toothed peaks and ridges surrounded us. Snow drifted across a cobblestone path that disappeared behind the bend of a narrow pass. At our sides, stairs climbed and wrapped around the entrance to a terrace holding more of the columns the Hortha perched on inside. It was the redoubt for watchmen—apes—carved into the mountain.

"We mighta seen that from the air, brah. Makes Mount Rushmore kinda underwhelming."

"So far, everything Kleeve Hartus told us has been true," I said.

The masterpiece of a hundred sculptors was chiseled in relief above the valley.

The crystal barge, its sails full, floated on a placid river. Carved on the deck were human and Tarn forms, some kneeling, some in embrace, all with eyes fixed toward a starburst sun, rays extended like outstretched hands. It was the sign to the pilgrim on the treacherous trail to the River Blix that their destination had been reached and the expiation of their sins would be accepted.

This was Celeste Hom.

"Yeah, yeah. It's what he didn't tell us I'm worried about, brah. He was a little light on details about what's waiting at the pearly gates."

Doug cocked an eyebrow. "What's got you worried, Dave? You never worry about anything."

"Think I'm wrong to be, Dougie-Doug? This morning, all was right in our world. You know—business as usual, picking up the pieces of a Ben misadventure. From the Furrow we rush back to the defense of what I thought was our home, only to have to escape a lynch mob led by a man I thought was our friend. Then, a psychedelic train to Santa's North Pole workshop where we slaughter all his elves. With a Shakespeare-talking ape to boot. Not to mention as many gunfights as I've had in a single day, and the day ain't even over. Brah, don't you think what's waiting at our next stop rates a little concern?"

"Screw it, homie. Every day on Mars is selection. At least, I reckon we're still on Mars. We been at least one weird place that wasn't."

The focused last rays of the setting sun flared over the top of the snowy peaks and stars awakened in the crisp sky. The pale glow of the first of the twin sisters was rising into view. "This train ride wasn't any hocus-pocus like that other trip," I said. "We're still on Vistara."

"Brrr. See, Davey?" Doug said as he rubbed his arms. "Nothing to worry about."

Dave's lips were taking on a blue tint. "Say what you will about the Harridan, brah, but the old girl kept the thermostat in her romper room set at a cozy sixty-eight degrees."

Doug's teeth chattered like a windup toy. "True dat, homey. Even the fur-squids liked to boogaloo in shirt sleeve weather. Let's get back inside."

I checked my watch. "Wait. I missed commo time with Karlo." To activate the link, I thought of him, tapped my wristlet once, then a second time. I convulsed with an uncontrollable shiver. "Brrr. That's the blind contact. He'll ping us back when he's safe to talk. Let's get inside and do post-engagement while we wait."

Warmth returned as we returned to the scene of our firefight. I found my 60-round mag on the floor of the carriage. It'd been a lifesaver busting into this mess. I pulled stripper clips from my ruck and started jamming, jammed my other mags full, and made sure every pouch was backfilled. Karlo still hadn't responded.

"Dave, could we be too deep in here for me to receive Karlo's ping back?"

"Dunno, brah. This has gotta be the farthest we've ever been. All the way to the top of the world. Or maybe, we're up against them running the same interference they used over the capital. Hate to say it, but we should give it another try again from outside."

So we did. The wind blew straight through to my spine, my lungs burned, and I thought the enamel would chip off my teeth as my jaws clicked together like a sewing machine. In the time since the sun had disappeared completely behind the mountains, it had dropped at least another twenty degrees. This time, a cloud with two faces answered my signal. Karlo and Cynar both scanned the landscape behind us.

"Ben, is that snow on the ground?"

Doug huddled down to stick his face in, stuttering as he shivered like a dog fished out of an icy pond. "Smartest guy in the room, my ass."

Karlo rolled eyes. "I love you too, Dougie."

Cynar stroked his beard. "You have reached the farthest north."

Dave joined our group hug. "Hear these chattering teeth, brah? If these aren't the Sharpa Mountains, I'm Marco Polo."

I gave a quick report of our encounters. "We're headed out now. Pretty sure we'll be out of commo until this over. What's your sitrep?"

"Not good. Not bad. I sealed the vault room and we're holed up in Cynar's lab. Kleeve Hartus is taking charge. We've denounced you guys, promised him we tried to stop you, sworn loyalty, all that stuff. Perrin Halser's backed us up, so for now, the first shield seems satisfied. He's going to summon us tomorrow when he seats the council. That's all I know."

"Did the Tarns leave?"

"We watched Double-K march two battalions of arkall down the Concourse of Diasemony. He never looked back. Sarkan Sell rode over to try to convince us to go with them. If things go bad for us here, Ben, that's where we'll be. One other thing—Beraal had your creche in her arms, Apache at her side, and a ring of Tarns guarding them all."

Our child was safe. My shaking stopped.

"We'll comm as soon as we can, Karlo. And when we do, it'll be because it's over. Keep the home fires burning."

A fire sounded good.

"Benjamin Colt." Cynar stepped closer. "If ever you think I doubted your intelligence, do not. Whatever manner of mind perpetrates this crime, they are no match for your sagacity. Do what only you and your friends can do, Warlord. Bring chaos into their midst."

The cloud vanished.

Back inside, the three of us beat and dusted the frost from our limbs. Dave bounced in place like a pogo stick. "Who thought there was snow on Mars? We should skin these things, brah. Their fur looks warm."

I pointed through the colorful mist to the crystal vessel and the canal of silvery liquid. "Where we're going, we won't have to worry about snow. That way leads into the mountain, not out."

"Wish we had a fire," Dougie said. "I'd like to be good and warm one last time."

Dave stopped his knee-pumping run in place. "One last time? Who's the worrywart now? What up?"

Doug banished the last of his chill with one final violent shake, then slung his rifle over his neck. "Cynar making nicey-nice with Ben-dog makes me rethink what you were saying, dude. That rah-rah speech could only be because he thinks we're headed for the last roundup."

"Then let's saddle up, cowboys," I said.

Dave thumbed at the waiting ship. "Brah, I think you mean, argh, maties. All aboard the *Flying Dutchman!*"

05

PLUSH SEATS LIKE THOSE ON THE CARRIAGE COVERED THE CRYSTAL deck. "They apportion their rides well, I'll give 'em that," Doug said. "I've seen first-rate Tijuana upholstery jobs not as good as this. We'll be cushy comfy for the sail."

"Negative," I said. "Just like that train carriage, someone other than us controls it." I grabbed two handfuls of the loose edge of the furled ball from my ruck and, just the way I'd seen Cynar do, gripped tightly and flung away. Out snapped the un-nautical shape of one of the wizard's canoes.

"Closest thing we'll get to a stealth delivery," I said as I laid it on the quicksilver. I stepped in, the bottom deepening, the beam widening in response, the same as it would on water. "Pass in the rucks."

Doug winced. "Shoulda brought one for each of us. We're gonna swamp it, dude. And that stuff looks like mercury. Hazmat to the max."

I groaned. "Don't make me do a Cynar, Dougie. I've had two people, a Tarn, and a gadron in one this size before. It'll hold us."

Any reluctance shed with a shrug, Dougie stepped in. After the challenge of a few bounces to prove the rim of our canoe remained high above the poisonous river, he pushed his ruck forward for a seat. "Wherever the end of the line is, I'm hoping it's far enough away they didn't hear the ruckus we caused."

Dave took a spot next to him. "Fat chance, that. You got the go-go thingy, Ben?"

I held up the small rectangle. "Cynar says this'll work even if they try some of their voodoo on us. He got all pissy with me when I asked

45

how he knew. Must be a chemical reaction. Or something. Bet he never planned we'd be using it in mercury instead of water. Hope it doesn't blow up."

"Maybe it'll do his turn-to-concrete trick and we can walk there," Dave said.

"Here goes." I placed it on the flat transom at the rear of the canoe. It held when I released it, then on its own, slid down beneath the surface. A silvery swell formed behind us. We were off.

Doug dug into his ruck. "Getting warmer, at least. Puffy clouds and harps, here we come."

"Heaven's not in a hole in the ground, brah. If it starts getting hot, then we know we're heading for the other place."

"Your granny teach you that, dude?"

"My tutu taught me a lot. Right now, I wish I'd have listened harder. Like how to pray."

"Bro-man, if we are headed to hell—s'all good. 'Cause the kinda heat we're bringing'll make 'em think we belong." Doug pulled out a MK 14. If spaces were tight, the six-shot grenade launcher would be dead weight. If they weren't, it'd be glorious.

This tunnel was crystalline and pulsed in colors more soothing than those along the Iridium Path. Doug grunted. "These guys sure believe in the wow factor, don't they? Who the hell do they think they're impressing? You got a take on all this yet, Ben?"

I'd learned nothing concrete before I abandoned my brief investigations into Vistaran cosmology. Though it started as little more than a hunch, my belief was growing even firmer. "They've got the whole planet suckered. And whatever happens to people when they reach the end of the Blix, it isn't something good."

"Hear that, Davey-Dave? I happen to know that where Ben-dog was raised, going to church was mandatory. If he don't believe this is some kind of supernatural deal, no way you should. Feel better?"

Dave settled in behind his carbine. "Don't worry about me, brah. I'm not confused about nothin'. This is some kinda mind-screw all right, pulled outta Psyops 101. Even Talis Darmon went all, 'yes, sir—

no, sir—three bags full, sir,' when some white goon told her to jump. Only way that happens is da kine cultural conditioning-type thing. On a humble day, she's as headstrong as a kid straight outta jump school. If they got *her* to surrender without a fight, ain't no one in Mihdradahl with the balls to tell some white goon to get stuffed if they came to take them away on their UFO."

It was true. Even Talis Darmon had been fooled. And she wasn't the believer some were. I'd thought the Blix and Farnest all metaphor until the day I saw four men get on an underground subway. All she'd said about it was, "They go where they dream."

Doug wasn't ready to let it go just yet. "Think they're running some kinda prison labor camps? Or is it some kinda Soylent Green thing? As long as this has been going on, how many people you think coulda ended up here?"

I'd dreaded the answer. "Dunno. Kleeve Hartus said there were more portals to the underworld around Vistara. But when I was Aetheria, I found out the Yellows don't play along with this. Neither does Pyreenia. But even if this is the only route in service, over so long, it must be a huge number."

"So, what happens to all the people who come this way, brah?"

"We're going to find out."

Doug scoffed, "I'm thinking that whatever kind of cult hides under a mountain and plays at being some kind of angels, they deserve to be shot first and asked questions later." He slung the grenade launcher around his neck and positioned it at his side. "And maybe we don't know much, but from what we've experienced so far, I think these Whites are gonna be overly confident. A gorilla Mount Olympus for their outer cordon of security? Clown shoes. Just more wow factor for the rubes. And since we ain't fallin' for it, that's gonna let us get the drop on them."

"Them apes almost ate our lunch, brah."

Doug's hands were back on the MK 46, positioning it to rest it over the bow. "And now they're peeling bananas in white ape heaven. End of story."

I pulled on the wide magazine again to make sure it was seated properly in my rifle, one of the hundred compulsive tics of a gunfight-er. "I think Dougie's got it pegged. We caught the bouncers flat-footed. Anyone trying to sneak into the club during ladies' lock-up would've gotten the same treatment they gave that priest. The Whites are certain to be overconfident that anyone making it through the velvet ropes and all the way to their VIP room are fully primed for the fleecing. What we're bringing? They've never seen."

Dave growled, "Da kine hate."

Doug laughed. "Straight up, dog."

We were agreed. I made my last oath on the subject. "Talis Darmon's coming home with us. And if the hole in the ground the Whites are hiding in isn't hell, by the time we're done, it will be."

✱ ✱ ✱

I finished by slinging a bandolier of 40 mm and another of frag gre-nades around me. With my rifle, pistol, the sword on my back, and enough demo in my ruck to bring the mountain down around us, I was ready. Dave was humming. Took me a second to recognize it. I had no clue Dave knew any classical music. "Classy, Dave. Spot on."

He stopped. "Huh?"

"What you're humming, Davey. 'In the Hall of the Mountain King.'"

"Seemed more appropriate than Slayer. Funny, the stuff comes to mind at times like this."

Doug disagreed. "Humph. Slayer's always the right call, dude."

The river never curved, and the light show interfered with any sense of an approaching end to it. Rather than calm me, the colors annoyed me like a commercial interrupting the movie at the best part. Or the guy who raises his hand to ask a question as the meeting's breaking up. The waitress disappearing just when you want the bill. Add them all together, and it didn't make me as irritable as I was when I thought about Talis Darmon being taken in by the Whites' existential charade.

Who would I get to punish for it?

We coasted on a mirror reflecting the rainbow light show. The parting of the mercury by the bow was the only sound, and it became as vexing as the music on the train had been. "We need to bag a live prisoner to help us find her," I said. "Talking to you, Dave." My irritability at his killing the talking ape was back. I caught myself. "Sorry, bro. Just feeling prickly."

"Yeah, yeah," Dave said back at me with a lilt. "I'll get us someone. No worries."

Doug spit angrily into the river, as if daring it to spit back. "First things first, Ben-dog. Anyone who don't give it up, gets schwacked."

"This isn't a hostage rescue. This is a raid to liberate a prisoner from an enemy fortification. They all get schwacked. And whatever happens, if there's only one of us left, get her out of there."

Dougie turned and grinned. "You're going to carry her out of here over the bodies of every silvered booger-eater under the mountain, Ben-dog. Promise."

"Look alive," Dave said. The shape of the vanishing point down the mercury river was developing into something new. The end of the line was approaching.

"Respirators and goggles on, bros," Doug said. "It's time."

Unexpectedly pedestrian and lacking the grandeur of what came before, the river dead-ended in a small chamber roughly cut into the rock. Adjacent the river was a narrow walkway. What reminded me of a ticket booth window sat beside the square frame of a portcullis. It was a fortified control point to the Whites' lair. I felt surer I was correct about what Farnest really was. We were out and charging.

Through the window appeared a lead-gray face cased in silver hair. He wasn't a welcoming angel. He was a DMV clerk, calling out a number.

"Through this door, Farnest awaits. Step forward and—"

Surprise cracked the ticket taker's mask like a dropped mirror shattering into a million pieces.

I was bringing my gun the last inch up when I felt the jolt of touching an electric fence. Despite all my efforts to move, I was locked in place.

A burst from Doug's gun chewed into the window with a *cha-cha-cha-cha,* and as instantly, I was released. His MK 46 had been leveled at the window and his finger must have been in the trigger guard. Whatever defensive measure had been meant to render us useless, when it hit us, it only served to spasm Doug's finger into perfect, deadly action. Dave sprinted to the window, M67 grenade in hand.

"Frag out," Dave said with voice muffled by his respirator. I dropped.

Ka-WHOOM. Shards of shrapnel and stone sprayed out of the window, and I was on my feet. On the floor, the clerk's body was splayed out in bloody bits. I put three more quick ones into the chest, proving to myself he wasn't going to zombie back into action. "I'm going in," I yelled, and made to vault through the aperture. There had to be an exit or a way to open the portal beside it. It was just common sense.

"NO!" Doug yelled. "Better living through C-4." He was already at the portcullis, running a strip charge down the middle of it. Before I could object, Dave was pulling at my ruck, Doug's wide back a retreating wall to herd us behind him.

"Brace for it. FIRE IN THE HOLE."

Before I had the chance for dread to build up from my pit of been-here-before, I assumed the position. Eyes squeezed shut, mouth open, yelling to expel all my air, our world became the fury that created the universe. I opened my eyes again.

On his hands and knees, Doug was down. Not even Thor could conquer the great god Overpressure. He paid the price of our admission, and it was no time to waste his down payment for our success. I stepped around him, flashbang already in hand. I tossed it deep.

As it made firecracker thunder, I slid laterally and peeked at what lay beyond. A short hall opened into a larger space, where blurred human shapes scurried away. One came from the opposite direction. The fish swimming against the school was always the shark. A muscular White raised something in my direction. I lit into him, and he reacted like any mere mortal. His shape changed from standing menace to a heap of dung in seconds. A riot of voices rose from within.

I hesitated, said "screw it," cocked the 40 mm and let fly with a smoke grenade. It would make it harder for us to see targets, but a lot harder for them to see us. Dave's tube followed a split second behind mine with the familiar *thoomp*, but the *kerblooey* that came at the end of his grenade launch announced to us all that he hadn't had a smoke in his pipe like I'd had in mine.

Nothing to be done about it now. Shit happens when you play roughhouse, and it was no time for tears. I had said we were going to shwack them all. It bought me a second to turn back to see Doug making it the last few inches to his feet.

"Shake it off, Dougie. Let's go!"

He lifted the chin of his mask and a thick waterfall of bloody snot spilled out. Blood leaked from under the cups of his hearing protection. As if jostling his brain even more would help, he shook his head like a dog with a rat in his jaws. No punch to the face could ring your bells like overpressure, and to get rid of that fog you'd try anything. I had the T-shirt for that one, too.

Doug expanded to full size. "RAAAR! Coming through!" He dashed to the mangled portcullis and before I could halt him, out flew the first round from his MK 14. The explosion ripped deep from the smokey cloud that filled the space ahead. There was indeed a big space beyond, I could tell by the echo of the explosion. Doug released the revolving grenade launcher in favor of his MK 46, and sprang. I was ahead of Dave to be on the big man's heels.

I rolled an ankle on the remnants of the portcullis, tripped, then found solid footing just as Dave slid past me. Doug was paused short of a corner, waiting for someone to be in his peripheral before stepping off. He chugged out a burst from his MK 46 at a gray shape in the mist.

It dropped, and what was on the ground did a good imitation of the funky chicken before it died.

Whatever the Whites were, they were no more god than a big black squid had been.

"Do it!" I yelled from between them, and we stepped out.

I took a step in, my left and right protected by the finest assaulters who ever lived. At last, we were in the kind of grand place I'd expected. It was the size of a stadium. One much too big for three men to control.

There was nothing fortified or defensive-looking about what I saw. We'd surprised a huge gathering in a space meant for it. Lounges, tables, cushions—everything gave me the vibe of a Roman estate laid out for a party. Runners dashed from behind the cover of furniture. Some wisely crawled.

Know how to eat an elephant? One bite at a time. From right where we were.

My first time in a shoothouse, and against instructions to do otherwise, I'd done what many do the first time they see there's something needs shooting. I'd charged at the target while pressing the trigger. The instructor laughed as he tapped my carbine with a finger.

"Know what the Indians call this? The stick that kills from long distance."

Call it bad taste, call it racially insensitive, call it what you will, but some indigenous person somewhere in North America, when first witnessing a European oppressor and their gun, had called it that. The stick that kills from long distance. The lesson was learned forever. From right where we were, with boom-sticks in hand, we could fight the whole space.

Those leaving our death zone, I allowed. My eye lighted on one of the many, many archways and deep spaces, waiting for more of the type who ran *to* danger to appear. And when the first lead-colored complexion with something in their hands presented, well, there's nothing fancy about the work. It's always the same. My dot settled and I pressed the trigger. And with me, my two brothers did their own work.

Until there was no one left to shoot.

The smoke settled. The quiet that comes with the cease fire is a disquieting interruption, not knowing if the last clap of thunder means the storm had passed, or if it was only the brief calm before the tornado appeared.

"Movement, nine o'clock," Doug said.

Feet and guns moved on line as one to cover the raised platform and the wall behind it, where a portal finished sliding open. Things accelerated to a blur. I saw the glow, I saw the outline of the man, and the arms of Moses parting the sea. I hesitated firing.

Because I couldn't.

My feet left the ground and my rifle was snatched from my hands. My sling kept it attached to my body to become a harness on a team of horses, me the wagon they pulled behind. I levitated forward. The commanding figure of a White was there on the stage, his arms spread wide, holding a staff glowing with power. An hourglass figure trailing a long gown stepped from the wings, a wicked smile spreading across her lips.

"Oblivion for you," the wizard said, and the glow of his staff flared brighter.

Killing someone with a pistol is damn near an accident. A pistol is what you have when you can't have a real weapon in your hands. And the most overemphasized skill in the world—the most bragged about, though rarely used of all the things a gunfighter practices—is the draw. Cold, I could draw and fire two rounds into a six-inch circle from ten yards in under a second.

My pistol was in my hands and recoiling before I'd even thought.

The White wizard's hands sprang to his neck. Geysers of blood shot out from between gaps in his close-packed fingers. Today, the over-practiced and never used skill was called from my subconscious repository like a memory recovered by hypnosis.

Our would-be abuser just learned the real deal—better be sure your supposed victims don't have a bad-touch worse than yours.

The wisp of his last threatening syllable hadn't escaped before I'd put the period on his sentence from fifty yards. I hadn't even tried. I landed on my feet, pistol in hands. Two pieces of brass bounced off the floor, their music a micro overture to the full symphony that followed. Two weapons beside me cranked to life, and the magician erupted in tiny bloody chunks. The firefight paused, and the wizard took on the last and best shape an opponent could assume.

The limp heap of dead meat.

If the woman had any magic tricks of her own, she abandoned them in favor of getting out of Dodge. Before the White conjurer had finished collapsing to the deck, Dave was already in the air and after her. Finally, there was space enough to be supermen again. I launched as well. By the time I landed beside the wizard's body, Dave had tackled the woman and rode her down like a bag of wet cement.

"Alive, Dave!"

I had nothing to worry about. She thrashed like a fish on the deck of a boat as Dave put a knee on her neck. "She's plenty that, brah." He twisted a wrist to the small of her back and pulled a flex cuff. She gasped as the other wrist was wrenched back, the ratcheting plastic clicks the assurance of a valued friend saying he wouldn't let you down.

Doug was there on our seized hilltop to join my search for the next White to need filling in. The slaughterhouse floor below us was placid for as far as I could see. Not quite a pastoral scene, as there were no shepherds and sheep, just stillness. Death's last sweet breath had caressed to sleep any White who had the misfortune to stick around.

Not gods at all.

"I've had enough friggin' magic to last me a lifetime, homies." Dougie peeled off his respirator and did the Detroit handkerchief, one nostril at a time, then wiped at the bloody stream drying on both sides of his neck. A little too loudly—deaf—the real wizard of destruction cracked his corded neck, and spat on the bullet-riddled corpse.

"How'd that work out for you, Whitey?"

06

Dave kneeled on our prisoner's back, his rifle up and ready to fight. She serenaded us with strained groans but no longer thrashed. "Got you a prisoner. One a helluva lot better than some talking monkey. All forgiven, brah? Where to?"

It was a good spot from which to view Farnest. Its welcome hall was as big as a football stadium. Dead Whites littered the field—enough bodies to make for two teams and their second strings. A battleground it was not. It was exactly what a good assault should look like.

A crime scene.

"Time to get out of this big open." Where David Copperfield with the Moses staff and his girlfriend appeared from seemed like a good bet. "Let's get some walls between us and all this big empty and ask our tour guide where to next."

"Whah?" Doug said.

I put my face where he could see my lips. "Hey, human blast blanket, we're going this way. How fricking large was that charge?"

"I wasn't having any more of that Taser shit. I figured my biggest door charge would get us in *and* futz with their gizmos. But that levitation shit, that was a new one. Nice shot, by the way."

"Nice shot *you*, Dougie. More than one, too."

Dave had the gal in the evening gown on her feet. "I got her. Let's move."

Doug and I went first. The room was a smaller version of what was outside. Lounges and tables piled with trays of morsels, like a talk show green room. If there was another exit, I didn't see it. It was time for answers.

"Give her to me." I pinned the woman against a wall while the guys tucked around the door to watch outside for any new arrivals. Up close with my first live White, the leaden tint made her smooth skin not ageless, but inhuman. Her yellow eyes burned with defiance.

"I haven't had a lot of success asking it this way, but I'm thinking you'll be the exception and understand. Wanna guess why we're here?"

I should've expected the spit in my eyes. "To make yourselves gods in our place? You're animals. Barely more than the primordial muck you were created from. How dare you—"

I am a slow learner. A firm palm into her chest, she got the message that with one good push, I could make her sternum touch her spine and turn everything in between to mush. She silenced.

"Let me introduce myself. I am Warlord Benjamin Colt. I'm the victor of every battle and conqueror of every land. I'm the mass murderer who used poison gas to kill an entire army, then slept like a baby. I killed the god Anso-Kylon and banished the Karnak, something not even Jawn Kurz could do. I've done what no man has ever done on Vistara. And I did it all to protect my queen."

She opened her mouth to reply, but against another ounce of my force, she closed it.

"Before you answer, let me make myself clear. You sent an airship to Shansara. Threatened our kingdom. Kidnapped our queen. Call me an animal? You have no idea. Give me Talis Darmon or what I'll do to this place, a hundred history mirrors won't contain the horror of it."

I released some of the pressure. The fire in her eyes was quenched. In its place was fear. At last, I'd made the right impression. I hate having to spell things out. "Now you know who I am. Your name?"

"I am Queen Lashura, benevolent light of beacon to Temple Farnest."

"Was that the king?"

She broke down. "My brother, my husband, my king, Zan-Sha. For eight hundred years has he ruled."

"Everything has an end, lady," Doug said from behind us.

I brought her face up. "I don't know what you've been up to here, but I know it isn't what the pilgrims think. You're going to walk me through it. Out there—you have some kind of welcome for them, yes?"

She nodded.

"Then what? Where do they get taken?"

"To meet their ancestors."

"I bet. Is that where you took Talis Darmon?"

"All pilgrims who arrive are welcomed with a feast, then are admitted to the underworld."

"Take us, Lashura." I thrust her in the lead, a handful of gown gathered behind her shoulders, my rifle in the other. Dave and Doug fell in on either side. "You guide us, we'll follow. Do anything stupid, and it's going to go rough for you. Where are we going?"

Hands still cuffed behind her back, her chin indicated the way. "Through the hall of reception, then on the left is the entrance to the golden path. There the pilgrims are invited to take their last steps to enter the paradise of the underworld."

I directed her down on to the floor and on a course through the carnage toward the farthest opening at the end of the hall. "Keep talking me through everything as we go." We'd broken up some kind of welcome feast, all right. Overturned tables, spilled foods and drinks, and Whites, dead at our hands.

This was a new role for me. I was the hostage taker. I was the bad guy. Hell, I was a terrorist. Think it was because I was desperate to rescue Talis Darmon? Sure, but I'd had to deal with situations like this too many times before, and I hadn't done anything like this. What was the difference? It lay in what I felt certain we were about to learn the Whites had been up to. And *that* I felt certain would make what I was doing a minor blip on my ethical radar.

Dave didn't take his eyes off his flank to speak. "We caught you with your pants down, didn't we, lady? How come you weren't expecting us?"

I jostled her to answer him, and she took the cue. "We gathered when the alert let it known that the Iridium Path had been used. But when no alert came to tell us that pilgrims traveled farther on the Blix from Celeste Hom, we assumed the Hortha had found the arrivals impious, so we retired to the feast. We should have suspected there was something amiss when no report came from the Hortha." She sniffled. "But a pack of roamak coming to bite the hands of the gods? This we did not give consideration."

Doug clucked. "Slaying gods is what we do, lady."

She'd said something interesting. "What does it mean to be impious, Lashura?" I asked. When she didn't answer, I gave her a shake of encouragement. I wanted Talis Darmon back, but I also wanted to understand the deception that brought her here.

Dave dismissed my question. "Pfft. No mystery there, brah. Anyone who sees the big monkeys and figures out this is a ruse gets ripped apart, amiright?"

Lashura bristled but answered. "We are not cruel, nor harsh, nor callous. Some of the pilgrims are—unsuitable."

"Sounds like I had it right," Dave said. "You let the apes knock off anyone who decides they want to take the return trip outta there and ruin your OPSEC."

We passed an avenue leading into the great room like the one we'd taken, and at the end of it was another closed portcullis. As we continued toward the arch of what she called the golden path, we passed another of the passages secured by a solid gate on the opposite wall. That made for three of them, including the one we came by.

"Brah," Dave said to get my attention as we continued our march. "You thinking what I am? Are those ways into Farnest like the one we came in on? More Blixes on the other sides of those gates? Where the hell do they come *from*? Do we gotta worry about QRFs of apes pouring in from them?"

Dave was right. From any one of these, an army of Hortha could come up behind us. I had the same intuition, but ignored the risk while

I tried to get us to Talis Darmon as expeditiously as possible. "How about it, Lashura?"

This time she answered without further threat. "Yes. From across Vistara they come, by one of the three branches of the River Blix. To join their ancestors, and receive the answer to the great question."

"What do we do about it, brah?"

The saying was, if you find yourself in hell, keep going. "We're too light. If we had more ass, we could do something about it. Our best bet is to plow through. I vote we keep our momentum. Sooner we find her, the sooner we can get out of here."

"Agreed," Dougie said. "But back up. What's this 'great question' shit? Like the meaning of life?"

Lashura's manner changed. With an eager perkiness she said, "Come, and you too shall have the knowledge."

We had arrived at the arch, framed by sculptures of more of the outstretched arms of all shapes, open palms welcoming and indicating the way.

"Hold up," I said as I pulled her to a stop. The floor was washed in gold and embedded with gems, another of the ostentatious touches meant to wow a pilgrim. The walls of the passage moved with the living images of white-robed Red and Green, walking hand in hand like a hippie Coke commercial toward a shimmering waterfall of light. The path ended in a similar curtain of rainbows. My spidey sense tingled.

"What's through there?"

"All you seek. She awaits for you on the other side of that curtain separating the world above from the way to the next."

Doug spat. "I'm worn out with this theme park bullshit. She thinks we're like all the other suckers. Hold up. Watch our back, Davey-Dave." Doug's MK 46 hung loose as he fiddled with something. "Ain't it always the same? The gun goes away, so does the fear. Then they think they can do you dirty. Let's try this." He held up a frag grenade, a loop of 550 cord around its narrow neck, and showed it to Lashura.

"You don't have to have seen one before to know it's bad, huh?"

She flinched as he placed the noose over her head, gasping as he pulled the sliding knot tight, until the grenade was an OD green pendant hanging below the soft divot of her throat. He worked quickly, then held up looped coils of green cord.

"I straightened the pin a little, and this is tied to the ring. I pull this," he made a pantomimed tug, "and off comes your head. Or you trip, or you run for it—kerblooey. Don't make him ask again. What's behind the door?"

Whatever hope she'd lofted by her confidence game came crashing down. She sobbed. "You are all our creations. You live to serve us. How could animals become capable of such treachery?"

Dave rolled his eyes. "And we thought Brandon Bryant had a god complex. You didn't create us, lady. We're not from around here."

I took her chin. "Tell me."

She was beaten. "It is the first of the preparation chambers. The rays of the curtain dissociate the will from the mind. Attendants wait to receive each pilgrim for the journey to the underworld."

Preparation chamber? That gave me memories of the room where my family hung our deer every season.

Doug took her by the scruff of her neck. "Anyone waiting for us through the light show's going to have the worst day of their life, Lashura. Move."

At the falling rainbow cascade, she spoke. The curtain evaporated to reveal a simple room in which were parked carriages like the one in Transspellum, but smaller, each meant for an individual.

"You first, Lashura. No tricks, or you're dead meat."

The grenade beneath her chin swayed with each of her carefully measured steps. The slack of the leash that tethered her to life played out its last inches when she stopped and pointed at the wall. It was a portal the width of the room, a recognizable panel next to it.

"Through there."

Doug tied a small loop at end of the cord for a secure pull, and handed the coils to me. "Don't like it, Ben. Let's let whoever's on the other side know we're not screwing around. I got another strip charge begging to peel that bad boy open."

"No!" the woman shrieked. "What awaits beyond is fragile. To bring the destruction you have wreaked elsewhere would be—detrimental to your cause. I wish to see your Red woman returned to you. She lies beyond. Take her and leave this place forever. I will see it safely done. In return we will abandon our call to Mihdradahl. You have my solemn promise."

Were she a Red, I'd say her desperation was genuine. But a White with a god complex?

"First, see us safely to Talis Darmon, Lashura. Then we'll talk about it. Unless you're ready to go to the underworld without a head." I dangled the cord as Doug had. "But I'm betting there isn't an eternal underworld, is there?"

"No deceit do I utilize. I am queen. It is my responsibility to secure the safety of my people from your vengeance. You have won."

"Find cover," I said. I took her with me to the forward most row of carriages and pointed at the panel, letting out all the play in the 550 cord. Like the guys, I knelt behind a carriage. "Do it, Lashura."

She touched the panel and the wall lifted. The entire room glided smoothly forward into the new chamber. Like one of Cynar's workshops, glowing panels and contrivances of all sorts lined the walls and benches. A forest of floor-to-ceiling cylinders bubbled purple fluid. Next to some of them were the same carriages as the ones we crouched behind, their empty cushions reclined flat.

On only one of them was there a body. Beneath a sheet lay Talis Darmon.

"She is there," Lashura said.

"We got the prisoner," Dave said as he and Doug rushed to hold Lashura.

I dropped the coil and shot like a cannon for the supine form of my wife. A spectrum of lights from above danced over her shape in a rotating pattern. After today, I'd never think about the colors of the rainbow the same again.

From behind a column of thick bubbling liquid, a White leaped out. In his cocked arm, he wielded some blazing red weapon.

"Animals!"

The attacker sprang his ambush from too far away to reach me.

"Don't shoot him," I yelled. Lashura said everything was fragile. Who knew if damaging any mechanism in the laboratory would harm Talis Darmon?

"Moving," Dave yelled, already airborne. I kept my attention on reaching Talis Darmon, to shield her with my body. Dave predicted the man's path, landing in time to intercept the White's wild charge. Dave thrust his muzzle into the lead-gray face. As if shot, the man flung backward. Feet in the air, he landed with a crack, his skull impacting first. The burning blade in his fist extinguished as it fell from his grasp.

Queen Lashura yelled, "You must not harm the Guarantor!"

Dave bent over his handiwork and grimaced. "That's on him."

On the only occupied bed, the tiny lights continued to prickle the sheet over her feminine form. Thin gold wires protruded from her bare scalp. Talis Darmon's face was unblemished and serene. She was breathing. I burbled anguish as I ran my hands over her to find what other indignities had been done to her. Besides taking her hair, I didn't see any other signs of harm. My fever rose again. I cautiously moved my hand closer to her scalp and the offending wires.

"What the hell have you done to her?"

Hefted aloft, Doug deposited Lashura next to me.

"Answer him!"

"She is not yet transcended. But you need the Guarantor! He alone knows how to return her."

Dave dragged the latest attacker over by a single heel. He scooped the limp and bound body onto a cushion, then peeled both yellow eyes back. "He's down for the count." Dave produced a slim handle from his dump pouch, examined it, then thumbed something. The red blaze of an energy ignited and sprang to the length of a knife. "This ain't no flashlight." He extinguished it. "Mad scientist is what this guy is, brah."

I raged at Lashura. "He can't be the only one who knows how to help her. Where are his assistants? There are always assistants."

She pleaded, "Fled, joined with the others to hide from your wrath. I appeal to whatever intelligence you may possess. Do not act rashly. We will recover her. It is not too late." She looked truly fearful. She correctly understood my desperation meant ill for her and her kind. She repeated to herself things which I heard only in snippets. "We are the beneficent peace and purpose."

I turned back and bent to Talis Darmon's ear. "It's going to be alright. I'm here." I laid my hand on her forehead. My palm brushed a wire and it fell off, leaving no mark behind. I touched another, and it did the same. So did the next.

Dave lowered beside me. "Ben, is that a good idea? Maybe we call Karlo and ask him?"

I brushed across her crown, clearing away all the offending probes, and flung the bundle of thin wires away. "It's done." The lights from above ceased twinkling.

As suddenly, her eyes opened. She gasped deeply. I spoke timidly in her ear.

"Talis Darmon, do you hear me?"

Slowly her face turned to mine. Her eyes cleared and she answered weakly. "I do, husband."

My heart started again. She breathed deeply to expand her chest, and a wrinkled, vicious scowl broke across her face. My voice had never brought from her such a visage. She raised up with such purpose and vigor, like a lioness disturbed from sleep in its den, that the suddenness caused me to shrink back from the bite to come. It was not the reunion I'd anticipated.

"I am at last awake from a dream."

Of the many Talis Darmons I knew, this was a Talis Darmon I'd seen but once. The one who'd torn apart a treacherous brother with the skill of a master assassin. An aura of red like the scientist's knife flared from her. An accusing digit found Queen Lashura.

"White! I know your secret. I know your deception. I know your crimes. And though there is not punishment fit, I will craft one. And my Warlord will see it done.

"For you have brought your end of days."

✖ ✖ ✖

She sprang off the pallet and grasped the sheet dangling from her, and tore at it with rage. The silken cloth rent to her force. Satisfied, she tore at another corner. I briefly thought her unhinged by anger, but it was with precision she took the remnants and tied them around her in a makeshift dress.

"Husband, listen carefully. The Whites are deceitful and treacherous. Do not hesitate to use all violence to subdue them."

Lashura cowered. "I promised cooperation to prevent further destruction. I beg you, do no more to us. I appeal to what animal intelligence you have."

Talis Darmon pointed at Doug and Dave who, like me, were transfixed by her miraculous revival from coma to command, like she'd had an IV bolus of adrenaline chased by a gallon of Rip It.

"Continue your vigilance! They have not the mettle for battle, but they will use terrible means to hinder us."

"We know, Talis Darmon. They tried some of their tricks on us," I said.

"And I take it that you punished them dearly for it, Warlord. Do not cease your readiness to do so again."

"Dave, take our six." I moved to put my body between Talis Darmon and the channel into a blackened corridor past the many instruments and various machines. I wanted to slow things down, but she was right. This moment was not about relief. It was about taking the last hill of the battle.

Doug tickled Lashura's composition B obedience collar, her posture that of a beaten dog. "She knows she'll die with us if they try anything again."

A corner of Talis Darmon's lips curled approval. "A thing wisely done, Douglas Knoblock. They think themselves above it, but force is all they understand. Our enemy does not yet comprehend how I answer violation, but soon my instruction to them will begin."

"We are no enemy," Lashura said. "We are your—"

My queen's aura flared again, enough that Lashura averted her eyes. "Our what? Gods? Creators? Emancipators? No. Zan-Sha boasted to me of your great secret. That his plan for me was interrupted is your undoing."

On the pallet, the man Lashura had called the Guarantor spat and coughed. He was still out but unconsciously strained against the flex cuffs. Talis Darmon's furious color dimmed.

"Benjamin Colt, were there time, I would seek forgiveness from you and your brothers for being so foolish and weak that you must rescue me. I was no queen to have submitted to their will as I did. But now I am strengthened and made vengeful.

"Our people have been enslaved. We have been deceived that what lay here is the afterworld. And when I make the truth known, forever will I be known as the Bloody Queen."

07

"Reverse route, Ben? Make our way to the boat, then find a way to take the train back south?"

"There's a faster way home, Dave. Doug, switch with me." Taking the leash in hand, I made sure I had Lashura's attention. "Take us to the airship you used to kidnap Talis Darmon."

Wincing, she gave a slight nod. "I will gladly see you passage from Astelaan."

That was new information. Astelaan?

"It is the true name of their domain, Benjamin Colt. Where the Whites have taken refuge for all the ages to act as parasites upon us. They consider us their domestic stock. And we have allowed ourselves to be." She menaced Lashura with gritted teeth. "Best to make our path a quiet one, lest my Warlord commence the immediate extinction of this domain."

"Queen of the Reds, I made a solemn promise that if you left this place, I would end the call to your lands. As you would sacrifice your life for the welfare of your people, so too would I."

Talis Darmon's menace came out loud and clear. "You think to threaten us, arrogant cur?"

Lashura shrank. "No! I mean only that you demonstrate great nobility. This we gave to you, just as we also gave you great reason, and obedience to the natural order of all life."

Talis Darmon drew her hand back to strike, but held. "You gave us nothing. You meddled. You deceive yourselves as to your role in the order of things on Vistara."

"I'm bustin' with curiosity," Doug interrupted, "but we've lost all momentum. We need to stop the chitchat and make our breakout. They've dialed 911 by now."

I agreed. "Lashura, if you mean to see us safely out of here, tell us how."

"I will command all of Astelaan to obey. I will see you to the ship, and you will depart. That will be the end of it." She turned slightly and wriggled her wrist to show me the flat bracelet, not so different from our own. "I can do so immediately."

I looked to Talis Darmon, who said, "White, you will speak only as you have, in Mihdra. I have no decipher and I would know if you think to communicate foul intent by speaking to your kind in your own dead tongue."

It was true. Lashura had spoken Mihdra, as had her king when he briefly threatened us.

Frustrated by our ignorance, the White made an appeal. "None but the welcoming court speak the derivative tongues of our progeny. It is foul to the ear, the vulgar noises made by the mouths of beasts. And none of the exalted wear deciphers. I must speak in the true tongue."

"Say something in your native tongue, Lashura." I'd try her language against my decipher. She spoke something in sing-song syllables, strangely interspersed with hums and lisps. Her words went unrecognized by my ear, but from deeper in, the decipher percolated meaning into my consciousness. I translated to Talis Darmon.

"She said something like—It is not by design that your development strayed so. The Green to toil. The Yellow to inspire order. The Red to moderate. Together, to survive and overcome the slow entropy that would engulf once sweet Vistara."

"I got that, too," Doug said. "Along with a lot of arrogance. It was thick enough to coat a battleship."

Dave frowned. "Does she believe they created the races of Vistara?"

"She does," Talis Darmon said. "Zan-Sha thought to subjugate me with the same claim. They are no gods. They are pimps, believing us all their property to do with as they will."

"We did create you," Lashura said.

Talis Darmon laughed dismissively. "We may all of us—Red, Green, and Yellow—be descendants of the White. Perhaps your ancestors wielded a meddling hand in our development, and did somehow breed us from a common ancestry. But Zan-Sha taunted me with something I *do* accept as plausible. The great secret is that the Whites saw the coming deterioration of the world. And in their arrogance to survive, they enacted a plan so foul, so monstrous and shameless, that from their hidden retreat they have watched in safety as the rest of Vistara struggled in creeping demise."

Lashura was again defiant. "Yet knowing this, you think to deny us as true gods."

❋ ❋ ❋

Lashura made the announcement as I dutifully translated to Talis Darmon, another first in our lives together.

"Exalted of Astelaan, the calamitous acts underway will soon be finished. The most exalted of all, Zan-Sha, has departed this plane of existence. But fear not, the way is preserved. I take his place as most exalted of our people. My wisdom is supreme. Interfere in no manner, and soon the disturbance will be gone from our midst and we may resume in perfection. Be at peace." She lowered her arm and Dave cuffed her again.

"What do you think?" I asked.

Talis Darmon reached out to the temples above the gray face. "Do not resist me." Lashura tensed, then resigned herself. Talis Darmon's eyes did not close in the manner I'd seen so many times, but instead fixed her gaze deeply into Lashura's. Satisfied, she pulled back.

"I do not trust her, but I do not sense the malevolence of subterfuge. She wants us gone as rapidly as possible. We are indeed the greatest calamity they have experienced."

"Bet your ass we are," Doug said.

Lashura's brows lifted. "What mutation do you carry that has resulted in something so unexpected—I would have it studied. Telepathy! Empathic sensibility! Is there more?"

"Some of your lab rats turned out in ways you didn't predict, lady?" Dave taunted. "People are just full of surprises. If you got out more often, you'd know that."

On the pallet and yet to regain consciousness, the Guarantor spat and sucked in a poor breath.

"Should we bring the mad scientist along?" Dave asked. "He might come in handy."

"He's an HVI for sure," Doug said. "No tellin' if we'll need him." Doug joined more cuffs to bind the arms and legs and heaved the tiny man over a single wide shoulder to drape like a rolled carpet. "Ready to move."

Head high, Talis Darmon said, "I would have your sword, Benjamin Colt. I will not be unarmed again. Ever."

I turned to let her draw Lady Vivamus off my back.

"Now, Astelaan recluse, if your claim to value the lives of your people holds true, guide us to depart your foul den."

With Doug in the rear and toting the Guarantor, Talis Darmon and me in the middle, Dave took the lead holding Lashura's leash.

"Lady, if you think you can go out in a bang and take us with you," Dave said, "know this: you screw with us, I'll toss you so far that your exploding head will just be entertainment for us."

"The exalted are not savage beasts. You heard my order. It will be obeyed. None will stand in your way."

"We killed some who tried, Lashura," I reminded her. "The gate guard tried some kind of paralyzing ray on us when he realized we weren't the right kind of tourist. Took everyone else a while to find their fight, but some did."

"They were among the few so tasked. The Hortha have never failed to separate any who were deranged or paradoxically affected by their journey to arrive unsuitable. The neuralyzing weapons lie ready for defense, as they have been since first emplaced for such a contingency.

Never have the ancient preparations been required, ever our method has succeeded so completely."

"All willing lambs, called to the slaughter," I said.

"Your interpretation is twisted. You do not yet understand."

Talis Darmon smiled in a cruel way I'd never seen before. "Pray that when I tell him more, my Warlord does not become the deranged creature you so rightly fear, White."

The laboratory behind us, we reached the end of the dark corridor. "What's next?" It was past tiresome, being completely blind to where we were.

"We enter Astelaan. The way will be clear of my people. We are near the haven where your transportation awaits. What you are about to witness will bring understanding that you have entered the realm of the truly exalted." With Dave's consent, she touched the door.

It didn't seem possible. Warm air, rich with scents of sweet blossoms and greenery filled my lungs. The starry sky tented the valley, its floor a vast city. The mountain slopes were terraced and ringed with paths bordered by lush growth. Habitations were spread throughout, and all of them flowered with inviting light.

"It's some kind of energy field," Dave said. "See where the snow collects above that perimeter of glowing lights against the peaks?" An unbroken chain of warm gold roped the mountains along a military ridge to make a continuous line just beneath the crests. Whatever transparent barrier it produced, it covered the enormous basin and the Shangri-La beneath. Karlo had once talked about building domed cities. Closed environments where extreme rationing and population control would be used to eke out a survival until the atmosphere of Vistara could somehow be synthesized. What he'd described was a bleak post-apocalyptic scenario. This was nothing of the sort.

The Whites had created a haven of splendor.

Doug was suddenly unsure. "Oh-muh-god. Is there where everyone goes? Did we get it wrong, Ben?"

Talis Darmon pounced. "Do not be deceived, Douglas Knoblock. This place is not the residence of Vistarans joined with their ancestors in eternal comfort. It is the sanctuary of cowardly thieves. It is made possible by murder, disguised in beauty, and built by lies. The force that maintains this sanctuary is by the harvest of the very rays of our lives."

"Do you mean to say—"

"The mechanism that makes this all possible is powered by Vistaran life, stolen and insinuated into a simulacrum where our kind live in dreaming deception, all to provide the means of the Whites' survival."

* * *

"A stationary target is the easiest to hit," I said. "Keep us moving, Dave."

Into Eden we went. Our curiosity was a million-lumen beam of light, one we had to switch off. There was no more time for questions. Escape, first. Answers, later. This was just another patrol. Ignoring the wonders around us, we reduced it all to shapes and danger areas, onto which we'd pour massive fire if anything got in our way.

We were the filthy homicidal orcs, raiding the peaceful elfin lands, traveling through a Thomas Kincaid painting of calm and beauty. With all caution, we left the perfumed scents of the vast, open valley to turn into a passage cut deep into the rock. Lashura had been truthful that the ship was near.

Perrin Halser had done an admirable job with his description of the ship. Across its spherical body projected crowds of quadrangular spikes of varying lengths. The ship resting on a tripod of three of the most massive of the spikes. The ramp leading into its fuselage was down, beckoning our escape. A tunnel as wide as the craft continued beyond.

"What in the name of all that is holy—" Dave exclaimed.

"Nothing sacred has been made by their hand," Talis Darmon said. "It is merely an airship. Greater than any in our possession, it is still naught but a mechanism."

"I have brought you to your means of egress. Take the craft and go in peace. It will obey your commands. Return to your kingdom and live your lives, and we will remain in our seclusion and do the same. None from your kingdom will enter Farnest again. Close the portal of Transspellum. Destroy it if you prefer. Do as you will. It is the word of the most exalted. Depart."

Doug laid the body of the bound man at his feet. "Too easy, baby cakes."

"How many more of these blimps you got, Lady?" Dave was on target. "You send the rest of the squadron to knock us down, and your problem's solved and it's back to business as usual."

Lashura denied it. "There are no other craft!"

"You're coming with us, Lashura," I said.

The self-proclaimed most exalted protested, "You made oath to me that if seen safely from Astelaan with your queen, you would depart peacefully!"

"I made no such promise."

Talis Darmon smiled with satisfaction. "The Warlord is correct to place no trust in you, Lashura. You and your fellow criminal will accompany us. I have plans beyond you serving merely as hostages to ensure our safe departure."

They call it panic for a reason. Lashura made a run for it. "No!" I yelled. "Dave, we need her!"

Dave cursed, releasing his handful of cord like he was bit by a snake. Profanities gushed as he took a leap. Dave easily caught up to her, lofted her by the waist, her legs still engaged in hysterical flight. Doug landed next to him.

"Hold her still, dude." Both hands on the grenade, he bent the pin down and loosed the cinch from around her neck. The big man blew out relief as he cut the cord off the ring and replaced the baseball in a pouch at his side. "Whew. That was close."

Lashura was returned with feet dangling, the two flabbergasted operators hefting her by the arms. Dave was pained. "Sorry. Shoulda had a hold of her before we called her bluff. Didn't think she was desperate enough to try the suicide thing. Live and learn."

Talis Darmon met their path. "That was your last chance at deceit, White. Inform your people that you and your Guarantor are on the craft. I have not yet chosen to destroy you all. If you test me again, you will have made the decision for me."

Lashura wilted to the ground, shrieking like a mad woman. Now I understood why straitjackets existed. Were they a thing on Vistara? If we'd had one, I'd have stuffed her into it.

"I will not! I do not suffer the command of beasts!"

"Just as well. It is my preference that your fellow conspirators hear it from the lips of the one they thought to enslave. Stand her, please." Talis Darmon returned, holding the band from Lashura's wrist.

"Benjamin Colt, can you communicate with Shansara? Does Karlo Columbo remain in the capital?"

I opened a channel to Karlo and he answered immediately. "Ben!"

"Listen up, Karlo. It's almost over." I nodded to Talis Darmon to go ahead. She held the wristlet to her lips.

"Hear me, all of Astelaan. I am Queen Talis Darmon Sylah of Mihdradahl. I depart your realm and with me, Queen Lashura and the Guarantor. Do not hinder us. They will be returned after they confess all crimes against us by your people. Afterward, all ties between us will be severed forevermore. Interfere in any way, and your complete destruction at the hands of my mighty army follows. Your predation upon us is at an end. Whether you survive to see another age is now up to you."

A voice returned, speaking Mihdra.

"Prove that our queen yet lives, beast. Allow her to speak."

Lashura's pained mumbles ceased, but the desperation in her eyes said she teetered on the edge of another break from self-control. Talis Darmon's voice remained sharp with menace. "In Mihdra, Lashura. Command them to obey." She held the band up.

"Obey me in earnest. Do not pursue. When I return, we will chart a new course ahead."

After a pause, the voice came back, this time in their language.

"We obey, Queen Lashura." Then in Mihdra. "Do her no harm, beasts, or there will be no peace."

"Agreed." Talis Darmon handed me the band. "We will see what Cynar makes of this. Let us depart at last."

"Got that, Karlo? Anything happens to us, drop an A-bomb on the Sharpas."

"Without a moment's hesitation, Ben." I closed the cloud. No matter Karlo promised he'd never do that, I was certain he was true to his word to make an exception.

We ascended the ramp. The cabin was spacious with many consoles and seats following the interior circumference. Doug deposited the Guarantor into a chair next to the bound Lashura. He seemed to come to a groggy realization of where he was, revulsion reviving with him.

"Debasers. Animals. Long ago I should have foreseen this."

Lashura whispered, "Hold fast. Our task now must be to save our people."

The man spoke groggily. "They may hold us as hostages, but their ancestors are ours, Queen. That power and more do we hold."

Lashura's grimaced shush to her friend told me much, but Doug distracted me. "Holy shit! Ben, check it out!"

Awakening above a console commanded by the largest chair floated a projection of Vistara. More so, in full detail, the first true representation I'd seen of our world materialized. The mountains. The gorges. A world of colors and places not even imagined came to life. My adopted planet was more than a world of red dust. And just as shocking, clusters of what could only be civilizations appeared. Cities of many shapes and sizes, scattered wide around the globe. They were by no means numerous, but more than I ever suspected existed on Vistara.

Talis Darmon traced a finger to a feature a hand's breadth above the Furrow of the Creator's Hand, to the representation that could only be Shansara. She touched it.

Doug settled into the large seat, the armrests closing around him. Talis Darmon said, "That was where the pilot sat, Douglas Knoblock. Beyond that, I am little help."

A panel protruded up slowly from the console and displayed a row of characters. "The decipher's telling me it says something like, 'Confirm destination.' Whaddaya think?"

I fixed Lashura with my frown. "If we crash this thing, my people will think you were to blame. I've told you what'll happen next." I made the noise that naturally went with hands pantomiming a mushroom cloud.

Her wide eyes said she needed no further explanation. "The craft will obey. You have identified your destination. Press the green stone and the course is then plotted and commenced."

"Give it a go, Dougie."

Over another console appeared a viewer displaying the tunnel ahead. The walls ran past, but no sensation of inertia betrayed our movement. We broke out into the night, floated to rise high above snowy peaks, and sailed, the twin sisters pale on the horizon. Dave muttered over another console, then took the seat paired to it.

Doug glanced back. "Dude, don't mess with anything. You might crash us."

"Brah, that's clearly the nav and flight control in front of you. This is, like, comms and stuff." He touched something below the screen and in a ring, the view outside appeared in a band around us. We were fish looking out of an aquarium. Retreating behind, the hidden valley of the Astelaan was just another arctic vista.

Talis Darmon touched my arm. "Zan-Sha bragged to me that their sanctuary was undetectable. He vaunted its undetectable nature among his list of reasons for my submission."

"Ben showed him what that was worth, Talis Darmon," Dave said.

For the first time, she relaxed. "I have been a fool." Her voice was as chilled as the air we flew through. "I vow to never again be the victim. Never again will you need come to my rescue."

"You did nothing wrong, Talis Darmon."

Her sour expression said she didn't feel the same way.

"Sun's rising," Doug said. "The rate this marker on the globe's moving, I bet we're home in a couple of hours. We must be doing Mach ten."

Dave rolled his eyes. "Like you'd know, demo-man. Been flying Vistaran milk crates for a few months and you think you're Chuck Yeager. You ain't even piloting this thing."

"Just sayin', dude. We're hauling ass."

I placed an arm around my wife's waist. At first, she stiffened, and my heart broke. She softened, but I made no move to pull her closer. I watched her as she watched the way ahead.

"Benjamin Colt, I have never told you what became of my mother."

She allowed herself to be coaxed by the gentle pressure of my fingers to move to seats away from our prisoners, and let me take her hands in mine. "I was there the day my mother took the Iridium Path. I was filled with sorrow, but inspired by the vision that she was on her way to live in peace with her ancestors, truly filled with the knowledge that her weary burden of daily existence would be lifted. And that I would someday join her there, that with her would be the child I never knew."

Her eyes teared.

"She was there. And so was my father. There in the underworld."

"You dreamed you saw them?"

She nodded. "A dream from which there is no escape. The Whites place the mind in a simulacrum. Zan-Sha tortured me with this knowledge before his minions set to lay hands on me. So that I would live for ages with the knowledge that I walked amongst ghosts in a realm where only I would know it was their prison for us. The rays of the life force of those taken to Farnest power their kingdom. And when the corporeal source of a life's energy becomes so corrupt that not even their science can prolong it further—they render what remains. All this did Zan-Sha reveal before he consigned me to join my ancestors as his living property. To punish me for an eternity.

"The transgression for which Zan-sha wished to punish me was that we have returned Mihdradahl to great health. Boredom, listlessness, and lack of purpose have been replaced with vitality. The desire for escape to a promised underworld of sweet breezes, green seasons, and freedom from all pain has dwindled so greatly, it threatens their survival.

"Mihdradahl's rise means extinction for the Whites."

08

QUESTIONS I COULDN'T PUT INTO WORDS WERE HOT COALS DANCING on my tongue, but I let them burn while she continued.

"Benjamin Colt, the realm of nightmares in which you fought to save Vistara, it was a place of reality. Even the Harridan's land was so. The underworld—it is a figment of the mind, created and perpetuated by an apparatus. It is grand in scale. I was in its antechamber when you found me. Had you not, a stasis chamber awaited me. A floating death beside the many thousands in the tunnels bored around their mountain valley. Zan-Sha and his Guarantor took great pleasure in showing it all to me, seemingly certain that the horror of it would shatter my pride.

"I fought. But there were so many hands. Pressing into my flesh. Some of them..."

She shuddered. "Caressing. It was as though they calmed an arkall being broken for the first mounting of a rider."

Doug and Dave kept their eyes fixed on their consoles, but there was no way they couldn't hear.

"My muscles burned and became useless. As the rays of anesthesia bathed over me, I surrendered my body. I could still deny them my mind, my animus, my true self. I retreated to my fortress. Its layers I built, stone by stone, room by room, firm and resilient. Always has it defeated the battering rams of all my foes.

"But with the blows of their sharp picks, the chinks in the mortar grew larger. The walls fell. Through a fallen section, from outside my body, I witnessed them remove my hair. The one who swept it off the floor gathered it to his nose and inhaled deeply. Another wall crumbled behind me, and through it, the ethereal cage of the underworld appeared. On a green hill stood my parents, beckoning to me to abandon my hiding place and join them.

"I was trapped on the edge between the physical world and the snare that would trap my soul. When disaster struck to panic my jailers, I knew it must be you. If not for your violent arrival and its cataclysmic disruption that ceased the Guarantor's fight to breach my walls—I would have floated away through the crumbling wreck of my redoubt to begin my eternal incarceration. Welcomed into the arms of my parents and all my ancestors with them."

"You really saw them?"

"And the many thousands. Thousands upon thousands I did glimpse through the ruins of my defense. On green hills and in tall forests. In gardens and the thresholds of homes covered in trestles bearing blooms." She dabbed a tear.

Lashura had been listening. "I told you it is as promised. And the distractions you led the people of your kingdom to embrace takes them away from their true purpose—to forget all struggles and live in joy. Don't you see your misguided desires have led you to deprive them of a life of eternal peace?"

Talis Darmon whirled on her. "They do not live at all! Your twisted logic is but warped rationalization. Pray when my people learn all that, they do not tear you limb from limb!"

The Guarantor spoke. "The underworld is a perfect construct, and those in it know ecstasy. It is the kindest of pastures for you. More so than a life wasted on the cruel surface of Vistara."

Talis Darmon was out of her seat, fist drawn back to strike, when I caught her. The Guarantor flinched, and rightly so. She shook off my grasp.

"If you must be held over flame in the fashion I learned at the hands of the Mydreen, if the skin must be flayed from your bones, you will admit all these things for the ears of Vistara to hear. Then will the same be done to all Whites. Silence our prisoners, Warlord. I will hear no more foulness from their lips until I rend more confessions from them."

Dave was on the move to comply for me. He caught my eye. His look transmitted a message that needed no cryptographer's onetime pad to decipher. Talis Darmon was making sincere threats about doing something severe. William Calley/Mỹ Lai Massacre kind of severe. Because when she revealed who the Whites were, it wouldn't take a queen's order to convince a zealot like Kleeve Hartus to become the kind of inquisitor she envisioned.

Or maybe, even to convince a Warlord.

I dismissed the vision of a red-hot poker in my hand and the screams of the Guarantor. I'd punish them for what they did to Talis Darmon and countless others. But it wouldn't be in the manner of a barbarous Green desert Tarn or maniacal subterranean White.

It would be one of my own crafting.

With the Whites gagged, blindfolded, and ears plugged, she said, "I know what you must think, husband. I am not unhinged. I am calmed and returned to reason. I think now of my responsibility to my kingdom. Tell me all that transpired after my departure."

From Kleeve Hartus's betrayal to the departure of the Korundi, it wasn't until I told her that our child no longer remained in our quarters that her composure broke again. Her grief poured out. "I have been no queen. I am a reed broken by the wind. What has my weakness wrought for all?" She wept.

I felt as weak as she mistakenly castigated herself for being. I put an arm around her and sat with her in silence. After the passage of an eternity, she sniffled and hugged herself.

"What they have taken from me, I will take from them. Do not fear that I am sincere in my visions of ugliest cruelty—though they deserve it. More pain than I can imagine how to inflict do they deserve. I promise their punishment will be fit to their crimes. But first, my kingdom needs its queen."

Her transition was a relief.

"I need to call Karlo. If the security situation isn't improved, we must decide on an alternate plan. Maybe we go to Pyreenia. Maybe to Califex."

"Do so, Warlord. But it is to Shansara we go. And we do not come home to beg the return of fealty by any."

The memory I had of Kleeve Hartus ready to give the order to fire to prevent us from rescuing her was front and center in my mind, and I told her my concern about facing him. Her decision was swift.

"If the first shield is a traitor, you will dispatch him, Warlord."

I gulped at her casual cruelty. "No one's without blame, Talis Darmon. And of all people, perhaps you can understand why he acted the way he did." She winced at my attempt to pardon his behavior. And hers. My regret washed over me like cold rain.

"I'm not trying to shame you. I just mean—I won't kill him outright."

If she had a job to do, so did I.

"Very well, Warlord. You will give him but one chance to show loyalty. If he fails, you will kill him. This is my command for how the queen returns to her kingdom."

And when she went on to tell us how it was going to go down on our appearance in Shansara, it was the woman who saw the twists and turns of the many paths that was at my side again.

✳ ✳ ✳

The guys spoke quietly to each other until Doug gave the warning. "We're slowing over the plains above the capital, Ben."

We studied the many panels in collaboration. We came to tentative agreements on the translations of the functions they controlled. I wondered if our assurances that we could do as she asked would match her demands. I least of all wanted to thwart her plan by our novice understanding of how to operate the strange craft. I whispered to Doug, "Any doubts about handling this behemoth?"

"No worries, Ben-dog. Except for a few extra gadgets, it's not so different from our own airships."

I tried one last time. "We can land at the army compound, Talis Darmon. We could go to the Korund instead. We could take time to make sure we really know what we're doing before we try something like this."

"I appreciate your counsel, Benjamin Colt, but now is not the time to act the husband of an injured wife. You must be your queen's Warlord. Proceed."

The towers and floating bridges of Shansara were in sight. Doug slowed us to crawl into the airspace over the capital. We were the same impending bird of doom that harbingered terror to the wondrous city just a short while ago. We hovered above the palace grounds until they became a floodplain of gawking red faces.

"Activate the device, David Masamuni," my queen commanded.

"Yes, ma'am." He stroked and adjusted crystals until the circumferential view of the morning sun was dimmed by the pulsing of our craft's exterior glow. "The indicators tell me we're at full effect."

She asked no forgiveness as she said, "I know what panic grips our kingdom by this assault, but it must be done."

The steps from the courtyard up to the central palace were packed with shriveled citizens, cowering in obeisance and fear. At their front, the gold helmet of a bowed head shone brightly above red-caped shoulders. The first shield was there, the prime emissary. Ready to greet the king of Farnest, no doubt returned to tell them the end of times was at hand.

The ship settled, and I commanded the door with a touch. She stepped to the ramp, and I took my place as her shield arm. We'd conquered this place once by blood.

She commenced to retake it with a different kind of shock and awe.

"Do not bow in fear. Do not supplicate before the imposters who terrorized our kingdom. No citizen of Mihdradahl owes obeisance to any save their queen. The ground beneath this kingdom is firm. Remember it, I say, and stand."

Eyes lifted from averted gaze, and with their rise, the groundswell of disbelief took voice throughout the crowd.

"It is Queen Talis Darmon!"

"Returned from the afterlife!"

"It cannot be!"

The queen silenced them with outstretched hands.

"The imposters who came to demand your subservience are not of Farnest! They are deceivers and murderers."

I took a step aside to let the guys hustle our prisoners into sight.

"Behold the ones who posed as lords of the afterlife, who use our sincere piety against us. They are not the gatekeepers of our ancestors' realm. They are not the guardians of the afterworld. They are criminals. And I have returned to expose their crimes and see justice done. Where is the First Shield of Mihdradahl? Where is the protector of the law?"

Kleeve Hartus rose slowly. The white shade of red he wore I'd seen in him a short time ago. The crowd retreated, leaving him exposed and alone.

"Whom do you serve, First Shield? Do you serve the queen who named you, or do you serve false gods?"

My rifle in hands, ready to become her angel of death, I pictured the red dot coming to rest on his chest. In the space of my own heartbeat, I would cease his from beating in the time it took to pump the last of his blood onto the plaza.

In the next second, he would decide if I did.

Kleeve Hartus returned to a single knee and placed fist over heart. I heard it as surely as I knew the sound of an oak felled, the snap of deep wooden grains, rendering might into splinters. With many oaths comes many loyalties. Between oath to the Guard and the queen, his faltering voice admitted to having chosen wrongly.

"I serve the Queen Talis Darmon Sylah."

The words were said.

My index finger touched the side of the receiver again. But would the one who said the words ever again be the man I'd once trusted like a brother?

For the moment, Kleeve Hartus would live.

A military voice boomed from the depths of the palace. "Make way."

From the summit of the stairs and the darkness of the grand portico, soldiers in uniforms the color of Vistara's red sands appeared. Leading them, ever the warrior, was Karlo. He commanded a soldiery who knew their own.

Karlo said it had taken little convincing to secure the loyalty of the troops. Most were Thorian. Doug knew Thorians better than we did, and assured Karlo that he'd find none of them fanatic believers in the underworld. Armed with M4s and ready to put down any insurrection by the Guards, with the Whites ray-killing field engaged, no one besides our army had any weapon more deadly than a blade.

She'd made me swear to her that if not by reason, then by blood—today her regency would be reestablished.

But how we would repair what the Whites broke? I couldn't see how.

"Generals, bring the prisoners. We go to council. This ends today."

✳ ✳ ✳

Karlo fell in beside me as a circle of troops surrounded us to protect our ascent to the palace. "Was that Pen Segus you left in charge of the detail to guard the ship?"

"Yes, Ben. He stepped in to command when the Korundi left. He's Clymairan, but the Thorians think highly of him."

"For how he fought in Pyreenia, they should. Good choice, Karlo."

Without breaking stride, Karlo moved to drape an arm around me and pressed lips to my ear. "He understands your orders. Shoot to kill anyone who tries to break the cordon around the airship. If a red cloak so much as raises a hand, it's their death warrant. How long will you keep the field running?"

"Until we're sure we're in control again. Then that prize belongs to you. You're going to take that bird apart and squeeze every one of its secrets out."

"Roger."

A familiar flock of the queen's attendants were waiting, tears and mournful praises shushed by Dureen Zell. "What have they done to your hair? A thousand deaths would I visit upon them that harmed your person." She threw her arms around the queen, who brushed her back.

"It is well with me, old friend."

"Then come, let us tend you. These rags tell a frightful story."

"Troopers, with me to guard the queen," I ordered, but she countermanded it.

"Warlord, we will be in my office but briefly. Form order in the council chamber, and I will join you presently." She was confident and at ease being in charge again. Any hint of disturbed confidence vanished like the morning mist in the sun of her strength. It made me whole.

"Yes, Queen." I snapped fingers, and a detail of fierce troopers surrounded her retinue to fall into a protective march around them, but stutter-stepped to an abrupt halt. From within their layers, her voice was a mountain mightier than any on Vistara.

"And, Warlord. Have the priests found. I would have them available when I summon."

In the wake of the queen and her retinue's true departure, the grizzled and gaunt Cynar appeared. "Benjamin Colt—" he began, then quavered. The master of life-giving waters never wasted a drop, but for the first time, he squandered the rare molecules to run from his eyes.

"I'm glad to see you, too, Cynar. I've brought you and Karlo a prize."

Cynar's emotional gauge had but two places where the needle rested. The first was on rage, produced whenever anyone seemed to question his abilities. The next pegged the needle over to the joy of a schadenfreude so intense, I was sure it was the fuel of the fire of his long life. Every time the failings of his enemies the air wizards came to light, he gained another decade. At mention of the prize—the airship—his eyes dried.

The moment had been evidence enough that he, in fact, had more than those two marks on his meter. He clucked.

"I once chose a box for you that contained the greatest wealth in the universe, Benjamin Colt. That one delivered your queen back to you. This box you select for me will I open to reveal the means to punish those who wronged her."

His devilish grin spread from a confidence born from besting a ghastly goddess.

"My intellect is the mightiest fortress in your service, and their regret of it will be short lived. Hehehe."

They say if it's true, it's not bragging.

"I know you will, Cynar."

The governance was an ant's nest of tense troops, shell-shocked nobility, and nervous government functionaries. Doug and Dave reappeared, our prisoners no longer in tow. Before I could ask, Doug reported.

"No worries, Ben. Those two aren't going anywhere."

I motioned Doug, Dave, Karlo, and Cynar into a close huddle. "We're a long way from done."

"We've been through worse, dog," Doug said.

"True dat," Dave said.

"Gods and monsters we have defeated. These pale tricksters are naught in comparison," Cynar said.

Karlo nodded. "By yourselves, the three of you just spanked a whole city. Together—there's nothing we can't do, Ben."

The storm winds that blew the human detritus around us became a minor breeze. The foundation of men that anchored me was denser than uranium. With this team of heroes beside me, what had ever stood in our way? Then, into the breezeway he appeared. The man who had once been a part of this circle. Kleeve Hartus wisely shied back, repelled by the bond of a group he was no longer a part of.

After what he'd done, was forgive and forget a thing?

Dave saw the gears turning. "He sent jailers and a medic to care for the prisoners, Ben. They're in the admin annex down the hall until you tell us what to do with them."

Doug jumped to add, "I know what you're gonna say, Ben. We searched his people before we let them in with the prisoners. Kleeve Hartus is still a pro, Ben. He knew our troops don't have the know-how to handle prisoners long-term. But don't worry, we left a detail of our troops to watch them *and* the Whites."

Karlo asked the obvious. "What are we going to do about the Guard, Ben?"

A dizzying fatigue suddenly hit me. My hand wiped it away with such firmness, my face stung from the roughness of it. "For now, we keep them under our thumb. Then it's going to be up to the queen. This ship's still taking on water, and we're trying to keep her off the rocks. We have to stay sharp. Here's what I want."

In the council chambers, the doors from the queen's office parted and two files of troops marched in. In regal garb with her head wrapped in silken knots, Talis Darmon accepted my arm as escort. Standing at their places around the council table were the core of ministers and functionaries.

The absence of the Korundi struck me. In their place, drab-uniformed soldiers lined the walls. As much as I respected them, they were not the equal of my departed Tarn soldiery. Then I pictured my fierce Green soldiers folding at the appearance of the Whites like the rest of Shansara, and my heat rose. I'd thought the Tarn religious about nothing besides their honor. The remainder of our Red army might be small, but the forge of Pyreenia had made them hard as nails. These soldiers cared nothing about myths.

These men knew legends could be killed.

Beraal's absence from the queen's elbow to conduct the liturgy of the council proceedings sent a pang of sadness through me. "Be seated," I said in her place. Talis Darmon's gravitas dispelled my brief despair.

"What I tell you now will be a shock. It will challenge the core of the beliefs you hold dear. This is the truth of it. We have been the unwitting dupes of a people who have insinuated themselves as the protectors of our faith."

Those gathered were normally self-assured, self-important, and immune to criticism. Mihdradahl's elite. And in their confidence, they had always shown contempt for any challenge to the order they embodied. I'd suffered their obstinance many times. Shaken by all that her presence represented, I saw in them the attention a child gave the one holding the paddle. A fear of something coming that they were helpless to stop.

"I will tell you of a great crime."

In plain language, she told them how the process by which pilgrims traveled to join their ancestors was not what they believed. Instead, it was a means by which a band of predators lured their victims, to then commit heinous crimes against not only those of Mihdradahl, but many more peoples across Vistara.

Succinct as only she could be, she set the first block in building up the truth.

She explained that those who traveled to Farnest were groomed and conditioned to arrive compliant. There they were met by those posing as guardians and invited to enter the underworld. As one, her audience was poised to react, her revelations the potential energy of a boulder at rest on a mountain, a placeholder for the kinetic force it held. They waited for the big reveal to push them to a momentous roll down the hill. She prepared them by saying the hosts committed terrible acts against willing and drugged Vistarans.

I anticipated the erupting volcano to come, when she told them the last.

"For as long as they have traveled the Blix, our loved ones have been the unwitting cattle of savages worse than the Mydreen we defeated. For in comparison, the desert Tarn act honorably toward their prisoners. Our loved ones journeyed to find paradise, and at the end of their path, instead met their slavers. Made to toil to their deaths in the mines beneath the Sharpa Mountains. And when their usefulness is at an end, their bodies become the fertilizer for the soil of the agriculture where they grow their sustenance. This the Whites have done in foulest conspiracy, in their realm beneath the Sharpa Mountains, hidden for all these many eons."

The room exploded. In that chaos, I shared silent looks of surprise with those who knew differently. Doug's eyebrows raised. Dave hid his face behind hands caked in burned gunpowder and dried blood. Neither truth nor lie, neither lie nor truth, what Talis Darmon told them was not the secret we'd learned. Not exactly.

When she'd formulated this, I didn't know. And why?

"This we have seen. The same crime was being committed on my person when I was rescued from the brink of death by the Warlord and his generals."

"Then it is to war we must go," someone burst out. "Our people must be rescued, the perpetrators destroyed, and revenge taken." Fierce agreement from around the table followed. Yet others protested in disbelief until one of the opponents took the lead.

"You have proof of this?" Dressed in a cloak as white as a pilgrim's was the minister of the purse.

My hand went to my sword as I rose. "Watch your tongue, Dalan Druse. It's not only the veracity of your queen you challenge, but that of my wife. Is that your intent?"

Though unsure why Talis Darmon's version of events had strayed, I was ready to kill. Her spirit was strong again, but her body bore the evidence that she had been greatly mistreated—her mane of rich locks, gone. Her face, gaunt. Her arms, bruised. My rage was fueled by what I thought should have been obvious to even a blind man.

Something terrible had happened to her. And Dalan Druse ignored it.

"Do you not see the assault inflicted on your queen? And when her kidnappers came, this august body of Mihdradahl's best and brightest abetted them. Not a one of you so much as dared question their theatre. You're all traitors in my sight."

Shamed faces fell low.

Dalan Druse saw where my hand rested and realized he stood on the precipice of his own demise. "I only meant—this is a tremendous shock. What it means for our faith is—"

I finished him. "The queen's word is both truth and law. As if you should need more evidence, you have the testament of the Warlord. Unless that is something you now suddenly find courage to question."

The minister bowed deeply in surrender. Whatever Talis Darmon was putting into play, she had a husband and a Warlord to back her. I only hoped that whatever that plan was, she'd let me in on it soon. Without dimming my fire, I sat to allow her to continue.

"For now, we are powerless against the weapons of this enemy. Our justice will not be swift. Vengeance must wait. Above all, the first duty is to protect the people. The device they used to silence the rays is in our possession. Our scientists will learn its secret, and how to thwart it. Until then, the Warlord assures me attacking them is unfeasible. And there are none to rescue. All that have travelled north have met a foul end."

Someone else found their voice. "I am not alone in shame and regret. Queen Talis Darmon's word is above question, as is her judgment. As the queen orders, so shall we be the hand of her will. What is your command?"

She knew these people. She had a plan. It was working.

"I will restore the tranquility of our people immediately. Our people will understand when I tell them that what occurred was this—another enemy sought to harm us, and we have risen triumphantly. In the meantime, as our first course of action, we will halt the pilgrimage and contain the Whites as best we can. Are we united in purpose?"

Kleeve Hartus shrank when her eyes came to rest on him alone. His head fell as if it were a weight too great to hold up. Removing the gold bracers from his forearms, he laid them on the table. "My failure demands I resign before my disgrace taints the Guard further."

Talis Darmon's tongue flayed him. "You do no such thing. If you wish my trust restored, you will perform your duties with diligence, not by retreating from sight."

"Yes, Queen," he said, chastised. He robotically replaced the armor.

She laid the next brick of the road for their path to her forgiveness.

"You are the cement that binds our kingdom. It is for the benefit of all that I seal you to secrecy. Under penalty of treason and pain of death do I hold you. The knowledge of the Whites' deception has great power to harm the kingdom—as much as another invasion. Until I orchestrate the manner in which our people are told the truth, you will carry this great burden with me in secrecy."

Someone asked, "And our faith? How will it be preserved?"

Talis Darmon didn't miss a beat.

"It is for this reason I hold your tongues. The priests will examine the prisoners and confirm they are not who they claim. The perpetrators will testify to their long ruse. The White imposters have admitted the ancient origins of their perversion of our beliefs. Their proclamation of this will be the way by which we restore our people's faith and tranquility. Even the priests themselves have been duped. Because this is what I have learned—the underworld exists. But the afterlife is not a physical realm below Vistara.

"And when this is understood, our faith can be built again on firm ground. And all will then understand what punishment I fit to the crime these imposters have perpetrated."

09

WALLS OF TROOPS SURROUNDED OUR OUTER CHAMBERS. PATROLS WITH harnessed gadron roved the grounds, their snuffles and growls at anyone not in a drab uniform restrained by their handlers. Another pang of absence struck me, this time with the thought of loyal Apache at Beraal's feet, her loving arms cradling a tiny egg. I let her attendants finish before I shooed them out of our bedroom. A tray of untouched food rested at the bedside.

"Won't you eat something, sweetheart?"

The strength she'd rallied to command her council was spent, her fire reduced to glowing embers. She didn't answer. Reposed in limp exhaustion, her blanket held her down like a restraint. It was through the fog of my own exhaustion that I tried to calculate how long it had been since I'd left this room to tempt a frivolous death at the mercy of gravity.

It had been the morning before yesterday. It was over countless eons that the continents of Earth had fractured and shifted.

On Vistara, it had taken only thirty-six hours.

"I wish to know our child is safe."

I took a seat on the bedside so she could see and be seen by the cloud above my wristlet. Beraal dutifully answered with a stuttering gasp sucked deeply between tusks—a Tarn response of shock.

"My relief is deeper than the Furrow! I was at my father's side when he received the news."

I'd tasked the guys to give Double-K a heads up and to start the process to reverse the damage that had been done.

"You child lies here, dear Queen. Do you see her beside me?"

The creche from our quarters held the growing egg, the skins of a field tent protecting and comforting them both. Beraal laid a tender sky hand on the speckled surface. "Speak to her, Talis Darmon, and I will feel her peace at the sound of you."

Talis Darmon smiled weakly. "Since I sent you to guard our child, I never once doubted, sweet Beraal. I yearn for you to be to our side, and our child again in her home. Will you return tomorrow?"

There was hesitation.

"My father believes it unwise to trust Shansara is restored to tranquility."

Khraal Kahlees stepped into view. "Talis Darmon, I am comforted that you again sit on your throne and that your hand guides the kingdom."

My wife found a tiny reserve of energy, and used it sardonically. "Yet you counsel my dosenie to keep away?"

"I counsel my daughter, who bears the highest of honors and responsibilities, that duty comes above all. Is it your Warlord's belief that all is set right in the kingdom?"

She darkened beneath a veil of disappointment. "It is so that the kingdom is not returned to equanimity simply by my presence. As ever, Khraal Kahlees, even from the Korund, no danger is concealed from your sight." She fell deeper into her cushion.

I hadn't expected to talk to him tonight, but since I had him, I asked, "Will you be turning the Korundi around and heading back?"

My friend defensively folded all arms. "As I told our clansmen David Masamuni and Douglas Knoblock, at this time Chieftain Parkus Laan does not foresee such. These are matters perhaps better discussed at an appointed time, Benjamin Colt."

"Does Chieftain Parkus Laan know we've proved the Whites false?"

"I have communicated with him. In his wisdom, he agrees that the fallen mountain must first settle before the pass can again be cleared, Warlord. There is much that needs to be considered."

I cursed myself. Had I not been away on a stupid task, would we even be in this situation? If I'd left Double-K behind that day, would the debacle of her surrender have gone unchallenged? Or would he have bent the knee to the Whites like everyone else?

"What needs to be considered? Is there doubt about what we discovered? Do the Korundi tremble at the thought of a visit from the Whites? Come to call you for being unfaithful? I thought a warrior of the Korundi feared nothing in this world or the next."

Double-K grimaced. "Your words are as firm as the iron of your sword. What comes from your lips carries no less power than the vision of my own eyes. And I forgive the harshness of their tone. I say, tend your duties in this time of distress as do my daughter and I. Trust that we do so in best service to you and the queen. Let time pass. With its passage, the course of things will be set true."

Talis Darmon intervened. "He is correct, husband. For now, our child is safest with them. I thank you both."

Khraal Kahlees nodded in receipt. "Benjamin Colt, news travels through the Korund that the Warlord has vanquished another mighty foe. By sunrise, many warriors will petition for permission to return to your service. The Korundi are free, and our chieftain will not deny such a request. It will not be two battalions returning, but those who hold bond to you will surely take the road to provide shield and sword. Such is their devotion."

I relaxed. "Tell my Korundi brothers they always have a place beside me."

In the background, Beraal remained with a hand on our growing child. Before she could say farewell, her father gave us his. "Then for now, there is nothing more to be said. When we reach Califex, my daughter will hail to assure that we arrived with your egg in our protection." He severed the connection.

I expected tears. When they didn't come, I laid a hand over hers. "We'll make things right quickly. I'm pained that our child is so far away, too, sweetheart. Just a little longer. You're a mighty warrior, my princess. No one's ever endured what you have."

Suddenly, my words became an overwhelming admission of my idiocy. I considered just how much she had endured. So many times. And my selfish and ignorant forgetfulness of her many trials shamed me.

How could I have ever left her side?

Her hands retreated from beneath mine to clasp her ears, to block my words from reaching her. "Do not call me that."

"Call you what?"

"Warrior."

I've flayed myself with recriminations for things I wish I'd done instead of what I did. Only a narcissist as sick as Brandon Bryant thought themselves perfect in decision and action. Teammates understand. So do husbands who've made mistakes they wish they could erase. "I know what you're feeling, sweetheart. You are not to blame."

She turned away. "We will speak no more of it."

I knew if I persisted, it would make things worse. I wasn't going to talk her down from this tonight. "Things will be better after some sleep. Do you want me to stay or leave?"

She said nothing until, "I am without hope of sleep. I must trace many lines in the sand, but only one can I make deep enough to remain once the winds of inevitability return to batter my works."

"Do you mean the lie you told the council about what we discovered? Can you please tell me why you told them what you did?"

"A queen need not explain herself. It is a Warlord's job to do her will."

The knife was aimed at my heart. I deflected it not with sword, but with her own words.

"I say this not to do you pain, but to plead my concern. You once told me if I became a phantom in your heart, you could not bear it. Are you trying to make me a ghost?"

I had her eyes back. I almost wish I didn't. The well of their pain echoed the blackness of her words.

"No, Benjamin Colt. It is I who I wish were a ghost. Had I not returned, all would be well."

The dam broke, the tears and sorrow she'd held back flooded out. She let me hold her until the lake emptied. Now I could try again.

"My princess, you taught me how such thinking poisons a soul. Had you not returned, it would *not* be well. You must never think that. And besides, it could never have come to pass. Even had I been in my proper place at your side, had you ordered me to stand down and allow the Whites to take you, I would have ignored you. I'll gladly bear that blame, if it helps."

She gave me a weak smile. "My orders are always but suggestions to you, husband. And I admit, your disregard has wrought good ends, every time. But, had I remained in their prison, the way for all would now be easier. For me, too. For what I attempt to do, I fear I cannot."

"Whatever it is, you don't do it alone. I'm here."

The comfort I thought to give her should have been cemented by my oath. It always had. Instead, it brought a shake of her head. "Always, your help. Do you not understand the price I pay for your help? How each time you come to my rescue it strains and tears at my confidence as deeply as any assault done by my enemies?"

"Huh?" I was truly confused.

"You shame me, Benjamin Colt. My reliance on you as has diminished me and placed you ever in harm's way. I continually ransom your protection by your pity of me. It was my own vanity that deluded me otherwise."

She waited for my reaction as if she'd revealed some profound truth, something that should have been self-evident.

"What you're saying makes no sense. I'm your husband, your Warlord. You're my purpose."

"I know. And what does it mean for me to be your purpose? That I am a child who needs constant rescue? A weakling unable to defend herself? Because that is how you make me see myself!"

"There's no truth in any of that."

She silenced me with a hand over my mouth.

"Do not think to deny the truth of these things! You see yourself as wiser than I! And I die inside to admit it is so! When protest and stirrings of evil occurred under my reign, I ignored your advice to follow the indolent ways of my father. I begged your patience, thinking my masterful skill would heal and join what discontent existed. And it nearly resulted in your murder by conspirators seeking to take my throne. Against your wishes, I accompanied you to the redoubt of Jawn Kurz. Had I not done so, I would not have placed you and your friends in even greater peril."

That was also not true, but she wouldn't let me speak. Her crescendo built to a fury, powering the loathing she razed herself with.

"I deceived myself I was a warrior. I am a fool. One so weak as to gladly obey the call of my own executioner. Just like the cattle they think us to be." She tore off the silk cap and dragged nails down her bare scalp. She tore at her bedclothes, laughing an anguished laugh of madness.

"I am no queen! I am nothing! And not even Benjamin Colt can save me from myself!"

A terror gripped me like I'd never known. And I knew no remedy for it. I only knew I needed help.

I thought of his face and Karlo's face materialized above my wrist. In the background, she shrieked as if the jaws of a jagged spring trap had closed on her. Karlo paled.

"I need you. Talis Darmon's out of her mind. She's trying to hurt herself. I don't know what to do."

I'd never said the word before. And when I did, it came with the epiphany that there was no word as bottomless in its frailty.

"Help."

✱ ✱ ✱

With gentle firmness he ordered me to hold her while he administered the injections with a calm I couldn't muster. She was out. But even in her sleep, I saw no peace. And I was still shaking. Karlo zipped up his aid bag.

"She'll sleep for some time, Ben. I gave her an antipsychotic and a sedative."

"What happened to her, Karlo? Did the Whites give her something to make her crazy?" I was ready to skin Lashura and the Guarantor alive until they revealed the antidote to whatever they'd given her. When had they done it?

"No, Ben. I'm pretty sure that's not it. Let's talk outside."

He forced me to sit with him on the couch where she and I snuggled in the few moments we found ourselves alone.

"She suffered a psychotic break. It's one of the things they prepare us for when dealing with liberated POWs. It's often not until they're safe and in a quiet place that the trauma of their captivity overwhelms them. As severe as her trauma was, it's a wonder it didn't happen sooner." Karlo leaned back and took a breath.

"Ben, you know that female POWs are often sexually assaulted." He stated it as fact.

"Oh my God!"

He left me to stew over those horrible visions as he went to check on her, but quickly returned.

"Her vitals are strong and she's resting."

I was numb.

He sat across from me again. "Tell me everything about her captivity."

I told her how Zan-Sha had tortured her with the knowledge of all the Whites had done. How they claimed to create all the races of Vistara. How they wanted her to live with the knowledge that she was trapped in a dream she'd never escape, knowing the predation of her people would continue. How she described watching from outside her body as they prepared her. Their hands all over her.

Karlo cringed. "Remember what you learned in SERE, Ben. A captor tries to break down all beliefs in God, country, family—attacks every institution of your faith. To tear away your confidence in what's just and good about you and those you serve. Pain, sleep deprivation, starvation, even rape—all of that's just a means to make you susceptible to those attacks."

All SF operators went through the school that taught Survival, Evasion, Resistance, and Escape. I'd used the lessons to withstand my own POW experience at the hands of Brandon Bryant. Until now I hadn't considered Talis Darmon had been the same kind of prisoner of war.

I'd been very, very wrong.

"Physical torture leaves scars easier to treat than the psychological ones. This was a violation greater than anything she suffered at the hands of the Mydreen. And she blames herself for being a victim. Between that and learning the monstrousness of what the Whites did, in less than a day she suffered an apotheosis and rape combined."

I didn't know what the fancy word meant, but I knew who to blame. "If I hadn't been screwing around, I'd have been here to stop them." I'd caused this. I shook like I was standing in snow again.

"Oh, boy. No." Karlo's aid bag was open again and he had a vial in hand. "You can't go down, too. You're going to sleep."

"The hell I am!"

Karlo's words were delivered in velvet, but hit me like a punch.

"Think you can't end up broken, too, Ben? Think your psyche hasn't been injured? I've got some idea of what kind of psychological problems you've overcome. You did it with her help."

I wasn't embarrassed that Karlo had pieced it together, and as a result, I knew what he was going to tell me.

"Who's going to help *her*, Ben? If you try to take the blame for this, if you try to Ranger through this, you're going to end up psychotic, too. And that can't happen. You've been running in the red for two days. You. Must. Sleep. You know I'm right about this."

Karlo the engineer. Karlo the alchemist. Karlo the healer. I slowly surrendered to the logic of Karlo. "Who'll take the watch?"

"As if you need to ask, brother."

I choked up. "If she wakes up, I want to be there next to her." If I was a superman, it was only when I was with her.

"Then let's lay you down, brother." I felt the prick, closed my eyes, and reached out for her hand. "Things are going to better," I told her and myself. Those were Karlo's words. Things would be better. I just needed sleep. The last I remember was Karlo speaking into the cloud.

"Ben needs us."

10

I AWOKE WITH HER HAND STILL BENEATH MINE. KARLO SLUMBERED IN a chair beside our bed, his head at an acute angle as he lightly snored. Her head was on the pillow, facing me with eyes open.

"Husband, are you well?" She seemed herself and her words released my pressure valve.

"I'm fine! How are you? I didn't know what else to do but call for help. You were—"

"The terrible things I said to you—it was from outside my body again that I watched a person I did not know cast invective at you. I felt as if I were still trapped between the simulacra of the Whites' underworld, watching what was done to my own my frail body on that laboratory slab. As I castigated you, I knew my psyche had lost its tether, but even knowing this, I was powerless to join the broken strands together. Not a single word I said holds the truth of how I feel. Do you believe me?"

"Of course I do."

"What are we to do, husband?" Her eyes moistened.

"You're going to rest." I kissed her forehead. "I'm going to check on a few things, then I'll be back."

"Tell me what you intend."

"I'm informing the council that you need some time. Everyone will understand. Until you're ready to make your move, everything else will have to wait."

"This cannot wait." She moved to rise, then fell back.

Karlo was immediately at her side. How long he'd been awake and listening, I didn't know. Sometime while we'd slept, he'd started an IV on her. He checked the bag, then knelt to her side. "I'm going to check your vitals, then I'd recommend eating something. Rest is the order for the day. Those are the doctor's orders."

"I feel very weak, Karlo Columbo. I am as exhausted as if I'd walked the length of the Korund."

"Food and more sleep are the cure."

"Benjamin Colt, come close," she said. "The priests are the key. I am unable, so you must do this." She told me what she wanted.

"You can trust that I will, my princess. Do what Karlo says, and by the time I get back, you'll be even better."

In our outer rooms, Dave was rolling up from a couch as Doug placed a cup into his hands. The last thing I remembered was Karlo calling them.

"How is she, brah?"

"She's better. So am I. Thanks aren't enough, guys."

Karlo closed the doors behind him. "Ben, with your permission, I'm going to send Doug to retrieve someone."

Doug explained, "Healer Shalees Parn's who Talis Darmon sent me to when I needed help."

Karlo shrugged. "I know my limits. When she's awake again, I'll ask her consent, of course, but I wanted to ask you first."

There were few in the kingdom who practiced the healing art that Talis Darmon learned as part of her maternal dynasty. I remembered Shalees Parn. Because of the deep personal connection that came with the touching of another's animus, Talis Darmon begged off being the one to help Doug recover from his deep mental distress.

"I trust you completely, Karlo. I was a basket case. I had no idea what to do." It was as if last night my wristlet had called him for me.

"You're always to call me first, Ben."

I got a lump in my throat and coughed it away. "I think you fixed her. She seems to be coming out of it," I said. I sensed he wanted to tell me something supportive, but, doctors were all the same. Truth, not platitudes, was the currency of their exchange.

"Ben, the pharmaceuticals I gave her were a tourniquet, not a fix. I stopped her from bleeding out, is all I did. I intervened in the physiology that let the break manifest. The cause of it—the drugs just hold back."

Doug cleared his throat. He was the most powerfully built man I'd ever seen. And there was a time when that strength hadn't meant anything in the war he fought in his head to keep from taking his own life. When he spoke, it was with an authority I respected.

"Ben, sometimes the greatest danger comes after the fight. And that battle takes a different kind of tactic to win. But Talis Darmon's a fighter, bro. And Shalees Parn's a gem. I know she'll want to help. She sure helped me."

I felt hopeful, and guilty.

"Sorry it's always about me and her, brothers. You guys need refit time, too."

Doug grinned. "I feel great, bro. If it weren't for Talis Darmon being a hostage, that little job wasn't nothin' but a good time. I'm ready to do it again."

Dave yawned. "Maybe not before coffee." He took a sip. "Blech. What the hell, Dougie? I thought you at least made some MRE coffee, not this porta-potty water."

I agreed the juice was a poor substitute. It was black like coffee, but sour and disgusting. Hot or cold, I wouldn't touch it.

"Whaaa," Doug whined like a baby, then took a sip. "Some green beanie you are, dude."

I remembered the good news. "Double-K says some of the Korundi will probably filter back. I'm betting Sarkan Sell and Jodal Jark will be the first."

"They saved our bacon, dude."

"That they did. When they do, I want them to form up the rest of any returning Korundi into a unit directly under us. Once again, we're a one-legged man in an ass-kicking contest."

Dave wiped his tongue on his sleeve. "There's a reason an A-Team has twelve members."

He was right. "When you're through bitching about the coffee, Dave, you're with me for an errand. First, we give a fragmentary order to keep the troops on task for security."

"Already done, bro," Doug said. "I was out early checking on things. I've bumped Major Tolan Garth from regimental ops to battalion commander. He'd already stepped in, but I made it official."

"The ship?"

"Right where we left it, a perimeter guard barricaded around it. I ordered the palace grounds to remain closed until further notice."

Doug had correctly anticipated a lot from my mental list. "Shoulda known better than to think you hadn't."

"Great minds think alike, duder."

"We meet back here, then you guys are on refit. At least until tomorrow."

Dave exchanged looks with Doug. "We'll see, brah. Where we off to?"

"The queen's given me a directive. Time to prep the battlefield for her assault."

* * *

Drab camouflaged soldiers saluted and held the door to the Guard headquarters. Cops were like soldiers—they followed orders. But both are supposed to know when it's their duty to disobey an unlawful one. We were spread thin, but until we knew the Guards were truly in line again, the army was going to be very visible. It was going to take time to sort out who was and wasn't worthy to remain a Guard.

Waiting for us was first among those I had to judge.

"I will take you to them," Kleeve Hartus said. Without being ordered, the first shield had already disarmed all Guards. He'd done the minimum to reassure me he had no immediate plans to carry out a fanatic's revolt. But I wanted more. I still saw him with his arm raised, ready to order our execution. I waved the soldiers back. There was no need for them to join us.

In the interview room, the munchkin priest who'd twice married Talis Darmon and I waited. With him was another white robe I'd not seen before. I burst into the room with all the subtlety of a dump truck speeding through the gates of a dynamite factory.

"It's with the full authority of the law that I have discretion over all matters existential to the kingdom. I hold the power of life and death. And which of those I choose for you is yet to be determined."

The munchkin was the pink of a Vistaran on the verge of collapse. His pal darkened to crimson, the color of rage, as he fired back, "We are the servants of Temple Farnest and the underworld. The carnal laws of the surface are but trifles."

Dave smirked. "Where have I heard that before? Oh, yeah! Why, it was just yesterday when the fat one of your trio said something similar, right before a Hortha tore him in two."

"What do you mean? What happened to Precept Turn Turndle?"

The obstinate priest's name had been as unflattering as everything else about him.

Dave cracked his knuckles. "We learned firsthand about the whole dog and pony show the Whites have been running at Farnest. That it's all a ruse to get people to travel north to be used by the Whites for all sorts of nastiness."

"Blasphemy!"

I took over. "We're thinking you didn't know, and that the Whites duped you like everyone else. But because you've been the enablers, whether you knew or didn't, if you want to save your skins, you're going to have to do what I tell you."

"You cannot levy punishment upon us."

"So you keep insisting. But it's not the law you need to worry about. Because when the whole of the kingdom hears what we saw, I'm betting your whole order will wish you'd played this differently. Being ripped apart by angry mobs is a rough shortcut to the underworld."

✿ ✿ ✿

Lashura and the Guarantor were kept in separate confinement. The scientist's bruises were dressed, eyes black like a racoon's mask. Both were clothed in the tissue paper–thin uniform of a detainee. Kleeve Hartus was subdued as he carried out the role of First Shield.

"There are no means by which they can avoid punishment and commit suicide. They are watched at all times. We recovered from their clothing and effects things suspicious, Warlord. Perhaps contrivances of violence or other devices."

"Have what you recovered delivered immediately to Scientist Supreme Cynar."

It was a blow, and I'd meant it as such. Hurt but faithful to duty, his protest made me remember the respect I'd held for him. "It is evidence that may be used in their trial, Warlord. If the chain of custody is broken, a defender could make the case that the kingdom tampered with the effects. The investigators need time to evaluate the items and to—"

I wasn't proud that I enjoyed shutting him down. "By order of the queen, your investigators are to stay clear."

He sank further. "But how will a trial be conducted properly without a full investigation?"

"They won't be standing before the arbiters, Kleeve Hartus. Theirs will be a royal tribunal. The queen alone will decide their guilt and their punishment. The Guards will continue to provide for the prisoners' safety and well-being until that time and nothing more. Is that understood?"

He nodded.

"Open her cell and depart."

He remained. "Warlord, I have much to atone for. Please, allow me to participate so that I may hear the admission of their crimes and begin my return to trust."

"No. The whole of the kingdom will hear of their crimes and the evidence against them at the same time. You are dismissed."

He held out a stone. "You may leave this with the shift leader when done, Warlord." He was gone.

"You're killing the guy, Ben."

Even in her weakened state, Talis Darmon was clear that she had only the beginnings of a plan. The marble block and rare pigments were all there. How she meant to turn the raw material from crude tracings into an unrivaled masterpiece, her method to create like da Vinci was yet undiscovered. But she told me she was working on it.

"Dave, these are Talis Darmon's orders. He has a role to play in what she has planned. I have faith she knows best."

I didn't tell Dave what she'd said to me concerning Kleeve Hartus. Because I wasn't sure what she'd meant.

"The fanatic always conceals the gravest doubts. And when their doubts are confirmed, their energies find a new direction. If Kleeve Hartus is such a fanatic, keep him off balance until it is clear to me where to direct his zeal."

I made a similarly abrupt entrance to Lashura's cell. She startled, as she was meant to. It was cold water in the face. A sudden shocking contrast from the bleak silence of a cell that reminded a prisoner they were not in control of their surroundings, and that outside their barren cell was a world of sound, color, and life. With imprisonment comes the fear that the walls around you may be all you'll ever know again. I knew. It was a kinder coercion by far than what her people had used on my suffering wife.

"Comfortable in your new home, Lashura?"

There was no rage in her. Instead, she let slip the wistful hope that told me she knew her life was in my hands. It came through in her plea. "What of your promise?"

"The queen is still considering how to ensure you keep your end of such a bargain."

"I swear, none will ever travel the Blix from Mihdradahl again. We will call only from elsewhere."

"No. The queen's not content to let you be parasites on any other kingdom either."

Lashura had prepared. "I have considered this. Even shut off from further pilgrims, the sanctuary of Astelaan can be maintained for many years yet. In that time, I can lead my people from complacency to find another way to exist."

"I'll leave you to keep thinking about how you'll convince the queen of your sincerity. But she's a very cautious ruler. It may take her some time." I closed the door to her cell behind us and watched her go fetal.

"You're getting to be a good interrogator, brah. I bet next time we show up, she'll have a ten-point strategy mapped out. Is Talis Darmon really going to send them back?"

"I think so, Dave. But make no mistake, there's a freight train heading for the Whites. And we just laid the first track."

I was certain of only one thing. Even more than the Kingdom's restoration, Talis Darmon's was dependent on a guarantee that the Whites were tied to the rails when I drove the train out of the station.

✷ ✷ ✷

Dave and I made the rounds, letting our new regimental commander know he had his Warlord's confidence, received the latest intel from around the city, and finished by contacting all the members of the council. This group was different from the council the queen inherited when first taking the throne. It had taken time to weed out the worst of them. The conspiracy to murder me had flushed out the most. Sure, they were still a bunch of entitled windbags, but at least they weren't a bunch of plotters. I was reassured in this because it was with care for the queen that each of them pledged to continue the work of the kingdom and to bring calm wherever they could. And they all seemed relieved there'd be some break from the immediacy of having to deal with the biggest crisis just now—how to explain to the people what had happened.

Or, maybe, it was from fear of my wrath that they faked it.

Either way, the most important tasks for the day were done. The only concern I had was behind the doors to our quarters.

I found Doug and Karlo waiting for me.

"Shalees Parn's in there, dude. Told you'd she'd jump to help."

I felt relieved, but guilty again. My two friends looked fatigued, no matter their protests to the contrary. "You guys beat it. Scram. Go flake out. Unless Yellow hordes appear over the horizon or an asteroid strikes and all our worries are over, we meet tomorrow no sooner than noon. Warlord's orders."

Karlo gathered his things. "I'll come back later and check on her, Ben. She ate and she's taking fluids regularly, so I can get rid of her IV."

"Leave me some stuff and I'll do it, Karlo. I promise to call if I need you."

"Understood."

I was alone and lost in thought until a woman I'd met only once before backed through the doors of our bedroom. She sealed the chamber, floating gracefully like a water bug coasting across a calm pond. She was either trained by an order of silent assassins, or was a professional in the art of bringing calm.

"Thank you for coming, Healer."

I'd surprised her. The cherubic face shed the minor shock, and brightened. Her layers of diaphanous gown made for modest dress by Shansara norms. If I were visiting a sick friend in the hospital, I'd say she struck me as the same kind of clinical professional on duty. Her smile was warm and empathetic. I liked her immediately.

She dipped. "Warlord Benjamin Colt, I am greatly honored to be called to the service of you and our queen."

"Won't you sit? How is she?"

She accepted my offer though she continued to hold herself stiff with formality. "She rests after our session. Warlord—"

"Call me, Ben. Or if you must, Benjamin Colt. I hope we'll be friends and I'd like you to be comfortable speaking to me. I'm also glad to be able to finally thank you in person for helping my friend, Doug. Without you, he was on his way to..." I almost said *ride the Blix.*

"Douglas Knoblock is a kind soul," she said. "It is rewarding to see him thrive." Her eyes remained gentle, but the light of her smile dimmed, making the atmosphere grow heavy. I sensed bad news.

"I know how intimately familiar you are with what occurred to Douglas Knoblock, and with all that has happened to the queen. But I must make this understood: to discuss the treatment of another is improper, and I will not betray the confidence of a client. What she and I discuss, I will not relay to you."

"Of course."

"You were witness to the traumas done to her. I would ask you to tell me of them. And also, to share with me what you know of other past physical or emotional insults Talis Darmon has suffered."

I blew out a deep breath. "I hope you cleared your schedule for the day, because it's a long list." There were her failed marriages. The death of her unborn child. The incompetence of her father's kingdom that led to her long imprisonment by the Mydreen. Our trial of survival in the Korund. I gave her the sanitized version of how she dealt with her brother's betrayal. Explaining Talis Darmon's sacrifice to gain the Harridan's cooperation was too much to explain, so I left it out.

I skipped to what had just happened, ending with an expectant mother's disappointment at having to remain separated from her unborn child. "She's been through more than anyone I've ever known, then bounced back as if made of rubber. But this time, instead of blaming the ones who harmed her, she's blaming herself for being their victim. And she's very, very angry at me."

One who dealt in hurt had to be a poker player, but after I laid my cards face up, not even she could hide her tell. The healer's eyebrows shot up like a pair of scrunched caterpillars.

"And how does that make you feel?"

I almost laughed. I wanted auras and Vulcan mind melds, and here she was doing a Dr. Phil. "Makes me sad. Hurt. I know she feels guilty for allowing herself to be deceived by her captors, but it's like she resents me for rescuing her."

The healer's nod made me think she agreed with my amateur assessment. "Not resentment at you so much as at circumstances. But your insight is adept. For now, let me reassure you she does not blame you for what happened. But the anger remains. And awareness of the irrationality of its transference to you is itself traumatizing her."

The cage to my penned fear swung wide. "Has this been one ordeal too many for even her to come back from?"

Everyone in my tribe knew of an operator permanently sidelined after one physical injury too many. But it was what had taken down Doug, the non-physical injuries, that shelved a guy in a way so much worse. The founder of our own SERE school had survived five years of captivity. I'd read the stories and even been lectured by POWs who'd been through the most awful things imaginable.

Few of them went on to happy lives.

"The stories of your exploits together and her rise to the throne are well known, but, I would never have suspected the full depth of how violent and awful were their conditions. She is ever an inspiration—even more so now, learning that she was able to shed these insults to return to grace after each experience. As resilient as she is, there has been much accumulated hurt. And this latest has been especially cruel."

"We had a name for it on Thulia. Post-Traumatic Stress Disorder. I knew people who suffered from it. Badly. If our counselors had the touch to heal minds like you have, a lot of them could've been helped."

Her eyes turned sad. "If only it were that simple. Your personal experience of Talis Darmon's skill may seem miraculous. One as gifted as her can seem to perform magic by firming the sinking soil beneath a path so that it is fit to again bear the traffic of coping. When success is so rapid, it is merely an indication that the underlying problem was one amenable to such correction. You must understand; there are maladies, and there are treatments. The proper treatment depends on the disease."

I thought I understood. "You're saying a hammer isn't the tool to fix every problem. I get it." And in telling me there wasn't a quick fix,

Shalees Parn was also trying to tell me that Talis Darmon's problem was worse than mine had been.

"While I share distant ancestry with the line of Sylah, I do not have the command of one as gifted as the queen. None but her can shape the rays of empathy and healing so profoundly. As you intimated, I must use other means. The good news is that—to use your words—some of the tools in my toolbox may be more appropriate to her treatment. At least, I hope so."

With a flash of inspiration, I snapped my fingers. "Can't believe I forgot about it. Maybe you don't have the touch she does, but our scientist has a healing ray. We've used it before. Do you think it could help?"

She maintained her reserve. "I am aware of its application. It may be another modality within the full spectrum of her treatment. It can repair some of the physical pain. Used properly, it will do no harm, but we should not force on her any treatment she does not desire."

"I think she'll be fine with it."

"Then the sooner the better. Mind, body, and emotion—they are inseparable. When one is attacked, the others suffer. To improve even one, bolsters the health of the others. If she agrees, please see her treated as soon as possible."

"I've seen it do miraculous things," I said.

She shook her head.

"I do not mean to dim hope for her sudden return to health. I only ask that you bear cautious optimism. The way ahead will be challenging. There will be days when she seems much improved, perhaps fully the person you know. But setbacks are certain to occur. If she is volatile, angry, withdrawn—when this happens, it is important that it is with the patience and understanding that you bear her hurt with her. Will you endeavor to do this?"

"I will."

"And when you need to discuss your fears and concerns, I ask that you rely on me. But remember! I will not discuss with you what she shares with me. It will be when she is ready that you will hear from her what she wishes you to know."

"I understand, and thank you. I know you probably can't say, but people will be asking. How soon do you think she may be on her feet?"

"My answer to you is… not today, Warlord."

"She'll have whatever time she needs. But there are very critical things happening, Shalees Parn. Some of them I can handle. But very soon, she's going to have to be the queen again."

"All the time, but not enough," she paraphrased my own words back to me. "The contradiction between your promise and the demands placed on her speaks to the uniqueness of my patient. I understand how necessary her recovery is for the kingdom. Which is why I will come tomorrow and daily for as long as needed. Though this latest invasion caused but a few hours of disruption, for many it has been the greatest tribulation of our age. Greater even than what occurred under the brief reign of Prince Carolinus Darmon."

"And for you, healer? May I ask how this has affected your worldview?"

Her professional duties fulfilled, my shift to something personal made her ease back. My invitation to comfort seemed accepted when she did something unusual. She called me by first name.

"Ben, I am from the stock of Pyreenia. I was not raised to hold the same beliefs as many in Mihdradahl. Though I maintain an open and accepting mind, the appearance of the Whites did not take me to knee in fear of judgment."

Not one Vistaran had ever called me by my first name. "I sincerely hope there are more who think like you, Shalees Parn."

Talis Darmon smiled as I stuck my head in like a cautious turtle. "Did we wake you with our talking? I'm sorry."

"How did you find the priests?"

"Are you hungry? The ladies left us dinner."

Her smile was brief.

"Please answer my question."

So much for small talk.

"I planted the seed, just the way you told me to."

"And Lashura?"

"I'd say she's cruising right through the stages of grief on her way to acceptance. Still got a little bargaining in her, but she's truly fearful that her cell may be all she's ever going to see again."

She sighed and dropped down again.

"I like Shalees Parn," I said. "She's a peach."

That brought back a tiny smile. "Your idioms amuse. Yes, she is pleasing and sweet. My mother was much like—" She trailed off. "Benjamin Colt. I am tortured with thoughts of her. She lives in a state of arrest, neither alive nor dead. As do countless thousands."

"We don't know that for sure, do we? What you saw could be something entirely different from what they claim. Just a mind game."

My theory was considered, and rejected.

"I am gripped with fear that what I saw was in fact a place where her very soul is held. That perhaps the Whites have indeed interfered with the order of things wherein souls reach their true destination, be it the underworld or elsewhere."

"Who would know? Maybe Cynar can figure it out."

"He cannot. When once we discussed similar after the encounter with Jawn Kurz and his queen, he impressed upon me that the nature of the soul was beyond him."

She sighed heavily.

"Husband, am I to hold this secret and spare my kingdom the suffering of this awful knowledge? As I think on how to bring destruction to the Whites, I realize that if what I fear is true—that they hold the souls of so many in a state of uncertainty—then to decide their fate without an eternity of guilt, I risk a worse madness yet."

11

I WAS REACHING FOR A CAN OF SNUFF WHEN SERGEANT GONZALEZ came from behind me. "Colt, if you're supposed to be pulling security, what's your hand doing in your rucksack?" The big man who was our cadre team sergeant snuck up without me ever hearing a thing.

In the two days since my student A-Team had made our night infiltration jump, there'd been no sleep. We'd still not been admitted into the safety of the guerilla camp. We stayed in our own perimeter, anticipating an attack from any and everywhere. I was wet, cold, hungry, and fighting exhaustion to stay alert. On my belly, I was so close to the soft earth where I just wanted to lay my head for a minute. That the guerillas kept us in our current condition out of mistrust seemed a little overdone. Maybe they just didn't appreciate the miracle by which we'd avoided broken legs, backs, and necks to get to them.

We'd jumped in from less than 500 feet on a moonless night to hit a drop zone that was the roughest-tilled patch of farmland this side of Afghanistan. The farmer had to be on the payroll of the Special Warfare Center, subsidized to keep his field in such shitty condition. The air that night was especially thin, my ruck especially heavy, and the night especially black. I'd no sooner finished checking that my canopy was full, was trying to find the horizon or some indication of how close the ground was, when I came to a stop that flexed every bone in my body to the point of snapping. I'd not even had time to release my rucksack. I laid on the cement-hard earth for a moment, reckoning that if everything hurt, it meant I was still alive.

I'd seen the guys held over from previous classes, hobbling around in casts—or worse—after bad luck on their own infiltration jumps into the remote North Carolina landscape. It was a lesson that you could be as strong as a plow horse. As intelligent as any scholar. Do everything right. Make no mistakes.

But still lose.

I'd avoided their fate. I'd arrived in one piece to free Pineland from oppression.

Gaining the trust of the guerillas we were sent to help, that was another matter still. Humping a hundred-plus-pound ruck on an endless journey through one swamp after another, we were led through briar thicket, over mountain, and blindly through dense forests to rest only briefly before being put on the move again. And each time, the guerillas tried to take our equipment. They cried that we insulted them by forming a security perimeter at each halt. They played their part to set us up for failure. We held fast to what we'd been taught.

And so far, we were still in the game.

It was all part of the final test—the graduation exercise in unconventional warfare that determined if the last year of Herculean effort would be rewarded with the green beret, or with little more to show for it all than the remnant of a house fire. Because after so much blood and sweat, that's what getting bounced out of the Q would be—a house fire, where everything you'd built was turned to ash in front of you.

I was not alone feeling like little more than dog shit hammered flat. And we hadn't even begun the real work in leading our guerilla force to win back Pineland.

The role players that made up our irregular army were a bunch of disgruntled clerks and jerks, highly pissed off and uncooperative because they hadn't joined the army to be grunts. Wi-Fi and hot chow was what their enlistment contracts had promised. Most of them hadn't been in field gear since basic training.

It was by design that these less-than-crack-troops were our pretend indigenous fighting force. The role of their leader—the guerilla chief—was played by a senior Special Forces operator. If he ordered it, every PFC and Spec 4 sentenced to spend these weeks freezing in the swamps and forest would commit our murders with glee. All the while, a battalion of the 82nd searched for us, joyfully ready to do the same.

If either happened, me putting on the green beret would become as unlikely as getting superpowers from the bite of a radioactive spider. To top it off, I'd just done something to make getting dropped into a vat of toxic waste seem like a happy accident. I was still in a perfect prone, and without taking my eyes off the wood line, I guiltily withdrew my hand from the top flap of my ruck.

"You shame that Ranger tab again, Colt, and your dreams of stacking a long tab on top of that one are history. Is that what you are? A badge hunter?"

I cursed myself. I'd relied on memory and touch alone to let my hand find the sweet tin that contained the heavenly shredded leaves and the brown go-go juice they made. I'd already gone through two cans. Not once had my eyes left the woods as they scanned for the approach of the hunters bent on our deaths. But I knew better than to say that.

"No, Sergeant." My hand was back on to my weapon.

"We'll see. As soon as you're relieved, you make your way to my CP. It's in the draw behind us. Your brain better be wired tighter than your ass has been, Colt."

"Yes, Sergeant."

Soon enough, my buddy Kyle Hill was there to relieve me. Making sure Sergeant Gonzalez wasn't behind us, I asked, "How was it?"

He looked like I felt. Frazzled.

"Brutal. Nothing I said was right. He's going flush me outta the Q course, man."

Unlike me, Kyle had a college degree, spoke two languages, and was brilliant. If a guy as smart as him was tail-tucked like a beaten dog, what chance did I have? The demands placed on us all were on a level different from anything I'd experienced. Rightly so.

The origins of SF were in the World War 2 OSS—the Office of Strategic Services. It was the precursor to both the CIA and Special

Forces. OSS operatives fought behind the lines with local resistances, from the deepest jungles of hellish Burma to urban occupied Europe where they conducted clandestine warfare under the noses of the Gestapo. The history of Special Forces was written in operations acknowledged only in rumor, to missions leaked by single photographs of operators on horseback in far-flung countries with foreign troops. For me, SF held the promise of a portal to a life of adventure.

How right I'd been.

The curriculum for this phase of training was a master's-level crash course in how Special Forces did what they did. Dropped into the mythical country of Atlantica, we were engaged in a last test of our ability to swim in the ocean of geopolitical instability. To put into practice how we would someday do the shadow-world kind of operations we all dreamed of.

As if what we had to do wasn't already difficult enough, Sergeant Gonzalez dropped extra weight into our rucks. Physical and metaphorical. Three books. And we were responsible for knowing them inside and out. If he was going to let us into SF, we had to prove to him we could do more than just meet the school's standards.

We had to meet his.

"I'll be back to spell you, Hill. What's left of me." It was time to get cooked under the spotlight of a Socrates produced by the school of unconventional warfare.

When I got there, the other half of the team was already cross-legged in a circle. Sergeant Gonzalez flipped open his camp seat. We'd all been assigned the same three books to read. And how we well we knew them and what we learned from them was going to weigh heavily on his evaluation of us.

"Your teammates have already given their book reports. Can't say I'm impressed. Maybe this half of the team is where all the smarts are hiding out."

Our team leader was in the group with my buddy Hill. The captain was a total stud. Multilingual. Master's degree. If he hadn't done something to make Sergeant Gonzalez satisfied, what chance did we have? I know they say you shouldn't beat yourself before the fight's even started, but when I measured myself against my fellow students, it was hard not to feel like a matchstick rowboat trying to stay afloat among the iron landing craft at the Normandy Invasion.

But we all bobbed in the same ocean where Sergeant Gonzalez would lob his mortars to sink us.

"Abbarca, start us out. What's the setting in which the book was written?"

Angelo was like me. All his real education came in the Army. Also like me, he'd been in the 82nd. Unlike me, he was motivated by more than just guns and explosives. He read this long-hair stuff because he genuinely enjoyed the study. I hit the switch to my brain like I would my readiness to hop in the ring, eager to prove to Sergeant Gonzalez that I could be better than what he thought of me so far.

A-A was well prepared. "The Japanese Imperial Army controlled China. The Chinese didn't have the conventional capability to expel them. The book is Mao explaining the tenets of guerilla warfare to the people as a means to enlist their cooperation to fight the Japanese."

Sergeant Gonzalez remained stone. "Nice, but not quite right. Where'd Abbarca screw up, guys?"

Our gatekeeper to the ranks of special warfare had made it known if he had to run the discussion, he'd downgrade the whole group. Right or wrong, as long as we could defend our opinions, it would count. He'd asked a question. He expected an answer without having to ask twice.

Mark Panther jumped in to take the heat off the rest of us for a minute by opening himself up as a target. Whether it's offering to hump the machine gun without being asked, or putting yourself out there to be ridiculed, you couldn't be here without having abandoned the old army dictum. Never volunteer. "It doesn't read like it was written for peasants. More likely it was aimed at the higher-ups."

"True, Panther. It was written for an audience of military and political leaders. Why?"

To be assigned as our evaluator, being a cadre team sergeant meant Sergeant Gonzalez had survived a career of the toughest schools and real-world missions. If he found us lacking in the skills of small unit tacticians or thinkers, going to an A-Team wouldn't happen.

I was time for me to try to get the stink of weakness off me.

"Because Mao was teaching them that guerilla operations are as much political as they are military. And that by themselves, guerillas can't win a war."

His forehead wrinkled in the tiniest amount. Neither approval, nor disfavor. I'd take it.

"Nothing new there, Colt. Everything you've been taught about unconventional warfare has emphasized that basic tenet. But, by reading it from the author of a successful guerilla resistance, my goal is for it to lend some weight to the concept. The question I have for you is this: why is guerilla warfare both political and military in nature?"

Abbarca was eager to get back in. "Because political power grows out of the barrel of the gun. At least, from Mao's perspective."

Sergeant Gonzalez's eyebrows raised in the way I'd hoped to inspire. "That's Mao, but not from the reading. Good. You've done your research. So, is that what we're doing here? Using the barrels of our guns to promote US national interests? Someone else."

The lieutenant spoke up. "Primarily, it's *their* guns we want used."

"True, sir, and we want to make our allies as lethal to their enemies as possible, as an extension of US goals and policies. If we can get them to do it for themselves, our whole war machine doesn't have to be spun up to do it for them. But, what did the book say specifically about the military action by guerillas? How is it different from any other military action?"

I stepped in again, ready to take my lumps or maybe give some to get the respect I wanted. "The book said military action by guerillas was for the purpose of attaining a political goal." Before Sergeant Gonzalez could take the floor of the forest classroom away from me, I flexed to show him my mental muscles were at least as big as my real ones.

"But when the Vietnamese used that model of political action, they used it to justify things like assassinating local officials. The tactic was politically successful because it achieved the goal of removing the immediate opposition to their insurgency, and it also generated fear in anyone else who might've thought about actively resisting them. But it outraged the West and brought us into the conflict."

My grandpa had told me all about the tactics of the Viet Cong insurgency. Connecting that example with the Mao we read, I'd thought to beat Sergeant Gonzalez to the punch.

"Okay, Colt. I know what you're doing. You're jumping ahead to the rhetorical question of the ethics of guerilla campaigns. Does helping a resistance to obtain their political goals justify any form of violence? We already know the answer to that. Our ethical and legal boundaries oppose the kind of statist inhumanity that believes the means justifies the ends. Not debatable."

He'd shut me down before I could grandstand to make myself look smart by answering the dilemma I'd presented. Sergeant Gonzalez knew all the tricks. Just as I thought I'd only succeeding in confirming for him that I was the spotlight Ranger he seemed to think I was, he threw me a bone.

"But we can go ahead and discuss it. What *if* our Pineland allies want to adopt the same kind of tactics? Plant bombs in public places? Mine trails to deter the pursuit by government troops? Attack nonmilitary targets? Do we accept it's their country, their fight, their right?"

Someone else beat me. "No, Sergeant. The law of land warfare, our values of freedom and democracy, they all go against us accepting any kind of terrorism on the part of our allies."

For the first time, Sergeant Gonzalez seemed human instead of all-knowing. "We'd like to think so. When you're by yourself with a platoon of indig, another American a hundred miles away, and the bullets start flying, it gets trickier.

"I can assure you that to those on the ground, bombs dropped by a marked aircraft from 10,000 feet don't produce less terror than an IED placed by an insurgent dressed in rags. And that's the other lesson to take from the reading. A G-campaign and its military tactics are a reflection of the political philosophy of the resistance it serves. But it's US political philosophy that determines how *we* do things. You all have a copy of the Declaration of Independence. If you ever doubt what to do—I want you to read it. There is no greater document to remind you of what it means to be an American."

The sun was getting low. Sergeant Gonzalez checked his watch. I thought he was about to cut us loose to get back to the perimeter. Instead, the message from his Rolex seemed to be that school had a few minutes left.

"And, Colt, the lesson to take from the Vietnam conflict is that we beat the VC insurgency. SF did. Not by ourselves, but our tribe can claim the distinction of having successfully carried out one of the few successful counterinsurgencies in history. South Vietnam fell to a conventional military invasion. But after so many years of prolonged conflict, the US was worn down and quit. So, whether or not terror worked as a successful tactic for the communist insurgency, it became irrelevant in the end."

"Yes, Sergeant," I said sheepishly. I'd meant to get there on my own, but my plan to solo to distinction like a prima donna had crashed and burned, my singing relegated to the chorus. I wondered if I looked like a bigger loser to him for the effort.

One of the medics, Brian Cutone, was a big muscled guy from Boston—complete with the accent. "Sergeant Gonzalez, aren't these kinds of communist revolutions all ancient history? Marxism is dead. Shouldn't we be more concerned about modern movements? The Islamofascists aren't going away. The old Eastern Bloc is re-forming under a kind of capitalist oligarchy."

"You might think the books on your list are outdated. They are not. They contain the guiding principles our enemies still use. And as far as being dead, Marxism isn't dead. Deception is an inherent part of their game. You can hide the essence of any revolutionary ideology by giving it a different name, but by studying these books, you'll be able to recognize them for what they are. We'll talk more about *On Guerilla*

Warfare before we move on to *Rules for Radicals*. We'll save my favorite read for last. That is, if the UPA Army hasn't caught you by then."

Then he gave a grin. "Not bad." It disappeared as quickly. "Your captain's going to meet with the guerilla chief to try to get your team into their camp and finally get this mission going."

Without looking at me, he said, "I'd keep hands ready. Anything can happen in Pineland."

✷ ✷ ✷

I woke from my nap a little disoriented by the dream. It was almost as weird as the dreams I'd had of Jawn Kurz calling to me through the ether. But these phantoms had come to me from memory. I wondered about the mysteries of my subconscious, when I felt eyes on me.

She was awake.

"My body rebels at the thought of lying on this bed for another second."

It was just a walk around the apartment, but it was a good sign her bed had become intolerable. More positive signs came when she agreed to eat. Working out more of the knots after dinner by pacing around our quarters, she pulled away when I tried to guide her to the bedroom.

"I am incapable of further sleep. I wish to speak with you."

Shalees Parn's advice was that when she wanted to talk, I should be ready to listen, mute and attentive. I was caught unprepared when she turned the tables on me.

"You have questions about how I have chosen to proceed. And that I did so without consulting you. Ask and I will answer."

Ever since her confabulation to the council, I'd wanted to do just that. Just as an earthquake dropping the roof on top of you made concerns about the appointment with the housepainters inconsequential, the terror of her psychotic break had put my curiosity on hold.

"When did you decide to withhold the truth from your ministers? And why?"

"It was as the women attended my abused state that my conspiracy took shape. In ignorance, Dureen Zell and the rest preened and prattled, all the while speaking in aphorisms of our faith, offering prayers to the ancestors who had seen me returned safely. They are common folk. But as I considered the oration I was about to give, I considered that the aristocracy and gifted are no less common in their beliefs. They would be no better prepared for the unfettered truth than would the simple women who surrounded me. To speak with complete candor would be no different from inviting the Mydreen to return, such destruction that would bring. So, I retreated to logic."

She was a philosopher. A scholar of great accomplishment.

"I retreated into my mind, ignoring the physical, and rapidly set the conditions to solve the problem before me.

"Firstly, did I understand the nature of the simulacra? And did that place truly hold the souls of the departed as they would have me believe? My immediate answer was that I did not understand it nor could I. Nor could I allow myself to believe any explanation rendered from the Whites. They are liars to their core. Nor, when I considered my second question, would it be likely that even Cynar could deduce an answer containing any certainty.

"Second was a question as old as any. What is the soul? What is its nature? Where does it go upon death? As immediately, my answer was absolute. I say with no arrogance that I am a scholar of a school from which there is none greater. No science or philosophy exists to answer that which I could not myself fail to answer. It is unknowable.

"Thirdly, accepting these questions have no answer meant there was no counsel superior to my own regarding how I should proceed."

I found no flaw in her assessment and kept silent.

"I foresaw that all would struggle with the same unanswerable questions. And that in causing this existential crisis, the struggle would paralyze us from taking action. And it is action we must take. So, I made my decision to tell what I could, while concealing what I must."

"Including your plan to restructure the entire belief about the nature of the underworld? How did you come up with that so quickly?"

"It was not a new idea. Nor is it to others of my time."

"You've always avoided telling me what you think happens at the end of the Blix?"

"Because… I had doubts. But never did I think it be something of the nature we discovered."

"So, you told them the Whites confirmed that the underworld is on the spiritual plane? And if we scapegoat the Whites and get the priests to go along, it will calm the faithful?"

"It was the best I could formulate in the crucible of the moment."

It was a diamond formed in only seconds by the terrific pressure.

"I understand why you went for it without asking for my advice. None of us are equipped the way you are to consider all the factors at play. What you came up with was as good or better than what a committee could have come up with after months of deliberations. Well done. It's bought us some time to get the rest of your plan together. Care to tell me what that is?"

Her jaw muscles clenched briefly. "The world must be protected from predation by the Whites. My dilemma is this—how to ensure such? If I order you to obliterate the Whites' nest and with them, the abomination of their prison, what is the result? If those currently incarcerated in the simulacra are living in the peace of an ignorant bliss—in a means beyond our understanding—then I am guilty of a holocaust more foul than the mass murder we unleashed on our enemy in Clymaira. For if the mechanism is destroyed, what happens to those within that ethereal creation? If they are truly extracted souls, would they go to the true underworld, or would oblivion be their destiny outside of the simulacra?

"This is what fueled the need for my deception, Benjamin Colt. Such possibilities would occur to all. Factions would form. Civil war would ensue.

"I then predicted the fruits of the only two courses of action available to us. To quarantine the Whites and leave them to tend the simulacra, or to destroy it all. It must be one, or the other.

"I search the memory of a life spent in study. No tome I know holds precedence for me to follow. Neither my father nor mother imparted on me the lesson of how to proceed. I was sworn by them to a belief that deceit can never be just. That duplicity is the death of nobility. But the more I consider the problem, the farther from an answer I seem to be.

"Because if I choose to let the Whites and the simulacra remain, the knowledge of it all will torture me forever. And if I destroy it, I live knowing that I have perhaps doomed thousands of souls to oblivion."

It would be enough to drive any but one already mad to the brink of insanity. Combining that with her already crushing feeling of victimhood, how was she now anything but a babbling wreck?

She was stronger than the forces that held the planets around the sun.

"We have time to figure this out. Together."

Her eyes came to rest on the pistol sitting on the table beside me.

"I want one of those. I have vowed to never be weak again. Teach me to use it. Or is there something better?"

"We have blasters." We'd taken to calling the fizzle pistols that after Karlo souped them up like he'd done the K-specs.

"The Whites can defeat devices that utilize manipulation of the rays. Their technology cannot interfere with the bullet-launchers, as you call them. Isn't that so?"

"Cynar's going to crack that nut eventually. But you're right. Guns are mechanical and chemical. If the basics are done correctly, one will go bang when you need it to." I tried to reassure her that we wouldn't be the Whites' victims again.

"We have our air defenses on alert and positioned to guard the northern approaches to the city. Anything bigger than a grain of sand blown by the wind is going to get lit up before it can get anywhere near enough to hit us with a silencing ray. If they even have another ship to send our way."

But she was resolute.

"I swore my oath before you already. I will never be unarmed again. I wish to start now."

✳ ✳ ✳

When I insisted that she rest, she insisted even harder that we continue. Finally, I felt confident enough with her dry practice and let her load the pistol. I checked the time. The sun would rise soon enough. "Shalees Parn will be here in a few hours. When she does, I need to go out."

"Yes. The Warlord needs to assert my will. And I should be rested for Shalees Parn's session. I know what it is to try to reach through exhaustion to do the work, such was your state when I first touched your animus." She still held the pistol. "This has brought comfort. Perhaps I will sleep until she arrives."

"It's meant to be comforting. I'll stay until she gets here."

With the healer's arrival, Karlo also appeared. Once Shalees Parn was out of sight, he handed me something. "Doug brought your computer like you asked. I would've bet it was your playlist you wanted." Karlo had found the file, translated it, and transferred it to a reading scroll. "Trying your Mihdra on a PhD level, Ben?"

"Hardly." I placed the scroll on the table and left.

The army presence around the city might quickly prove to be unnecessary if things kept up like this. If the city was not operating normally, it was at least operating. Functionaries filled the governance quarter and were about their business. The Whites' airship was drawing no more attention than the other pieces of art around the promenade. I wanted to get it out of there soon, but first I had to run it past Talis Darmon.

At the army headquarters compound, Dave had good news. "Regiment got a buzz from Jodal Jark. He and Sarkan Sell are on the move back and bringing a platoon of volunteers with them. More will follow."

"Wish it were more," Doug said. "But we'll put them to work."

As the sun rose higher, my expectation that I'd be prematurely called back to our quarters dwindled. I told myself it was because she was doing well, not because she'd renewed her anger at me. Before a stomach full of anxious butterflies accompanied me on my return home, I had a final task planned. A solo one.

In the Golden Hub was a small fabricator's shop, buttressed by warehouses and factories making mundane necessities. I took the exterior stairs to the sub-basement. Weaving through a collection of barrels leaking a toxic lime-green substance I was careful to not get on my boots, I arrived at the dark utility room door. Recent events had put me behind, and it was time to catch up. My palm print recognized, I entered the den of the Plumbers.

No one on Mars, not even the guys, knew who G. Gordon Liddy was and why my name for the surveillance specialists should be amusing. It was enough that I did.

The woman rising from the monitor wore laborer's coveralls, stripped out of the arms and tied to her waist. I'd have done the same as thick and oppressive as the air was, like most industrials shops I'd visited in my life. I waved her down and pointed to the next room to indicate my destination. She correctly sensed I wanted to go to work and made her report without pleasantries.

"There's been much increased wristlet communication as of late, Warlord. Summary analyses are prepared, but you may find the raw transcriptions more interesting than usual."

We'd been eavesdropping on the conversations between Bryant and his girlfriend—the head of the Yellows' security apparatus—since I'd let Bryant extort one of Cynar's wristlets from me. It was when we questioned the possibility that Bryant had been doing the same to us that Cynar cracked his own tech to make it possible. The Plumbers had monitored and translated the clandestine communiques into Mihdra from their two parent languages—US-of-A English and Annamese.

At first, I'd checked the products of the surveillance daily, excited by the prospect of hearing secrets from his own mouth. After the first few weeks, I stopped. Booty calls weren't the kind of state secrets I cared about.

Bryant: When?
Tourmaline: Tonight.
Bryant: Time for dinner?
Tourmaline: Time for something.

Most of the conversations were as abrupt and lacking intelligence value, other than to let us know they were still in intimate cahoots. With a gun at the head of my friend Zaylin Twee, Bryant had made a leveraged ask of me—support for a new and improved leadership in Annameria in exchange for a lasting peace between Yellow and Red. With no indication that their play for the supreme magnate's seat was taking shape, nor a plan to fly north and attack us, I defaulted to reading a summary of the exchanges whenever I remembered to.

There had been the occasional gem amongst the unpolished pebbles we mined.

Tourmaline: Be warned. She's ordered Kai Sar and his staff picked up. Keep clear, just in case.
Bryant: Thanks. I was going to drop by and check progress. Is it because they're so behind on [Indistinct. Could have been *Acelyx*. Mythical winged predator that ate children who lied to their parents.]?
Tourmaline: Yes.
Bryant: Serves him right for overpromising and underdelivering.

That had been two months ago, and there'd been no further mention of the incident or whatever Acelyx was. I skimmed ahead to find the latest traffic. On the way to the most recent week, I found a brief but curious exchange.

Tourmaline: He's at it again. He's going to die by his own misadventure. We won't have to do a thing.

Bryant: I'd rather kill him myself. But we'll celebrate that day, any way it comes.

It was me they were talking about. It sounded like they discussed my near death over the Furrow. That they both wished me dead wasn't a shocker. Not at all. It was that they even *knew* about it. Only the closest of my closest were with me to test the new gizmo. I checked the date-time group, and relaxed. The pair of ill-wishers were referencing a different incident where I came close to personally investigating the realm of the underworld. A month ago, I'd been assisting with training when a short round sent me tackling two novice Korundi mortar men to the ground.

In all fairness to them, our mortar program was in its infancy. When the anemic round plopped out to nosedive about ten meters in front of their position, the two Tarns gawked like it was their first trip to a peep show. The shrapnel tattered my plate carrier, but at least my last set of Cryes missed needing more darning by Dureen Zell.

What we learned—the energy released by the propellant eroded and fouled the tubes faster than we predicted. We increased the centrifugal arming distance for the rounds and toughened the tubes.

Such is the trial and error of learning from scratch the industry of making things that go boom.

Anyway, the method for that tale to reach Bryant's ears had an explanation more logical than Annamerian spies in our army. It was evidence that when drunk on the town, troops bragged. Some cantina spy overheard slurred tales of the Warlord at work, which made it into a report sent south. I'd make a point to have the Guard review counter-intel operations in the saloon district.

I skimmed through to the morning the Whites appeared—the day I was caught away at play with my friends. The Whites' arrival, her kidnapping, the departure of the Korundi, and our rapid return would no doubt fan the flames of secretive and rabid gossip between Bryant and his girlfriend. Unless they'd succeeded in overcoming the communications gap in their tech, it would take a minimum of three days from the day a trade caravan left Shansara before it reached Aetheria.

The first transcription indicating they knew anything was from yesterday. It started with a harried one-way transmission.

Tourmaline: Meet me. Now. [Speaker seems more distressed than usual.]

More exchanges followed, more than Tourmaline and Bryant had risked by using their clandestine means of communication than any other time since they'd been under our observation.

Tourmaline: The time isn't now, she says.
Bryant: Can't she be convinced?
Tourmaline: You're the one who cautioned we were still behind in the arms race, and we'd most likely suffer devastating losses if we attacked them. So, congratulations. She's still firmly in your camp on that.
Bryant: Maybe when their greenies went home, they took all the best stuff with them? Maybe they're at their weakest right now!
Tourmaline: Until I have something hard to suggest that, I won't bring up the idea. Don't you do it either.

It was proof Tourmaline and Bryant would screw us the first chance they got. On word of the Korundi departing, their first suggestion to the supreme magnate was to attack us. But she shot them down.

An hour later came their next conversation.

Tourmaline: Whatever it was that paralyzed the city when the Whites appeared, it's in their possession.
Bryant: How's that?
Tourmaline. The report says that just like the first time the ship appeared, everything went dead again when the craft returned. The craft is parked in the governance quarter. Means it's under their control now.
Bryant: If it has that kind of effect, how'd they beat it to get her back?

Tourmaline: No idea. I must report this to her.

Bryant: [Sighs] We're already at fifty percent alert. Are we about to be ordered to a hundred percent?

Tourmaline: It's likely. You know her. She's going to bunker down when I tell her. We won't see each other for some time.

Bryant: Maybe this is our time to move against her.

Tourmaline: No. We'll talk about this later.

They were quite the pair. One moment they ran the odds for success at hitting us, then the next, the same for their coup d'état. I was right to remember they were scorpions, no matter how they promised to be well behaved while they rode my back across the river.

Putting it all together, it meant that the product of the spies' collections continued to be reaching Tourmaline only at the crawling pace of the floating convoys. The other good tidbit to come with all this—the ultra-paranoid supreme magnate thought we had a new super-weapon acquired from the Whites. And the fear of it was buying us some breathing room until the guys could figure out the nuts and bolts of it.

There were a few more exchanges. They contained less meat and were even murkier in the soupy broth made from the reports of what happened over those thirty-six hours.

"I'll be back tomorrow," I told the analyst. "Anything critical, I want to be informed immediately."

"Yes, Warlord. Most of their traffic occurs during the day when the two are engaged in separate activities. Indications are that most nights they are co-located and the wristlets unused. If something of importance comes through, you'll know at once."

It was late when I returned. On the couch and deeply engaged in reading, her eyes reluctantly drifted up and away from the light of an open scroll.

"Did you leave this for me to find?"

"I did."

Her color was wonderfully strong. She'd gone to Cynar's healing bed today for a treatment, but what she held in her hand I thought might have as much to do with her vitality. I didn't want to break an arm patting myself on the back just yet, but it made me think maybe the groundhog's shadow was absent and winter was coming to an end.

"I find it puzzling. It presents a philosophy of political machinations that I find most unsettling, but strangely enticing." Cynar's tanning bed treatment had also accelerated the growth of her hair. She absentmindedly stroked her scalp like a buzz-cut recruit, locks returning from stubble.

"I thought the same when I was first made to read it." It was the book Sergeant Gonzalez had savored as a graduation exercise and gift all rolled into one.

"You left this for me to discover in some subtle ploy?"

I'd been found out.

"Guilty as charged. I thought it might be helpful."

A flowery bouquet might have been the conventional gesture. But for the woman whose scholarly brilliance outshined her beauty? I gave silent thanks to a scheming sixteenth-century Florentine diplomat and to a twenty-first-century Puerto Rican–American professor of deadly chaos. It was too long since I'd done anything to make her smile. Her perfect white teeth shone and the first hint of thaw tickled my bones.

"I wonder what my father would have made of—how is his name pronounced?"

"His name was Machiavelli."

12

SHE STARTED TAKING MEETINGS AGAIN AND DOING THE BUSINESS OF the queen. Shalees Parn came daily. But the days of that next week were no easier. In a way, they were harder. Even during our trek through the Korund, each cold night held the promise of a respite with the inevitable sunrise. Since the brief beams of pleasure shone from her interest in the new reading material, there'd been no repeat breakthroughs of sun to warm our gray domicile.

How to bring more from her again, I was at a loss.

If there was a time each day when it seemed she neared another breakthrough, it was when cooing to our child through the cloud that joined us to Califex and the creche Beraal guarded. But even those brief moments were quickly shadowed when her storm clouds of anger or rain of sadness blew over us again.

There was one other time when she seemed unburdened, and I entertained hope that she might yet truly come home. Talis Darmon insisted our training continue. She was frustrated at first because her concentration was scattered. But as her health improved, so did her shooting.

"It's a kind of meditation, is it not?" she said after today's practice. In just a few range sessions, many small holes now combined on the target to form one large one. "Is it so for you?"

"It is. And the more your skill becomes learned and unconscious, you'll find you think less and less. Your mind floats in the same way as in the deepest meditation. Your awareness opens up to everything around you. And as you find your performance improving, with it comes a deeper sense of well-being and confidence."

"Well-being. Confidence. You see me as I see myself. Lacking those qualities. I do not believe with ten thousand shots will I regain them." The darkness was back.

"I was speaking about myself and what I feel when I practice. If it makes a simpleton like me feel that way, I'm just saying you're right to think it can do the same for you."

Shalees Parn reminded me that though she was improving, the road I traveled with her would be booby-trapped with mines, some of which I would inadvertently set for myself. That last one I thought I'd disarmed, but always, I feared I'd unintentionally say something to bring out her hurt. The only way I could avoid that would be with my silence, which the healer had also warned was as potentially wounding to her.

Shalees Parn summed it up for me. "You're damned if you do, you're damned if you don't." Some idioms are universal.

It was when I shared with Dave how things were going that he hit me with a suggestion. "Tranya Olan. She's got a side you haven't seen. A lot of sides, actually. I've already brought it up, and she's super ready to try, brah. You don't know the full extent of what she's been through. If anyone can relate to Talis Darmon, it's her."

Tranya Olan was a painted porcelain doll who concealed a core of Tasmanian Devil. As talented at mayhem as she was at combining Vistaran invectives in unique and awkward ways, Dave had found his own soulmate. It was another accidental blessing to our exile on Vistara. And in the brief peace of the months since we'd killed one—maybe even two—gods, Dave had admitted he wasn't no longer rolling with the punches. He was happy. If Tranya Olan could be a help or even a friend to Talis Darmon, I was all for it.

"I haven't been much of a buddy, Dave. I know hearing about our last scrum had to have worried her. How's she been?"

"Mopey. Got nothing to do with me getting in tussles. She's resigned from the Guard."

"Because of the Kleeve Hartus thing?"

"Yeah, brah. She was full-on pissed off about her boss drawing down on us. If she'd been on the scene, she'd have beat the Tarns to it and lit her own people up."

"So, we're her people now, not the Guard?"

"Brah! We've been her people since you guys came back from Annameria. She feels like the Guard abandoned her. Know what I mean?"

"It's just, I know what a shake-up it is to have to question your own tribe." We'd had a team abandon us when they decided to leave our principles by the wayside. "But I'm not sure how to put the two of them together. Dinner and wine doesn't seem like the setting to talk about PTSD."

"I got an idea, brah."

I tested the waters with Talis Darmon soon as I got home. "How would you feel about getting back into combatives? You and Beraal worked out daily."

"Just today Shalees Parn inquired about my return to an exercise regime. My body craves it. Even before the—incident—I had allowed myself to become lax. I feel ready. All right. In addition to our other practice, you shall teach me your method of fighting."

"Not me. I have someone else in mind."

When the protection detail announced the general was here with a guest, I brought them in. Next to Dave, the elfin woman I'd seen kill men many times her size dipped deeply in the formal curtsy reserved when in the queen's presence.

"I sense David Masamuni has had a hand in offering your services as warmaster, Tranya Olan."

I knew my former accomplice in espionage was fearless, but her voice trembled as she rose and said, "It would be my honor, Queen Talis Darmon."

"I have meetings today. Will you be available tomorrow?"

"David Masamuni has already shown me your private gymnasium. I will be there at your leisure."

"Benjamin Colt, will you make the arrangements for her access? Until then, Tranya Olan." I knew she had no meetings. It was the time when she retreated into the empty nursery to call Beraal and then cry. She preferred to be alone.

Now that my wife had retreated, I said, "Thanks for this, Tranya Olan. And there's no need to be nervous with Talis Darmon. She's a humble student."

"I do not doubt that, Benjamin Colt. My trepidation lies elsewhere." My diminutive friend was troubled. "You see, David Masamuni and I have no secrets from each other."

I knew what she referred to. At the mention of Tranya Olan's abuse, Dave looked as uncomfortable as I felt.

"I too was once victimized. The violation I suffered while exercising my duties was of the worst variety. I struggled greatly to regain my composure."

That's what Dave had meant when he said she could relate.

"You don't have to go into details, my friend," I told her, while thinking, *and rumor was you stayed on mission and when the time was right, spilled your rapist's guts as the signal for the rescue team.*

"Just so. David Masamuni has told me what happened. If the climate becomes amenable in such a way, I will share my own experience with her. If such does not present, then it is solely in the role of her trainer that I will remain. It was with a wisdom and maturity I do not usually credit him with that he brought the idea to me."

"Hey!" Dave protested good-naturedly.

She gave him a smile reserved for children and puppies. The two were truly well matched. "I felt it necessary to tell you what intent we conspired. Is that also your desire? That I act to potentially be confidante of your queen?"

"It is. If nothing else, if by training her you can help her restore physical confidence, I'd be indebted. Thank you." And if Talis Darmon accepted her as more than a trainer? I was rich because of my friends. There weren't enough gems in all the mines of Tranya Olan's people to equal the value of what such a friendship might mean for Talis Darmon's future—and mine.

"Then I accept. If I am able to aid her, then I would not think my trauma solely a curse to me, and it will be me giving thanks. But if you are looking for a spy... the saying comes from your world, Warlord. You are shit out of luck."

✳ ✳ ✳

Talis Darmon had a full day planned, and none of it included me. In just days, Tranya Olan had added to her role as warmaster that of personal bodyguard and companion. Talis Darmon was a library of many volumes, whereas I was the simple tree that produced the pulp for their blank pages. She needed more than the soil, sun, and water that nourished me. With Beraal gone, I was not enough. I was not saddened by that realization. I was relieved that Tranya Olan was filling the void. I was alone when Karlo buzzed me, in the middle of deciding which of my duties to shirk in order to get some workout time for myself.

"Ride shotgun with me, Ben."

"Where to, Karlo?"

"I got the call. Tyreen Sorell's ready for my help."

The Supreme Guild Master of the Atmosphere Wizards had been trying to reach the source of the alchemic process that produced the very air of dying Vistara. We'd taken to calling it "Element X."

After Tyreen Sorell's full mea culpa, I'd sided with the queen to forgive his treasonous actions and allow him to attempt to isolate the material from the air works in Maleska Mal. If the lost process for making Element X could be duplicated, all the atmosphere works could be returned to bountiful production. That the work was moving at a snail's pace only served to make me consider Cynar's opinion as correct—that the air wizards were clueless and stalling for time.

"I can't be gone for a week to Maleska Mal, Karlo. You understand."

"We'll be back tonight."

It was days of flying to reach the eastern frontier. The ancient and once wondrous city of Filestra had decayed to become the wreck of Maleska Mal, occupied so long by the barbaric Mydreen, until their destruction and near total abandonment of the city left it to slip closer into a state where it disappeared beneath the red sands and into memory.

"Tonight? How's that possible?"

"I've got the Silver Surfer running again." I was puzzled until he reminded me. "You already forget about the brand-spanking-new hot rod you guys flew straight into a gunfight? It still had that showroom floor new-flitter smell when I gave it to you."

"I didn't know it had a name. Or that you'd fixed it up. It's that fast?"

"We'll be there in three hours. Another couple on the ground to make sure the containment is solid, then we button up and speed back. Thought you'd want to go along. Get eyes on the ground and whatnot."

I didn't have a better offer for the day. "What the heck? Why not. Be right there."

In Karlo's skunkworks sat the sleek silvery ship, none the worse for wear. He was stepping out of the hatch, with Cynar following closely behind. The old wizard gave a grin as sparse of teeth as his potato sack clothing was of any decoration. He just refused to completely abandon his hermit persona. "Benjamin Colt! Coming with us to witness if there is in fact any product of the atmosphere fools' labors? Or to render execution on the spot for their failure? Hehehe. One can only hope."

My mom had a demented aunt who liked to put her old lady panties on her head at holiday gatherings. Our family learned to roll with it. But even she could break from the routine if the occasion was something important like a wedding. I didn't bother to sidebar Karlo away in an effort to spare Cynar's feelings. "Is this why you asked me along? To ride herd on snarky Gandalf? You want Don Rickles agitating old Beardy while we haul him and this precious cargo back? I thought

Element X was like super volatile or something? I'm supposed to keep those two from wrestling in the backseat?"

Karlo's sheepish look was enough of an admission that I was here for just that very reason. "I need Cynar to monitor the containment. He's just having some fun while he can. He's got a new perspective on things. Tell him, Cynar."

The only time the old codger didn't pepper me with insults was when death was imminent. That he hadn't launched into his insult comic routine could only mean the trip to shepherd Element X had the potential to be just one-way. His perpetual frown and wrinkled forehead smoothed into as saintly a mask as his burlap hide would allow.

"I have neutralized the poison in my veins toward the guild of the atmosphere wizards. Karlo Columbo's wisdom has won out—all of us sort the pieces of a great puzzle. We each hold shapes unique and necessary for its completion. The air wizards hold knowledge of rays I thought did not exist. I in turn have an understanding of much that they lack. Their guild preached a jealous and insular philosophy, as did my own. These attitudes are contrary to all that science represents. My time is short. I would see this thing done."

I turned for the exit. Karlo called after me with concern. "Ben, where're you going?"

"Outside. I need to check to make sure the sky isn't falling."

Karlo snorted. He got it. The butt of my joke did not.

With balled fists and face scrunched wrinkled again, Cynar fumed, "Tyreen Sorell admitted fraud only when facing execution for treason. You do not congratulate me for my evolved viewpoint and its evidence of my superior reason. I am the savior of the kingdom, and you would not show me half as much consideration? After all I have done to prove my intellect, you would give him the benefit of doubt and not me?"

"I was just joking, buddy. But without a diploma from an anger management seminar, you can't convince me you'd pee on Tyreen Sorell if he were on fire. How are you going to tolerate being cooped up with him for the trip home? Because I'll gag you if I have to."

"Again, you show me so little consideration! Can I not vent with a comrade? Pah! My self-control will stun you. *I* will be exonerated, and *you* will be forced into yet another apology. But be warned! Though I may have learned to acquit the atmosphere buffoons, you, Benjamin Colt, I will never absolve."

"For what?"

"For being the torturer who ever discovers a new raw nerve to exploit. For spoiling the sweet contentment of a life lived in solitary. For being the weaver that entangled so many lives with mine. I should never forgive you."

Like a seizure ended, his mad cackle returned.

"HEHEHE. Admittedly, life was rather dull. Shall we go? I promised Dureen Zell I would be home in time for dinner."

From my brief time behind the controls, I'd not been able to appreciate what Karlo's new flitter was capable of. The sealed cabin did more than shield us from the elements. From an altitude over Vistara not traveled by any craft in centuries, the ground sped beneath at a rate I'd never imagined. The peaks of the distant Korund danced past like fence posts along the highway.

In less than three hours, we slowed over Maleska Mal. Two henna beards waited outside the passage leading into the impenetrable wall of the atmosphere works.

Cynar mumbled, "Officious boobs, hehehe." I gave him the look. "My last, Benjamin Colt. I promise. Unless he starts. The right of self-defense is absolute, yes?"

"If he does, Cynar, just turn the other cheek. I'll put him in the penalty box if need be, okay?"

"I won't turn the other cheek save to blow him a kiss when I raise robes for him to pucker up and plant his lips on my—"

"Stop hanging out with Dave!" I hissed. "Bring the thing and let's go."

The interior of the atmosphere works was an intricate nest of wires, tubes, and crystals, surrounded by ladders, passages, and platforms. I followed Tyreen Sorell and his assistant deep into the core. With each turn, our path became an even narrower trail through a hoarder's house. Bits, pieces, and sections of mysterious mechanisms were stacked against the walls.

"They've got a lot of spare parts," I said. Karlo was quick to correct me.

"No, Ben. Tyreen Sorell wanted you to see firsthand why it's taken so long. Without damaging anything, they've tunneled to the core by disassembling what was never meant to be disassembled."

It suddenly made sense. The pieces and parts were actually tailings of an excavation. One sorted and catalogued by miners with OCD. Each fragment and pebble of the tunnel would need to be precisely restored from where it had been chipped.

"Tyreen Sorell didn't even know *where* the core was at first. He's kept me updated as they've played blind man's bluff."

As we went deeper into the interior, our course deviated up and down, turning and twisting. Were we beneath the surface? Were we high in the towers? I was truly lost. Cynar was behind me, carrying the shoebox that I supposed was the containment device. At the risk of setting him off, I brought up something I'd had something on my mind since we'd entered this labyrinth.

"The place where you made the waters was very—organic—compared to all this. Why is it so different? Isn't H_2O more complex than just oxygen?"

Expecting my intelligence to be insulted, it again unnerved me when he passed over the opportunity.

"My process releases the water bound in other forms from within the deep strata, and amplifies the quantity. Their guild uses another process entirely to create the elements of the atmosphere themselves—which are many. That it once did so and may do so again is—fascinating."

"You mean, it's more like the Blue Fairy?" The engine of creation Earth's scientists had cobbled together from alien technology—without really understanding how it worked—sat in the vault room, little used these days. Karlo was saving what life in it remained in hopes it could duplicate Element X.

"No. Not like it at all. It borrows nothing through the flux of time. The last rays are manipulated to truly create from nothing."

For the time being, it seemed his curiosity was keeping his resentment for the air wizards in check. "Thanks for keeping it together like you promised, Cynar."

"Humph. It is the ability to adapt to new environments that separates us from animals. Fortunately, not all of us are like you and have only one coping mechanism—to kill what you don't understand, hehehe."

My back thanked me as I followed Karlo to rise to full height. Without a "Ta-daa" or other fanfare, the ball of black electricity at the center of the spherical chamber was its own barker to herald that we'd arrived at the main attraction. If you didn't know a badger's reputation, you might think it cuddly as a cat. On the other hand, a spider—you don't have to teach an infant that a creepy crawly like that means danger.

The crackling condensed sphere made the caveman in me leak a few drops.

I hugged the wall to keep all the distance I could as I pictured frying to a crisp if I brushed the floating Element X. The air wizards were within an arm's reach and seemed unconcerned. His assistant busied with their own device as Tyreen Sorell nodded to Cynar.

"Master Cynar, I believe it is time. Would you evaluate the essence and make your determination, please?"

"Indeed. Please assist me."

I nudged Karlo and mouthed, *What gives?*

He smirked back and mumbled, "They've been collaborating remotely for months. Pretty cordially, too."

"Wait, you already knew Cynar was chilled out?"

The evil grin he gave I'd never seen before. "Just a little fun at your expense. Cynar's rubbed off on me."

There were books full of stuff I knew nothing about. Here was one more. Karlo was capable of carrying out mild sadism if there was a laugh at my expense waiting at the end of such a lengthy con. Such is the humor of a genius. I preferred bathroom humor and pratfalls.

"You seem nonchalant. Isn't Element X deadly?"

"Sorry if I let you think this would be risky, Ben. I would never have brought you here if that was the case. Water'll kill you if you drink too much. A big enough boulder might crush you flat, but it has to roll over you first. And it's the amps not the volts that'll do the same. Element X in its current state of power is safe. But notice there's only one air wizard with Tyreen Sorell?"

There had been three.

"You mean… ?" I drew a finger across my throat.

"Yup. He volunteered to be first into the chamber to attenuate its radiation. Cynar thinks it was a kind of cellular degeneration that killed him. Did it in a day. You'd have been proud of Cynar, Ben. He really was quite consoling toward the air wizards."

Now the shoebox was on the ground beneath the fist-sized ball. Cynar manipulated the pad in his hands as next to him, Tyreen Sorell observed. The ball disappeared. The shoebox glowed amber, then red, then a cool green. Cynar's pad went into the folds of his robe, then he squatted to pick up the container.

"We'd best leave. The essence will remain contained until placed in the larger vessel waiting in the ship, but it is best we do not test the portable device to its fullest."

I waited for Tyreen Sorell as he said his goodbyes to the lone subordinate. The portal sealed again into flawless concealment and he fell into silent step with me for the long walk to the ship.

The newfound congeniality between the two scientists was welcome, but I knew Cynar. He held a grudge like a cat, just waiting for the day to claw you, long after you'd forgotten you'd stepped on its tail. The trip might be a fraction of what it once was, but whether it was a few hours or a few minutes, a scorpion and a tarantula in the same box always fought. There wasn't much more I could do to persuade Cynar to keep cool. Considering my own history with the air wizard, maybe there was another way to ease the tensions I felt building as we neared the cramped cabin of the Silver Surfer.

"I only just learned that your guild brother was killed. I'm very sorry. It was a great sacrifice he made."

"It was Gent Farla's insistence that he enter the chamber first. If there was another way to attenuate the energy of the essence than by the mechanisms within the chamber, I knew it not." He paused and took in the city a last time before we mounted. "Entombed in the depths of the works, as the works themselves are buried in this crypt of a city, I have come to feel the decay creep into my own bones. May I ask of you, Warlord, have you often seen death so close?"

There was a time I'd have bet the house that nothing mattered more to this man than his own comfort. Heavy with the conscience of a leader, he mourned his role in a decision that sent someone to their death. Like a soldier would.

The twisting columns of the air works stood out among the other towers, most of which were decaying, ravaged by the ages.

"My own walk with death began very near to where we are now. My first sight of Vistara was the towers of Maleska Mal. It awed and thrilled me with the mystery of what it had once been. I escaped from its dungeons vowing to speed the process to raze it once and for all—neglect and indolence were taking too long to do the job. Now, I come again to see the promise of a wonder hidden beneath its collapse. Master Gent Farla's sacrifice will be remembered as the rebirth of not only Maleska Mal, but all Vistara."

He stood taller. "I've frequently misjudged you, Warlord, but never have my errors been more apparent to me than now." He bowed. "I wish I had but equal consolation with which to return your kindness. I do not envy what you and the queen do to soothe a kingdom's soul. The task of our hands is petty by comparison."

I dropped next to Karlo. Behind me, the two scientists were deeply engaged in conversation, a multitude of glowing pads laid out around them. "Don't think I have to mediate the peace between those two."

"So, get some more stick time instead. Because the Silver Surfer's yours. Just wanted to make sure she was back to flawless function before I handed her over to you. Happy Birthday, Merry Christmas, Mazel Tov on your wedding and the baby and any other occasion I may have missed."

"Really? You can spare her?"

"I already have the production line going. She's just the first in the fleet."

It was another incredible remedy to one of our many problems. Aimed for Shansara, I relaxed. "What happens next?"

"First, Baby Blue tries to analyze Element X. If it can, we go for a duplication run. Then we're on the fast track to Tyreen Sorell reassembling the factory and firing it up. If it works, then we make Element X until either we run out of room to store it all or the Blue Fairy conks out."

"What if Baby Blue can't even analyze it?"

"You want me to say it? Then we're on the road to try to figure it out for ourselves. And if we can't, the option we'll be left with is asking the Whites to show us how they built their Shangri-La."

13

THE DAY'S EVENTS BUBBLED INSIDE ME AS I RUSHED HOME TO POP THE cork off the good news. My exuberance vanished. Kleeve Hartus paced in front of the palace doors, guarded by a cordon of soldiers. Even before our falling out, apropos of our relationship was that the man was ever the bearer of bad news.

"Warlord, I have something for your eyes alone." He held a scroll.

The queen used the outer chambers to conduct the affairs of the kingdom in a social setting. To be invited there was a reward, conferring an air of informality and inviting familiarity with her not possible in the council room. Kleeve Hartus had always been first among those welcome there. He had to feel the sting as the captain took the first shield's weapons before allowing him through doors where he'd once been freely admitted.

I remained torn between mistrusting a traitor and empathizing with the man's severe sense of rectitude. I didn't want him in chains, but the knife's sharp cut of dismissal would be kindest and best for everyone. Talis Darmon was resolute he had a role to play at the head of the Guard—though she'd not yet shared why or how.

Coming from the other direction were Talis Darmon and Tranya Olan.

On sight of the first shield, the smile breaking on Talis Darmon's face that I hoped had been meant for me, disappeared. As an undercover operative, Tranya Olan was an actress unmatched. But at the sight of her old boss, her neutral countenance gave way to similar distaste. To be perturbed so greatly at the sudden sight of him, the two must've been in discussion of things far pleasanter. If my tank of grievances had partly drained of misgivings about the man, it surged and replenished at being robbed of the ladies' delight as both turned sour at the sight of him.

The queen was cool and distant as a glacial peak. "I had no word you were in waiting, First Shield."

Kleeve Hartus saluted. "Forgiveness, Queen. I waited for the Warlord, not wishing to disturb you with this." He lofted the scroll.

"I'll take it," she said.

He obediently placed the scroll in her hand, but as he did so, his eyes met mine in apology. It did not escape her attention.

"You may be seeking to regain the confidence of the Warlord, but it is by my dispensation you remain as First Shield."

He averted his eyes and, as if it explained all, said, "It is from the Plumbers."

She read as we waited in silence until finally, she closed the document. "You may go, Kleeve Hartus."

The first shield would normally have been part of any discussion about the contents of such an urgent piece of intelligence. Likely, he would have been the hand of any will to act. Her dismissal was another slap, another test of his obedience, but also an opportunity to prove loyalty. Between my treatment and now hers, were I in his place, I would have resigned—and be damned whether she accepted it or not. Yet, with a crisp salute, he answered this latest test and was gone. She wanted him outside looking in. For how long?

She handed me the scroll.

Tourmaline: The reports agree. The craft remains in Shansara and under light guard. We should risk it. If it holds the weapon responsible for the disruption, we want it before they have control of its secrets.

Bryant: Sophena Pah, you're the sharpest blade in all Annameria, but to pull off something like that and to do it without them knowing it was us, we don't have the assets in place I would need. It's a prize, but one we can't steal brazenly. It's going to take time.

Tourmaline: Numerous sources confirm it is practically unguarded and in the open. We must risk it now, while we know its exact location. So, if not covertly, then a surprise attack to take the ship. What matters if they know it was us who stole their toy?

Bryant: Now who's going off half-cocked? Because a plausible deniability is the only way to keep them from come straight at us in retaliation. And they'd be justified. They could do the same thing to us they did to the Mydreen. Or worse. Total war would be in our laps. Anyway, you just don't appreciate what I'm saying about those miniguns. They've created an air defense artillery that'll clean the clocks of any airborne raiding force. Anything less than a total invasion, our losses would be too great. We'd never land with much of a force left with which to take Shansara.

Tourmaline: Then perhaps our counsel should be that the time is at hand for just such a total war with the Reds. With a weapon of this power in their control, how long until they attack us?

Bryant: True. But they have the ability to use weapons of mass destruction against us now if they choose. Look at it like this—if they do have this new weapon that can shut off all power, it's not us they'll use it against. The visitors from the Sharpa are the threat they're worried about. And we don't know what we don't know about them. Could be they're a new enemy for us, too. Chances are if we lay back, the Reds take care of them just like they did the Karnak. It will give us time to complete the project. Then we choose the time and place to act.

Tourmaline: [Makes extended sigh.] You're right, handsome man. But what a prize it would be.

Bryant: Patience. The Annamese are great because of their patience. When an enemy is in turmoil, let them struggle in their disjointedness rather than become the reason for their unity of purpose.

Tourmaline: You are a better student of the analects than most any born of the true race. And if the fools succumb to their religion and are made impotent by these events, then they deserve what comes to them. It will only make them weaker when we finally do invade. My assistant comes. [Transcript ends.]

We'd been expecting this. It had been by design we left the craft where it was. They'd mentioned "the project." Was that the same as the other thing they'd referred to—Acelyx?

"I do not have the context to understand some of their exchange, but it seems their spies in our midst have done their work. It also seems we can delay no longer."

There were a lot of things we had to decide, and quickly. "Tranya Olan, you'd best leave us. The queen and I have matters to discuss."

Talis Darmon snapped, "Benjamin Colt, your queen decides who is to remain, who is dismissed, and what information, if any, need be filtered by you. We were coming to greet you when inadvertently stumbling into your meeting. Fortuitous it was. Would you have otherwise withheld this intelligence, thinking me still feeble?"

The reflex to hit back harder is one I never had to train. And it carries over from the realm of physical combat to verbal. In fact, I'd been proud of how I'd learned the control to suppress it. Especially in trying to support her during her tumultuous recovery. But even after a deep breath, the tension holding my counter-punch broke like the rubber band stretched too far, too often.

"You assume wrongly. I didn't even know he was here. I was hurrying to bring you good news. So much for a happy homecoming. I'm not your enemy. Stop treating me like I'm anything but your greatest supporter."

Talis Darmon made a pained face. Dammit. The reunion couldn't have gone more awry.

Tranya Olan cringed in discomfort. "I should go."

We both answered, "NO!" Poor Tranya Olan shrank further. I was busy composing my apology when hers came.

"My shrill and bitter words belie that I know you do your all for me. You are correct to bring my ingratitude to my attention. I disappoint not only myself, but you. It is only too clear that I am still far from self-possession." She sighed deeply. "Kleeve Hartus's presence was unexpected and unbalanced me. It was a sudden reminder of the dilemma I've ignored but cannot escape. Accept my reason, not as an excuse, but explanation. I am sorry."

She let me hug her. "I want to go back in time and hear what made my beautiful wife light up. What were you coming to tell me?"

It was a fraction of what it had been, but her smile returned. "I was anxious to show you the new fashion we've developed." Grateful to move past the awkwardness, I held her at arm's length. She wore a broad shouldered tunic above a long flowing skirt. "Tranya Olan agreed that a change in my mode of dress had to occur if I am to truly live the maxim, 'Before all else, be armed.'"

I knew who she quoted, but left it alone. *The Prince* was still her close companion. We'd not discussed the moral ambiguities within, and I didn't correct her that in the pithy quotation, Machiavelli referred to the state rather than laying foundations for a libertarian consciousness. But the result was positive.

"She's the expert. Where's your pistol?"

She parted her tunic with a grin to show her pistol lying pressed against her abdomen. Accommodated to the waist of her dress, it sat a little higher than I would wear it.

"Appendix carry, we call it. It has its uses. If that's your choice, we'll work on it."

"Do you approve?"

"I do. It's functional." It was time to gild the lily some more. "And very attractive. You also did something with your hair." Her hair continued to grow and had rapidly become long enough to merit attention.

"Tranya Olan wears hers short and had suggestions. Do you like?" It was evenly trimmed and much like the professional's next to her.

I winked. "What's not to like? You look great."

"Do you mean it?"

"Of course I do. And I'm so lucky you care what I think."

If I read Tranya Olan's tiny smile correctly, it was approval. I didn't have a silver tongue, but it was nice to get some props for restoring the peace as best as I could. This time, and for the first time in a long time, it was Talis Darmon who reached out to hug me. I'd rushed to start tonight's reunion like the first climb of the roller coaster. Kleeve Hartus had been the peak to a frenzied downhill crash. Finally, the furious ride was done, and at last we coasted into the station.

"What news were you bringing, husband?"

"We've got Element X. Soon we'll have the answer to the big question."

"It is good news." Then her brow fell heavily. It was a single-point lead in a tight game. Not enough of a margin to bring confidence of a win. "Word from our enemies makes clear, we can delay no longer. And before the sun rises, we will brace the Whites with the ultimatum for their salvation. By this time tomorrow, we will be on a new path. And there is no greater danger—no uncertainty to be feared more—than when a prince leads to introduce a new order of things.

"Which is why none but us will know the destination it is to which I lead."

✹ ✹ ✹

Much as the appearance of the Whites had brought the city to a standstill, public invitation to the royal tribunal brought something similar. The spectral hall was hastily prepared and all seats filled. Throngs crowded the palace grounds at the promise of bearing witness to the trial of the imposters who'd kidnapped the queen. I returned from the wings to see her attendants fuss over the last details of her costume. Sensing the time had come, Tranya Olan brushed them back and left us alone.

"Lashura and the Guarantor seem ready to play their part, sweetheart, but what will the city do?"

"The afterlife of the underworld cannot be held in contempt. But the Whites can be, and must be."

Her plan was intricate. From the perspective of friend and enemy, subject and opportunist, devout and indifferent, she predicted the
coming reaction of each.

"How can you be sure the people will agree with your penalty?" I
asked.

"I am highly regarded by my people. Only a prince can understand
the nature of the people, and to understand a prince, one must be of
the people. In their affection, those that love me will see the sentencing
as justice meted out with great wisdom. If there are those who lose that
affection and think me weak, by the end, they will see it otherwise. The
final harvest of this strategy will not be reaped in a day, but with time,
it *will* be collected in full. For both in fear and love will all consider me.
First, we do this. I am ready, Warlord."

As her shield arm, I escorted her to seat the throne and took my
place to stand beside her. Looking every bit like they were being fed to
the lions, the Guarantor and Lashura were ushered in by the bailiffs.
The silence of the thousands in attendance made the air more electric
than if their contempt for the accused were communicated by snort
of disgust or gasps of revulsion. For how many eternities would the
Whites be satisfied if they had the rays of all those lives powering their
machines? She began without introduction or preamble.

"The crimes committed against our kingdom are great. So great,
there is not proscription in law for them. By the mandate of my regency, I am the protector ultimate. I must sit in judgment. So that
nothing be concealed, all will hear of the crimes from the perpetrators themselves. Lashura of Astelaan, queen of the realm beneath the
Sharpa Mountains and criminal conspirator against Mihdradahl and
all Vistara, step forward and speak your admission."

The bailiffs brought Lashura forward, her silver-gray complexion I
thought even more sallow and gaunt. Would she play ball, or did she
have a trick up her sleeve? I still thought Talis Darmon's plan an incredible gamble, and the multitude of sayings governing such ran through
my head. The more unlikely the plan, the more likely it is to succeed.

Who dares, wins. But my favorite came from my imaginary mentor, Patton. "A calculated risk is quite different from being rash."

If ever there were his equal, she was there next to me. Her plan was all of one and none of the other. With fingers crossed, I waited with the rest of the kingdom as Lashura stepped onto the platform, the pedestal illuminating jade green to indicate the accused stood in the light of justice.

"I make this admission honestly and in hope of mercy. Long has my race hidden themselves. We have survived in craven isolation by means of a deception perpetrated not out of hatred, but by desperation. On behalf of my people, I ask the forgiveness of all your kingdom when I reveal what has been insinuated upon you."

She admitted truth. The Whites were not the guardians of the underworld. The paths to the Blix ended in their realm. Deceived pilgrims did not enter the underworld. Then, as instructed, she repeated as she'd been ordered.

"Those who came to Farnest came under the deception that it was the promised underworld. Instead, they were sent to toil as slaves in the mines and farms. When their usefulness was reached, rather than their bodies be allowed to become corruption, their mortal shells were reduced to elements to enrich the soil that sustains the life of our own people."

The crystal ceiling shook with tremors of the crowd's outrage. The outburst continued until the queen ordered the horn blown.

"And why was this done? The one called the Guarantor will make admission."

The bailiffs brought the other White forward. "For many thousands of years, our population has dwindled. We became unable to sustain ourselves. The deception to lure pilgrims to the northern pole was just as long in the making. Those who arrived became slave laborers and lived out their days toiling like beasts of burden. The society I inherited was one also deceived—that all life save White is lesser. That Red, Green, and Yellow are no different from the other beasts of Vistara."

The crowd gasped.

"The sophistry of our ancestors' perversion of the faith and their cruel rationalizations for it has long gnawed at our souls. Whether your timely incursion had happened or not, a change was upon us. Before the queen and those like myself could coerce the king to accept a new path, the evaporated pilgrimages sparked Zan-Sha to the desperate act to terrorize your kingdom with yet more deception, to kidnap you... it was not the will of the people. It is with relief that on behalf of all Astelaan we stand before you today and accept judgment for our crimes."

I marveled at how well the contemptible creep had memorized his lines.

The audience gnashed their teeth and mumbled curses. The queen waited for them to quiet.

"Your admissions bear evidence of an evolving shame and regret. Lashura, tell what transpired in Astelaan at the return of Zan-Sha."

The woman stepped again onto the platform. "It was the outrage of your kidnapping which pushed the opposition and I to take action. The time for change was long overdue. It was fortuitous that your rescuers came to us. The people of Astelaan rose up to join with your soldiers. The revolution your military led was brief but thorough. Zan-Sha and all of his order were killed, bringing your freedom and our own."

A murmur of surprise broke out before she continued.

"I have admitted the ugly truth, knowing that no matter what we did, at the end, it is little in recompense after so much wrong. I plead for the lives of those whose only crime was apathy. I beg you stay the hand of their destruction. As queen, I vow to lead a people committed to a new way of life."

The crowd could contain themselves no longer.

"Thousands they have enslaved! Murdered! Butchered like animals!"

"They must suffer for their crimes!"

"Wipe them out! Wipe them all out! It is the only just punishment!"

When their fury descended from its peak, the horn sounded. The queen indicated for the bailiffs to take the accused to their seats again.

"All of this, do I also bear witness of," Talis Darmon said. "Discovering that the underworld was a ruse shattered the foundations of all beliefs I held dear. But through this tribulation, a much greater truth was revealed. Or rather, established anew. While perverting our faith, the Whites have kept the true faith to themselves. The underworld is a place of the spirit, not the body. At life's end, by whatever cause, all go to join with the ancestors in the eternal underworld. Priests, step forward and speak what you have learned."

The pair of priests did as ordered. The tiny one stood on the pedestal and, once bathed in its light, answered, "It is as the queen says. In deep study we have found where this deviation in doctrine took origin. We beg the forgiveness of Vistara for allowing ourselves to be deceived, but we too are victims. A reformation is at hand, and a restoration to true faith with it."

The queen nodded with dispensation. "And your commission is to do just that."

A lone voice carried above all, one I knew well.

"Not good enough!"

Kleeve Hartus.

Fueled by the zealot's fervor with which he'd readied to kill me before I could desecrate his beliefs, he strode onto the floor. My soldiers hesitated to restrain him, such was his commanding presence. The sergeant of the detail recovered from his latency, only for me to hold him and his men in place by my outstretched palm.

"Not good enough by far."

Kleeve Hartus put himself between the queen and the Whites, facing the gathered. I caught the twinkle in her eye, the one that came with her sorcery. The spell she'd cast for so long to transmute the first shield into something new was in its final throes.

"I stood witness when the Whites came for our queen. They accused her falsely! Leveraged her ancestors against her! Pierced her as if by a sword with the reminder of a child who did not live to hatch.

How could the Whites have known these things? By their own admission they are not representatives of the underworld! It could only be because the priests were in league with these imposters! The priests are not victims—they are conspirators and betrayers of our faith and must be held accountable."

Ever the investigator, Kleeve Hartus was right. The priests were conspirators. Blind conspirators never knowing why they were doing it, but conspirators nonetheless. In the desperation of her cell, Lashura admitted it to us. The priests regularly sent a detailed census of all births, deaths, marriages—all that and more, north on the Iridium Path. They were the Whites' spies among us.

But I had a role to play, too. I stepped in to assert a Warlord's privilege—protect the kingdom from all existential threats. "First Shield, the Queen forgave you for once allowing your oath to be perverted. It won't be forgiven again. The royal tribunal has standing, not the Guard. Take your place."

The first shield obeyed my command, but did so without timidity. His fire against the priests still burned.

The queen said, "I will now render my judgment."

The horn sounded to clear the air.

"Such atrocities as the people of Astelaan have committed can never be forgiven. To order their total destruction would seem just. But I do not believe their people to be as one and equally guilty of these crimes. Evidence of the contrary is enough to stay my hand.

"Instead, my judgment is thus: you will return to your realm. Your crimes will be made known everywhere on Vistara—to any with ear to hear and eye to read. Predation by your kind upon any Vistaran will bring your complete destruction by my hand. Neither will any be permitted to render you aid. In one hundred years' time, your realm will be inspected for compliance. If found wanting, then will your quarantine continue. It will be in the isolation your people wished themselves that you will survive or perish. Depart at once."

While the crowd remained confused as to how they should react to her decree, I descended. If any dissidents wanted to start a riot, we were most likely to avoid it by acting quickly. Sarkan Sell appeared, leading a squad of Korundi. The crowd could part, or be trampled beneath corded green thighs. My soldiers surrounded the prisoners with a wall of Tarn flesh. We were off.

The spiked ship waited. At the base of the ramp, I removed the manacles from each of their wrists. "By order of Queen Talis Darmon, depart Mihdradahl and the surface world of Vistara forever. Go."

The Whites ascended, the ramp retracted, the doors sealed. The craft rose silently above the city and headed north, vanishing over the spires.

"Citizens of Mihdradahl!"

Eyes turned to Talis Darmon on the balcony.

"It is with firm faith that we have acted and defeated another enemy. Now we can heal the deep insults they inflicted, without fear our wounds will fester and abscess by the seed of repaying evil with evil. In this way will we return to robust health and achieve our greatest prosperity. This is the promise we share together."

A woman's voice started it. "Queen Talis Darmon reigns!" Like a cloud burst to relieve the drought of the most sweltering summer, their cheers drenched and cooled the heat of the kingdom's angst, leaving behind only a people's love for their regent.

She knew her people.

And by knowing them, her deceit couldn't have found victims better suited to her manipulation. With arms spread wide, she cast her beneficent smile down on them. I was proud, but saddened. Relieved by the unity of the crowd, but repulsed. If I was to have the comfort of time to reflect on our duplicity, I had to do my part.

My abrupt departure went unnoticed by the crowds still fixed on their beatific queen. I was soon behind the yoke of the Silver Surfer. I kept low and slow until I broke out of the city and turned her loose. If not for my task, I would've been amazed how the jagged rim of the Ha Shur depression was in sight in minutes. Flitters and drab uniforms surrounded the exterior entrance tunneled through the rim. I'd arrived so quickly that I was on the ground to see for myself the spiked ball growing above the low horizon like a rising sun at it approached. It came to a hover over the peaks and eased into the depression like a cannonball rammed down the mouth of a cannon made of rock. But this missile would never again launch into the air.

I was through the tunnel to watch the craft settle onto the valley floor. In a few zigzag hops down the switchback trail, I was there to meet the lowering ramp. Doug and Dave flanked Lashura and the White scientist as they descended the ramp. During the spectacle of the tribunal, the two had waited inside, ready to pilot the ship away with none aware. Cynar and Karlo appeared from the temple entrance to complete our send-off gathering.

Once placed in the carriage, the White prisoners were bound in restraints anew. I trusted that Talis Darmon knew best, but as Lashura protested, I couldn't help but feel she was getting off light. Remembering Talis Darmon's suffering and the terrible fear I imagined she felt at their hands, made the base part of me want to hurt Lashura in kind.

Maybe this would be a close second.

"Release us as promised. We performed as demanded!"

"Which is why we're returning you to your own cage instead of a cell here. You have other conditions to meet if you're to keep us from destroying you outright. Remember?"

The Guarantor answered for them. "The simulacra will be maintained. Those who exist there will continue to do so. Protected and unaware."

Alone together that long night before the tribunal, Talis Darmon had made her decision about which of her two choices she would take.

"I have found solace in the knowledge that a prince may by necessity lie. But I cannot lie to myself. If what I experienced there was real, and their mechanism holds the disembodied consciousness of so many of our ancestors, I would go mad to know its destruction at my hand meant oblivion for so many souls. Cynar promises to continue his consideration of the question. For now, my decision is to make no hasty decision. I will secure the sanctity of the simulacra as best I can while hiding the knowledge of it from our people. This way is the path to lesser evil until another solution can be found. But no more shall join them. That we must guarantee."

The Whites were trussed like turkeys for the oven. "Karlo, is everything set?"

"It is." He addressed the soon to be parolees. "When this carriage reaches Celeste Hom, you two best hop quickly to board for your trip up the Blix. The explosives on this will drop the mountain on top of the portal temple and close it forever."

Cynar cackled. "Hehehe. It is I who monitor your progress and I who will send the command to destroy the way station where you enslaved the innocent Hortha. It is on their behalf that I take great pleasure in giving you this warning—your kind's science is weak compared to mine. The secrets of your ship are yours no longer. For such perversion of the rays you should earn greater punishment. You have no means for revenge on us. Should you try, it will be I whom the queen unleashes to see you turned to dust for good."

If Lashura's lack of emotion failed to satisfy my ugly passion for revenge, the memory of the Guarantor's whimpers would console me if I ever questioned whether we'd been cruel enough. I was the last off the carriage.

"The queen concocted a whopper of a lie in order to spare people the truth about what you've done. Your reward for cooperating is we spare you an invasion of grief-maddened Reds to burn you all alive while you cluck about what ungrateful animals you created."

"Animals you are. Cruel, vengeful, and above all, brutal." The carriage started its glide, but not before Lashura's curse ended with a mouthful of spit landing at our feet.

Doug waved in glee. "You ain't even seen us at our worst. Bon voyage, shitbags."

The carriage was gone.

Karlo'd been busy. "We've got a mule loaded and ready, Ben. We'll drop this end of the tunnel about a mile ahead. As we locate the other transits around Vistara, we'll drop them too."

Dave spoke for the first time in a while. "I don't get it, brah. I mean, why doesn't Talis Darmon ask Karlo to make a nuke and we just end them? You would, wouldn't you, Karlo? There can't be a better reason than this."

Karlo answered him with complete detachment. "Talis Darmon doesn't have the sangfroid about killing that you do, Dave. Not even after what they did to her. Because she can't be sure she wouldn't be responsible for annihilating the souls of thousands who've already been violated."

Doug shook his head. "If you destroy the Matrix, doesn't everyone just go to heaven? I'm very confused."

"Don't be confused about this," Karlo said. "In case anyone's forgotten, I'm not making a nuke. And not that anyone's asking, but if you want to know, I respect Talis Darmon's belief and her conscience. I'm proud of what she's done. Proud to serve someone so worthy. This is as good an answer as there is."

I got a lump in my throat. "Thanks, Karlo," I said.

Dave grinned sheepishly. "Me, too, brah. Don't mean nothing by it. Just thinking out loud, ya know? Hey Cynar, do you really have a lock on the Whites' tech already? Got us a ray-killer cannon yet?"

"I do not. But if left to work undisturbed, I may soon."

I led us outside. The giant craft took up most of the valley floor. It would remain hidden from prying eyes, as if the deep depression were custom made for this express purpose.

"The Yellows' spies will report the ship went north with the Whites. It'll keep them off-balance, wondering if we cracked her secrets or if the Whites may come after them someday. In the meantime, Cynar— you're now the director of Vistara's very own Area 51."

14

THE WHITES WERE GONE. IF FAITH HAD BEEN CHALLENGED, IT HAD not been destroyed. Her Machiavellian scheme—an ugly but accurate description—had worked. At first, it was as if she was on the same path to normalcy as her kingdom. She'd resumed most duties. Her public confidence seemed returned—her daily practice and friendship with Tranya Olan being no small part of that. I took the reduced frequency of the sessions with Shalees Parn as another sign of improvement. But as her tortured nights continued and our amity failed to return, it was a stab when I learned she'd stopped seeing her therapist altogether.

It was during one of our silent dinners together that I brought it up. "I haven't seen Shalees Parn in some time. Is she well?"

"I released her, with my thanks."

"But why?"

"It is a waste of her time and mine, Benjamin Colt. I should not need to explain more. You know what it is that haunts me."

It was the conundrum of the souls trapped in the simulacra. A problem as unsolvable as the unworkable solution to prove some arcane theorem of math. Though her answer to the problem was pragmatic, it had not resulted in bringing her peace. Instead, while her public days were spent in victory, with each night, an invisible enemy sapper tunneled beneath to undermine the rebuilding of her fortress.

Shalees Parn welcomed me not with the warmth of an intimate, but with the suspicion of one finding a salesman appeared at their door.

"I know why it is you come, Warlord. I have told you. I am bound." Conspicuously gone was the "Ben" I heard from no other Vistaran. She was about to close the door when I placed a hand out.

"She may have dismissed you, but don't you have a responsibility still? You know she's not well. I don't need you to break confidence. I know what it is that's hurting her. I need to know who I turn to next?"

She raised an eyebrow. "Are you asking me as a client? As one seeking to deal with his own grief? Or as the husband of a client?"

I recognized the loophole in the contract she was trying to bring to my attention, and jumped into it. "I'm seeking you out for my own benefit. As your client, Shalees Parn."

She visibly relaxed. "Please enter."

Seated, but far from comfortable with the ball of razor wire in my gut, I listened. "Often when there is a tribulation, my work is to guide a person to the realization of where perception differs from actual circumstance. I believe you to be one appreciative of directness, and I will be so. If your peace is predicated on her return to a previous self, then it is my counsel that the way forward for you lies in acceptance that it may never occur. I can aid you in coming to terms with this likelihood."

An invisible fist landed one in my gut. My world crashed down around me. "That's not what I was expecting to hear."

"Just so."

From my first day on Mars, survival was my mission. When Talis Darmon appeared in my life, my mission became her. The healer was telling me that had to change. I didn't really hear her as she spoke platitudes about grief and healing, and suggested we meet weekly. I left numb and without commitment to continue with her to explore what she offered as my new way forward. The destination of such a road was a place so bleak to make the red deserts rich and joyful in comparison.

We'd been so close to winning a world, a family, and a promise of peace. The night had started out with such promise. Talis Darmon wasn't getting better. I was just told to expect that she may never. My worst realization was this—if anything, she was getting worse.

I'd hoped to rekindle the comradeship she'd knitted with our friends on the flight to Jawn Kurz's fortress. I was tired of so many days and nights filled only by the absence between us. I thought if she could touch that comradeship again, it would—I don't know—help her reconnect to me, too. So, I invited our friends and their significant others—in Doug's case, all three of them—hoping that it would bring her out of her gloom.

With our home filled by friends who'd literally gone to the ends of the universe for her—the kindest, most caring people I'd ever known—maybe together we could dispel the last of the gloom that should have departed with the Whites.

At first, she was the gracious hostess. Doug's Thorian lady friends had never been to our home before. They all curtsied, then flocked around her like fans invited backstage. Talis Darmon stiffened, repelled by their compliments and adoration. Without the hint of the same noblesse oblige she'd taught me, she glided away without explanation, leaving them perplexed.

She'd managed little better with anyone else. Like a flower burned by a sun that once made it blossom, she wilted. Talis Darmon disappeared only minutes into the celebration.

I am the king of bad ideas.

A short time later, the gathering uncomfortably broke up. I'd not slept next to her in our bed her since the night we were both tranquilized by Karlo. I was on the couch, failing in the pointless meditation to bring my own sleep, listening to Talis Darmon pace the bedroom, when Doug called.

"Ben-dog. You look like hell."

It was my embarrassment as much as my exhaustion. "Sorry about tonight, Doug. She didn't mean to be rude to the ladies. I don't even know what to say."

He waved away my apology. "Don't give it another thought, bro. The girls understand. See, that's why I'm calling. When we saw how shell-shocked Talis Darmon was tonight, they said she reminded them of… me. When all I wanted was for my pain to go away. I was willing to do anything to make that happen. Brother, I see the same in her. She's on the verge of, well, something bad."

He was right. "I know it, Doug. But I don't know what else to do."

"I'm the poster child of 'been there, done that' for PTSD. I'm no Karlo and I'm sure as hell no Shalees Parn, but I'm willing to try. Would she listen to me?"

"Shalees Parn's no Shalees Parn, man. She gave up."

Doug's eyebrows shot up. "I didn't know. Wow. Dude, I know I'm all up in your business, but if I didn't at least offer, I'd never forgive myself. If you want me to try, I'll come by first thing."

"Thanks, Dougie. We got nothing to lose by trying. Yeah, man, come by first thing. What'll you say?"

"The truth. Hurting herself won't end the pain. It'll just make more pain. For you. For all of us. No matter how badly she's hurting, her heart's too big to want that. She loves you too much, bro."

"I'm not so sure, Doug."

"No, Ben-dog. You can't let yourself think that way. If you stop fighting, so will she."

"I know, bro. It's just that I've been patient and tried to do everything Shalees Parn advised. It's made no difference. It's like it's all the wrong treatment because it's the wrong disease." I'd thought often about Shalees Parn's paradigm. Maybe we still didn't have the right disease. Or the right healer.

"Ben-dog, this ain't gonna be a one-battle war. I didn't get there all at once, either. If she'll listen to me, that's what I'm going to tell her. I never thought things would ever be better. And now, my life's good in ways I could never have imagined. If it could happen for me, it can happen for her."

"Thanks, Doug. I want you to try."

"Cool. Get some sleep, homie."

I was a lucky man to have so many people who cared about her and I both. But as I drifted off, I was puzzling over a woman other than Talis Darmon. One who'd been as much antagonist as ally.

I awoke still on the couch. Sometimes she left the bedroom, seeking the awkward and distant comfort of pacing the living room with me as silent witness. It was not the sound of her trudge which woke me. A terrible moan of distress came from behind the doors. Without hesitation, I burst in.

If I'd ever been closer to death, it was only because I'd not known it.

Her pistol was aimed at the door when it barked. Gone was the calm focus she'd learned on the range. Eyes squeezed shut, she fired with her pistol clutched close like it was a crucifix warding against a vampire. Had I not kept moving, it would've been my chest filling with blood rather than my nostrils inhaling the copper wind of a bullet passing by my shoulder. More than my exclamations, it was the report and recoil that brought her into the present.

"Benjamin Colt! I did not know you! I saw only him! Zan-Sha, laughing as he told me the souls of my kin were in his prison."

She collapsed, gasping, weary, her shoulders trembling. I climbed onto the bed next to her and pulled her close. It was all I could do. That I held her and she did not retreat was a hollow achievement. There were no tears left for either of us to shed. She was asleep when I snuck out at first light. I put the pistol in Tranya Olan's hands, who accepted it with grim understanding.

"I too went through such terrors and was separated from tools of self-defense. Rightly so. It was difficult to accept I could be a danger to others. It was not until I realized the truth of my predicament that I became truly frightened. My counselor aided me to see that with such worsening hypervigilance might soon come a desperation. The worst kind of desperation. Until I was safely past such a turn, I had to be separated from means to—harm myself. I never reached the edge of such a fall. Do you know that she has dismissed her therapist? I am a poor substitute, Benjamin Colt."

"Shalees Parn didn't have any advice for me. She thinks I should move on, as though Talis Darmon will never come back from Astelaan.

Neither you nor I can watch her every minute, and I have to go away for a little while."

"Then we must be practical. When a prisoner is in such a state, they are not left alone at any time. None but us know her private distress. Ever do ears and mouths in the palace prove disloyal. What of her dosenie? Can she not return?"

I'd brought it up many times, thinking the return of her best friend and our child would be a magic salve for her wounds. It was only at this moment I realized I failed to heed the warning that hid within her reasoning to keep them away.

"The time isn't right to have our child here," she'd said. "It may not be safe yet. I may not be… safe… as a mother."

She refused to say more.

"She doesn't think the time is right," was all I said to Tranya Olan.

"Then I wish to call to trusted friends for whom loyalty unto pain of death is their code. Shasa Karin and Keshin Tellest are both disposed as I am. They have left service of the Guard since questions as to its… proper role has manifested."

Like Tranya Olan, the two women were gifted undercover operatives. "I didn't know they'd resigned. What about Zaylin Twee?" The commander had been their senior in the Guards.

"We think the first shield's actions have greatly strained their personal relationship. Though we all served closely, she was our superior, not a peer or a confidante. She remains sworn to the Guard. This is why I did not bring her to your attention for consideration."

We did need help, and the women would be utterly reliable and uniquely gifted, just like Tranya Olan. "Please call them. I trust you to tell them whatever they need to know."

"They would perform any task for you without need of reason, but I thank you for your trust, Warlord. To be fully read-in to a situation produces best results."

"Your coming has been the best thing to happen to us in a very long time, Tranya Olan."

"David Masamuni would not burden you, but he frets over your welfare constantly. I am fortunate to be called to the service of so many dear to me." She was gone, before the quaver of her trailing words made my own thanks tremble in kind.

✳ ✳ ✳

The great cliffs of the Furrow were on my right. I followed them until the steep escarpment gave way to the wide terraces of the ancient port city of Shelasa.

I didn't know if what I was doing was crazy. I only knew what we were doing wasn't working, and it was a worse insanity to do the same thing over and over to hope for a different result.

Shalees Parn had made a terminal diagnosis. The rays of Cynar's healing bed didn't penetrate as deeply as where her hurt lived on. Neither did my love.

It was just me and my thoughts, alone together in the cockpit of the Silver Surfer. I almost wished the ship weren't so easy to pilot. If I'd had to work harder to keep it on course, I wouldn't have been so consumed by dark thoughts.

My destination was the cove set far apart from the stone city. Its isolation lent an extra sadness to the arid estate. I set down in sight of the giant shell that was a landmark from a half-remembered dream. The organic shape was a remnant of Vistara's vanished sea. From out of it appeared the living and ageless reminder that nearby, the Amethyst Sea once licked at long absent shores.

Clothed only by tattooed skin and body jewelry, her purple mane was the deep color of the evaporated waters of the sea she and her sisterhood hastened to become dust. She appeared from her sanctuary not as Aphrodite from her shell—but with the fierce scowl of Poseidon, angered by the sailor who'd offered no sacrifice before the journey. At recognition of me, her arms uncrossed. She dragged at her bottom lip with the pad of a single finger, then purred.

"I knew you would not forget me. That you would tire of her. Even Jawn Kurz was just a man." She closed on me with swaying hips, playing the role of temptress. She stopped short and narrowed her eyes in reappraisal.

"It is not that. You seem gravely burdened! Diminished from the Warlord I once touched. It can be only one thing. Tell me quickly. What of your queen?" The sorceress held concern in her voice that convinced me it was not a different kind of theater she affected. It was genuine.

They say a guilty man sleeps soundest once finally caught. And like a murderer confronted with an exact accounting of their crime, I stood transfixed. She had me dead to rights. I felt no shame when I practically prayed to her.

"I need your help, Mother Oceansong. I don't know who else to turn to."

Amber light seeped through the translucent shell to bathe us. From the ceiling dangled the dried skeletons of myriad ancient life-forms. Like the duality of the decorations that inspired contemplation of creation and death, she'd once used her allure to test my resolve while flaunting her sex to insult Talis Darmon. They'd fought. Then, in a chaotic shift, the temptress took the role of mentor when, in our time of greatest need, she transformed into a compassionate healer.

Her turbulent nature reminded me of an unpredictable sea. Talis Darmon thought she fought an internal battle across a border that separated great passion from great wisdom. For the moment, the waves stirred by that battle seemed in her control. She received my revelations without passion, and with my question was the evidence that she was truly the learned sage I sought.

"Nothing in my experience lets me entirely refute or confirm her fear, Warlord. But surely, standing in the presence of the Warlord Jawn Kurz and his queen served as comparison to what she experienced in the underworld created by the Whites?"

The regal pair in the mirrors—who gave their dispensation for me to wield the powerful tools of the Warlord with which to battle the evil awakened beneath Vistara—had been ghosts.

"At the time, she said Jawn Kurz and his queen spoke to us from Farnest. But even I thought they were—absent, in many ways. Once we weren't so overwhelmed by our experience, she became more convinced they were some kind of interactive recordings. They'd said as much to us. That they were—shadows."

"What is preserved of them is that, but more. A replica of their essence with some echo of sentience. But it was not their disembodied souls you spoke with. Yet, just the possibility that her experience in the underworld was not something similar has wrecked her."

"She fears that the Whites really have stolen the souls of her ancestors. Could it be?"

Mother Oceansong's brow was troubled. "The Whites disappeared long before even I hatched. Is it possible that they could have learned to do such a thing? If so, they are an evil worse than the Karnak or even the Harridan herself. It is a terrible burden she carries by this dilemma. But that it continues to corrupt her with such grief is puzzling."

"Then I'm not crazy to think she should be getting better by now?"

"Her insults were many. If she were ordinary, such traumas would permanently cripple her. But your queen? For one so young, she is studied and of great facility. Her path to transcend such transgressions and deny them power over her—it is well within her ability. You were wise to suspect that there is something amiss. I think it some interference that works to make her hopeless. A forlorn she cannot shake off."

Her choice of words could not have been accidental. "The Great Forlorn?"

She frowned. "What is that you say?"

"It's what took her mother. It's what led to her father becoming king. It sometimes runs in families, a kind of disease that makes people hopeless and drives them to ride the Blix."

She shook her head dismissively. "I know of the Great Forlorn and what is believed of it. I did not mean her malady was the same when

I spoke of forlorn. I have navigated the anima and minds of so many. More than you could conceive. All while Vistara turns to dust around me. This so-called Great Forlorn manifests as a disease of the mind, but never have I found evidence it is such." She squinted in deep consideration.

"But, with the knowledge you bring of what the Whites have been up to—"

A lightning bolt struck me. "The Great Forlorn is not a disease. It's a weapon."

If the Whites put some kind of time bomb in her head, I'd beg Karlo to change his mind about weapons of mass destruction. They deserved to fry in the fury of nuclear devastation.

A single clap of her hands filled the shrine. "The Whites did more to her than she realizes. This is the impediment that ails her. And one cannot fight an enemy that evades detection."

The finish line seemed in sight. "What a relief! Now you can help her!"

My horse broke a leg.

"I cannot. She would neither accept my help, nor would I offer my sorcery to aid her."

Like that rider thrown from the crippled mount, I got to my feet. "She's not so far gone she doesn't know it! She'd welcome your help! Or is it you're still holding onto your grudge against the Sylah?"

The sympathy she'd shown turned ugly at my accusation. "For all your might and deeds, despite your partnership with me in affairs fantastic, you have the understanding of a child."

"Then you need to explain it to me like I'm a child. I can't just stand by and do nothing. Every day, the light goes out of her a little more."

She softened. "Your warrior's tenacity and virtue are what touched Jawn Kurz through the ether. But whether born of Vistara or of distant Thulia, not even a Warlord is so equipped to understand these things. But I will try."

She gestured me to take to the cushion again.

"When I aided her to take the last step to free herself from the Harridan's box, I did not touch her animus. I released the lock on the doors to the prison she'd built to protect herself."

"And it couldn't be the same kind of thing again?"

"It is not." Suddenly, she was parroting Shalees Parn, reminding me that the disease determines the treatment, not the other way around.

"Even with her permission, the touch of my animus to hers would be as an assault—one she could not help but defend from with all her might. Though old feuds between her maternal line and mine have been abandoned, our very essences are unchanged. We would be two volatile substances placed in dangerous proximity. And if her current state is as troubled as you say, with her having lost reason and control, disaster for both of us would result. That is why my sorcery would not suit."

"I'm not taking her to the Whites to ask their help!" I blurted. "If that's the only option, it's a nonstarter. She'd die before she let them touch her again."

"I do not offer that suggestion."

"Then what?"

"Not what. Who."

Her aura welled forth in a purple so deep as to be almost black. It bathed me in trepidation, as though I stood on the shore of an ocean as deep as the color, one that concealed dangers. I knew she was not what she appeared from the first time her dark aura battled Talis Darmon's. Beneath the artistry of her painted skin were rocky shoals to tear the hull out of any ship she lured to her shore.

The aura I associated with only her remained for only a moment. It changed to a lighter shade, soothing like the lilacs of spring. The color inspired me not to search my memory for their sweet smell, but to touch the well-being I felt in the presence of the one who I knew owned the pigment as their own. Its energy hinted at an empathy perhaps even greater than Talis Darmon's.

Mother Oceansong taunted me to speak the name.

"You cannot have forgotten her. She has touched you. You know her." The aura she affected imitated that of the kindly goddess who hid in the sour neurosis of the Yellow Kingdom.

Sister Wavecrest.

"But if your essence is incompatible, wouldn't hers be just as wrong?"

"We are sisters, but her essence is as unalike to mine as mine is to Talis Darmon's. She is the kindest and most lawful soul to ever grace this world. She alone may be able to help."

The wind went out of my sails. Choking help out of the Whites seemed an easier solution. "They'll never let her leave Aetheria. She's like a captive. And no regent of Mihdradahl has been welcomed there in a thousand years or more."

With her seductive grin, it was never clearer to me that her greatest pleasure was her ability to cause turmoil.

"Then here lies a task fitting for a Warlord."

15

I was ready to bear the fury for violating her privacy, sharing her condition with someone she thought of as an adversary. Honestly, it would be an improvement. Apathy wounded deeper than hate. Injured me more than her irrational accusations. Or the confusion of the surreal attempt to kill me. It was her indifference that for so very long had hurt me most. But learning the source of her continued decline elicited an emotion I did not anticipate.

"How could *she* have seen what I could not?"

Jealousy.

"Oh my God. What's it going to take for you to bury the hatchet with her?"

"Peace treaties do not have the power to erase all enmities. The matriarch of their order is correct that at our essences, she and I will ever distrust each other."

"You've never told me what that's about."

"Now is not the time, either." She massaged her temples. "Yet there is much here that makes sense."

Shining through her resentment was the realization that we had a diagnosis for her ailment.

"Good! Don't you feel better knowing what's happening to you is something beyond your control? That you're not responsible? "

My attempted words of comfort brought back her spite. She assumed the role of a desperate creature backed into a corner, with no choice but to fight a predator to the death. Only I was the predator. My prey, whatever it was that possessed her. The demon within her reared.

"More proof for you that I am a hapless victim! She aids your quest to see me confirmed feeble."

I was never more certain the Whites had done something to prevent her from regaining health.

"Listen to yourself. Your mind's been tampered with in a way we hadn't suspected. And Sister Wavecrest may be able to help. This is our way forward! Wake up!"

I was exhausted. And frustrated. I restrained from acting on the mental image stolen from some old movie. Shaking someone by the shoulders was violence, not medicine. Whatever begins in anger ends in shame. But as if the image was stolen from me, she committed the act on herself.

She shook, flinging her head and body back and forth, winding and unwinding as if to shed something stuck to her. Startled, I grabbed her by the shoulders to calm her, but she fought me off. Like some frustrated slave who could bear her oppressive shackles no longer, she sprang up, screaming.

A radiance built from her. It required great concentration to manipulate the energies around her, and for the first time in an eternity, she was trying. Like an athlete putting all their effort into pressing the heaviest weight overhead, her crazed effort yielded results. A yellow glow covered her, then burned orange, and finally red. It faded, and she relaxed.

Her eyes cleared, but her voice was tiny and distant.

"It can only be that I suffer because someone has tampered with my mind, damaging my reason."

The dots at last, connected.

"Yes! Hallelujah!" I witnessed her epiphany and nearly cried when it came.

"I am not at fault."

"And I'm going to keep reminding you of that until we have this thing beat!"

She sat again, leaving the place of her inner reflection to find my eyes.

"I am lucid, Benjamin Colt. But it will not last. When we are together, I slip into an unreality. From outside, I watch myself act toward you in an alien way—in ways I have never entertained thought of. None of these afflicted moments reflect my love for you." She placed her hands over her heart.

"In one of her last moments of tenderness toward me, my mother once admitted the same. I am on the same path. It is the Great Forlorn."

"We think so."

She seemed to clear even more as she considered the memories. "With others, she was capable. When with my father or me, she became so dark, it hurt. The healers prescribed her to separate from our presence to preserve her clarity. Eventually, even separation from us was no palliative, and she succumbed to take the walk. It was not until that final manifestation that the healers called it the Great Forlorn."

Mother Oceansong and I had worked it out. "The affliction that sent your mother and so many others north—it's not an organic condition. We think it's a weapon engineered by the Whites. I don't know how they did it to anyone else, but we know how they did to you. Those wires, that laboratory. When they had you, they altered your mind in some way."

Her jaw clenched and unclenched. "Their victimization of me continues, but it no longer hides from me." The Talis Darmon I knew returned as her face became kindly to me.

"I am not so ill to fail in gratitude for your tenacity, Benjamin Colt. Despite my irrational bitterness, it has not deterred you to fight for my recovery. I am the most fortunate of all to have you."

For the first time in too long, I had real hope.

"We're going to beat this."

"Is it truly possible that Sister Wavecrest could rid me of whatever parasite has infested my mind?"

"Mother Oceansong thinks so. And so do I."

"But how will we accomplish such a convergence? I may be not myself, but the supreme magnate of Annameria is—"

"Completely bonkers." Paranoia and mistrust permeated every part of Annameria, and she was the fountain from which it sprang.

"I would say, unfathomable in her motivations and perceptions. Her counselors would distort, misconstrue, wield accusation of subversion at any advance for a meeting if its purpose were to visit Sister Wavecrest. At best, anything I revealed to the Yellows, they would find a way to use as weapon against us both. Her true identity is unknown to any but the supreme magnate. If we unintentionally brought attention upon the sorceress, it may cause her harm. What circumstance could we create for our meeting without unwanted consequence?"

"You once told me you saw—what was it?—the complexities of many courses. Paths that you see and influence from their divergence and steer toward harmonious union."

"Lest you think them my own words, I was quoting the Queen Diaphel Soarus Sylah. I borrowed that lofty claim from her. But for all her many observances, few have been as helpful as those of your Machiavelli. I felt guided by his words as I formulated my scheme for the theater of the tribunal. If only his words still spoke as clearly to guide me again. I feel certain he would advise you to do what you do best. You've infiltrated their midst before. Is it daring military action you plan to take to liberate her and bring her here?"

"I'm no Machiavelli, and I'm certainly no Talis Darmon. I'm just a tired soldier. Tired of all the mysteries. Tired of so many enemies. Tired of waiting for the next war. Mostly, I'm tired of what I don't have—you. So, I'm through with all of that. It's time to lay our cards on the table."

"Yes. While I am capable and in my right mind."

I wished I'd had a tenth of her formal training. Philosophy and logic were the last thing on my mind in the days when all of life's questions were solved by another hundred push-ups.

"I'll lay out my logic." Copying her method, I started. "First, the Whites and the Yellows mean to see us destroyed."

"The Yellows have the ability. But the Whites? Have you not removed their poison sacs? They can hate, but are they able to act on it?"

I shook my head affirmatively. "My only evidence is that Lashura folded so easily to cooperate with your ruse. All I need to know about the Whites, I learned on that day in Astelaan. They are the most malevolent beings in the universe. Right now, Lashura's scheming some way to get revenge on us."

She sighed. "I must concur."

"Just as I'm sure I understand the Whites, I'm sure I do the Yellows. But them, I have evidence on. Eavesdropping on Bryant and Tourmaline has been the peek behind the curtain of things we'd only guessed at. Before that, we were living in a truly blissful ignorance of the unpredictable danger that lies in Aetheria. Between my experience there and our surveillance, it confirms we're never going to be out of their gunsights. They may think of themselves as masterful tacticians, but, one day, something as random as the alignment of the stars could tell them it's time to invade. They are unpredictable except that they mean us ultimate harm."

"The perniciousness of their mistrust of even themselves makes your assessment logical."

"Two enemies. Both of them want our blood. If we take eyes off one, the other is sure to strike. And we don't have the resources to fight both at once."

We'd had a fraction of the army we'd needed when we cleaned up Pyreenia. We had superior weapons—and perhaps another on the way—but against a million Yellows at our front and an unknown White danger to our rear? We weren't capable of a two-front war.

Nonetheless, I'd made up my mind.

"But I will destroy them both."

Her pained face returned.

"You know the conflict that prevents me from proceeding against the Whites."

"Accept that I truly do. Even if Karlo agreed to make me an atomic bomb to drop on them, I know you can't carry the weight for ordering the destruction of the simulacra. But I see another way. One that frees you to come back to me, and removes the danger to our north and south."

Her eyes widened. "Then you see such a future to which I cannot imagine the way."

She let me take her hands in mine.

"The question is, how much guilt *can* you live with? Because I can't live with the guilt of not trying. There's a child that needs us both. And I need both of you."

She teared up.

"I also lay my cards down for you to see, before the aberrancy returns. If there is even a tiny chance for your vision to succeed, then take it! I beg you! And as my illness returns, do not allow anything I might say in my irrationality to alter the course you steer for us. Because I cannot continue this way."

"You won't have to. Not for long. I'm going to get you to Sister Wavecrest."

"How?"

"The same way I'm going to get the Yellows to do our dirty work for us."

I retrieved the scroll she kept near. Machiavelli had been her comfort and guide. I thumbed through until I found the quotation and passed it to her. She read aloud.

"It is a double pleasure to deceive the deceiver."

✻ ✻ ✻

Bryant heard me out, but in return, gave up nothing about what he'd believed had transpired in Mihdradahl. Butter wouldn't melt in his mouth as I told him my story. It was a lie. But a lie too good for him to discount outright. Because at the end of the rainbow picture I painted was the ultimate pot of gold he and Sophena Pah wanted.

The means to dominate Vistara.

Tourmaline was next to Brandon Bryant in the cloud. It had taken the rest of the day for their machinations to create the conditions for her to be alongside him for a prolonged, secure conference with us. Her feistiness, contempt, and superiority were on full display.

"You succeeded in convincing Brandon Bryant that the risk of such a communication would be worth our while. I will give you the briefest amount of time to make good on the claim that you made to him, Warlord Benjamin Colt. How is it that we should make your enemy our own?"

Bryant looked ready to burst.

"So, you lied to your own people about—everything."

"Just so," Talis Darmon seemed to admit.

Sophena Pah reveled in the admission. "Your open society and freedoms have crushed you from within. You had no choice but to console your people back to sleep with the deception that their fantasies are secure."

I laid out the breadcrumbs of the trail I wanted her to follow.

"The stalemate we have with the Whites is temporary. We made a bargain to leave them alone if they left us alone. But they have a technology superior to any either you or us holds. At will, they can kill the rays that power everything. We beat them with our old-fashioned Thulian weaponry, but if they come for us again with any kind of army, we don't have the numbers to fight them. We lost our army, and not even the queen can order a conscription."

Sophena Pah smirked. "Such is the weakness of your so-called enlightened form of benevolent governance. The belief in the individual over the state. Pathetic. And it has made your society so decadent, none step forward to serve."

"Not in the immediate numbers we need. No," I said.

"All because religion weakens your people. Why would we not rejoice to watch your kingdom crumble beneath an invader's heel?"

The queen answered. "Because they will appear on your doorstep next."

Tourmaline's ambition might have made her a standout among Annamerians. I didn't believe the Whites' claim they'd engineered the races of Vistara, but if they had, it explained why the Yellows all carried the paranoia gene. I was exploiting that trait. And—if Sophena Pah was half the snake I knew her to be—her ambition to be supreme magnate coupled with the fear of a more powerful enemy, she would see this as an opportunity.

And the ray-killer was just the tool to create the circumstances she needed.

"So, what is your proposal?"

The queen was still in control, focused by her need.

"I am composing an appeal to the supreme magnate. In it, I use language not used in diplomatic communication between our states for an age. I make the overture for a summit meeting between her and I. And as a measure of my sincerity for an end to any enmity between us, I offer to travel to Aetheria."

Tourmaline's smirk disappeared. "This is why you sought this secret meeting? You desire my influence to add weight to your appeal."

"Exactly."

The wheels started turning in Tourmaline's head.

"You spoke true. Such a meeting between our political principles has not occurred in many lifetimes."

I stepped in. "You asked us to be receptive to committing ourselves to your cause if the opportunity came for you to—step in to a new role. What we're asking from you is something far less risky."

The wheels in her head were about to fly off their spindles.

"We must discuss this between ourselves. We will be in touch." She extinguished the cloud, abruptly swiping her hand across Bryant's wrist before he could react.

Talis Darmon pursed her lips.

"It is an avarice for the access to a treasure she could not otherwise find a way to obtain."

Dave was first to his feet.

"Like chocolate cake in front of a fat kid. She wants that ray-killer for herself."

From the other side of the room, the rest of our cabal broke from their repose. Dave, Doug, Karlo, and Cynar had borne silent witness to the clandestine call. Behind them, Tranya Olan, Shasa Karin, and Keshin Tellest had also overheard everything. The last person to be inducted into our circle of trust was also the last to step into the light. Perrin Halser.

"How long till you have the ray-killer sussed out, Cynar?"

"It is done, Warlord. Its secrets are revealed to me. It cannot be separated from the Whites' ship, but it can be reproduced."

"And how long to turn it into a weapon for us?"

Karlo pointed to Perrin Halser. "That's for you to answer."

If the engineer had been overwhelmed in any way, he hid it well. "With Karlo Columbo's and the scientist supreme's assistance, and the three of us sequestered in the secrecy of the works and unmolested by other distractions, it may only be a few weeks. Nothing ever works as desired when in its first form. It is an inviolable law of engineering."

My wristlet buzzed. I turned so it would reveal only Talis Darmon and myself while our conspirators hid from sight. Tourmaline and Brandon Bryant reappeared.

"Send the diplomat carrying your request. Be prepared to exercise patience. The supreme magnate makes no decision rashly, no matter how simple the issue. I know who will stand in opposition. I hold something over all of them. I am willing to expose myself to risk in order to leverage their favor in recommending she agrees to the summit. I will want much in return."

The queen dipped her head. "And you will have it, Sophena Pah."

She couldn't suppress the pleasure of her victory and practically cackled. Bryant laughed too, and took a last shot at me.

"I'll be in touch, Ben. These wristlets have been beneficial for us both, don't you think?"

The cloud collapsed, his white hair leaving an afterimage burned onto my retina.

Talis Darmon breathed out with relief. Or maybe, it was with the anticipation of a new toil.

"So we begin."

16

A STATE VISIT WAS NO SMALL AFFAIR. I KNEW THIS FROM EARTH. BEFORE I'd joined them, my old team had done advance work in many countries where the US president was going to visit. With the negotiations for the summit almost complete, we began preparations for the massive undertaking. We didn't have an FBI, Secret Service, or CIA. We had the Guard.

I thought the message from Zaylin Twee must have something to do with the summit.

"Warlord, this matter requires your personal attention. Alone. Please meet me at once. It is best if you come cloaked. Do not be seen. Please hurry."

Commander Zaylin Twee was one of the Guardswomen who'd accompanied me for the mission to Aetheria to recover the treasures left by Jawn Kurz, the first (and only other) Warlord. It was there I met Sister Wavecrest, and had been touched by a goodness that surpassed any I'd ever felt.

I'd not spoken with the Guardswoman in some time. Despite her relationship with Kleeve Hartus, I wasn't conflicted in feeling favorably disposed toward her. I'd seen her in action. After Annameria, all of our team had the bond that comes with sharing the kind of danger we experienced together there.

But the split loyalties created by the Whites' intrusion meant Zaylin Twee was on the outside, while the other three women from our mission were on the inside of my circle of trust. But I'd leaped at the chance to bring her close again. The Guard would handle the details of security for the state visit to Aetheria, and Zaylin Twee was who I ordered Kleeve Hartus to assign to the task.

That she was buzzing me before the sun was up didn't yet strike me as necessarily odd. Early bird gets the worm, and all that. When she gave her terse message, it left me with the uneasiness I should have had from the first.

I landed the flitter at the outskirts of the Amber Quarter. It was the old center from which Shansara had grown. When the deserts around her had been lush fields, and the grains from her silos traveled on barges down a river whose bed no longer existed, to the port of Shelasa, where the sailors of the Zi-Shan chaperoned goods across the Amethyst Sea to all of Oceania.

The quaint buildings reminded me of pictures of some Scottish village, or maybe the town where Harry Potter purchased his school supplies. I chuckled about the reminiscence as I walked, though the gravity of whatever circumstances had summoned me there probably should have kept me from such silliness.

Earth was gone, but its cultural pollution still permeated my brain.

The streets were narrow and winding, none of them wide enough to permit more than two to walk abreast, making the entire quarter a pedestrians-only section of the city. At this early hour, the arts and entertainment borough was dead, but the smells that permeated it all were there. My memory recognized flavors of tangy liquors and charred meats. I passed thresholds with heavy stone lintels draping massive doors reinforced with metal strapping, the thick barriers made of some extinct wood-like fiber.

It was thought nostalgic in the inefficiency of its design. I knew as much about the ancient history of Vistara as anyone currently alive— which is to say, pathetically little. Still, I knew better. The civil engineering of the time was purposeful. It made for a mechanical breacher's nightmare. No battering ram could be brought to bear against a door in a city with such architecture. It was a hidden testament to the times the builders of the original city lived in.

What were once the strongholds of clans, merchant guilds, political dynasties, and the money brokers who profited from them all, now housed galleries and restaurants, museums and exclusive bars. I was nearing the only large open space in the borough, where the largest open area was a depression excavated into a sunken amphitheater. The city hadn't fully recovered, the fine red coating of dust on the tiers of benches the proof. I took the path behind the bowl sheltering the stage.

Close to the center of worldly tastes, yet hidden from sight, my destination was a metaphor for the institution itself.

The plain white block building stood out amongst the other construction in the old quarter. It was meant to from the beginning. The temple was small, in the same way I'd once erred in thinking its importance in Vistaran life was also minimal in its footprint. The building could be accessed from the offramp just a hundred meters beyond, where it descended from the floating skyway that wrapped the edge of the old quarter. But Zaylin Twee had counseled me to be my most invisible in my choice of routes. Beneath the full covering of a desert-colored cloak, I was as discrete as any person could be, conspicuous only because I was the lone person to be on the streets.

The path to the entrance was along the cramped sidewalk that held off the encroachment of the surrounding buildings. I made the sharp turn around the corner to find her waiting at the entrance. Though she was covered from head to toe in a concrete-gray cloak, I knew it was the Guardswoman. The rigid, female form of one alert for danger.

"Prepare yourself, Warlord. You have seen much, but even for me, this was a shock."

With no other warning, Zaylin Twee took my elbow to hurry me in beside her.

The clear crystal skylight focused its rays on the alter. Splayed above it hung the crucified bodies of two pale men. Or what was left of them.

"The act was done in a ritual fashion, Warlord."

The skin had been peeled back. The muscles beneath were the next layer of anatomical exposure. Beneath them, their rib cages were spread wide from split sternums, and the contents within hung loosely by their attachments. Evidently, the release of death had brought no peace. Their visages were locked in the white pain and black terror they'd suffered.

"I believe this was done to them while they lived."

I'd seen a lot. But not even among the Mydreen had I seen anything like this.

A red-cloaked Guard stood in the shadows, backed as far away from the central display as the space permitted.

"Guardian Setch Krayman discovered this only an hour ago."

The man stepped into the light. "I was making rounds, and thought to meditate for a moment in the sanctuary. I'm not given to such, but it seemed—appropriate, given what has happened. My father was devout, though I have not been..."

She stopped him. "Thank you, Guardian. You acted correctly to contact me first."

"Does anyone else know?" I asked.

"Only the three of us. And of course, the one who perpetrated this."

The bodies were lashed to thin crosses, themselves expediently formed from broken furniture. The pair were hoisted from the ceiling by rope and blocks. "You mean to say, 'ones,' don't you? Not one. Whoever did this brought most of these props with them. Even for two or three men, this required a lot of work."

"One. I know who did this," she whispered to me before raising her voice. "Guardian, wait for me outside. Let no one enter."

"Yes, Commander."

She placed a hand gently on my arm to caution me to remain silent. When the doors closed, she relaxed her touch. "He was distracted by the butchery and did not see what I hid from him."

At the base of the altar, a bloody blanket lay in a limp pile. It was embroidered with a scene similar to that sculpted over the snowy entrance to Celeste Hom. Tarn and human, riding the crystal ship over the Blix. When I'd last seen it, the artistry was not drenched in gore, but was carefully placed over the altar. She peeled the copper-stained cloth back, revealing the gold braces, chest plate, and helmet of a Guard hidden beneath, and one wristlet.

"There are no others like them. These are the marks of office belonging to the First Shield of Mihdradahl. It was Kleeve Hartus who committed these murders."

"You'd better tell me everything."

Her detached poise broke, and she rubbed her eyes as if to clean them of the scene. "You are right to suspect me. I am not innocent in prior knowledge that there was much amiss with Kleeve Hartus. But I never suspected him on the road to a madness such as this."

It was my turn to guide her. The priests had a study. I led her there, took a quick look around to make sure I wasn't stepping into some undiscovered nightmare, then brought her in. I sat next to her in the high-back chairs where I'd once half-heartedly listened to the smaller of the priests instruct me in his faith.

"Make it quick, Zaylin Twee."

She regained composure, the horror she seemed convinced done by her former lover—and death's odor of blood and shit—held at bay beyond the small room's door.

"Since the event, we have been distant. It was he who began separating himself from me. When I voiced opposition to the role he created for himself in the reorganization of the governance, he shunned me. I was relieved from service and sent home. After the queen's return, I took it upon myself to step back to my duties. He welcomed me, but kept me at a distance. We were immediately subordinate and superior once more.

"As many took leave from the Guard, I resolved that though I did not condone what he'd done, I owed it to the institution to which I've dedicated my life to try to see it made reputable again. And I hoped that he too would regain his reputation.

"His confidence waned. I saw it in him daily. The Guard's relegation below the army, his own to being a minor cog, unable to apologize to the queen for what had been a result of his love of Mihdradahl—all wore at him. It was the night when the royal tribunal concluded that he came to my apartment for the first time since before the Whites appeared. He was more distanced from the man I loved than ever I could conceive.

"He said, 'The priests are not the subjects of the same deception as the faithful have been. They are in collusion with the Whites. I am sure of it. It was my solemn duty to step forward and decry them for the collaborators I suspected them to be. The irregularities of their story demand an investigation. But I am commanded to ignore the obvious. I cannot determine if it is simply the queen's pleasure to emasculate me, or political convenience to see everything swept away into the desert sands, to be carried off into the winds, and forgotten.'

"I thought like him. I'd have preferred to see the priests in cells, and their collusion made public. I understood her manipulation to quell the crises by suborning the priests' perjury, but thought they deserved more than a slap on the wrist.

"Apparently, so did Kleeve Hartus.

"I tried to console him that the queen surely knew best, and it was the duty of the Guard to see her will carried out. He grew more morose and said, 'It is not for any to subvert justice. As a woman, she may choose to forgive what was surely espionage by the priests to provide such painful a leverage as the knowledge of her still-hatched child. But as regent and protector of this land? She cannot. It marks this land as ignoble, and further defiles us all by her refusal to punish the wicked.'

"I used all I knew to convince him otherwise. I offered my body to soothe him. He refused me. When I asked why it was he had come to me, he gave me his confession. 'I have been an errant knight. I have shamed myself and the Guard by my actions. I have lost all that was dear to me. I must make amends. I am not allowed to leave and walk the desert in shame. I cannot travel the path to Farnest—it does not exist. But I at least want the one I hold in highest regard to know that no matter what happens, please remember me as true.'

She wiped a tear. "I did not forget what he said to me that night. But I kept it apart from my interactions with him as I worked to do my duty and see the Guard do theirs with rectitude, all in hopes we would be restored in the queen's sight. I was greatly heartened when the first shield called me into his office to tell me I would be responsible for the queen's security on her diplomatic mission to Annameria.

"Then... this."

It was still hard to believe that Kleeve Hartus had been the monster that committed the crime next door.

"Are you sure the watchman hasn't contacted anyone else?" I asked.

"I know Setch Krayman to be resolute in his oaths. If he says he has not, he has not."

I was ready to go into action. "This all goes away. We're going to sterilize this crime scene and make the whole thing disappear. And, Zaylin Twee, if that means Setch Krayman has to disappear too..." I let the rest hang.

"I called you first, Warlord, because I knew the gravity of what it would mean if this crime were discovered. Whether Setch Krayman sees the implications we do, he nonetheless recognized his discovery as being a situation that demanded the utmost of caution."

"We lucked out then. Because I think Kleeve Hartus meant for this to be discovered, and word of it spread far and wide. He may have been a zealot about his beliefs, but now that Farnest has been exposed as what he most despises—a lie—he's a zealot for a different cause."

"I think you correct. It is the first act of a man who seeks to bring justice to the guilty. And such ritual that went into this can only be meant to terrorize the priesthood, and perhaps inspire as a beacon for others to follow."

I buzzed Dave. "Get Doug. We have an emergency to deal with." I thought quickly. "Who else can we absolutely trust with a secret?" I'd caught him off-balance with my contextless verbal rapid-fire.

"Huh? Uh, there's the crew we put together for the other thing. What's this about? You need gunfighters or brains?"

Perrin Halser wasn't a crime scene kind of guy. Cynar and Karlo were, but were busy with Perrin Halser. The Guardswomen? I wanted them close to Talis Darmon. Plus, I'd have to let them in on who we thought the perp was.

"I need janitors. We have a cleanup job. A bad one."

"I took the morning off. Later I'm supposed to pick up Dougie on my way to the compound. We're getting together with the Tarns to—"

"Say no more. Move it up to now. Get Doug, Sarkan Sell and Jodal Jark, and meet me at the temple. Oh, and bring all the cleaning supplies you can carry. Tarps. Towels. I need Winston Wolf."

"Your handiwork?"

"No. But this looks even worse than what the Wolf had to clean up. More like what Dr. Manhattan did to Rorschach. And we need to make it go away."

If nothing else, our common pop-culture upbringing had left us a secret vocabulary. Wristlets or not, there's just something about doctoring the crime scene of a ritualistic murder that makes you want to be sure if anyone was listening, they'd have no idea what you're up to.

"Oh, boy," Dave said. "I get it, brah. You can fill us in when we get there."

"Make it fast, Dave. Put down right at the front door. Before the city wakes up."

"Yikes. Moving!"

All I said was, "Explanations gotta wait. We need to make this place spotless. Daylight's burning."

The Guardsman who'd discovered the scene remained outside. Zaylin Twee and I'd already lowered the bodies and piled all the other evidence onto the same bloody stack. With a raised eyebrow, Doug said, "All right, boys, you heard the man. The inspection team from regimental headquarters could show up to white glove the barracks at any time. GI party. Let's move."

Dave reached the edge of the congealed pool and stopped. "Yech."

The Tarns were spreading a tarp. Doug moved to one end of the mess. When Dave didn't take the natural position across from him to help hoist the first of the bodies, he mistook the reason for Dave's hesitance.

"Dude, what up? You've killed more people than cancer. Let's go. Chop, chop."

Dave twisted the side of his face. "Forgot my gloves. You know, when Ben called, I'd just gotten cleaned up. Tranya Olan has the morning off."

"Yeah, yeah. Hey, Sarkan Sell, switch with Dave, okay?"

"I might still make it home in time before she leaves for her next shift, brah. I used half of the day's water ration so she'd have the rest. Won't be any when I get home."

"We'll get our hands dirty. Jeez. You could shower up at the barracks, you know? Take a stone and start zapping everything behind us then, dude."

With every iota of evidence gathered and wrapped tightly, the doors opened, and we rushed everything into the flitter. Everyone but Zaylin Twee and I piled in. Dave was shaking his head as he lifted the flitter. It was not how he'd planned to start his day. Doug waved goodbye and made a big, stupid grin. The Tarns picked at their nails, uncaring as ever. They were gone.

I checked the sanctuary a last time. I ran the rays of a stone over our tracks as we backed out, the sterilizing light removing any last trace we'd been there. I pulled my hood up, and we stepped out.

"We'll speak later," I told her. I went back the way I'd come, and she with the Guardsman to resume his beat. Since I first set foot in the Bosch-esque recreation of a scene from Dante's *Inferno*, forty-five minutes had elapsed. The Amber Quarter still showed no signs of life. Had a worshipper stumbled upon the grisly scene, the entire city would have known of it in minutes.

We'd been lucky.

I found Talis Darmon in the gymnasium, engaged in exercise with the women. Her color was strong, and she seemed well.

"Sorry to interrupt," I told the ladies. "I need a moment with the queen."

At my appearance, her demeanor changed. My presence was again invoking her subconscious drive to repel me. In three days, we would start the journey to Aetheria. And soon after that, I would no longer be the cause of her alienation.

I hoped.

Her face was sour. "Why do you disturb me? You of all people know it one of my few times of peace."

"This couldn't wait."

Though she stiffened as I did so, I placed my lips to her ear and told her. It took some time, and she fought her revulsion of me to not pull away until I'd finished. I waited for her to say something. Without reply, she turned on her heels to return to the women locked on the mat in a grapple.

I called after her. "Talis Darmon, is there something else you wanted done about this? What do I tell her?"

She turned back.

"Tell her that her wisdom restores the confidence of her queen. By my word, she is now in command. And it will be as first shield that she accompanies us to Aetheria."

Shasa Karin and Keshin Tellest stopped their tussle. Talis Darmon could tell them what she wanted. I wasn't ready to spill any more beans.

"And him? Do you want him pursued?"

Her affect remained ironing board flat.

"No. It is well. The bitter seed I sowed within him has taken root. It may have been preferable if it had sprouted for all to see in the morning light, but what's done is done. It is difficult to control all the myriad variables. The germ of this he will plant elsewhere to bud deadly poison to those who think they have escaped justice."

I let her go.

Kleeve Hartus had it wrong. There was neither forgive nor forget in Talis Darmon's plan for the priests. *He* was her plan for them. Was there lore on Vistara to describe a golem? A malevolent creature fashioned of clay and ill intent. That's what she'd created. Made to be the instrument of her desire.

Of course, when we were done, the one I planned to give life to would be far worse.

17

I DEBATED US TAKING THE SILVER SURFER. WE HAD A SMALL FLEET OF
them now. Karlo's latest evolutionary leap to catapult Vistara's tech
wasn't meant to be kept a long-term secret. But, appearing at the gates
of Aetheria in less than a day would send the Yellows into fits of apo-
plexy caused by the neurosis of their inferiority complex. It would put
the kibosh on the summit before it could begin.

So, it was in the slow, creeping wagon train of the flying convoy of
barges and flitters that we set off.

As I looked at our armada over the Furrow, it seemed like we were
bringing half of the capital with us. I was a little surprised that the negotiations regarding the composition of our contingent were so easily
agreed upon. After only a tiny amount of perfunctory exchanges about
the demand, they had capitulated. Sophena Pah's influence, I suspected.

Annamerians were renowned for haggling and the intentional confusion they injected into any negotiation, like carnies engaged in a
fight for the crown of craftiest swindler. Prices were not fixed or adver-
tised. Every transaction was a battle between vendor and purchaser. I'd
gotten a lesson about this pervasive part of Annamerian culture from
Shasa Karin.

The Guardswoman's grandmother was Annamerian, and she inherited enough of their features and language skills to be the perfect operative for our mission into the xenophobic kingdom. One morning,
she returned to our safe house laden with foodstuffs tied together and
draped around her shoulders like a hunter's kill.

"What took so long?" Zaylin Twee scolded. "We sent you to the market to get a few things. I was beginning to worry you'd been captured by the Yellow Roamak."

Though we wore their uniforms, the thugs of the secret police were obsessive in their suspicions and questioned random citizens on the streets in great detail about their activities—even members of their own department. The secret police were a machine for accountability and control of the populace, especially in the capital.

"Nothing's so simple, commander. Not even buying groceries. I had to play the game. Luckily, Grandma taught it to me. Otherwise, I would've stood out like a Thorian courtesan on a Pyreenian street corner."

"What game?" Keshin Tellest asked.

Shasa Karin held up a roast.

"Like this, for example. I asked the vendor how much. I made a counteroffer for half. She scoffed, like she was supposed to. Then I asked her if she'd give me a discount if I bought all three of the roasts hanging in her stall. The unit price came down. So, I said, 'Fine. Just give me the one, but for that price.'

"We haggled some more until the price was something closer to fair. Then, after doing the same for these," she held up a bunch of something that could've been bananas—only they were red with green blotches and shaped like hot dogs, "she tried to shortchange me. Gave me a bunch of singles, asked for them back because she didn't want to run out of small bills so early in the day, gave me back a tenner when I'd given her a twenty, and on it went. I caught her every time. Finally, she knew she wasn't going to get one over on me, and shook my hand."

Tranya Olan was rarely impressed, but cocked an eyebrow in appreciation. "Did you have to do that for everything?"

"Of course."

I was also impressed. "It's a wonder you weren't gone longer. Is everything so difficult?"

"You don't know the half of it, Warlord. You should hear my grandmother talk about the negotiations for the dowry of her first marriage. There was almost a war between the clans."

That a similarly exhausting amount of bargaining hadn't been required to arrive at the agreement to let us bring so much of our own security only meant that the prize we dangled in front of them was that tempting.

But I hadn't completely shed the notion that there was another possibility behind their acceptance of our well-armed contingent. We could very well arrive at the borders of Annameria to be met by a hail of anti-aircraft fire. It would be the perfect opportunity to decapitate Mihdradahl.

Our biggest ships were the trade barges that made their way to and from Aetheria. Slow, ungainly, but capable of the biggest payloads, we had a company of troops and Guard spread between two of them. Irrespective of the hostilities, the caravans took grains from our underground farms south and returned fertilizers, tiny payloads of spices from rare Annamerian trees, and the products of their mines—amber stones and other ray-focusing gems used for a myriad of tasks.

Why Annameria depended so heavily on our food exports—especially when they were supposedly far wealthier in oxygen and water resources than Mihdradahl—was often debated.   Having   been there, I knew why.

Farming is misunderstood by virtually everyone who relies on the work of those doing the farming, but has never done it themselves. It's just sticking seeds in the ground, right? The so-called intelligentsia not only discount the exacting science and mechanics behind real farming, but the economics of it. Every statist regime or classed system of landowners who ordered a serf to till a piece of arable land, produced miserable little compared to the free farmer who worked the ground to feed his family, selling the surplus to finance next year's harvest.

A harvest can't be legislated into bounty. Farms can't be centrally controlled. Quotas, threats, and punishments don't bring the best yields. A peasant class can't be chained to the land to work it with any kind of predictable success. The collectives of Mao and Stalin starved millions.

Think farming's an unskilled activity? It took someone like my grandpa, an intellectual if I ever knew one, who planned, studied, fretted, worked from before sunup until after sundown every day just to bring in a crop. I grew up seeing how hard he worked. It drove me into an occupation I thought easier—combat.

Mines could be worked by laborers, directed to dig wherever the wealth was located, and their products collected and traded. Farms also required laborers, but more so, they required farmers. And farmers were not the bottom rung of a society. Unless it was a society that enjoyed famine. In Annameria, everyone not in the inner kingdom was the bottom rung of society. Especially the farmers.

Despotic systems are run by despots. And despots need control to remain in power. Which means that everyone has to know they're a bug to be smashed beneath the despot's boot. It didn't matter how much arable land and resources Annameria had. What mattered was that the despot was in control, no matter their ordered society couldn't feed themselves, despite the necessities being available to them to do so.

Show me a politician that thinks they understand farming better than a farmer, and I'll show you a despot in the making.

I stayed off the royal barge to spare Talis Darmon the stress of my presence. Surrounded by the three former Guardswoman, she'd seemingly remained even. But at some point, I had to confer with her in person. There was still much we had to prepare for. I hoped she could hang in there for just a little while longer.

Doug, Dave, our new first shield, Zaylin Twee, and I huddled on some crates below deck.

"Before we get to it, can you finally spill on the whole Hannibal Lecter scene, dude?" Doug had found some chewing tobacco substitute and was spitting green juice into a small piece of pottery.

"What's that?" I asked. I dearly missed dip.

"It's like mint. Kinda."

"Don't even bother trying it, brah. It's like the coffee. Disgusting. And it's got no kick. Might as well be nothing."

Karlo was more adamant than ever that Baby Blue be conserved for one purpose only—the manufacture of Element X. He wasn't yet sure the Blue Fairy could even duplicate the mysterious power source of the atmosphere works. As important as it was, the project had been put on hold while we focused on our current crisis.

I wished for a world where plentiful air *and* Copenhagen were possible.

"And if it did have a kick, I wouldn't be using it, bro. It's like near beer for me. I still like going through the motions. And the girls say it makes my breath sweet." Doug was a recovered addict. It made sense.

Zaylin Twee grimaced. "Baku leaf is a spice. We use it in soups, mainly."

Dave shook his head. "I told him what he was doing wasn't any different from smoking oregano."

"Leave me my dignity, dude. Back in the day, I'd never have been fooled by someone trying to pass that off on me."

No matter how serious our situation was, I couldn't suppress the grin these men always brought out of me. If I'd have had to do this without them, it would've been a much lonelier, mirthless, and anxiety-ridden task. Maybe it wasn't exactly like old times, but when had it ever been? I was glad I'd fought my instinct to leave them behind. We had capable subordinates charged with the protection of the kingdom. My mood was lightened by their dependable and good-natured ball busting, but it was time to make the donuts.

Zaylin Twee had also sensed the moment was at hand to get back to business. She answered Doug's question about what they'd helped us clean up in the Amber Quarter. "It was the work of Kleeve Hartus. There is no doubt. Nor is there doubt that he has departed Shansara. His apartment is missing essential personal effects, as if he chose but a few things needed to sustain him to travel lightly for a rapid departure. A flitter is missing from the Guard Headquarters."

"Where's he gone?" Dave asked.

"A similar vehicle was routinely sighted leaving the city in the pre-dawn hours the day of the incident. Westward bound."

"Pyreenia?" Doug wondered aloud.

"Good place to hide out, I s'pose," Dave said. "Still pretty chaotic there. Not a lot of cops about. But I'm sure the Guard could sniff him out."

"She doesn't want him found," I said, not needing to explain who "she" was.

Zaylin Twee opened her mouth, then closed it.

"Out with it," I said. "You don't need to filter anything with us. Being in our inner circle means you always say what's on your mind. Because we're going to do the same with you. We don't hold grudges. We don't get hurt feelings."

Doug winked at her. "Not for long, anyway."

She nodded. "It is an unusual invitation to insubordination."

"Isn't like that at all," Dave said. "It's how we work. We trust each other. If one of us needs help 'cause they're conflicted about something, it's how we know it. How we keep the air between us clear. Any other way's nuts."

I tagged on. "Speaking freely promotes the best ideas to come out. You see a potential flaw in a plan—say something. Don't keep it to yourself. It can save lives."

She relented. "I doubt I will save lives with what I was going to say, Warlord. But if your way is to forgive the aired grievances of a comrade, I was about to say that her twisting of Kleeve Hartus into a weapon against the priests—it is cruel to treat him as such a disposable commodity. Even in light of what he did."

"You're not wrong," I admitted.

Doug frowned. "So, what, bro? She made Kleeve Hartus into the Punisher? And he's out there doing his thing, getting revenge on the priests?"

Zaylin Twee said, "I know Kleeve Hartus better than any. The depravity of what I saw was not driven by psychosis. It was done with purpose. He is ever the investigator. I believe in his work, he extracted the truth from them, however awfully it was done. And though we disturbed that part of his plan, he surely intended that scene to strike terror into the priesthood everywhere."

"Yikes," Dave said.

"I also know something of which I doubt any of you were aware. Kleeve Hartus's first wife was lost to him because of the Great Forlorn."

Dave ran a hand over his head. "Sheez! She really had him figured out. Wow."

Doug wasn't convinced. "So, he's just going to be left alone to run amok, dude? He gonna come after us?"

"She wants things to run their course. And she's not worried that we're a target for him. That's all I can say."

"Wha'? You holding back, brah?"

"I wish I was, Dave. She hasn't told me more. We're not communicating so well…"

"Sorry, Ben," he said. "Just—sorry's all."

I shrugged it off. "But I see the genius in her manipulation, and the good that can come from it. And I don't disagree with you, Zaylin Twee. What she's done to Kleeve Hartus is terribly cruel. But the priests have to be dealt with. There's no doubt in my military mind they conspired with the Whites. And without the turmoil that investigations and public trials will cause, they're getting justice. And Kleeve Hartus gets his chance at redemption. Sort of. The queen remains blameless. To the people. And, to an extent, herself."

"Holy shee-it," Dave exclaimed as he rocked back like the world shifted beneath him, catching himself before toppling off the crate. "I just got it, brah—what this whole thing you're trying to pull off with the Yellows is. I mean, I dig it. It's a peace summit kinda deal. Hands across the water. Making alliances and all that. But, this is *you*."

He pointed at me, poking his finger with each syllable.

"You're trying for the same thing as what *she* did with Kleeve Hartus. You want *them* to do the dirty work of exterminating the Whites so she doesn't have to bear the responsibility for what happens to the underworld. Goddamn, son!"

Doug's mouth dropped open. Zaylin Twee straightened and pulled back her neck to avoid catching the jab of the surprise on her chin.

"Keep it down, will you," I said at the volume I wanted everyone to continue with. The hold of a barge was not a SCIF.

"I wasn't trying to hide it from you, but, yeah, that's about the size of it. More importantly, there's a very urgent and more tangible mission. I have to get Talis Darmon to Sister Wavecrest. Before it's too late. So, I need us to stick to the nuts and bolts of how we're going to get secured in Aetheria and create some space for me to pull that off. Because I don't know how to do that yet. The rest has to take care of itself. For now."

Zaylin Twee fretted. "With David Masamuni and Shasa Karin occupied elsewhere, our best operators for clandestine action in the city won't be able to assist in that endeavor."

Doug snorted. "We're gonna be busy, yo."

✷ ✷ ✷

"Take a ride with me, Dave? See Tranya Olan?"

"Sure thing. I'll drive."

We hopped into a flitter parked on the top deck and lifted. The sun was rising to mark the second day of our slow procession. The royal barge was in the middle of the armada, protected fore and aft by the massive haulers, our flanks covered by squadrons of flitters with K-max waist guns and miniguns on the prows.

At that crawling pace, it was an easy piece of piloting to come abreast, match speed, and tie off to the cleats. The flitter strained the ropes only slightly as Dave eased back the power, leaving our shuttle to float alongside like a towed dinghy.

The royal barge was decorative and comfortable. Plush, wide benches and wingback chairs were arranged on the deck to permit tête-à-têtes. Skins, blankets, and parasols sat handily within the reach of any needing respite from the exposure of the open deck. Vistarans wore little, neither the sun nor the wind causing them discomfort. The weather was always mild, but even after so much time here, I required more protection and preferred the uniform of the new army. Our desert camo might not be as good as multicam, but the material was as comfortable and resilient as my Cryes.

The rear deck was the queen's retreat. A canopy and tapestries hung over spans sheltered a bed and the sitting area with her desk. It's where I thought to find her, but my eyes were quickly drawn to a chair, the backs of her red-tanned arms draping the rests. She faced the Furrow, the three bodyguards splayed on furs around her like the painting of some Oriental court. There was no reason they should not be relaxed and conserving energy that was surely going to be needed when we arrived in Annameria.

The women stood at my approach. Tranya Olan lifted a hand in recognition of Dave, and the other ladies smiled at me. I thought nothing of the fact that Talis Darmon remained seated. But as I neared, she arose. Without turning to face me, she took a firm step to the edge of the gold gilt railing, her gaze fixed on the undulating pattern of the barren floor far below us. She was stepping onto the top rail when I sprang.

I grabbed her waist at the moment her feet left their grounding.

On both sides of me were many hands. The women were there with me, my explosive leap driving their attention away from our approach and to the focus of my action. So quick it all happened, that it left me speechless.

I'd fallen back on the deck, gripping her tightly on top of me. I hurriedly set her down and scurried myself around without letting my grasp completely leave her. A trance-like expression held her face calm as her friends kneeled around us, exclaiming their shock in gasps and hummed sustained notes of concern.

She blinked and met my eyes, seeing me for the first time.

"Benjamin Colt. I dreamed I was falling. The Furrow of the Creator's Hand has a voice, and sings an alluring, peaceful song to me both day and night. Do you hear it, too?"

The comforts of her craft were rapidly moved by a platoon of men to occupy the hold of my barge. For the moment, she seemed to be comforted by me sitting on the edge of her bed rather than aloof, and not, as she'd grown lately, abhorrent of my presence. I said it as gently as I could.

"What were you thinking?"

"I was not. I've been consumed by thoughts of leaping to my death. Images of falling from an impossible height as you so casually do. You are ever above me, your hands outstretched, yet you never reach me before the blackness swallows me. It was truly a waking dream."

"Why haven't you said something?"

"I am in a constant battle against some intrusive thought. Which one of the jumble should I choose to take precedence for me to explain?"

Dave and Doug huddled with Zaylin Twee and the three women, just beyond earshot. What they discussed in guarded tones could only be how they would proceed to ensure Talis Darmon could not again attempt to hurt herself.

Talis Darmon wilted. "I wish Beraal were here."

"Let's call her."

I didn't wait for her to agree before I had the cloud formed into Beraal's face, a cozy Korundi home of stone around her.

"I am so very pleased to see you, Talis Darmon. It has been some time since you've reached across the distances between us. I tried not to worry. Word of your epic diplomatic mission reached Califex, consoling me. I knew the reason for your silence was due to your submergence in the demands of such an undertaking. Are you well?"

"Yes, sweet Beraal. I am sorry for my truancy. You must think terribly of me, a mother who allows her egg to be separated from her care for so long."

"Shush, hatchling, and look upon your beautiful egg. See how it grows?"

The egg beneath Beraal's touch did seem larger. Talis Darmon burst into tears and buried her head. I stepped away.

"How much longer, brother? Is Shansara not yet restored to safety well enough for us to return? Surely, there are ample warriors to protect us, even if we must barricade within the palace for another annual around the sun."

"I don't know, Beraal. But we're getting closer. I'm sure."

"Do you have a message for my father?"

"Tell him, he's missed." I did miss him. And our former army.

"With the alliance dissolved, it is as our people have returned to a time prior to our first meeting, yet the feeling in the Korund is one of its greatest unease. He feels it, as do I. He works in his way to be ready for whatever comes, Warlord. Be assured."

"Then tell him I look forward to a time when we ride together again."

"I do not wish to add to your worries, but you do not look well, either. Take care of each other until I can be there to care for you both." She ended the connection.

Talis Darmon's eyes were puffy, but no longer wet. "While I am able, we must speak. There are things that must be said before the chance disappears forever. Things I want you to know and that I must know from you. Things we have never spoken of before."

I stayed silent.

"What know you of the mists of time? Do not evade. You may think that I have forgotten about Cynar's clumsy revelation that you have viewed them, but I have not. I have my own reasons for ignoring that incident, and I will make them known to you. First, I want to know. What did you view when you peered into the mists of time?"

There was no reason I could think of it to keep it from her any longer. "I saw myself on the throne, with you at my side. A crown on my head, and the crowd hailing me as Warlord."

The revelation seemed to satisfy her. "Not unlike what I had been warned about the mists from my professors, and just as Cynar reinforced. They do not see a perfect future. The mists deceive, and warp one's desires. Your own vision was close to what eventually transpired, but no throne or crown were your reward."

"That's true. But I didn't seek out the mists of time to tell my future. And when I looked into them by accident, it wasn't with desire to be a king, or a Warlord. I didn't even know the title existed."

"I believe you, Benjamin Colt."

"Why are we talking about this?"

"Because I too once viewed the mists of time."

When she was her best self, like she was close to being now, she conducted discussions like this one so that by the end of her dialectic, the participants left feeling enlightened. I'd seen her do it many times. I gave her the courtesy of not asking the obvious questions—*what had she seen and why was she looking?* She'd get there in her own time and manner, because *how* she would tell me was as important to what she wanted me to understand as was *what* she was telling me.

"You know of my second husband's death, and the subsequent death of my unborn child. I have told you what a blow those things were to me. But I was not honest about the extent to which I was affected. I experienced a period where I was so inconsolable in my grief, that I found it impossible to believe I could ever recover from its grip. I wanted to die. Not join the afterlife, but to erase my existence entirely—and my pain with me—by embracing oblivion.

"It was only my mother's intervention that prevented this. Her method was one available only to the privileged people we were—the royal family. Her ploy was to place me before the mists of time. She believed it was my destiny to regain my strength and return to a full and wonderful life. If only I could see what yet awaited me in this life, then I would abandon my desire to end my life, having seen that there was a happy future that held me in it.

"Do you not find it ironic, that she was once so full of hope and belief in the love of life, and that she succumbed to the Great Forlorn?"

I did. And I was bringing justice to the ones who imposed the paradoxical transformation on her.

"Do you know what I saw, there in the tunnels below the library in Clymaira?"

I remained silent.

"I saw a small child with hair of spun gold, held to the chest of a mighty warrior. In his other arm, it was me he held as tightly as he did the perfect child. My mother's therapeutic method to make me believe as she did, that with life there was always the chance for wonderful things, had proven correct. When the mists of time showed a beautiful future for me, I abandoned my thoughts of death, and eventually moved forward. It did not occur overnight, but over time, I returned to a useful life.

"And over so many years that followed, the face of the warrior who held us both became blurred and unobtainable in my mind's eye. Until I one day saw the face again. In a palace in a faraway land, when I was in my most desperate hour of need. He appeared then to save me.

"I swear this is true, Benjamin Colt. It was you I saw that day in the mists of time. And now I know without a doubt, I will not survive to make that image come to pass. I will not be there with you and our child."

I had to speak. "No, Talis Darmon, you *are* going to make it. We're very close now."

"You fail to see. Your own experience in the mists of time proves it. If the mists are incapable of seeing the future as it truly develops, then what I saw cannot become a reality. Given my predicament, the logical conclusion can only be that I do not return to equanimity. The image of the three of us together cannot come to pass. It is inescapable."

My protests did not infuriate her as I thought they might. Instead, she became the loving, caring person I missed.

"My love, I tell you these things for your own good. And to secure your promise. If it is so that I must die, then you must do everything in your power to be there for our child. Promise me."

"I will not."

Her eyes were wet again. "Think on these things, Benjamin Colt. Now, you must leave me before I become ill-disposed toward you again.

I have some of the medicines from Karlo Columbo. I will use them to drive me into a dreamless sleep. If I can regain even some of my internal strength, I will then attempt to enter a deep meditation and remain in such a state for as long as possible. Do not be alarmed. I must realign the last of my energies for the task ahead. There is a kingdom with two enemies, and they must be removed so our child will be safe. Go so that I may rest. I know the women will be in even closer attendance of me now, but I must not be disturbed."

"Yes, sweetheart."

Already, she winced at my affection. From a bag at her bedside she retrieved a brown plastic pharmaceutical bottle that could only have come from Karlo. I watched as she took two of whatever pills they were and swallowed them.

"Benjamin Colt. If I should plummet from your grasp, do not follow. Complete the task and live so that our child is not an orphan. Promise me."

I relented.

"I promise."

When she was asleep, I'd come back and take the bottle. An OD was not going to be the next of possible perils to worry me. I herded the gathering a little farther away from her expedient bedchamber. The women were all doe-eyed and subdued.

"Enough of that," I said. "There's no need for apologies or recriminations." Like good soldiers, they didn't protest my order. I told them what to expect from Talis Darmon as she prepared, and the rest of us made for the top deck.

"Brah, how hard can it be for us to wrangle some kinda alone time for your friend to do her thing to Talis Darmon? Won't there be some big luaus and stuff where they can sneak off to the ladies' room together? A sightseeing tour? Or we sneak the sorceress into whatever quarters we'll be billeted in. I thought Bryant and his girlfriend are like all up in the secret police and what not? They gotta be able to pull something as simple as this off, just for the asking."

Zaylin Twee naysaid him. "You do not yet comprehend the restrictiveness we are to encounter, David Masamuni. We will be under intense scrutiny. Each of us will be watched. And the watchers will have watchers of their own. Neither can we depend on our conspirators. Sophena Pah is the embodiment of unpredictability, except in her pursuit of advantage. And I have experienced the duplicity of Brandon Bryant. The Warlord is correct to see this as the most difficult of tasks."

"And Mother Oceansong led me to believe this will be no quick laying on of hands like we saw in Shelasa."

Doug scoffed. "Dude, I was pulling off second-story B-and-Es in middle school. Never got caught once. Heck, I snuck a chick out of the female barracks and got laid behind the battalion HQ dumpster during basic training. I can get in and out of anywhere, and do the same while smuggling someone else. Getting those two together? I don't care if it is North Korea. Piece o' cake."

Zaylin Twee slapped her forehead.

"What Doug's saying is that opportunities multiply when they're recognized and taken."

"And when we have to, we make our own opportunities," Dave said.

Doug bounced his eyebrows up and down. "And with the right motivation, you can make damn near anything happen."

The first shield looked as if she'd just learned her parents were the kind of criminals she spent a lifetime chasing. "How is that as I ascend to the heights of responsibility, I fall into ever lower company?"

Dave puffed. "Ha. You're not the first to say that about being running buddies with us. She's getting the hang of it, isn't she? Welcome to the team, sister."

18

AETHERIA BY DAYLIGHT WAS A CURIOSITY NO LESS UNSETTLING THAN IT had been when I last floated over it, witnessing its oddities through the green and black shades of night vision. Concentric rings of walls separated the wide tiers of the partitioned city. Sprouting from the masses of low tenements in all the ringlets were towers, random cornstalks jutting above fields of soybeans. The skyscrapers were capped by heads of massive stone authorities which faced in different directions. Elongated chins and stretched noses cast suspicion on those below, their almond frowns and wrinkled sneers passing judgment from above.

"Big brother's watching," Dave said over wristlet.

"You and Shasa Karin gawk while you can," I said back. "Be below-decks by the time we head in."

"Yeah, yeah, dad."

"Check it out. I count three atmosphere works," Doug said from behind the pilot's console. "Is that grass? And trees?"

A single patch of green space occupied one of the middle tiers—the park I'd used as a drop zone. Dotted throughout Aetheria were trees with fluffy tufts atop skinny trunks. The way their foliage contrasted to break up the flat rooftops gave the city a golf ball pattern. Until the rounded tree tops reminded me of skin, puckered and thickened because of the cancer growing beneath it.

Behind the tallest and thickest walls of the innermost ring lay the palace and the section reserved for the first caste. And in a secluded and ignored zone within that lay the district containing the relics and antiquities, and among them, Sister Wavecrest. I lowered my binos, our descent and the rising walls causing me to abandon my search for the shell where she secreted herself.

"If it's gonna happen, it'll happen in the next minute," I said.

"They know how much ass we have," Doug said. "My bet is, not."

Our gunships flew layered in altitude around the hover of our central formation, giving them all unrestricted cones of fire. The Guard were still our air force, and their gunnery had only improved with the numerous opportunities for practice they'd gotten supporting the army in so many conflicts. From this distance, we could render the port and every ship in Aetheria's airspace to Swiss cheese.

An officious gold flitter left the port, streaming yellow banners hoisted from its rear deck. It passed the last wall to float over the chasm that was the northern border of the city, and halted to a hover at a respectful distance from where our armada hung.

"Time for the handshake," I said.

Doug eased us off the deck of the lead transport , piloting our runabout flitter to a perfect nose to nose with the welcome wagon. Black-uniformed Yellow Roamak crowded the deck in perfect files, like the stiff bristles of a brush, a single central sprout at the head disturbing the uniformity by the replacement of a green-cloaked woman. There was not a male among them, not even the crew. I stepped to the point of our bow and saluted. Dropping my salute, I said nothing. In their culture, the one who spoke first was at the disadvantage. The woman met me at the point of her own craft's bow. After an interminable stare down between us, both hands darted from her wide sleeves to shoot skyward, then brought them down abruptly to join in front of her heart.

"By her benevolence and wisdom, the supreme magnate of the eternal imperial kingdom of Annameria bids welcome to Mihdradahl."

The guards did the same in unison, their hands joining together in a single clap, and sang in a perfect chorus with a drawn out hum, "Mother of us all."

"I am Shō-Fell Tō-An. I have the blessing of being chancellor of rites to the immortal wellspring of Annameria, author of all destinies, seer of providence, architect of the perfect path."

I didn't believe in fancy titles. The bigger the title, the less impressive the person. If you were the assistant to the regional manager of undersecretary affairs for the department of strategic toe counting and asymmetric navel gazing, it meant you and your boss occupied the same closet in the Pentagon.

"Warlord Benjamin Colt." I didn't dip my head or render any other pleasantry as I said it. She knew who I was.

From her sleeve, she produced a scroll and thrust it in front of her like a ward. "The seal of the supreme magnate binds the etiquette for this occasion. The diplomatic retinue from Mihdradahl is to follow."

I saluted and stepped back.

The homecoming queen float that was their vehicle veered off, and I gave Doug the high sign to follow. We'd be leaving the protection of our flitters. They would hang off the coast to watch as we took point to lead our flying sandwich made up of the first transport, the royal barge with the queen, and the second of our transports to fall in behind.

The port was sheltered behind the outer citadel walls. When once the Furrow had been an ocean, sailing ships had bobbed there. Separating the port from the city was another wall as grand and topped in parapets. Docks and wide quays accepted the large ships that carried the trade between our two kingdoms. Warehouses lined the base of the walls. At one end, a tunnel large enough to permit vehicles to travel in both directions was the point of access between the port and the outer ring of the city's first tier. The portcullis to it was lowered.

A smaller tunnel lay closer ahead of our berthing area. Its entry was open, the sharpened spikes of its gate hefted precipitously high and restrained from gravity's pull. Soldiers bearing spears and short shields lined the way. Manning the walls above in all directions, shoulder to shoulder, was an unbroken ring of the same soldiery.

The last of our transports passed beneath the bridge connecting the outer walls, and the massive port gates ground to a close. To aircraft, they were more symbolic than restricting in their security, but the feeling of enclosure was hard to overcome. These people loved their cages.

Doug and I were on the quay to meet the royal barge as it set down. The chancellor of rites was there with her cordon of state police. A grand palanquin with two gold chairs rested on the ground, a throng of stout Yellow men fore and aft, eyes averted groundward.

I sidled closer to the green-robed official, her security (or were they her jailers?—was there a difference?) watching me like hawks.

"I won't be riding beside the queen. My place is leading her procession into the city."

The chancellor wasn't diplomatic in her tone. "Men do not ride palanquins. I will be beside Queen Talis Darmon as her guide through our illustrious city. I am surprised that a military commander of such renown has not memorized the protocol of the march. But of course, you have no matron to oversee you."

Snooty tones, discourtesy, and Yellow sexism didn't play well with me. I wasn't lying down for her, not even surrounded from high ground on all sides with more Indians than Custer and the 7th Cavalry.

"Join me to welcome the queen," I said as I stepped off with one of my gravity-defying moves, one of my unique combinations of glide and hop that when I pulled it off, had the effect of dazzling an observer because it looked like I expended zero effort—which was true. Without telegraphing anything, in a flash, I was ten meters ahead of her.

Dick move, I know. She started it.

I had combed through the protocol for our arrival, but where there were specifics, there was also vagueness. The clear lines in the sand of the document's language—Tarns were not welcome. And beside myself, no men would be allowed past the last wall and the corridor into the Serene Sanctuary where the palace lay. No weapons were permitted to leave our ships. But now that we were here, I worried about that proviso the least. With our gunships floating just off the coast, at a word, they would rain dragon fire over anything and everything at my command.

A negotiation, by definition, means neither side gets everything they want.

Within the vagaries that seemed meant to benefit the home team were the flowery concords to insist on the harmonious presentation to the winds, the acknowledgement of the dignity of the most serene race, and more meaningless babble. I signed off on all of it once we'd secured the right to park our air force off their twelve o'clock for the duration of the visit.

Our Guard had already hustled to form a wall between the royal barge and the esplanade. They remained an unyielding barrier to the protesting foreman of a detail carrying an arched gangplank wound in flowering vines and lined with crepe paper lanterns. It was a beautiful work of art, worthy of a distinguished visitor.

But not good enough for my queen.

From our transport, a squad of camouflaged soldiers trotted in time, hefting a walkway with crystal rails above jewel encrusted risers, a runner of gold spun silk carpeting the middle of the ramp.

I arrived just as the First Shield snapped to attention and barked, "Detail. Part formation. Move."

The Guard formation swung open like a pair of gates, herding the flustered protests of the foreman and his crew bearing the garden gangway to one side. Our desert-clad porters flowed seamlessly into the funnel to seat the ostentatious ramp against the royal barge.

The chancellor arrived next to me, harried like a hen squawking because there was a fox in the coop. "The feet of the Red potentate must touch the cleansing path of the wholesome first flowering to absorb any foreign radiations that would clash with the tranquility of this auspicious ground."

I dismissed her protest with indifference. "She'll wipe her feet on the welcome mat before she enters the palace."

At the top of the ramp, as though out of thin air, Talis Darmon appeared. Straight and muscled, deeply red and exuding vigor, the many colored jewels of her crown split light to bathe her in their spectrum.

The morning light pierced the sheen of the diaphanous cobalt cape to reveal her figure. Laced gold armbands covered her forearms. Falling from a high waist, a split skirt revealed the length of her thighs and legs. Gold armor cupped her bosom as if held by some magic. She paused.

The buzz coming from the Yellow reception, even the complaints of the chancellor, vanished. Like them, I was a deer captured in the headlights. Trailing her at both sides by a breath were Keshin Tellest and Tranya Olan. Both were dressed to complement their charge, revealing enough skin to suggest that their beauty was what selected them for close service to their queen. But beneath the pleats and extra material of their more modest dress would be concealed a plethora of sharp fangs and deadly implements. The braided gold wires that crisscrossed and caressed their arms could twist a neck shut. Jewel encrusted nails could pierce an eye, open a jugular, or penetrate flesh in stiff fingered stabs. Their edges could remove tender appendages with a slice or open bellies to spill guts.

Her descent broke the mass trance.

I let the chancellor keep pace with me to the foot of the ramp. Talis Darmon's gaze saw everything and fixed on nothing, though mine was locked on her. The chancellor made a deep bow and started her obsequious routine.

"The most exalted and serene mother of Annameria, the living creator and thread of life that binds all authentic peoples of Vistara in harmony, the Supreme Magnate Yi-Zun Bao Shu-Wen Dō Gwen, the light of the morning sun and sparkle of the night sky, welcomes the Red queen to the domain of the blessed."

With chin held high, not gracing the chancellor with the personal attention of her gaze, she spoke into the air and in the third person, something she never did. "Queen Talis Darmon Sylah has traveled a distance not crossed in history to accept this courtesy. Lead her to the supreme magnate."

The queen accepted my hand to escort her to the palanquin. On steps formed by the backs of the litter bearers, the queen ascended the platform, her attendants holding the train of her cape to arrange it around her as she took her seat in regal fashion, then assumed places behind her seat. The chancellor sat beside her and lifted an arm. The platform rose with the silent exertion of the bearers.

Now, the fun would begin.

The black-clad women of the Yellow Roamak fell into a perimeter around the hoisted gondola. Before the order to march came, Doug stepped to the rear and barked from his diaphragm, "Post."

With me on one side and Doug on the other, two lines of soldiers followed as we wedged between the Yellow Roamak and the palanquin. We towered above the women and the porters. Agitated, bewildered, and unbalanced, black uniforms parted to the sides like waves. Our soldiers inserted themselves between the porters on both sides, took charge of the palanquin, and hefted it smoothly another foot higher to rest on their shoulders. The unburdened porters looked about in confusion as to what they should do.

Before the Yellow Roamak could recover, a new layer interposed between them and the float. Red-caped Guards filed in. Their arms raised to grasp the shoulder of the man in front of them, forming an impenetrable wall of muscled Mihdra might around our queen.

At the head of the palanquin, Doug and I assumed attention, but not before I saw the tiniest smile touch the queen's lips. The chancellor gasped. For someone who spouted words like a thesaurus, she was at a loss. Footfalls of hobnail boots tapped the stones in a stampede. From the tunnel ran the detail of spear carrying soldiers. The man at their head wearing the distinct epaulets of an officer yelled, "Halt this assault on the representative of the most serene—"

Before he could continue, the chancellor lit into them. In rapid-fire syllables, too fast for my decipher to translate, his men halted in their tracks. The man with the green boards on his black shoulders took a threatening step in front of Doug and threw out his chest.

"This disrespect will not be tolerated, Red."

Dougie's chin dropped to meet the man's eyes.

"Eat a bowl of unwashed dicks, tiny."

The officer wore no decipher, so Doug's dining recommendation probably wasn't understood.

From over our shoulders, another machine-gun burst of orders came from the chancellor. The man flushed, then returned to the disarray of his troops to fire his own orders to them. They hastily performed an about-face, formed into a tight square, and marched.

"More like it," Doug mumbled, then drew a breath. "FORWAAARD. MARCH."

We were off. The black uniformed state security we'd displaced sped ahead to fall into a similar formation behind the marching Yellow soldiers. Out of the tunnel, we came to the first tier of the city. Both sides of the street were lined with citizens, proctored by black uniforms on every block. From bowed waists, they threw petals onto the streets to greet our procession.

"I want this kind of welcome everywhere we go," Doug mused as we both snapped a hand salute to acknowledge this block of well-wishers.

The two formations marching ahead of us were as unnecessary to guide our route as it would be for the first float in the Macy's Parade to find its way on the route. The walls of Annamese folding at the waist on both sides of the street were like tunnels of forest ferns, fronds curling at the touch of our presence.

It was a long march through the layers of the city. The chancellor droned endless narration to the queen, who occasionally lifted single finger by way of reply. I counted each gate as we passed the concentric rings to reach the last wall. There were wide tunnel entrances interspersed in the walls making up all the rings, but the one we halted before leading into the palace grounds was a narrow pedestrian tunnel.

The Yellow soldiers that headed our procession fell in with the troops waiting alongside the entrance to the last passage, and the contingent of Yellow Roamak fell back in around the palanquin, waiting for it to come to rest and our human wall to part and permit the inevitable descent of the queen and the chancellor.

"Hang loose, Doug. Once we're out of sight, the protocol is for the Yellows to get our troops quartered. I'll buzz you later and find out where. Give me a heads up if there's any shenanigans."

"Won't be nothing we can't handle. Good luck, homie."

"You know the go-to-hell plan."

He smirked. "I've always dreamed about what it'd be like to call in an airstrike on myself. Hehehe." He sounded like Cynar.

The queen accepted my hand to descend from the platform, using the human step stool that had reappeared. I fell in as her shield arm to move to the red silk runner heading into the tunnel, the tongue of the dragon's mouth. We would soon be in its belly. The chancellor met from the right as we crowded into a staggered file to enter the tunnel.

I was the only male. Squints of suspicion painted me as I passed the checkpoint of female sentries to take my place behind the queen. The tunnel was long, the longest yet, and I strained to see past the chancellor and Talis Darmon, curious about what we would walk into.

Shadows from the surrounding spires cast prison bars across a courtyard filled with robed women, organized into green, gold, and red echelons, standing in quiet welcome. The trail between them to the steps ahead formed another narrow causeway. The chancellor gestured the queen to take primacy and fell in at her shoulder. Keshin Tellest and Tranya Olan followed, and Zaylin Twee fell in beside me to exchange a sideways glance before making a tiny bounce of her chin to indicate she saw something ahead I should also see.

Through a gap in the tall columns supporting the portico at the top of the stairs, was a grand hall. Past groves of crystal trees that shaded more silk-robed armies of women, a dais waited. It rose so high, I could not see what waited on its peak.

Center-faced women turned in unison to face the dais as we passed their row. At the pinnacle of a platform twenty feet tall was a gold throne wound in twisting beasts with ruby eyes. A permanent guard of statues chiseled from straw-colored marble stood in a line behind the ruler. They were the mythical representations of the ideal of Yellow feminine warriors, meters tall, muscled, and armored—all sculpted from stone of a color near that of the living people below them.

On the seat waited the supreme magnate.

She was consumed by the immensity of her throne and the statues behind her, all of it only emphasizing her diminutiveness. Purple robes flowed from her to cover the floor, themselves engulfing her in their folds. Her face was painted stark white. Black metallic-flecked makeup circled her eyes, and her lips were the brightest crimson. Her crown was the unmistakable skull of a jeweled Tarn plated platinum, the jaw split so the tusks rested at both of her ears.

On the floor beneath her was the presentation line of her council. To my right, in latex black uniform, was Sophena Pah, emanating a cloud of malice and intimidation contrasting the colorful robes to either side of her. Near the opposite end of the line was the bookend to the head of state security. A purple-haired goddess whose yellow saffron skin radiated the light of a morning sun above her high neck gown, covered in pearls and sequins. Sister Wavecrest found my eyes for an instant and a butterfly spread its wings in my chest.

The chancellor broke the silence with a throaty, musical note that she sustained as all heads dipped.

"In our ignorance, we waited as unformed clay to be delivered into perfection. She descended in the form of an authentic, to give birth and bring order to the true people. The supreme magnate of the eternal kingdom of Annameria, Yi-Zun Bao Shu-Wen Dō Gwen, showers welcome on the Red queen of Mihdradahl."

I wasn't sure what to expect, but it wasn't the squeaky voice that came out of the sickly doll above us.

"Queen Talis Darmon Sylah, you have come to rest in the heavenly kingdom of Annameria.

"May you never leave."

19

"THE SUPREME MAGNATE GIVES THE WELCOME OF ENDURING ACCOMmodation. Never has such been extended to a Red regent," the chancellor whispered.

That was one way to interpret it, I guess. Sounded more like it was an invitation to the six-feet-under club.

Fortunately, my queen was at her best—politic, sardonic, and virtuous.

"Then we are especially pleased for it, if the walls of heaven are so tall as to concentrate such joy behind them."

The chancellor smiled broadly. Telling someone to go to hell in such a way that they'd enjoy the trip was a skill I didn't have. Doug was sure lacking in the finesse department, too. I wondered if he'd instigated his first fistfight yet.

I stood behind to travel down the receiving line for the introductions to the council, but was not presented. The whole second-class citizen thing I couldn't have cared less about. With no attention on me, I stole a surreptitious glance upward to check out Mount Olympus when I thought I could get away with it.

The supreme magnate was zoned out, noticing neither me nor anything happening below her. I checked to see if Sophena Pah would send me any sort of sly recognition, but her agate eyes avoided me entirely. The supreme magnate had an air wizard on her council. I was surprised it was a man, the only man on the council. Other than the color of his skin, in every other way he had the mark of his brethren. Henna-dyed pointy beard and a self-satisfied look that made me want to smash him in the face. Another step down the line and I snuck in another look at the line of statues behind the throne.

I stifled my astonishment. The statues that I thought were either bronze or stone were neither. Taught muscles over abdomens rippled and ribs raised with respirations. A slight rhythmic sway to their stance indicated hearts beat and blood pumped. The scant armor and clothing, the close cropped hair, the eyes—all were the monochromatic weak yellow of their skin. On their pedestals, they easily towered three meters. Off the platforms, they'd be as tall as Doug and as wide.

Somewhere in Annameria, a village produced a race of Amazons.

We were nearing the end of the line. "I present the keeper of antiquity and counselor of record, the imperial scholar and aedile memorian, Amelyn Tōpara Sī-Shan."

Sister Wavecrest dipped in a curtsy.

"Your reputation as the great scholar of your age is known even so far across the Furrow, Queen Talis Darmon. The humble libraries of the kingdom are yours."

The queen's voice quavered the tiniest amount such that I doubt anyone else but me would have noticed. "That would be a most welcome visit." Her hand briefly touched the tiny pendant at the hollow of her throat—the branched, silver plated curiosity of ancient coral life.

Sister Wavecrest met my eyes for a fleeting second, and the purple irises shone hope. Whatever she knew, she knew, and she beamed assurance to me in that briefest of moments.

Everything was going to be okay.

The chancellor continued with the protocol as planned. Centered again and facing the dais, she raised her hands high before bringing her palms to her heart.

"Mother of us all."

The crowd did the same, as did the council. All bowed deeply. I stole a glance up to see the living statues step off their pedestals and form an escort around the supreme magnate as she rose and exited the wings. When the platform was empty, the chancellor left her deep bow and the room relaxed.

As we flowed outside through another colonnade, I took the opportunity to slide next to Talis Darmon. The rustle of silk gowns made a blanket of noise, and I risked speaking to her in prison yard tones. "You're doing great."

Likewise, without turning her head, she answered in a wispy breath, "Her aura beams tranquility. We must—"

The chancellor turned to speak, preventing her from finishing.

"A chaperone will guide your consort to sit with the males. You will sit beside the supreme magnate. Come."

Three tables as long as the cavernous room were piled with arrangements of foods and roasted animals I did not recognize. At the central table was a version of the throne we'd just seen and next to it, a smaller one meant for Talis Darmon. I moved to escort her, but the chancellor stopped me. At her elbow was a slight man in crimson red silk, a decipher around his narrow arm.

"I present the first consort, Eidolon Sah. You will dine with him." Without finishing the introduction, she offered her arm to the queen, who placed her hand on top of the chancellor's and departed.

"As first consort, I welcome you. Follow." I was relieved he didn't offer a hand in the same way, and I followed him around the tables to where in a deep set alcove, a table and three couches were tucked. Around them stood six equally slight yellow men, all dressed in the same lighter shade of red, the color of pinkish blood from a lung-shot deer. And, like a tarry, upright turd capped by a marshmallow, there stood a larger man in the uniform of the Yellow Roamak.

Brandon Bryant.

He looked—different. His silver hair had the sheen of some hair gel he'd acquired in Aetheria. He was thinner.

"Welcome to the kid's table," he said. He sounded different. Not smug. He was almost smarmy.

I was short of friends at the moment, but, accepting his offer of the space beside him, I was still short one. We stood at attention as an invisible orchestra broke into twangy chords and the supreme magnate and her giantesses appeared. She glided into her seat and the guardians filed around her to their posts.

A herald made an incantation as all of us besides the supreme magnate remained standing. It went on for some time, stopped, and the chancellor bade Talis Darmon to sit, then took a place beside her as the rest of the party took their own seats. At the queen's elbow, Tranya Olan didn't come up to the waist of the Amazon next to her. I wondered if their parents had to feed them with slingshots. An army of servants carrying pitchers appeared from behind tapestries and flooded to the central tables.

"We can cop a squat now, Colt. The pageantry's over for a little while until the supreme magnate leaves the party."

I took the middle of the couch, Bryant on my right, the first consort on my left. It seemed like a good arrangement from which they could each slip knives into me. The other members of our dining party crowded three to a couch. None wore deciphers. A central table was piled with food and sweating decanters.

"Dig in. It's self-serve for us. Like this." Bryan tore off a blackened leg from something that had six of them and poured himself wine, filling my goblet as well. "Eidolon Sah's okay. Consorts two through seven aren't much for conversation, are they?"

The man to my left chortled. "They all conspire my fall to assume my primacy, but we may converse without their ears on us." He spoke in Mihdra.

"News travels fast, Colt. You caused a hubbub with your wiseass maneuvers for the procession. If you're coming hat in hand, that's not the way to show it. Dick."

"No one respects weakness, Bryant. Tell me I'm wrong."

"S'pose."

He was acting like we lunched together every day. I got a vibe off him I'd not experienced before. Bryant was a lot of things. Conceited. Manipulative. Deadly. But unless he'd become better at camouflaging his emotions since he'd been with the Yellows, when he was building up to do violence, he always telegraphed his intent by bleeding off nervous tension by running his mouth with subtle threats like the bully he was. Instead, his plate was the focus of his energy.

So, I tore into my meal. The consorts to my left and right were taunting the one whose plate held a conspicuously small portion and only sipped a water glass.

"It's a pity your number comes up tonight and you have to starve yourself." One of the others tore off a huge chunk of meat and dangled it over his mouth in front of the dieter.

Another chuckled. "Leave him be. He chooses life over a full belly and flatulence."

"If she even sends for him. He might be missing out on the feast for nothing."

"At least have some gold berries so your soldier stands at attention."

The subject of their teasing shrugged them off. "I'd rather go easy today than miss tomorrow. We'll be feasting all day at the games. Then it's you'll who'll be singing sorry while I'm stuffing myself."

The one who'd first teased the man apparently on call to provide the supreme magnate with diversion gave a shrug. "True. But chances are, we'll both see more feasts. This visit won't conclude before we're up in the rotation again."

The other consorts all nodded in agreement.

My closest companions kept up their graze until Eidolon Sah took a slurping sip. "This vintage hasn't been uncasked since my ascension forty years ago. Another forty years and it'll be vinegar." His Mihdra was flawless.

"It's good timing for your visit, then Colt," Bryant said. "This is the good stuff. They'll keep rolling out all the finest while you're here. Gotta keep your queen in her place, and all that. Make you peasants think we live like this all the time. But it'll be back to plain fare soon after. Stoicism is the religion here."

The first consort put a scoop of something on my plate. "Pickled carlet tongues," he said as he doled himself out a healthy portion.

I didn't know what a carlet was, but if these were their tongues, the things must be the size of hummingbirds. It would take a thousand to fill the bowl he scooped them from.

Eidolon Sah watched as I tried the delicacy. Chewy. Tangy. Otherwise, innocuous. I made the yummy face, and he raised eyebrows in approval at my agreement that the delicacy was, in fact, a rarefied treat.

"There is more. Don't be shy."

"The real dog and pony show starts tomorrow," Bryant said through a mouthful.

Eidolon Sah's attention was back to his own plate. "Tomorrow will be a great day of entertainment and feasting. It is propitious timing for the state visit. It coincides with the decennial festival of glorious prosper."

"What's that?" I asked, easing the rubbery ball from my mouth into my napkin. The gourmet morsel had taken on a putrid aftertaste, like each of the tiny tongues had waited until I was about to swallow before vomiting into my mouth.

Bryant continued to eat. "Once very ten years, the shackles are loosened on the proles for a day. Haven't seen one yet, obviously. But it's a big deal. Games. Races. Bread and circuses. That sort of thing. A big drunk goes down afterward."

"You'll sit with us in the lesser box at the stade," Eidolon Sah said. "Not the best seats in the house, but plenty good."

"When does the summit start, Bryant?"

"When the supreme magnate decides. Your barbie doll had better be on her best game. If Talis Darmon doesn't inspire the right mood to strike the empress, she may just wake up one morning, decide she's tired of your presence, and send you all home with a boot in the ass for a door prize. She's unpredictable like that."

I kept my napkin close to cover my mouth. "But doesn't she want the—ice box?" On the spot, I stammered out a phrase to indicate the ray-killer. He made a subtle frown and turned his head slightly away as he radiated vibes for me to shut my trap.

"Dummy," he coughed into his fist.

The first consort commented on all the dishes as we continued to eat for hours while Bryant and I ignored each other. A chime sounded, the band built up a sour plucking dirge, and we all popped to our feet. The moving forest of Amazons surrounded the dwarfish figure of the supreme magnate as their pod departed.

I faced Bryant. "What are those things?"

He shook his head. "Don't mess with the Guardians of Heaven. I've seen some shit. Tougher than a Tarn. Stronger than Doug on steroids. Watch your P's and Q's around them. Not that it wouldn't be fun to see your arms torn out of their sockets like they did to the minister of the bounty when he didn't have the grain tally."

Eidolon Sah took my arm. "You'll be quartered in the consort's wing."

The queen was already being escorted away, her two shadows and Zaylin Twee with her.

"I need to be close to the queen."

Bryant shook his head. "Ain't gonna happen, Colt." He leaned in close. "This is as free as you're gonna be for a while. Don't try and use your—" he tapped the wrist at my side. "Eyes and ears on you everywhere. See you tomorrow for the hootenanny."

I turned back to the first consort to find a platoon of Yellow Roamak waiting, and his previously serene face turned bitter. "Sophena Pah has personally assigned these women for your protection." For the man placed closest to the supreme magnate, he'd seemed unusually simpatico to me. Maybe it was an oppressed-to-oppressed male kind of thing. But I suspected he and Bryant had their own understanding, and it was extending to me for some purpose. But now that we were under the eye of the Yellow Roamak, he became hostile, and continued to scold me in front of the harsh escorts.

"We expect even an inferior culture to adapt to the comportment of serene Aetheria. Act like a proper guest and follow."

Black uniforms surrounded me and marched us off through mazes of corridors until we reached the wing of the consorts. At each arch, a pair of Yellow Roamak stood. The first consort stopped in front of one and I was herded inside.

"You will remain here until sent for in the morning. Anything you require, you may ask of the women, though what you could lack would be only some lesser barbaric comfort. The luxuries we bestow could not be matched in the hovels you hail from." He dipped his head curtly and was gone. Half of the squad of black uniforms left with him and posted outside my door. The rest spread around the periphery of the room and faced inward to the raised bed, a sheer netting around it.

"Sleep there," one woman said. "The wash closet is in there. Do not deposit your waste freely, as is the way of your filth. If you do not know how to use the toilet like a proper person, you will be instructed, man."

I had about a hundred comebacks ready, but let it go. I stepped behind the curtain, stripped, and got between the sheets.

"You ladies can go now. I don't need tucking in."

"The Yellow Roamak remain, man."

Bryant said I'd be under the microscope, but this was more than that. This was payback for how we'd ruined things earlier. "Draw the drapes, huh? It's still light outside."

With a gruff wave from the one who insinuated I'd take a hunch-back growler in the middle of the floor like Apache, two of my minders complied. I lay in the semidarkness, the eyes of the women hidden by the thin curtain, but the heat of their gaze on me.

This was much worse than I'd thought it would be. How would I orchestrate the meeting between Talis Darmon and her physician? I drifted off, picturing myself a fish in a bare aquarium.

✖ ✖ ✖

I ignored the buzz of my wrist while remaining motionless, wondering if it was Doug or even Talis Darmon trying to reach me. Perhaps everyone but me had some privacy for their night's rest. The tickle was noiseless, but I nonetheless watched for some response by my watchers.

When none came, I returned to sleep, comforted by thoughts of Sister Wavecrest's aura bathing over Talis Darmon.

Droves of anxious people filled the streets, heading to the outer ring and the farthest edge of the city and the stadium oval. Corner vendors offered food and handed out tiny triangular yellow banners from their carts, which children waved overhead as they rode on their parents' shoulders. The cotton ball trees that peppered the walks dangled streamers. If it was only once every ten years these people got a tailgate party going, then it probably was more than my imagination that the oppressive air of Aetheria seemed lighter than usual.

I rode with the consorts in the rearmost ground car of the motorcade. Doug marched behind us with the troops, our pace slow through the streets because of the crowds. The stadium rose from the horizon above the surrounding sea of tenements.

Crowds packed the stands, and the usually constrained citizens laughed and expressed themselves in ways I'd never thought possible. Jugs were passed between men and women, unsegregated wherever I looked. I was about to ask about the huge obelisk in the center of the open stadium field, and the glistening gem at the top of it, when horns blared and all noise and motion ceased. I turned to face the box above us as the chancellor stepped onto a riser and made her announcement for the entrance of the supreme magnate.

After the ceremony I'd come to expect came the grand entrance of the dragon lady herself, with Talis Darmon allowed the honor of walking at her side. Finally, we were released. Bryant nudged me. "This is the safest we're going to be for a while. No one watching us or listening in."

He dragged me with him to the buffet and started piling.

"You look thin, Bryant. Are things that bad in Annameria? We send a ton of food here a week from our underground farms in exchange for the fertilizers you send north. I never understood how that is. You have better land, air, and water."

"A lot of mouths to feed here, Colt. The big hot-house thing you say they have going at the north pole has captured some imaginations. More than that ray-killer you're dangling in front of us as a prize."

"So, you think the air's favorable for an alliance to hit them?"

"You're here, aren't you? Sophena Pah's made the case for an expedition, but Empress Pol Pot hasn't tipped her hand. Like I said, she's unpredictable. Just try not to do anything antagonizing while you're here. You know? *Don't* be yourself. C'mon, might as well settle in. This is supposed to go on all day."

Eidolon Sah sat next to me. "The demonstrations and undercard bouts will fill the morning. The big event won't be till this afternoon after everyone's had a nap." He seemed genial again.

"Do I have to look forward to an audience watching me sleep every night like last night?"

He gave a scoffing laugh. "Ha! You brought that on yourself, big man. You insulted the Yellow Roamak. Look! Here come the acrobats."

It was the first of many performances. After them, archers took turns launching flaming arrows at each other, the shafts landing at the feet of the bowmen on the other end of the field, who did the same back. The oohs and aahs came fewer and fewer as the show continued, and a sort of disappointed groan went out when it became clear no one was going to be skewered and flambéed.

The next act was ushered out. Arkall riders played a kind of polo. The jockeys nudged the animals with nail-covered batons that they also swung at the other riders as the animals collided with a huge ball to send it across a goal line at either end. The audience cheered especially loudly when an arkall trampled a fallen rider or one rider successfully bashed another with their club.

"The real blood sports'll start soon," Eidolon Sah said. "That's all anyone really cares about."

A theater troop of all males, some dressed as women, put on a costumed performance complete with fireworks and mock fighting. It was a bland course to clear the palate for what was coming. The audience received them tepidly and some even booed when the performance went on too long.

On the opposite side of the stadium in a large box as low as ours, Doug and the troops were watching. I picked him out and gave him a wave, which he returned. I'd find a way to get over there at some point.

"Here we go," Bryant said. "Heard about this."

Guards brought in chained gadron, frothing at the mouths, and set them to fight each other. When they didn't, sword and spear wielding men herded them into proximity to the cheers of the crowds. Ringmasters rewarded the survivor of a bout by slaughtering it, bringing even louder cheers from the crowd.

The same was done with gazraal. Three of the lions were brought into the arena, each surrounded by several fighters, lightly armored and carrying a variety of weapons.

"Now things get a little more interesting," Eidolon Sah said. "But I'm holding my coin for later. No one bets on a gazraal. And choosing which fighter will stand or fall? There's no handicapping these things. I'll tell you when there's something worth betting on."

The bout nearest us was the liveliest. A truly big cat was doing a formidable job, leaping at one tormenter, then another, keeping them from reducing the circle and bringing points to bear from more than one direction simultaneously.

The crowd drew sharp breaths when a gladiator fell to a lightning fast explosion, enveloping a tormentor with all but the rear set of its claws, fangs tearing the man's head off. My testicles retracted all the way into my stomach. Decapitation by gazraal—that had almost happened to me once.

"Maybe this one time I'm wrong," the first consort said as he leaped to join the standing waves.

The two remaining gladiators hesitated, and the gazraal got the next one.

"Someone's going to make a better killing than that gazraal," one of the other consorts said.

The last spearman backed against the wall, and we lost sight of him. In a box next to us, a man cursed. "First interesting thing to happen all morning, and we can't see!"

The crowds with a good view from the opposite side of the stadium cheered loudly, but it was not yet apparent who was coming out on top. Above the battle, a lone woman leaned over the edge, then expanded to the crowd and made a banshee shriek, her arms lifted high.

"I won! I won! You all thought I was crazy! Pay up!"

And the gazraal struck.

Four tan limbs with foot-long razor claws shot over the wall and closed around her. Her head disappeared like a hot dog bitten off in an eating contest before the lion dragged her down onto the sands.

Hysterical laughter broke out. People collapsed and grasped their bellies, laughing fits and back-slapping breaking out everywhere. In our box, the consorts were on the ground, laughing until tears rolled down their faces. I checked the imperial box. Even the supreme magnate had broken her wax museum poise to chuckle. Talis Darmon's eyes were glazed over. Whether it was the spectacle or her illness, she appeared to be losing the ability to maintain the front she'd presented yesterday.

"Bloodthirsty lot, aren't they?" Bryant said. "It's always the same, even on Earth. It may be entertainment, but subliminally, the people know it could be them getting butchered and are grateful it's not."

"Speaking of, the prisoner event is next," the first consort said.

There was little that was imaginative about it. Women clad in decorative armor with a smorgasbord of weaponry—long, jagged swords; hooked spears; chain whips; and more—worked in twos and threes to surround and slaughter lightly clothed men armed with short swords.

"If they'd team up, they'd stand a chance," Bryant said with rapt attention. I didn't point out the obvious that, in his own experience, teaming up hadn't necessarily worked. Instead, I decided to take a chance on him.

"I need your help."

"Hmm," he replied without looking away from the carnage.

"I need to get Talis Darmon and Amelyn Tōpara Sī-Shan alone together."

He still didn't look at me. "Good luck. Sophena Pah's kept close tabs on your purple goddess friend since you were here."

I fumed. "How come? Sister Wavecrest wouldn't do anything to harm your girlfriend."

"Because she was hiding weapons powerful enough to let you do whatever it was you did to the Karnak. If she's got something else squirreled away that could benefit us, Sophena Pah wants to know what it is. We don't buy your saintly story about her. But, we can't just go busting down her door. She's the supreme magnate's fave."

The council sat below the supreme magnate and Talis Darmon. Sister Wavecrest seemed withdrawn and subdued, no doubt as appalled as Talis Darmon looked to be witnessing the spectacle below. Sophena Pah was bent to the supreme magnate's ear, engaged in some lengthy report, to which the ruler simply nodded.

"Once they clean this up, the main card will be announced," Eidolon Sah said. "Then refreshments and naps before the big event."

I had Bryant's attention. "Does that mean you can't or won't help?"

"Why's it so important? Is it like Sophena Pah thinks—more mystical gizmos you're trying to sneak out?"

"No." I was weighing telling him that Talis Darmon was ill and that Sister Wavecrest could help her, making an appeal to his compassion, but he didn't have any. Before I could come up with another explanation, the chancellor was above us on the platform.

"The great contest will soon commence. From each canton comes one champion. The supreme magnate herself will crown the victor with greatest favor, and their clan will receive a benevolent ten years' grace from taxation. Second finisher, a double share of their annual water store for one year. Third place, a year of portion increase from the granary.

"From Hidalla, their clan's champion, Kai Doon."

A man dressed only in a loin cloth trotted onto the sand to many cheers, made the heavenly bow to the imperial box, then stood at ease.

The chancellor announced another twenty competitors onto the field. No wonder they had lunch and a nap planned as an intermission. The introductions alone were taking forever.

I eased to Eidolon Sah's side. "What's the big event? Gladiator fight?"

He was still feeding his face. "Nothing so dull. It is a foot race through the city. But with many twists and turns. It will end here, but the course gives entertainment to those not fortunate enough to be seated in the stade. All is broadcast, but there's just something about seeing it for yourself, don't you agree?"

The chancellor made the statement indicating the intros were coming to an end. "And finally, representing Aetheria, the dominator of the Heavenly Guard, Xa."

The crowd gasped. Clad as the men in only a loin cloth and a thin strip across her chest, the muscles beneath her pale yellow skin rippled as she strode onto the sand. The mob of competitors parted for her. A half meter taller than the tallest man, she outweighed even the most muscular by double their weight. She made the sky bow, then slammed knuckles of a fist into an open palm, raised them to the imperial box, bowed again, and took a series of kicking handsprings backward to land in a crouch before rising to the same position of attention I'd seen her hold on her pedestal.

"Guess we know who's taking home the trophy," Bryant said.

The first consort was in my ear. "The competition taking the field is always kept secret until the last moment. She's the safe bet. I'll spread a little around, just in case. That guy from Plennah looks pretty tough. I'll check the odds on him when the bookmaker shows up. You never know."

One of the consorts counseled the others. "Xa will certainly place first, so the real decision is choosing who takes second and third. A three-split option is the best hedge to take home some winnings."

The chancellor continued. "But for these decennial games, there is another representative, from a land far away, come to uphold the honor of his queen and her people."

A sensitive part of me puckered. From above, Talis Darmon's voice reached my ears. "This is not acceptable. It has not been agreed upon."

The chancellor continued as if she'd heard nothing, and her voice revved up like a good Vegas ring announcer. "The white man from the barbarian red land of Mihdradahl, Benjamin Colt."

Bryant turned to me, mouth agape. "I swear, Colt, I knew nothing about this."

For once, I believed him.

20

Beneath the stadium, the waiting area was a series of cells, and we'd been ushered there to prepare as the bets were laid, feasting continued, and the canopies extended for shady, full-belly naps before the main event. Dressed in a loincloth, I limbered up, as the other competitors did the same around me. All but the giantess, Xa, who sat on a bench, arms folded, her glazed yellow eyes baking me the whole time.

The message was crystal clear. She meant to take me out.

As if we were no more than horseflesh, a pair of attendants argued about the participants.

"Listen, hatchling, I was here the time when, right at the last minute, the Supreme Magnate Fō Lassen declared winner-takes-all for the great race. Think that didn't make the handicappers pucker their poopers? With no second- and third-place finisher, the bookies were in a frenzy to cover all the long-odds bets. I put it all on the one with the longest. I made a bundle. A hundred and twenty years ago, it was. I can still hear the screams of the losers as they did the dance of remorse on the sands." He sighed wistfully. "Now *that* was a tyrant you could rightly brag on."

His younger partner paced with him on the other side of the bars. "Just saying, having the surprise of one of the old gal's personal monsters in the race kinda puts the hinkey-dinkey on things. Same as this other foreign bugger."

"He's no wild card. Plenty muscled, but sickly and pale-looking, isn't he?"

"Who you spreading it around on with this lot, then?"

"Shh, not here. Any one of these twiggers can hear us and still get word to their clan before the bets close. I don't want the odds to crash on my picks. What's this here?"

The march of feet preceded the appearance of the Yellow Roamak, and the two jailers snapped to before getting out their way and then out of sight, such was the fear the state security produced in even rough men like them. Talis Darmon was in the center of the escort, accompanied by the women of her retinue.

"Benjamin Colt, there you are!"

The black-uniformed women ordered the other competitors to step away, and Talis Darmon reached out to me between the bars. I took her hands and pressed close.

"What were you thinking! You did not need to accept the challenge. We would have departed for Shansara immediately and later found another way." Concern poured from her, and I melted. She was herself.

Until she wasn't.

She squeezed my hands with a crushing force. "You were so brazen in your craving for the adoration of the crowds, that you deafened yourself to my pleas from above." She threw my hands back at me.

The crowds had booed when I didn't stand at the announcement of my name. Once I'd gotten over the initial shock and stood, they booed even louder. I climbed onto the edge of our box and conjured the ghost of every wrestling bad guy I'd grown up with that had made my childhood awesome. I clasped both hands overhead, pumping them to my left and right as I turned in all directions. When I had their attention, I cupped a hand to my ear and leaned out, daring them to boo louder, which they did.

The Iron Sheik, Rowdy Roddy Piper, and Sergeant Slaughter had nothing on me.

If you're the heel, be the heel.

The Warlord was about to enter the ring.

"I thought it best, that's all," I said nonchalantly. "Begging off is what they would have expected, and I wasn't about to embarrass us by backing down. These people are all about face. Plus, if I wussed out, it would give them a leg up on you in the summit."

"They mean to kill you! *That* is the advantage they seek over me. And you dare them to do just that. You are the greatest of fools."

Stepping away, she turned her back on me.

Zaylin Twee pushed close and whispered, "Douglas Knoblock is a bit unhinged, as well. He had to be restrained by his men from charging in to take your place. He may yet begin a war by himself."

Good old Dougie.

"Tell him I'm fine. Did Dave and Shasa Karin get on their way?"

"Yes, Warlord. The watch is bare-bones everywhere in the city. My spy smuggled them from the port before twilight."

"Then we've got nothing to worry about. This won't take long, and once I win, with a little extra respect heaped on us, we'll be better placed to get what we want. She'll see. Please, take her out of here."

Zaylin Twee was grim. "Remember when you told me one should speak up when one disagrees with a plan? This is a bad one, Warlord. Have I not heard you say that as an exercise, running promotes cowardice? This is a race! You are in no way trained for such."

"Yee of little faith. Too late now, Zaylin Twee."

"The queen is correct. They will attempt your murder. In front of the entire city and protected by the rules of the competition."

"Not when I do it to them first." I winked.

Her eyes grew wide. "You are not brazen. You are a homicidal opportunist."

"Luck favors the bold. It's called making lemonade out of lemons."

Talis Darmon allowed herself to be led off, but she turned to find me a last time. The woman I knew was back—in her brief glance, hurt, regret, shame, and love gleamed in equal measure. I countered by sending her a farewell of my widest, stupidest grin. She grimaced. I was going for a projection of confidence, but Tranya Olan and Keshin Tellest shot me the same look you'd give a toddler pulling a gift out of his drawers to show to the dinner guests.

I'd only succeeded in looking like a smiling idiot in a big boy diaper. Great.

I turned back to find the yellow giantess was still eying me. The other contestants didn't have marathoner builds, either—all were muscled and coarse, and there was a platoon of them. Of course, there'd be some kind of hand-to-hand nastiness. Nothing I couldn't handle. But just then, the possibility nagged at me that my corner crew's trepidation about my chances was a better assessment of the situation than mine. I gulped down my rising stomach contents.

Maybe I'd let my ego write a check my body couldn't cash.

Nah. I'd whipped a dozen Mydreen bare-handed without breaking a sweat. I could leap a tall building in a single bound. Sorta. And there was always some kind of mayhem implied with this kind of contest.

Mayhem was my specialty.

I was Warlord.

I went back to warming up. No one wore a decipher, so unless they spoke Mihdra or hillbilly English, I couldn't ask anyone a question they could understand. My Spanish was long gone, not that I missed it or that it would've helped me. I'd only just become proficient with my first second-language before we came to Vistara. The boys and I could speak to each other using it, but what was the point? Anyone with a decipher could understand us. Only Dave's Pig Latin fooled a decipher, and if we kept it up long enough, even that nonsense language would reveal its pattern and be translate by the device. I listened in on the banter.

"I hope it's not you and I in the lead, craftsman, but I won't spare you if I get to a weapon first."

"Nor I you, metal smith. Good luck to you out there."

"Good luck to us all to bring what prosperity we can to our clans."

"Even if I secure a relief from the tax, there's no ore left. We've worked the mines empty in Sulla this last year. We'll all be refugees to Aetheria soon."

"Not if my clan beats you there. The Yellow Roamak took all the technicians and fabricators from of our factories, and they sit all but empty, bringing no exchange back to us."

"We work three shifts to strip fertilizer! Never before have we dug so deeply. We reach the dregs of the known deposits. If we don't receive as much back from the Reds in the way of grown food, I don't know what will become of my village."

Sunlight spilled down the ramp to the sands of the stadium as the doors swung wide, and I fell in with the mass of other contestants to trudge out. The chancellor was on her perch.

"The race begins. The rules are firm. No contestant may assist another to complete the race. Leaving the course to attempt a shortcut will be punished. When the skull is held aloft, those on the obelisk place in rank by height of ascension. The first to retrieve the crystal skull wins. Prepare."

The supreme magnate moved to the speaker's stand, hefting a purple silk handkerchief high. The stadium was silent and my heart pounded in my ears. I had no idea what I was supposed to do. Race? Where? The gates at one end of the oval field parted, and soldiers poured in to form a line on either side.

That way.

The silk dropped from her hand and a horn sounded. Before I knew it, my feet moved with a will of their own to join the gush of the runners around me.

I was in the middle of the pack. First to the exit by a dozen body lengths, Xa sprinted like a thoroughbred, roostertails of sand kicking up from her heels. I took a bound over the pack to the gasps of the crowd and landed at a run just behind her. I could overtake her at any time. Piece of cake. All I had to do was stay on the course, and I was guaranteed to win.

Through the gates, the streets were lined with people waving yellow pennants, making the course route obvious. I made my move and took a spring over Xa's head and landed at a full sprint. I made another leap, putting plenty of distance between us, and at the first ninety-degree turn, slowed to check the course ahead.

Something hit me dead over my left eye. My world went temporarily white, and I staggered. More projectiles pelted me and I shielded my face as I weaved to get out of the kill zone while trying to figure out what was happening. The spectators were joyfully hurling rocks. I was blindsided with a kick that sent me flying into the crowd. Xa whizzed past me, dodging rocks as she went. Hands pushed me roughly back into the street and more rocks came at me, the wild pleasure of the missileers with them.

"I got him good, Mama!" a little boy said gleefully.

"Don't waste all your rocks on him, bubba, there are more coming."

More racers caught up and were speeding ahead, the ones on the periphery taking the most abuse as they shielded their faces and poured on the speed. The kid who'd been so proud of landing one on me had followed his mom's advice and saved a nice flat one that barely missed my head.

"Nice aim, kid," I said.

Screw this. I went back to running and bounding, and was quickly leaping over the herd of racers again. More rocks careened in arcs across my path, failing to intercept me as I went into overdrive.

Xa was out front by herself, headed for the citadel wall and the tunnel to the next tier of the city, more soldiers marking the way. Blood gushed down my forehead into my left eye, making me a cyclops. I surged and made up the distance to reach the tunnel only a few seconds behind her. Through the darkness and out into the light, a train broadsided me and I took another tumble. I rolled up but before I got my feet under me, a vicious kick landed on my kidney, and I dropped again. With a sideways view to the world, I watched Xa take off to the cheers of all.

No rocks pelted me, and I took a second over bent knees to retch out the morning's feast, as the body of the pack pounded the pavement to fly past me. I had my breath again, and was off. I caught up to them, but stayed to the back, wary of the crowds of yellow flags ahead. When nothing came flying at the pack from the multitudes, I did another spring over them, and set my sights on catching Xa. I had a maneuver custom-made for her ass. The next wall was in the distance and with a huge lead, Xa was halfway down the straightaway to the next tunnel.

I poured it on, my lungs and legs burning as I closed the distance. Soldiers held frenzied spectators out of the way of the entrance, and she was just reaching their cordon when I launched. I landed with both feet square between her shoulder blades. She crashed to the ground, a one-giant pileup. I stayed on her, bending my knees deeply to dump all my momentum down through her and into the stone pavement. The best Martian chiropractor couldn't have gotten more cracks out of her spine, and she made the groan of a beached seal. Very satisfying.

"Payback's a bitch, huh?" I said before I sprang away.

Paraplegics can't lay an ambush.

I knew to be gun-shy for some kind of surprise on the other side of the tunnel, and braced as I broke into the sunlight, my arms ready to ward off the welcome of whatever flurry of things to come. When they didn't, I pumped my arms hard to power my sprint down the street. Up a slight hill, I was at full speed when I broke into the intersection. I blew through the crowd, bodies flying from my collision, the rest scattering. The course had made a ninety-degree turn, but I couldn't stop in time. Pissed off spectators shrieked.

"Kill him. Kill him! He leaves the route. Cheater. Cheater!"

A black-uniformed spearman lunged at me. I barely stepped out of the way, caught the shaft at the limit of his lunge, and tore it away. Another came at me. I parried with my own, gave his thigh a quick swipe with the tip, and was rewarded with a howl. I threw the spear down as I turned and blasted off in the correct direction. I glanced behind me as I ran.

Xa was gaining on me.

If I thought she looked mad before, the way her narrowed eyes fixed me as she pumped arms and kicked heels made me reconsider my life choices. I'd taken out Tarns with less than I'd given her. I directed full attention ahead and kicked into high gear. I had the hang of it now.

The secret was, don't get caught by the Amazon, don't blow through any more human barriers, and I had it made.

I ran down yet another endless street, and it occurred to me that this city was much larger on the ground than it seemed from the air. And as to what everyone else in the city who didn't have a seat in the stadium was up to? They were on the streets where the real action was. I came to a long stretch leading to the next tunnel and knew there was something up.

Where were the flag-waving, cheering mobs?

Spear-wielding guards hugged the walls of the apartments on either side, backed away from the thoroughfare, the rabid throngs conspicuously absent.

I stutter-stepped to slow as the spearman lowered tips to menace me, and something exploded at my feet, showering my legs in shards. I skipped to one side, dodged the jab of a spear, just as another piece of air mail crashed onto the street in front of me. It was a clay tile. Behind the parapets of the roofs appeared squat figures, all hefting square pieces of roof overhead and aiming for me.

It did seem like a good time. Why sit in the stands and watch others shed blood, when you could do it yourself? I varied my course, hopping as unpredictably and fast as I could through the gauntlet, and was clear. I hobbled to a stop and checked my legs. Sharp clay fragments peppered my shins and rivulets of blood streamed down them. I jogged off, wincing as I did.

The next tunnel lay ahead. Through it, the route veered left to a street curving to parallel the citadel wall. Thick crowds cheered my appearance, and I searched their hands for rocks and the roofs for ambushers. Seemingly without extra risks, I picked up my pace again as best I could.

But I was slowing. My breath was heavy and my head was light.

After another winding street where I almost repeated the deadly mistake of blowing the turn, the terrain opened up and ahead was the park I'd once landed in. In the widest clearing, reviewing stands were

packed with spectators, standing, pointing, and cheering in my direction.

"There's the first! It's the foreigner!" Yellow pennants waved furiously. The route between the standing crowds indicated the way ahead
passed between the stands. The grass cushioned my footfalls, and I was
able to add a little more speed.

I followed the curving path into the field created by the reviewing
stands and slid to a halt. Palisades of sharpened poles stacked twenty
feet high blocked the way out of the area. It was the end of the line.
Maybe there was some maze through it? In two big hops—much easier
than running—I landed short to keep from impaling myself on a stake.
The roar of the crowd on both sides was so loud I couldn't think. My
left eye remained blind, and I wiped at the dried blood sealing the lid
shut, hoping to alleviate my handicap.

A searing pain and a *whoosh* brought me out of my daze. A spear
shaft bounced, rattling off the palisade ahead. I whirled.

At the opposite end of the field, Xa recovered from her spear throw.
Leering at her close-but-no-cigar handiwork, she spat. The burn of a
wound across my shoulder completed the picture. She sprinted to a
rack of weapons. I suddenly realized I'd blown past several of them on
each side of the field. She chose a wicked-looking halberd and turned
to find me again, but I was gone. Already in the air, I bounded for the
nearest rack on the opposite side of the field.

"Now it's a show! The foreigner's got a sword!"

I had a jagged two-handed blade as long as me, the first thing that
had come into my grasp. Xa made a run for me, but then—like some
gift from the heavens—a rock whizzed out of nowhere, hit her on the
side of the head, and toppled her. At the end of the field, another gladiator was loading a rock into a sling to wind up for another shot, this
time at me.

In no time, what remained of the pack poured onto the field, dashing for the racks to arm themselves. What followed was a free-for-all.
Every man against every man. I fought singles and pairs, parrying,
thrusting, spinning to watch my own back, dodging and leaping away

from and into whomever I could, until a loud whistle blew. Rifle-bearing guards stepped onto the field and fired into the air.

"Back to the course, all of you!" a commanding voice yelled.

The palisades parted. I threw down my sword and bounded. I'd picked up another dozen pinks and minor slashes from pointed and edged weapons, but none of them had laid me open. I couldn't say the same for some of the others. They wouldn't finish the race. I'd lost track of where Xa was.

The course led through another tunnel in the citadel wall, back toward the outer tiers of the city. Perhaps the melee in the park had marked the halfway point. I could only hope. The return leg was less eventful, but my energy was seeping out with the streams of my blood, and for the first time I could remember in a very long time, my lungs couldn't keep with my muscles' demand for air. I'd given up on running as exercise. My bad. Still, I should've been doing better, being from O-2-poor Mihdradahl.

If I hadn't been so faint, I might've wondered how it was that Xa was in close pursuit and seemed to be gaining.

I rallied as the heights of the stadium grew closer until they finally passed above me. The obelisk lay ahead. The mouths of the crowds were open like whales feeding on krill, but I heard nothing except my own wheezing. A last spring and I landed at the base of the tower. It was not as smooth as it looked from a distance. Finger and toeholds sprouted along the sides. All routes up looked the same. I started climbing and was a dozen feet up when a grasp took my ankle and yanked. I pushed away from the surface, passing a grimacing Xa on the way down. I landed with both feet and knees locked together, and rolled up to see Xa climbing. A few more runners entered the stadium, but for now it was just her and I at the black tower. I could spring for her and give her the same treatment she'd given me, but instead chose a different face, took a breath, and leaped with all my might.

I made it halfway up the forty-foot tower and amazed even myself by landing a grip with both sets of fingers. On a good day, I might have been able to make it to the top in one bound.

This was not one of those days.

All I had to do was not be hasty, keep a steady pace and find secure holds for my climb, and I would win.

I reached the next taper, the pinnacle of the obelisk in sight. The finger ledge on my right hand made a *click* and a stiletto blade shot from the wall at my face. It was square, tapered, and dull on everything but the tip. I got a very good look at it, protruding an inch from my eye. Had I been shorter, it would've gotten me in the chest.

From around the face of the tower, Xa's long muscled arm swung at me, a small knife in her grip. I batted it away and heaved myself higher to land a foothold on the spike. I spotted the peak of the obelisk and scurried up. I expected to trigger another spring-loaded stiletto with every handhold, but never did. I reached the summit, alone. I balanced on a flat ledge just wide enough to stand on, staring at the red crystal mound in front of me.

Xa sprang onto the summit. From her loincloth, she pulled the small knife and, in one continuous slash, tried for the move that would spill my guts. I sucked my stomach in, threw my hips back and my chest forward. I pinned her backslash with both hands, rolled her wrist as she fought to keep her balance, and took the knife. In an ice pick grip, I stabbed downward. A hand shot under my vision to grasp my throat. Her arm deflected my stab to her neck, and I dragged the blade along the same arm. I sawed inefficiently downward over her bicep. The flesh and muscle peeled away and beneath it, a smooth metal gray bone fell exposed, the edge of the blade tinking off her metal skeleton.

She grinned, unaffected by my filet job, blood seeping down her face from the many gashes she wore. I dropped the knife and drove both thumbs into her eye sockets until they would go no deeper. Her grip released. I pushed, and she was gone.

Alone on the tower, I swayed and almost followed her off. I crouched and put both hands on the garnet-red crystal and for the first time, could see it clearly. It was in the shape of a Tarn skull. I hoisted it from its cradle to hold overhead.

A horn blared, but I didn't hear it. I plopped onto the tiny flat the skull had occupied, cradling the heavy stone, and waited. I became aware when a flitter floated next to me, and arms pulled me off the obelisk and onto the deck. It was a short, floating ride down. Hands hefted me to my feet, the prize still in my hands.

The same hands guided me over the sands. The Heavenly Guard were forming ahead, but I had nothing left to fight them with. The chancellor stood at their lead. They parted, and out stepped the supreme magnate. She opened palms to me, and I placed the crystal skull in her hands, bowed without toppling over, then took a retreating step back.

My hearing returned, and I was drowned in the storm of the cheers of thousands. The giantesses and the purple-robed empress evaporated, and the sands flooded with people pouring from the stands. I was hoisted on desert-camouflaged shoulders, and Doug was propping me up from behind.

"Holy shit, Ben. Holy shit! They broadcast whole thing into the stadium. I thought you were a goner. Incredible, dude!"

My world narrowed to one of the black tunnels I'd run through, until only a tiny dot of light remained, and everything faded to a heavy blanket of night.

21

I WAS ON A LITTER IN THE CELLS BENEATH THE STADIUM, THE SMELLS OF the sawdust floor, blood, and sweat thick in my nostrils.

"Get the hell back, Bryant."

I opened my eyes to see Doug's hand on Bryant's chest.

"Easy, Knoblock, easy. I brought my aid bag. The imperial physician is on her way."

A tussle was underway between our troops and Yellow Roamak trying to break the protective cordon around me.

I croaked out, "Let 'im in, Dougie. S'alright."

Bryant kneeled by my head. "Colt, goddamn! That was something. This is going to work out!"

Eidolon Sah was in my other ear. "The supreme magnate is beaming. I have never seen her so flushed. This is most auspicious."

I was confused. "How? I mean, I killed Xa…" At least, I thought I had. What I did to her would've killed me. Had I seen metal where a bone should've been?

The first consort clucked. "The supreme magnate won a treasury's worth. Brandon Bryant sent word that she would be wise to bet all her holdings on you. When my friend assured me you would easily win, I hesitated, but the odds on you were forty to one! It was a once-in-a-lifetime opportunity. I also have a hoard waiting to be collected. No one has ever seen such an upset occur in the race. What excitement!"

"Glad not to disappoint, thanks for the confidence, Bryant," I said, sucking air as he sprinkled Quickclot on my gashes and pressed a field dressing onto my shoulder.

Bryant grinned. "You almost screwed the pooch a couple times, but you pulled through. I made a bundle, too, Colt. Good going, not showing off before the odds were set. You totally sandbagged them."

Doug reached across my supine body to shove the kneeling Bryant onto his ass. "Get the hell away with that shit, Bryant. You're such a bravo foxtrot. You offered Ben up for this, don't deny it."

Yellow Roamak sprang to hold Doug, two women per arm. He grinned as he flexed, lifting them all off their feet. Bryant rocked up, waving hands wildly. "It's okay, it's okay. Release him, Roamak."

Sophena Pah's voice pierced the scene. "Withdraw, Roamak."

Doug looked disappointed as he let the women down and they stepped aside, daggers shooting from their eyes.

Bryant dusted himself off. "Same old Dougie. Knoblock, believe what you want. This whole thing was a surprise to me, too. I just went with it and made the best call I could. And it paid off. Most important-ly, it paid off for the supreme magnate. Gambling is about the only vice allowed around here, and the old girl hasn't had a big hit in a while. We're all going to be better off now."

I raised to my elbows. "It was you, Tourmaline. I saw you putting a bug in her ear."

Sophena Pah ignored me. "Come, Brandon Bryant. There is work to be done."

"That's my boy, Colt. You didn't let me down." Bryant shot me a thumbs-up, and I fell back as black uniforms departed and the ring of our camouflaged soldiers closed around my litter again.

"Where's Talis Darmon?"

Doug said, "Last I saw, she was herded off with the dragon lady and all her Amazons. The local bonesetter's here." He dropped close. "Bro, your friend's with her."

I rallied back to my elbows, anxious to find Sister Wavecrest. A stern-looking woman in yellow robes came through the parting of des-ert-clad warriors, and erupted, "What idiocy has been inflicted on my patient? Poultices soaked in urine? Unguents of mud and spit? Aiyee!"

She threw off her outer coat and with a palm on my forehead, forced me down. I surrendered.

"Even an animal deserves better treatment than this. First, I must undo what has been done. A Tarn's neglect would have been better than this Red affront to medicine. Left as is, these wounds would fester in a day." She fiddled with bottles from her satchel, laying them out on a bench.

Karlo and her would get on like old classmates.

A sensation like a spring breeze filled my nostrils with renewal, and I opened my eyes. Sister Wavecrest was over me. She smiled and my pain lifted like fog beneath the sun.

"Warlord Benjamin Colt, how is it with you?"

I checked around me. A wall of Red soldiers protected me, no black uniforms in sight.

"It is safe to speak, Warlord. Physician Terellah Sansen is a friend, my only confidante. You may trust her."

Her presence brought me strength. I couldn't remember her Annamese name. Whispering, partly from fear of being heard, partly because I was spent, I said, "Sister Wavecrest, Talis Darmon is dying. Your sister said there wasn't anyone but you who could help her."

Her eyes welled sympathy. "There was great distress in your lady's aura. It was not the life force of the person I had so long imagined meeting. It was the discordant energy of one engaged in a tumultuous struggle. There was a churn of darkness in her that should not be. She has been sundered in two by the Whites, has she not?"

"How did you know?"

"What transpired in Mihdradahl was reported in council. There has been much debate as to what it all means. But in our brief contact, her soul spoke to me with clarity. The Great Forlorn calls her, and her will to resist it is almost spent."

I grunted as the doctor vigorously scrubbed my legs, cursing at my wounds as she worked. "What filth is this on these wounds? Ridiculous." I ignored the new pain as she continued her assault.

"I knew you'd understand, Sister Wavecrest. Can you help her?"

She sighed, her shoulders drooping. "I believe so, but it will require circumstances so difficult to arrange, I cannot conceive how to affect them."

"Can't you arrange a visit for her to your shrine?"

"It is not there where her cure lies. Only in the Tears of Oceania can she be made whole again. Allow my touch, and I will show you what is required."

She moved to cradle my head between her hands, bending deeply until her sweet breath blanketed my face and eased the pain in the wound over my eye.

"Look into my eyes and allow me to see you."

I swam in the pools of her amethyst eyes, and I smelled the salt of the ocean, tasted the water, and felt the summer warmth of the Gulf of Mexico bathe me as I floated in their waters.

After an eternity, I saw her again.

"This is where I must take her. Do you now understand?"

I did. Just the image of the pool of pure, lavender waters had filled me with calm and resilience. My aches were gone. If this is where Talis Darmon had to go, I'd get her there. "Where is this place?"

"Far from here. It would take many days travel, which is why I am confounded. If I cannot bathe her in those waters, I cannot conceive how to cleanse her. Her soul shrinks to a point so diminished, the hour of its death looms."

My wounds were sealed by the crinkled glue of some bandage. The doctor muscled her way in. "Let me attend his head, Amelyn Tōpara. Your work can do nothing more on a skull this thick."

She set to scrubbing the laceration over my eye. I gasped, and she scolded me as she produced a needle and thread.

"This needs the same mending as did the deep wound on your shoulder. Fearless you were, fighting that abomination to all flesh, yet a tiny needle makes you cringe! Stop being a baby and lie still while I sew it, or you may lose an eye."

Karlo cussed us the same way when he worked to repair the result of stupidity, as if we'd earned the injury and therefore also the derision. When she was done, I sat up, a little woozy, but better.

"I have a way to fly us there and back, maybe before anyone would even know we were gone. We have to try. I just need to get you and her to our fleet."

Doug said, "The royal barge flies out nightly to rotate fresh troops to the air armada. No sweat."

Sister Wavecrest shook her head. "You do not understand, Warlord. Even by air, the journey there and back would be many days. How to disguise our absence for so long, I cannot fathom."

"I can have us halfway around the planet in a day. If the Tears of Oceania are anywhere in Annameria, I can get us there in hours."

Doug snorted. "You look like you came out second in a hatchet fight, dude. You aren't in piloting shape."

Terellah Sansen spoke. "He is a beast of the field. I deem him ready for service. The festivities will rage on and tomorrow is Purging Day. Few will be on their feet. If ever there were a time of distraction, surely this is it. I will be tending the headaches and ill stomachs of all the imperial court and first caste. This one, I can exempt from sight by admitting to my infirmary. Perhaps the queen needs to be indisposed as well? For a diplomat extraordinaire, she seems to be ill company. All have commented on how sullen and remote she seems. The celebration is not in her honor. If she were to take her leave, it might even be greeted with relief."

The doc was suddenly knee-deep in our conspiracy.

Sister Wavecrest smiled. "I told you, she is my confidante. As for me, the supreme magnate does not require my sustained attendance at such events. Once the celebration is underway and the spirit of imbibing spread, I can maneuver to remove Talis Darmon. If she begs ill, then my departure to escort her away will not be thought unusual."

The physician was packing up. "I will assist in this charade. The supreme magnate will be in her cups and think little of it. As for Sophena Pah and her Yellow Roamak, I can browbeat them into retreat. I have treated all of them for numerous ailments, many of them of an embarrassing nature. They conceal from others the rites of their secret sisterhood of pain. All of them would be loath to question my judgment and anger me."

"There's going to be a shindig for the men," Doug said. "Red and Yellow soldiers celebrating together. Fuhgeddaboudit. If it's like any other host country event I've been to, it'll be drinking games and all kinds of shenanigans to see who's the toughest. We can keep a lot of eyes on us while you guys do your thing."

"But you'll coordinate the handoff?"

"Nothing but a thang. The ladies'll have to go disguised as gear. I've got a couple of big duffels that'll hide them. Won't be comfortable, but last night's escorts weren't too curious about anything when we ferried out the crews."

Sister Wavecrest was still troubled. "But how is it that you are so certain we can travel so swiftly?"

I swayed a little as I stood, thought better of it, and propped against the litter to let the dizziness pass. "Because our uniquely Thulian-produced half-Italian, half-Cherokee genius and his eternally pissed-off, half-crazy Vistaran hermit partner produce genuine miracles."

✹ ✹ ✹

I was littered to the hospital, and it required no acting on my part to play the casualty. The physician and I were alone.

"Eat. Let my medics attend you. Your compatriot will come soon to see you escorted to join your soldiers. I will be in the grand hall with the council and the first caste. The festivities have already commenced, so it may not be long before you make your departure. Rest while you can. I wish you luck."

I slept for a while, tended by Terellah Sansen's medics, not a Yellow Roamak in sight. I awoke to Doug's voice. "Up and at 'em, Adam Ant." The sun had set. "Here. Got a change of clothes for you." He handed me a set of desert fatigues. "The streets are full of drunks. Soon as I get you delivered, I'm back to the barracks. Gonna have to break sobriety, but since it's a mission necessity, it'll be a freebie on my count of clean days. Can't stand out, you know—it'd be suspicious."

"I won't rat you out to Shalees Parn."

"She'd understand. Sure you're going to be okay?"

The wooziness was gone, but there was a vice squeezing my skull. "Good to go. What's the movement plan?"

"I've got a private for a driver who's like any Joe—anxious to get his orderly duties done so he can get to the party. We've got one more detour to make. Your lavender pinup smuggled a note for me to give to the driver. Tells him we're picking up supplies from the mess on the way to the port. The ladies are supposed to be waiting in the kitchen."

I followed him to the truck, two squads of Guards and soldiers in the back. He put me in back and jumped in the passenger seat next to the driver. "Take us here on our way to the port." He thrust the note to the driver.

Annoyed, the driver said, "I don't understand your gibberish, Red."

Doug tapped the note.

After the driver read it, he sighed and lifted. "Be quick about it. I want to get back before all the best stuff's gone. My mates said they'll save me a plate, but they never do."

We floated through back alleys and stopped at a service entrance. The driver thumbed. "I'm not your slave. Form your own work detail. Be quick, now!"

I jumped out with Doug and a half dozen troops. Crates and kegs were stacked, and Terellah Sansen was there, waving us to her as she commanded the detail with a vexed tone.

"Barbarians. Enjoy the fruits of the people's labor and give thanks to the supreme magnate for her benevolence and pity as you do. Off with you. I have many injured drunks to attend to. There'll be no feasting or drink for me."

I squatted to lift a crate, and she whispered, "Mind the casks."

Loaded, we glided away. Guards waved us through the tunnel checkpoints and soon enough we pulled into the port. The royal barge waited, and at the gangplank stood Brandon Bryant and a squad of black-uniformed goons.

"Going somewhere, Doug? Lemme guess. Colt's in the back. I knew this was some bullshit." As one, his troops leveled guns our way. "Think I'm stupid? Just the time to try a sneak attack on us when everyone's partying."

I eased out of the back to join Doug, my hands held wide.

"And there he is. I got word the second you left the infirmary. Colt, I played straight with you, and now you're blowing it."

I swallowed all my pride. "I am playing it straight. I told you I needed your help. I just thought it best to save you the exposure. I need to make a milk run, and I'll be back before sunup. That's all."

"What kind of errand?"

"Can we talk alone?"

"Keep your troops where they are, Knoblock," Bryant ordered. Doug scowled, but stood fast and relayed the order. Bryant pulled me aside. "What are you pulling, Colt?"

I had no choice. "I've got Sister Wavecrest and Talis Darmon hidden with those supplies. We're going to load on the barge with the crew rotation, and once we're out there, I'm flying the three of us to a place where Sister Wavecrest says she can help my wife. Talis Darmon's very ill and our only chance to get her better is to let Sister Wavecrest take her to a place where she can treat her."

He frowned. "She seemed off. Where's this place?"

"She's going to guide me there. It's somewhere south, down the Furrow and inland."

He shook his head. "Best I can do is take you all back and we pretend none of this ever happened."

"Bryant. She's dying."

"And keeping her alive helps me how?"

I blistered inside, but kept my rage in check.

"You need her alive. To get what you and Sophena Pah want. It'll take her to convince the supreme magnate to cooperate. She's going to let you bring your whole army into Mihdradahl to take out the Whites. Whatever's there—the ray-killer, the environment shield—it's all yours."

"Sophena Pah thinks we just do it without your permission, Colt."

"If we don't make it back, you'll never make it past the Furrow. Our ADA will knock down every one of your ships. We may not have much of a ground army left, but we outgun you in every other way. That's not what we want, Bryant. It's not what you want."

I waited while he bargained with himself. "How are you going to get wherever this is and back before anyone knows you're gone? You've got another secret, don't ya?"

I nodded. "I do. We have hypersonic flight capability. I can get us there and back before anyone wakes up from their hangover. It's our best opportunity."

The smirk I hated more than anything was back.

"I know you. You wouldn't risk your stuck-up queen with a half-ass plan for all the tea in China. Or that purple bitch you're so enamored of. Okay. You can go. But with one small provision.

"I'm going with you. Whatever secret your priestess has, if it's more ancient weapons or some kind of tech that'll give Sophena Pah and I leverage, then I'm getting read in."

Some bargains with the devil are made for more than your own soul.

"Deal."

22

I PULLED THE LID OFF THE CASK. SHE ACCEPTED MY HAND WITHOUT recoiling and let me lift her onto the deck. In starlight, she looked as ghostly as she sounded. Unsubstantial. Distant. Wispy.

"Benjamin Colt, it was as if I had stepped into her box again. The lid closed and I was in darkness. I tried to picture our child. I tried to remember your face. I once knew how to form a blockade to my fears. But the weight of the blackness fell on me, and the stifling heaviness of the air grew worse. I found escape only in the call of the Furrow. I am falling. Let me go." She collapsed.

Sister Wavecrest was there to help me catch her.

"I must anchor the thread of her attachment. It unravels faster. We must hurry."

"Almost there," Doug said over my shoulder.

The royal barge slid next to the service tender, the next largest ship in our armada after the ostentatious luxury craft. Doug was over the side before the ships were tied together, barking orders to crewmen. I cradled her and was ready as the bulwarks opened and the walkway extended.

On the rear deck of the tender, Doug and the crew pulled off the tarp to reveal the Black Widow. Twelve meters long, pointed like a bullet, a black so dull it resisted even the light of the stars and rising moons, she was a wonder.

"Karlo," Bryant breathed wistfully as he shook his head. "It was a mistake I didn't work harder to keep him happy. Hey! Get your hands off me!"

From behind him, Doug levitated Bryant in his grasp, pinning arms at his sides. Joined together, Doug plowed forward, releasing Bryant in time to ram him chest first against a crate. Pinning him between the shoulder blades with one arm, Doug tugged the sidearm from Bryant's holster and tossed it to a soldier.

"I'm the one you gotta worry about making happy, chief. Because every time I think about Marky shoving a gun in my face and you laughing, I wanna do this." He bear-hugged Bryant from behind again, heaved him off his feet, and walked to the edge of the deck.

"Colt!" Bryant screamed, kicking and fighting to get free.

"Okay, Dougie. Enough. Please."

Doug halted in his tracks, dumped Bryant on his belly, put a knee to his back and swept his body, producing only a small knife, which he tossed over the side as he stood up.

"Just so you know, Bryant. You or any of your Yellow stooges points a gun at me again, they better use it. Ben says you can go with him, fine. But he don't come back, or you pull some other kind of shit, don't bet that Karlo won't let me WMD your whole goddamn continent." He reached out a hand, which Bryant accepted, and hefted him to his feet.

"Remember what it means to be SF," Doug growled. "Or at least, act like a human being. That's all I'm gonna say. I'll take her, Ben. You get the Black Widow prepped."

I passed my wife into Doug's arms, Sister Wavecrest flowing in to feel Talis Darmon's forehead.

"Bryant, come with me. Take the right seat," I said as I bent to climb in. Bryant did as I asked, slinking past Doug as though Thor might change his mind and bring down the thunder. I started my checklist as he belted in.

"I'm not trying to rile you up, Colt, but… you're no jet pilot."

"I'm the closest thing to one on Mars. You can stay behind. Won't hurt my feelings."

He seemed to consider it. "I want to see whatever it is Amelyn Tōpara is hiding. Plus, you wouldn't risk *her*. What's wrong with her, anyway?"

I ignored him as Doug hollered, "Ready to button you up, Ben."

"We don't make it, you know what to do, Doug."

"It's all copacetic, bro-man."

I knew it would be. Doug would make sure to retrieve Dave and Shasa Karin from Annameria before he took our contingent home and to safety, ready to prosecute a war against all fronts as best he could. The hatch sealed and Doug's fist pounded the fuselage to tell me I was clear to lift.

"Are you ready, Sister Wavecrest? Where are we headed?" I asked.

She was cross-legged on the deck, Talis Darmon's head cradled in her lap.

"Follow the course of the Furrow in the direction of the sunset." Her eyes were closed in concentration. "You know the home of my sister in Shelasa. Ta-Far is as ancient, but unlike my sister's home, it shelters no remnant of my own people. The guardian of the harbor once stood facing his brothers across the Amethyst Sea. When last I saw him, he remained in silent vigil. Get us there, and I will guide you further."

I strapped on my helmet and pulled down the PVS-31s. "There's a set for you beneath the seat, Bryant." I eased us up and away from the deck of the tender.

"Colt, you go blasting off, it's going to raise a ruckus. Not everyone is drunk or asleep."

I continued to ease us to sink slowly deeper into the canyon. "Give me some credit. We're creeping out of here like the mystery gang before I light this candle. Your people run any ground patrols in the Furrow?"

"Hell, no. The only thing ever down there were Vermeel, and the Yellows wiped out every Tarn for a thousand miles around a very long time ago."

"What about coastal observation?"

"Not so much. You get us a good forty klicks south, the last city near the Furrow is Pella. We have outposts in the surrounding workers' villages that provide the labor for the factories, but it's a banishment posting. They keep the workers in. There's nothing to keep out. Everything past that's wasteland."

He caught himself. "Now, don't go thinking I gave you intel on where to attack us. Before you take your leave to go north, I'll have a division parked across our southwest flank, bet on it."

"The thought never crossed my mind, Bryant. Got your NODs on?"

"This helmet fits perfect. Can't be Doug's."

"It was Mitch's."

He should've been able to guess. Doug had chastised him to remember what it meant to be SF. When he didn't say anything in the way of regret or remembrance for our teammate, I put it away for another time. "I'm going to hug the face of the canyon until we're far enough past any observation posts to get some altitude. Then I need you to help me navigate and spot for landmarks."

"Can do."

The console was the usual panels of stones, but along with the more conventional yokes for control, there was a very simple air speed indicator and chronometer mounted. I did some fourth-grade math as we coasted along, and when the clock reached my countdown, I set us on a gentle rising trajectory.

"We should be clear. I'm taking us up."

We rose high with the plains to our port side, and I leveled us off. "Here we go." I swept the forward vector controls and watched the indicator climb. "Air's so thin, there're no sonic booms. If anyone looks up, all they'll see is a tiny dark blob against the stars, and they won't see it for long."

Bryant lifted his NODs to focus on the gauges. "Two thousand miles an hour! That's impossible."

The ride was smooth as glass. It was time for my tease.

"You fly a flitter, right? Want to learn to drive this beast? It's not much different."

I'd gotten his interest.

"The air cars are pretty basic," he said casually, "like steering a fishing boat. But I think I can handle this. You know, I got pretty good at flying a little bird. One deployment, our team had support from the 160th. One of the rotor heads was an old teammate of mine before he got the flying bug. He let me have a lot of stick time. Heck, I'm probably the most experienced pilot on Mars."

Leave it to Bryant to make it sound like he was more entitled to fly than the guy offering to teach him.

"Take the yoke." I coached him through the basics. "On the way back, I'll put you through the whole program. It's easy."

Bryant was captured.

"If Karlo could invent us a GPS so it wasn't all dead reckoning and celestial navigation, we'd be golden. This is a game changer, Colt."

The lure was jigging in front of him. I'd set the hook before the sun came up. With temporary simpatico, it was like we were teammates again. I let him keep the controls as I searched the terrain. It was flat, and the undulations of the canyon edge stood out against the depths in sharp cutouts. At thirty minutes, I took the controls and eased us back to a crawl. Our best flitters moved out like Grandpa's fifty-year-old Buick. This was faster than a 230-grain bullet from my MK 22.

"We should be near. Help me keep an eye out."

"What are we looking for?"

"It'll be a dry harbor. There should be ruins around it of the old city. There! Something's coming into view."

Rising above the everything around it, a monolith stood out. As we neared, the moons shone on the stone colossus.

"Sister Wavecrest, can you come look?" I lifted my chin to peer below my NODs. Even without them, the giant guardian was visible, as were the outlines of a crumbled city.

"I never knew this was even here," Bryant said. "I don't know if anyone does. No one comes this far."

Her head poked in between ours. "It is a place the supreme magnates have all protected. They believe in nothing but their own omnipotence, but even they must acknowledge and respect what once was." She gasped. "And the guardian outlasts them, standing against the ravages of time!"

It straddled the mouth of the dry harbor, as the Colossus of Rhodes was purported to have done, but didn't. The helmet dangled in one hand, a double-edged sword was held horizontally in the other, the flat of the short blade touching the forehead in reverent salute. He wasn't a menacing watchman. He was a hardened soldier, rendering honor to welcome the dutiful weary on their return home.

"The monuments in Shelasa are just wrecks, but even so, they were nothing like this," I said. I put us in a wide bank over the drifts and shambles.

She brought the dream below to life for us. "The glow from the lanterns in his eyes hailed sailors from across Oceania. Ta-Far was a city that never slept, bustling with energy and activity at all times beneath the light of the guardian."

I could almost see the ships in her harbor and feel the warm breezes blowing off shore.

"Where to next?"

She pointed past me. "The twin peaks in the distance. Aim for them. It is not far. It was but an hour's ride on arkall. There will be a ravine that once was a river, and you will find a wide chasm along its path. It is there we find the well of tears."

"How is she?" I asked as I set us on the new bearing.

"Make haste, Warlord." She disappeared.

"Colt, 'fess up. What the hell's wrong with her?"

I gave him the abbreviated version of what the Great Forlorn was, and how the Whites had infected her with their weapon.

"So, if the Aztecs don't get enough virgins to volunteer to have their hearts ripped out, they zap them with their mind-bug. How do they do it? Is it some kind of ray?"

"We don't know. But they've got to be dealt with once and for all or none of us is safe."

"And they tipped their hand by taking her? Didn't know what they were getting themselves in for, huh? You must've kicked the shit out of them. Three guys. In and out hostage rescue. Impressive. But, I get it. Not enough to take on a whole city by yourselves. But if you had their ship, why didn't you just go back and waste them with their own weapon? Why'd you give it back? Why didn't you make *them* fix her. You had hostages."

"It's complicated, Bryant. It was Talis Darmon's decision to negotiate a peace with them, with the threat that we'd come calling if they broke the truce. We didn't know what they'd done to her until a lot later. Then we figured out the Great Forlorn was their doing all along."

"Why didn't you at least keep the ship?"

"It was no good to us. We couldn't crack the tech. Plus, we figured your spies would know what we were up to, and it might precipitate an invasion."

Bryant humphed. "I mighta played it differently, but I see your logic. Mars. What a shit show this has been."

For a second, I thought he had a mea culpa for me.

The moment was broken when he said, "That's gotta be the river, eleven o'clock." He pointed. "Looks like a fault line."

I turned to put the terrain feature on his side and headed upriver. Bryant kept his attention on our course.

"You know what screwed up the U.S. so badly? Having so much hidden from the people who actually made the whole country work. The hair lips? Someone knew more than they were telling, right from the get-go. If we'd stood up to the overeducated, brain-dead losers who were running things a long time ago, we'd still be on Earth."

I let him go on. It was an insight into his pathology. He saw himself not as a dictator in the making, but as an enlightened reformer of everything that was wrong with the world we came from and the land of our birth.

"I'm not satisfied to let any secret stay buried on this rock, Colt. I wanna see whatever's down there, and I wanna crack open whatever the freaks at the north pole got buried. I'm not saying Sophena Pah and I can force things to go the way you want it to, but if your queen can make a convincing case to Grandma, we'll help by pushing as hard as we're able without risking the dance of remorse. Fair enough?"

"Fair enough," I gave him.

We both spotted the widening in the fault.

"That's gotta be it, Colt."

I flew over the chasm. The moons were still low, the widening gap in the fault just a lake of shadow. I made a low racetrack around it and spotted the lines of something manmade on one shore. I set us down.

"What happens next?" Bryant asked as he unbuckled.

"We do what she tells us." With Talis Darmon cradled in my arms, the dark pit waited.

Sister Wavecrest breathed the night air deeply. "The salt of her living tears touches my memory. Follow."

I kept my NODs down, but she set off with steps as sure as if she walked them in daylight. Low walls guided to a path, and stairs descended along the edge of the basin into the bottomless canyon. I hugged the wall with a shoulder as I learned the steps one by one. I was about to halt for fear of tripping and say we needed a light, when Sister Wavecrest spoke in a singsong chant and a faint glow came from the walls.

"Use your own eyes, Warlord, to see what no other has seen besides one of the sisterhood."

"I got 'em," Bryant said as he tipped my goggles up for me. His were already up. "This you gotta see."

As the chasm deepened, the bowl also widened on all sides, the lips above us far narrower than the space they sheltered. The narrow clefts of the canyon tapered on either end to let in only a sliver of the night sky. The stairs continued down, and on the next landing, I turned to carefully peer over the edge.

There was a shimmer of starlight on water far below us. At the farthest end of the Furrow we'd witnessed the rising lake. There had been Cynar's underground rivers. Even found a black subterranean sea at the center of the planet.

I smelled brine. If all the other waters of Vistara were rare diamonds, what did that make this reservoir of the last remnants of the Amethyst Sea? Unobtanium?

I followed her down one span after another, until the opening above us was a tiny swathe of stars. The smell of minerals and salt grew stronger, and the sound of our footfalls echoed off the pool below. The lagoon was as wide as the basin, a smooth stone shore reached from the bottom of the stairs to its edge. As she stepped onto the landing, pale stones came alive around us.

"The Tears of Oceania, the last well of the Amethyst Sea. It is kept alive by the essence of my sisters, all departed save for myself and the last mother of our order. Here, too, will we someday add our life force to join theirs, and know the bliss of its waters."

Sister Wavecrest waded into the pool and opened her arms wide. "Bring her to me, Warlord."

I eased the unconscious Talis Darmon into her arms. "Here she will be kissed by their touch. If she hears their call, she will know the way back." She waded into the waters until Talis Darmon floated. The soothing aura of lilacs that I'd anticipated awakened at last to bathe them both. As if responding to her, the waters answered with the same glow, and the surface rippled with a current from some deep source.

I trusted Sister Wavecrest, but fear struck me as she released Talis Darmon from her arms. Her supine body floated effortlessly, perfectly suspended like an angel asleep on a cloud. Sister Wavecrest moved to placed hands on her floating temples. I watched her fingertips melt beneath the short black locks and felt the memory of the same touch, as hers penetrated deeper into Talis Darmon's tissues.

I paid no attention to Bryant's mumbled amazement. At a loss for words from what we witnessed, his sounds of genuine awe angered me and tainted my hope. I'd waited so long, dreaming of this moment, and he was spoiling it.

He was evil. As malevolent and deceitful as any demon. Then I thought of my own deceptions and manipulations, and suddenly, I felt as unworthy as him to be here. I became mindful of my own ugliness and failures. In the presence of such magnificent beauty, I was ashamed to be the callous, cruel, and vengeful soul I was. By no other grace than Talis Darmon's love could I ever be witness to such reason-defying splendor.

To make amends for my defilement, I concentrated all the goodness I could find with me, wishing I too could form an aura around me, to hide the beast I was.

From the lavender below, swirling currents took shape. Feminine hands raised from the ripples, the palms and graceful fingers nothing but water themselves. Talis Darmon floated away from Sister Wavecrest's hold, drifting from the shore on a string of pearlescent hands.

"She is in the arms of the sisterhood. They will care for her now."

She came to rest in the middle of the pool. The light from below her body darkened to a deep purple, so intense in its richness that the waters became unfathomable. Her body turned in a slow whirlpool, sinking slowly, submerging beneath the ripples, leaving her gossamer drape floating by itself on the surface.

She was gone.

"She is held in the embrace of the Amethyst Sea and the Sisters of Oceania."

I panicked. "She can't breathe!"

"She has all she needs. If her soul awakens, her essence will return, and so shall she rise."

"And if she doesn't?"

"Then know that she will be at true peace at last. Her suffering has been great, more than can be endured. What was done to her was a violation so vast, I would not have believed it possible that a trace of her remained. If she can see the light and follow it from that eternal night and into day again, it will be by the glow of their essence that she is led. Now, we must wait."

I held my breath in sympathetic time with Talis Darmon's submersion, and watched helplessly from the shore. Until the oxygen starved frenzy of acid burned my chest.

I dove. Headfirst. And swam.

No magic would keep me from bringing her to the surface.

I took my last breath and kicked. Down, down, down. A light pierced the pleasant murk. I kicked harder, the familiar squeeze building in my eardrums. She floated in a fountain of light. A dozen maidens encircled her, their hands joined, singing a song I heard through every cell of my body. Their purple manes danced with them. I felt at peace. I drew a deep breath. Water filled my lungs and with it came no panic, but instead, a rich warmth.

The eyes of the water nymphs were on me.

"I need her. We need each other. Please, sisters, please help her if you can. Or take me with wherever you take her. I can't live without her anymore."

A smile came over them all. The circle opened, and the ones to break their hold waved me gently ahead to admit me. I kicked and stroked closer, and then, with arms plunging ahead, I captured the suspended Talis Darmon in my arms. I looked into her face. She opened her eyes and smiled. A dazzling light pulsed brighter and brighter as the nymphs sang, until I was deaf and blind.

All was dark.

The pressure of being submerged came back to me, as did the burn in my lungs, and I knew not to try to draw another liquid breath. I kicked hard as I pulled her with me. I broke the surface, and with all my might, heaved her with me up through the liquid plane and into the air.

Her eyes were closed again and water streamed from her nose and mouth. I drew her close in one arm and side stroked hard until the shallows told my body to stop. Sister Wavecrest was there beside me.

On my knees with Talis Darmon floating in my arms, I breathed into her mouth. And again. Once more, she spat water, then gasped. Her eyes opened wide.

"I was floating. I was warm and without pain. They asked me to stay with them. They accepted me as one of their own." She placed a hand on my cheek. "And then, you were there."

Sister Wavecrest helped her rise from the waters.

"The sisterhood released you into the arms of the one who risked all to bring you to the light. They would not keep you to themselves. They are neither selfish nor ignorant of your deepest need. Yours was not the need for release and the peace of ultimate rest. Your need is here beside you."

Talis Darmon swept hands across her face, spreading the water from her eyes, then flinging drops from her fingers, as if casting away all that Sister Wavecrest said.

"But that is not so." She turned to face me. "I do not *need* Benjamin Colt."

My heart shattered into a thousand pieces. An old hurt returned to me, then magnified a million times into the deepest pain I had ever known. I dropped onto my knees, ready to let the waters drown me.

She reached down and lifted my face in her hands.

"I *choose* Benjamin Colt."

She bent and kissed me deeply.

"I choose you above all others. And when this is at last done, my brave hero, I will spend every day of the rest of our lives together proving it to you."

23

"WHAT IS *HE* DOING HERE?" SHE TURNED AND CAST A FIERCE FINGER AT Bryant on the shore, who did the only humble thing I'd ever seen him do. He took a knee and bowed his head. Surely, he'd been touched by the goodness as well.

I said, "It's alright, Talis Darmon. I think he understands now."

Bryant looked up. His eyes were wet and his voice reverent in a way I didn't think possible. "I don't understand. It was a glimpse of—something sacred. Something we need to protect."

"Perhaps you do understand, Brandon Bryant," Sister Wavecrest said.

When I reached for Talis Darmon, she reached as fervently for me until we united in full embrace. "How do you feel?"

She beamed. "I am myself. Whole. Returned."

"Can it really be true?"

"It is so, husband. The darkness has been expelled from me. I alone am the mistress of my faculties, no other.

I took Talis Darmon's hand. "Can you walk?"

Far from retreating, she answered the clasp of my hand with an iron grip and laughed. "I can run. I have never felt more alive. But you? Are you not wounded?" She touched my head, but there was nothing there. I ran my hand over the laceration, or where the stitched wound should have been. I checked the rest of my body. There wasn't a mark on me.

Sister Wavecrest hugged herself. "Only the true Warlord could have inspired the sisterhood to accept you into their circle. Your service to their cause is known, and honored. Truly, a multitude of old wounds have been healed."

"We have to go," I said.

We actually giggled as we ran hand in hand up the stairs, both of us renewed, courageous, and ready to shape the future. At the ship, she kissed me again. "The culmination of so much comes near. Return us to Aetheria and I will commence the accomplishment of this final act. No matter the outcome, we will make it well. Together."

I marveled. "You're really back, aren't you?"

"Never to fade again. I promise it is so." She gave me another peck. "Now, be my Warlord and I your queen, and let us fly."

I was already belted in by the time Bryant slid wordlessly in next to me. I almost lifted us, but stopped. I checked the time. We had a few hours until sunup. "I promised to give you the full package, Bryant. You'll need it, because when we leave, I'm leaving the ship with you."

Bryant sputtered. "Why would you do that? After all that's happened between us. Why would you trust me with so much?"

I set the hook.

"Because you're going to need it. It'll cut down on the travel time between Aetheria and Shansara, and you're going to be making a lot of trips back and forth. Staging the Annamese army in Mihdradahl for the war against the Whites will be like coordinating the Normandy invasion. Let me show you."

I kept coaching him as we flew. He had the Black Widow figured out in no time. I checked over my shoulder. The two women sat hand in hand like long-lost sisters, until Sister Wavecrest ran a hand over Talis Darmon's cheek.

"I knew Tashara Denara Sylah. She was the greatest of your maternal line. You are so much like her, but even those who knew her would agree that your strength and conscience are second to none, not even to her."

"What happened between her and Mother Oceansong? The stories from my mother are no better than myths."

Sister Wavecrest's tears rolled down her cheeks in tiny rivulets as she unburdened herself. "It is all true, not myth. The sisterhood and the Sylah were ever at odds, but especially how to cope with the rise of the Karnak. The Sylah alone had the knowledge from the distant worlds that was needed, but refused our plea to construct the means to dry the oceans and remove the sanctuary of the ancient evil. They accepted all as true—that Vistara was dying around us, that the evil beneath was rising, and that the one would kill us all sooner than the other, but resisted the answer our sisterhood presented.

"As the heads of their orders, my sister and her fought."

Talis Darmon was shocked. "My mother said it was as fierce a battle as has ever been waged, but never said why! Only that our two dynasties were old enemies with old hatreds, so long held that no one remembered their origins."

"There is some truth in what she told you, but there was nothing before that so firmly secured us as foes as what happened that day. My sister won the battle. With her last energies, Tashara Denara Sylah sealed the power into the device as she vowed to do as the loser, then died.

"As we consecrated the death of the Amethyst Sea, it was not only for our beloved waters that we shed tears. We cried for Vistara, and for your dynasty, and for the ignominy we brought on ourselves through our desperate actions. There was nothing but regret to result from any course we might have taken. With the aid of Jawn Kurz we succeeded in much, but we also wrought so much tragedy."

I'd learned a lot about hatred. Hatred for others so often starts as hatred for self. I wondered as Talis Darmon did when she asked, "After so much time, does Mother Oceansong not see the nature of what drives her ugly passion?"

"You see what she does not—that my sister's enmity for your line is always aimed back at herself. Perhaps someday you can mend her with your forgiveness."

Talis Darmon wiped her own tears away. "I know what it is to hold such poison. There is much to be healed. I promise I will do my portion to make it so. But first, there is a final enemy who must be dealt with. Are the Whites who they say they are? Gods? Creators of all the races of Vistara?"

"Pah. I am the memory of this world, as poor as they both may be. Like us, they are also children of the stars. Ignorant and forgetful. Wielding bits of a greatness lost. In jealousy and fear, they retreated from the surface a very, very, long ago. After the Karnak, the sisterhood and the Sylah should have joined to dry the life from *them*, had we only known."

"And the promise of Farnest? The underworld they have created? Is it…"

Sister Wavecrest poured out empathy. "I have seen all from your eyes. I only know that I do not know."

"What would you do?"

The tears were dried and she returned to the countenance of a peerless philosopher, imparting the wisdom of a pragmatic mind, a giving heart, and a beautiful soul. "Make a choice. And live with the consequences. This is the lesson to take from the conflict between our maternal dynasties. That, and to forgive what can be forgiven."

"They cannot be forgiven."

"Then your choice is clear. When judgment such as this is made with a heart attuned to the needs of others, then there is no reason for doubt."

It was far different from what Machiavelli taught us both.

Bryant had been listening as well.

"This is too much, Colt. I still don't understand."

"Maybe there's nothing to understand. Maybe we just try to do what's right. Why don't we start by you calling Sophena Pah? Tell her what's happened. Then let's stop hiding and playing games."

We settled into the port and stepped out to meet the reception committee. Even in the dark I could pick out Sophena Pah by her outline, hands on hips, her Yellow Roamak at her side.

"Bringing such a weapon to our doorstep should be a call to war!"

Bryant made a quick salute. "Not when it's a gift."

271

She exuded curiosity. "Is it truly so fast?"

"Take her for a spin, Bryant. Seeing's believing."

She motioned a subordinate forward and spoke in an unusually gentle way. "Escort them all to their proper destination, with respect and discretion. Draw no attention."

The ladies were by my side. Sophena Pah nodded to both. "The supreme magnate has let it be known that she is amenable to begin the summit. Today marks a day of rest after the festival. I will come to you later, Talis Darmon. We have much to discuss." Her eyes found Sister Wavecrest.

"And you, Amelyn Tōpara? Is there dissension in this?"

"No, Sophena Pah. As the archivist, I will give counsel as to what is known about the Whites. I will leave no doubt that they are a perilous threat, little different from the Karnak."

"Until then." She lifted an eyebrow to me, then took Bryant's arm to enter the Black Widow.

We rode through the city, chauffeured by the Yellow Roamak. Sister Wavecrest parted from us with a bow to return to her domicile. A bevy of maids met us at the palace grounds as we dismounted. I moved to go with Talis Darmon, when the senior among them stepped in my way.

"He may not enter."

The queen brushed her back. "I will not be commanded. Wake your chancellor if you so choose. Wake the supreme magnate herself. My Warlord is ever at my side."

The Roamak commander spat something rapidly, and the matron of the servant girls bowed and stepped aside. Sometimes, you have to use outrage to out-rage the outrageable. Black uniforms posted outside her quarters, but none entered. Zaylin Twee, Keshin Tellest, and Tranya Olan were on their feet as we entered.

The doors closed behind us, and Talis Darmon spread her arms wide to take them all into her embrace. Even little Tranya Olan wiped at moist eyes.

"Are you restored, Queen Talis Darmon?"

"Thanks to you all, I am." She put a finger to her lips. The women moved quickly away and returned carrying red stones. Once arranged around us, they pulsed in unison. Zaylin Twee nodded. "It is safe, Talis Darmon."

"What of Shasa Karin and David Masamuni?"

"Nothing is known," Zaylin Twee said.

"It might've been Dave that buzzed me the other night, but I haven't been in the position to open a cloud with him. Do we know if they made it out of the city?"

"No," Zaylin Twee said. "It is maddening."

"It is," I said. "But we knew them being incommunicado was going to be par for the course."

"We will continue our mission as we hope for the success of theirs," Talis Darmon said. "They have excellent help, do they not?"

When we departed the Yellow Kingdom in a firefight after recovering some of the artifacts of Jawn Kurz, the Guardswomen and I took four refugees with us. They had little choice but to accept my offer. It was that or stay and be pulled apart by the Yellow Roamak.

Selen So-Pan had been the caravan master who smuggled us into the desert. With a brother and two daughters, he escaped with us. His gratitude to Mihdradahl for accepting his family came back to us in a way that had value beyond just his thanks—when approached to become Zaylin Twee's agent, he did not hesitate to volunteer. He'd been smuggled back into Annameria with a wristlet and a mission.

"Selen So-Pa has been invaluable," Zaylin Twee said. "He is confident that the massive allocations of so many resources to the industrial complexes beyond Pella are significant for some strategic activity. With Shasa Karin acting as their matron, he felt he could lead her and David Masamuni to investigate what mysteries develop there. I think our trust in him is well placed, as is our confidence in the two operatives chosen for this mission. There are none more suited, by appearance and because of their tenacity and resourcefulness."

The conversations we monitored between Bryant and Sophena Pah about Acelyx, a project so secret they hesitated even speaking about it, could only mean danger. If I asked Bryant about it, it would immediately reveal we had a method for deep espionage in Annameria. Maybe, he'd even suspect that it was the wristlets we used to gather our information. He might be acting like he'd come to Jesus tonight, but I wasn't convinced that this new spirit of cooperation meant he was a convert to a new ethos of fair play.

A snake's always a snake. And it's never truer than when it's bulging with a mouse. Bryant and his girlfriend were freshly fed by my gift of the Black Widow. That was all. Whatever was going on and whatever Acelyx was, we needed to know by our own covert means.

"I saw the region around Pella when we flew past it on our way to Ta-Far. Getting into the restricted zones beyond it won't be quick work. If they left the city two days ago, they're probably just now starting their search. They need time."

Tranya Olan was back to her matter-of-fact self. "And if their mission is not complete by the time we must depart? Isn't the intelligence crucial?

Her impassiveness couldn't hide her real question—what if we had to leave without them? Without the man she loved?

Dave was *the* SF operator. Ostensibly, he was the easygoing muscle-head who had nothing to prove—which was true—but at his genuine core was the engine of a driven, calculating professional. If he chose, he could crush other men with his intellect or his might, but like a rabbit snare on a trail, he reserved those gifts to use against those he aimed to trap. He'd go anywhere, do anything, anytime or any place, but cuss about it so you didn't feel like you were wrong to feel the fear he didn't.

And if he got a laugh out of you by his performance, so much the better.

I once got a peek at his two-dash-one. He'd been distinguished honor grad at every school he'd ever been to, and there wasn't one he hadn't. And he'd been sent to *that* place with *those* guys—the three-letter ones—to learn the stuff only they knew. A Silver Star was listed on his personal qualification record. If I had that award, it would be framed and hanging over my mantle in place of a wide-screen TV. He cared nothing about any recognition save one—being known as the guy who got the job done.

James Bond was the ultimate wannabe compared to Dave.

"Dave will holler when the time's right. I'm not worried."

Of course I was, but sometimes a lie is the greatest kindness. And, by the way, two things can be simultaneously true. I could be anxious for my friend, *and* his prowess could make him an invulnerable stud. What they were doing in remote Annameria was the most dangerous thing any of us had done.

"Is there word when the summit will begin?" Keshin Tellest asked.

Talis Darmon said, "We have only just learned that it will at last commence the day after tomorrow. Meaning that now returned to full capacity, and not one moment too soon, I have but a day to prepare. Sophena Pah promises to come calling, bearing information I hope will aid me. Since she may show up at any time, I suggest we all rest." She smiled. "I no longer require minding, Guardswomen. My husband will see to my needs."

We were alone.

"Lay with your arms around me so that your heart beats against mine and your breath is ever in my ear. Even if I do not sleep, I will never be more content than to have you to myself for even a few short hours."

"Someday, wife." I held her without need to say more. She drew my arm deeper over her.

"Someday, husband."

✶ ✶ ✶

The summit's commencement was heralded with even more pageantry than our arrival. A troupe performed, dancers costumed in rags and skins shambled clumsily to clash with other players to give the impression they were somehow afflicted or stunted. A shimmering forest of silks entered the chamber and parted to reveal a statuesque figure with her face painted a ghastly white, her lips red and eyes black. Despite the costume supposed to evoke a clear resemblance of the dictator, the dancer was as unlike the crone who watched from her throne as a Ford Agency supermodel was from a monkey wearing lipstick.

The goddess made grand gestures, casting silver dust to sprinkle down on the primitives. In the best tradition of magicians everywhere, the dancers shed their rags to reveal a transformation into finery, their movements now strict and graceful.

Floats bearing representation of agriculture, industry, scholarship, and science circled the dancers as they weaved their steps. The message was clear. The supreme magnate was a deity, responsible for the evolution of all things Yellow, from the people to everything they created.

Yawn.

I was almost sorry Talis Darmon put her foot down that I'd remain at her side. Not really, of course, but I'd had enough of the Yellows' cultism. I surreptitiously inspected the line of Amazons behind the empress. Had the Yellows figured out how to make Terminators? Or were they more like Wolverines? Bryant just said they were to be avoided. If any of them took notice of me or held a grudge for killing Xa, it wasn't apparent in their inhuman lack of expression.

The chancellor introduced each minister, who rose and gave an oratory extolling the virtues of the supreme magnate. I grew old as the program dragged on, until the chancellor took center floor again.

"It is by the divine grace of the mother of us all that we gather. She has had enlightened vision. The wealth and perfection of Annameria can be a beacon to all of Vistara. Having bid the regent of Mihdradahl to bear witness to the paradise that is our empire, the supreme magnate gives me dispensation to invite Queen Talis Darmon to speak."

Suddenly, the moment had arrived.

Talis Darmon stood. As much as the gathered tried to feign indifference, the gentle amber aura that framed her brought an electric interest, and coaxed their taut and distant postures to tilt forward to receive her.

"The auspicious and historic nature of this invitation was so great, it brought unparalleled joy to my person and to that of my entire kingdom. The gentle yet powerful nature of its wording commanded my obedience, in hopes of uniting our humble land in harmonious cooperation with yours. The flowering of a lasting friendship has begun, thanks to the mother of the great Annamese race."

I was as affected as the corpses she raised around us. She was at her best. She kept up the prose for a while, and when it seemed she'd outdone them all in their attempts at grandiloquence and planting smooches on one posterior in particular, she weaved the simple tapestry of her statecraft.

"Your warnings about the Karnak and your invaluable assistance allowed us to destroy a malevolence that would have brought an age of despair to us all. This victory could only have been accomplished because of your wisdom."

Giving the Yellows the credit for our moves against Anso-Kylon was like saying the guy who pointed out that Hitler was a little pushy was responsible for us winning W-W-Two.

"But as you are aware, another great threat has arisen. We have achieved a respite. But destruction looms from the farthest north. I have shared all concerning the calamity that occurred in my kingdom. The time has come to speak plainly. It is to your superior wisdom and might that I make this appeal. We are incapable of fighting this foe alone. I ask for an alliance, for your aid. To commit with us to the cause of life, to ensure the future for both our peoples one secure from this threat. I invite your great army to Mihdradahl, to lead the destruction of the Whites, to our eternal gratitude."

She sat.

The room was silent until the supreme magnate spoke in her squeaky, monotone way.

"I will accept advisement. Sophena Pah, how does the head of state security perceive this matter?"

The black latex clad woman rose. "I lend credence to all that has been revealed by the Reds. The hidden dwellers beneath the Sharpa have weapons we cannot defend against. They are a creature with a venom for which there is no antidote. To allow them the opportunity to sting means death. Knowing this, their complete destruction is necessary and justified. To strike them in their den before they stir to seek new territory in which to nest in is wise."

The supreme magnate raised a finger to silence her.

"You delve into matters beyond your ken, Sophena Pah. You are not a military expert. What advisement for me has the Imperial War Khan? Cannot the mightiest army to ever exist defend Annameria if attacked?"

A woman in the drab green uniform of the army stood. "Your army numbers as the stars themselves. Every woman, man, and child in the empire would take arms to fight without hesitation, before the mother of us all would even speak her desire. But there is much to be considered in what Sophena Pah says. To defeat an enemy in their land rather than at our own gates is the greatest of wisdom."

The supreme magnate pursed her crimson lips sourly.

"Useless platitudes. An infant from the egg strategizes no better."

The general flushed, then bowed and sat, remonstrated.

"But there is merit in the obvious. I command the aedile memorian to share the counsel she has given her empress."

So, Sister Wavecrest had already given the old girl an earful? And, the dragon lady was so swayed by the advice, she allowed the woman to tell us herself, rendering credit to her counselor—which I bet was a very rare thing. If I were any judge of Annamese, the gathered were just as much the chihuahua I was, trembling in anticipation of the mailman coming down the street. Amelyn Tōpara rose from her place beside the ruler.

"The Red belief in mysticism and myths is common knowledge. But there is record of the ancient White race, all but forgotten in their irrelevance. They were banished by the celestial empress in the dawn of days, during the first incarnation of the Supreme Magnate Yi-Zun Bao Shu-Wen Dō Gwen, the light of the morning sun and sparkle of the night sky. She fought the Whites, they being evil in her sight, and in her mercy, allowed them to retreat from the surface of this world to live in eternal darkness beneath the Sharpa."

The supreme magnate gave Sister Wavecrest leave to sit.

"After so many manifestations I admit I cannot remember all of my deeds, and the aedile memorian aids me in remembrance of this great feat, so many they are. In my wisdom and beneficence, I once removed the disease of the Whites from Vistara. But it appears my mercy to them has been forgotten and now is mistaken for weakness. I am reminded of that which I already knew, and esteem the service of the aedile memorian, as should you all. I need hear no further deliberations from my mortal advisers.

"The Red queen has been sincere and forthright. Gifts of great value she has shared. All has been done in a manner so acceptable, that I am amenable to the justness of her plea. Any walls between us will be as glass. Our path together shall be shared. The Whites will be destroyed. My army will see it done."

We all rose and bowed, Talis Darmon making the deepest curtsy, the honor usually reserved for her reception alone. The silence ended and the room broke into nervous exclamations. I drew close to my queen.

"It seems Sister Wavecrest was the real secret weapon," I whispered.

"She is that and so much more," she replied. "Now, to the details. We invite that which we have guarded against for a thousand annuals around the sun. We lay open the gates of our home and welcome the Yellow enemy into our midst."

24

After three more days negotiating with the principal players of the supreme magnate's council, we were headed home. At last, we were free from the eyes and ears of the oppressive Yellow kingdom. In comparison, the barren Furrow below seemed like a welcoming land, and the air of our northerly course carried a scent of freedom.

If watching her wither and fade had brought us low, Talis Darmon's vitality was a medicine that rejuvenated us in surplus, bestowing all with a bounty of well-being so much more than the sum of our past hurts. She was clear as a Vistaran horizon, sharp as my sword Lady Vivimus, vigorous as a thoroughbred mare, her skin a rich red, the color that the wild Indian paintbrushes of my youth only aspired to exhibit in their proudest blossom.

We had a hostage. That's not what the Yellows called him, but that's what he was. Eidolon Sah was sent as a "witness of good faith" by the supreme magnate. The other consorts could barely contain their glee at the announcement, just as the first consort could hardly disguise his revulsion. It was an act, of course, and one he was the master of.

Do you know why you always invite two Mormons fishing and not one? One will drink all your beer. Once we were off, the first consort's two-faced coin flipped from the head side of the loathing xenophobic—to the tail side of the top-popping spring break co-ed.

"Yeah, took him about two seconds to settle in, bro," Dougie said when I called to check in. He had the first consort with him for the ride home. "Guy's eating us out of house and home, and drinking like a fish. He's M-F'ing everything and everyone in Annameria. Is he a guest, our conspirator, or a spy?"

"All three, I think. He's out of jail for the first time in his life. Buddy up to him, and let's see if being in the land of the big PX doesn't loosen his lips with something useful. I'll send over some of the queen's best vintages."

We conferenced over the cloud to bring our Shansara inner circle up to speed on all that had happened and what to expect. "It's game on, so I'm hoping you've got progress to wow me with."

I'd asked Karlo, but it was Cynar who pushed in to answer.

After a thousand years of secret labors, his desire for recognition had taken him from resentful recluse to insufferable egomaniac. But for every boast, he'd delivered on his bombast and continued to prove his genius was no fluke. I prepped for his usual bluster to proclaim his intellectual supremacy.

"Progress? Pah. Completed. Karlo Columbo and Perrin Halser are peerless in their abilities. With our combined talents, how could you have doubted, Warlord?"

Nietzsche's dictum that hell was other people was Cynar's personal creed. As the hermit struggled with acculturating to a life outside of his dungeon, his derision was sometimes a geyser of diatribes about the faults he found. The air wizards, other council members, dead architects, the masons who laid the bricks and the street sweepers who vacuumed the sand from them. Me. But voicing loud respect for someone else's competence?

I had to bust his stones about it.

"Cynar! First you cooperate with Tyreen Sorrel, now you're praising coworkers? Karlo, have you been slipping Prozac into his Fancy Feast?"

The old goof blew me off with an air of calm superiority. "We criticize in others that which we most detest about ourselves, you muscle-bound oaf. My greatest pleasure you will supply when you are forced to acknowledge my brilliant leadership in delivering to you this latest achievement with which to prosecute our aims. None of which would be possible without me, need I remind you."

"There's the mad scientist I know and love. I take it that means you cracked it?"

Karlo gave a hand salute. "Affirmative. Perrin Halser has teams building from our prototype as we speak."

"It works?"

Karlo snapped his fingers. "Like flipping a switch." He changed beats. "About that other thing… Dave?"

I shook my head negatively. "Not yet."

"I'm your first call when you know something, 'kay? I'll run the recovery myself."

"Roger."

Talis Darmon led me to the railing of her yacht. "I have great concern for David Masamuni and Shasa Karin. Your arms are not there to pull them back from the abyss as they were for me."

"Not true, sweetheart. You'll see."

There was a song about how waiting is the hardest part, but other than the title, I couldn't remember the words. There's another even older one, about being tired of being kept waiting. I sang it, unembarrassed as always about my inability to carry a tune.

She laid her head on my shoulder. "It was never my wish to keep you waiting. Did you grow weary for my return?"

"But I never gave up hope. And here you are."

"Here *we* are."

We stayed like that for a moment.

"I love you, husband, but you should leave the business of song to the bards. If David Masamuni were here, he would tell you to stop swinging that cat by the tail."

"Who's busting stones now?"

"Are you truly not worried for them?"

I hadn't gotten so much as a three-buzz tickle from him to let me know he was at least alive. I told her what I'd been telling myself I thought it meant. "If they were captured, he'd have gotten a distress message off to me. *Not* hearing from him means they're working the problem and doing it well."

"Then while absent comrades are heavy on our thoughts, we should show appreciation to those whom we can." Zaylin Twee, Keshin Tellest, and Tranya Olan were with us on the yacht. No longer body-guards-slash-suicide-watch-orderlies, they nonetheless remained close.

"I have much to thank these women for. Come, husband, there will be time later to fret and tread many more times over all the treach-eries we anticipate from our new allies and our contingencies for them. If you promise to let us have this day of respite, I promise to make it worth your while."

"Then I promise to let you."

We took a meal together, and after orders from both their queen and Warlord, the ladies took on an affected and strained attempt to relax on the luxury yacht. Talis Darmon and I gave them space and stretched on a lounge together, the ladies nearby on cushions. After some time, the command took hold and the ladies talked among them-selves.

"I found my nerves stretched tight. It was as taxing as our last in-cursion amongst the Yellows. At least then we worked in the shadows. There was no hiding this time. A thousand eyes rested on us every-where," Keshin Tellest said.

Zaylin Twee seemed comfortable with the ladies, and they with her. "I no longer harbor hatred of them. I have pity for their people and the ignorance enforced upon them. They suffer mass delusion about their own society's perfection. They criticize anything foreign without question. Of all their derangements, that their empress is a deity is the most bizarre."

"Surely, they know it to be a fantasy forced upon them by the state," Tranya Olan said. "Why do they tolerate such oppression? One great uprising, and afterward, they could emplace a just monarch."

Something about her statement vibrated in me like a tuning fork. I spoke loudly enough to let them know I'd heard. "If you were going to all the trouble of a revolution, why put another king or a queen in charge? Aren't there forms of government besides dictatorships and monarchies on Vistara?"

Talis Darmon stirred. "What do you mean, husband? Like the Korundi? Choosing a single leader by the consensus of their clans? Or the Mydreen, where the chieftain gains position by violence. Both are very tribal. In the case of the Mydreen savages, the chieftain's rule is—was—obtained by brute force. The position is maintained by placating all followers with treasure and by slaughtering any challenges to leadership. I witnessed Domeel Doreen do both in my time in his cages."

She continued. "I spent much time among our Korundi friends, too, though under more pleasant circumstances. They are far more evolved and even egalitarian in some ways, but their chieftain is largely chosen for the same attributes of strength and ability to bring prosperity. Almost always, their leader is chosen from one of the clans with the most familial tie to others, and gains power by the implied threat of a majority force to impose their will. Neither has the legitimacy of a royal bloodline."

The ladies were all attentive from their cushions as she lectured, and I motioned them to bring their cushions and to come sit close.

Once they were comfortable, I said, "I'm not trying to stir up trouble, I'm just curious. What makes a bloodline royal?"

"If I may, Queen," Keshin Tellest offered. "It is well known to all educated in Mihdradahl, Warlord. Those who trace lineage to the first king, Arsacius, are of the ruling class. There are the Partell, the Darmon, and the Sylah, of course. There are a dozen dynasties who can prove that lineage and actively cultivate their progeny in the responsibilities of the aristocracy."

It sounded like the Hapsburgs, Burgundys, and Kennedys.

"And what is it that all Mihdra find agreeable about the right of some leaf at the tip of one of the branches of that family tree to sit on the Spectral Throne?"

Talis Darmon drew into a cross-legged position on the couch. "It is tradition, but more so, because those of the aristocracy are raised with the expectation to serve if called. The necessity drives those families to train and cultivate their members with a sense of nobility and service.

All are trained in the principles of governance, law, philosophy, strategy, and other requisite fields of knowledge."

Zaylin Twee spoke up. "Benjamin Colt, do you not perceive the essential differences between the aristocracy of Mihdradahl and the common people? Our society values everyone, but each knows what inherent ability suits them for their distinct and particular roles."

I was feeling feisty, and tilted to Talis Darmon. "Did that include your brother?"

She frowned. "You know he was an aberrancy. In no other age save the one we lived through would he have risen to the throne."

Tranya Olan fixed me with her steely eyes. "In this life, we are not all of equal abilities, especially that innate quality that inspires people's devotion and trust such as we give our regents. I celebrate the talents I have been given, but I know myself. I have none of the gifts of one from a royal line. I rejoice that we are blessed with those of such grace."

I almost didn't say it, but I couldn't let it go. "Zan-Sha and Lashura crowed about them being the gods that created all the races. She let slip something about 'the Green to toil, the Yellow to inspire order, the Red to moderate.' Remember that? You're essentially saying they had it right. That everyone is genetically bound to some nature and purpose."

The ladies' eyes shot open at my low blow. Talis Darmon smiled wryly. "I know what you construct, Benjamin Colt. You attempt to point out what you think is a logical flaw in our beliefs. But the example you try to mock us with is an extreme and inappropriate equivalence. Still, I am pleased to see you exercise your intellect so. You are as much a scholar as a warrior. I would expect nothing less from my Warlord. Someday, when peace again reigns, I think you will enjoy discourse with the philosophers of the university."

She seemed to think she'd defused the situation and purred, "Now, let us recline and enjoy our respite." She tried to coax me to lie down again. I almost did.

"I'll be back."

To her puzzlement, I went to find my gear. I dug through my ruck. Folded in a Velcro pouch was a wrinkled and mostly ruined booklet.

I thumbed through it as I returned to the couch. Some pages stuck together, the print unreadable on others, but near the end, was the masterpiece I'd hoped had survived. I pointed to a line.

"Can you read this?"

Deciphers allowed a kind of subconscious translation of symbols. It was slow, not a word-for-word conversion like a good app would do, but I'd been able to read Mihdra through its magic until the symbols became known to me. I don't think we'd ever tested it this way, having a Vistaran try to read from the English alphabet.

She was a scholar, always curious. Machiavelli had captivated her. Maybe she'd find this inspiring in some way. She took it from me, then wrinkled her nose. "It stinks of sweat and grime, like all of your Thulian equipment."

"Sorry. It's been in my ruck for ages."

She made the *yuck* face, but took it anyway. Her lips moved silently as she read, then recited.

"We hold these truths to be self-evident, that all men are created equal, that they are endowed by their Creator with certain unalienable rights, that among these are life, liberty, and the pursuit of happiness. That to secure these rights, governments are instituted among men, deriving their just powers from the consent of the governed—what is this document? It comes from Thulia, does it not? What sentimental drivel! It reads more like romantic prose."

She turned it over in her hand, examining it, like the booklet itself was as strange and unfamiliar as the words she read. I was impressed that she flubbed not a one of them.

"Just a little light reading for you. It's probably the only copy in existence, so be careful with it. But it's my gift to you."

Always polite, she accepted it like a pretend cup at a child's tea party, sugary in her condescension as she received the booklet. "Thank you for this. I will give it just such care. But come, it is time to rest. The air is as sweet as the wine, and I prefer to surrender to the warmth of your arms than to intellectual pursuits. After so long held in the center of clashing furies, I'm filled with a need for slumber and sheer laziness. Besides, you promised."

"You've got me there."

But when I awoke, she had rolled away from our spoons. The booklet was open, and my stirrings went unnoticed.

It was dark when my wristlet buzzed and I ignited the cloud immediately. Dave grinned like a madman.

"Yo, brah, wuz happenin'?"

Talis Darmon sat up beside me.

"David Masamuni! Are you safe and sound? Where are you?"

"Hello, Talis Darmon. Yup. We're in a hide site so far out in the desert, there aren't even rat holes. First chance I've had in a while to risk a contact. Dude, we had to ditch everything in a cache including our wristlets to work our way in. Say, looks like you guys are airborne. Headed home? How'd it go?"

I spurted out my words. "Holy moly, Davey-Dave! I'll get you up to speed later. I was worried, brother. Are you ready for a retrieval?"

"Roger that, brah."

"I'll buzz Karlo. He'll fly a Black Widow himself for your exfil."

"Good copy, brah. He should have no problem taking a loop south over all this nothing to make for a cold extraction. Between homing in on my wristlet and IR beacon, it'll be a pretty simple exfil."

"Thank God! We're only a day out from Aetheria, you'll beat us home, bro-man! What'd went down?"

The irrepressible grin evaporated. "It took a while. We played caravan teamsters, and conned our way into hauling a supply train, then got all sneaky Pete–like and infilled one of the factories disguised with a party of laborers. Total strip searches, paper uniforms, the works. I make a convincing deaf mute. Getting in wasn't so bad. Getting out, that was a little tougher. But, s'all good. We got close enough to get a peek, not like they could really hide those things."

I was ready to burst. "What things?"

Dave shook his head. "Biggest I've ever seen. A pair of them. Bigger than the aircraft carriers you see at Norfolk."

"Troop transports?"

"I'm guessing between the two of them, they could carry a division—more, even. I figure this is the Chief's contribution. He's given them a whole new paradigm to work off of. It's gotta be. But that isn't all. Selen So-Pan and Shasa Karin got wind of what else they've been doing. They have bomb factories. Old-school solid chemical explosives. Five hundred–pounders. They've dedicated the whole of Annameria to build these two monstrosities and all the trimmings to go with them. They're strategic bombers, troop transports, aircraft carriers—the whole ball of wax. They could only be for one thing, brah."

"To pull off a blitzkrieg," I finished for him.

Talis Darmon said, "What are these things, Benjamin Colt? Some of the Thulian terms are not clear to me."

I gave her a brief description.

She mused aloud. "Such war machines as these we have never seen on Vistara. To drop crude destruction from the edge of the ether, then land and seize whatever they have destroyed. Such could only have been inspired by a Thulian. And Brandon Bryant let none of this be known to you, despite all you shared with him! Transparency and common path, pah! All gadron droppings! Their intentions are all too clear. How do we continue with this plan? It is inviting our own destruction!"

Dave raised an eyebrow. "I take it they agreed to help us wipe out the Whites?"

"Yup. And they'll be staging in Mihdradahl in a week."

"Showing up with two Death Stars like butter wouldn't melt in their mouths, trying to catch us with our pants around our ankles."

"I'd so say, Davey-Dave."

But I bet they wanted whatever the Whites had as much or more than they wanted to see us dead.

"Time to chew on that later. Buzz Karlo and get your team out of there, brother. Let me know when you're safe. And don't worry. Bryant's from Minnesota."

"Huh?" Dave squinted.

"He grew up with hockey and ice fishing. I grew up in woods so thick they can swallow you whole."

"So what, brah?"

"His Maw-Maw never taught him Brer Rabbit and the briar patch."

25

"Bryant always said he hated Star Wars, dude, just like he dissed everything the rest of the team dug. But those are friggin' Imperial Star Destroyers, bro," Doug said.

"Told you they were the biggest things I've ever seen," Dave said. "Not very graceful looking. They sure love their Easter Island heads, huh?"

The battleships were blocky, little more than huge rectangles that tapered un-aerodynamically toward the aft, the same elongated faces that watched over Aetheria were reproduced as superstructures nearer the bows. The two ships were coasting into the flats northwest of the city. Far, but not far enough away that the entire city couldn't see them.

We'd prepared Shansara for the coming of the Yellows, but what reassurances could have prepared anyone for this sight? It was one thing to be told what an aircraft carrier looked like, another to see a picture. But the first time you see one in person, you're just glad it's your side that has them.

And if your side doesn't?

It was the same message as the Charles Atlas ad in the back of the comic. Big muscle-man kicks sand into skinny guy's face, then mocks him in front of his girlfriend, telling the little guy he'd smash his face in but for fear the scrawny man would just dry up and blow away.

We were underweight for a beach fight with a bully.

Cynar appraised the unaesthetic qualities. "This is what a unified effort can accomplish. When all the hands and elements within a kingdom allocate resources into a single purpose. Who knows? Had our people done the same, Mihdradahl might have remained a garden."

"It almost sounds like you admire that kind of system," I said.

"Pah. Perhaps my guild was driven by a philosophy I now see as ill advised, but intellectual freedom they held dear. What I see there is no more than the work of drones."

Karlo peered over the scientist supreme's shoulder. "But it's all tech based on the same harnessing of the rays, correct?"

Cynar lowered his tablet. "Oh yes! They must have used every stone, condenser, and transformer in their kingdom. Massive, but they are just crude expressions of the fundamental science. Their immense size does not offset the base and unimaginative design. If we had such resources, I would craft something far more refined and efficient."

A trio of dots lifted from the back of one and headed for us, until the lead craft resolved into the unmistakable bullet shape of the Black Widow I'd given Bryant, two Annamerian flitters in trail with it.

"The first chance he gets, he's gonna stick the knife in, Ben-dog," Doug said. "You need someone to watch your back. Lemme go with."

I esteemed Doug as highly as I did Dave. His drive was ninety percent the same as the rest of us. To be the best. But that last ten percent—he was the kind of SF operator who needed a regular fix of the rare juice that had only two sources. One was squeezed from a fruit plucked by cheating death every time he jumped, dove, or busted through the door. The other source?

Hate.

He hated Bryant like I did. I didn't doubt Doug's honest intent—not the tiniest amount—nor his assessment of Bryant's. But in close confines with our former chief, well, Bryant was unlikely to have forgotten Doug being a step away from throwing him into the Furrow. They would be two parts of a binary explosive coming together. If my goal was to die with my hands around Bryant's throat, that would be okay. But my plan was to live.

"Doug or I could show them the way to Astelaan just as well as you, brah. You should be the one to stay here and run things."

"It should be we who are at your side, Warlord," Sarkan Sell said. "They would not dare attempt treachery with us in attendance." Jodal Jark tapped his dagger and sword with his lower hands.

"Noted, but it's been settled. You all have important jobs here. This is how it's going to be." Bryant and Sophena Pah were marching toward us, and I was glad for the distraction. "Look who he's got in tow." With them marched a detail of the Amazons.

"Those are the creatures you spoke of, Warlord? Hardly anything to be intimidated by," Jodal Jark said.

Something odd was happening, and it caused all of us to put hands on our pieces. The automaton giantesses spread out, sniffing the air like animals, hunched like wolves with their hackles raised, and made throaty growls.

Bryant yelled ahead to us. "Colt, you didn't say anything about Tarns! I thought they all booked it north. Get rid of them, quick."

Sophena Pah cupped hands to mouth. "The Guardians of Heaven are mortal enemies with the Tarn. Have your slaves withdraw. We cannot be responsible for what may occur." She turned to the pack, hands on her hips, and barked commands, seemingly to no effect.

"Let them come, Warlord," Sarkan Sell said. "Korundi bear the countenance of steel against any fool enough to boast themselves our enemy."

"Get on a flitter. Now. I don't know what the deal is, but we've got bigger concerns," I growled.

Jodal Jark bared his tusks. "We do not run from a challenge."

Dave stepped closer. "You follow orders, though."

Both snapped to attention and were soon lifting away as Bryant and Sophena Pah held the Amazons in place. With their departure, whatever gripped the straw-colored giants passed, and they fell into formation, emotionless robots again.

"I love those guys," Dave said, "but, man, Tarns are stubborn."

The head of the Annamerian security apparatus would have been an alluring woman if it wasn't for the rotten core spoiling in putrescence inside the shapely shell. "Had we known, we would have given advisement for you to keep your Greens in their cages. Apologies for the misunderstanding." The amusement she suppressed said it was no apology at all.

"What do you think, gents?" Bryant said, the cat that ate the canary. It was obvious he referred to the pair of mammoths resting behind them. Two klicks away, the ships were even more impressive grounded. I folded arms across my chest, stern like the farmer who found a trespasser on his favorite hunting grounds.

"You said you were shuttling twenty thousand troops and arms in your armada, not that you were bringing it all in two Noah's arks."

Sophena Pah made a smug, tight-lipped smile. "The supreme magnate promised to commit fully to this endeavor. She has held true to the agreed terms. Are you prepared to do the same?"

Bryant brushed his silver hair back. "Only the three of you know exactly where these turds camp. So, who's our Alamo scout? You, Dave? Or is it Doug?"

I hefted my ruck. "Me."

He and his girlfriend glanced at each other. I'd surprised them.

I pulled out a scroll. "I've got a navigation plan with the major waypoints and landmarks. There's a thousand valleys and they all look like. It may take a cloverleaf or two to guide onto the right valley, but I'll get us there." I memorized every jagged peak and craggy draw of Astelaan, dreaming of the day I'd come back to turn their hidden valley into a bigger crater.

"Frickin' Mars," Bryant grumbled. "Shitty maps. Not even a compass. Someday we'll get that solved. Let's get a move on, Colt. The Whites aren't getting any less creepy."

Bryant flew and I peeked between him and Sophena Pah as we circled before landing. Flitters covered the top of both ships like F-18s on a flattop. "Your air cars are all open deck."

He waved away my observation. "Who needs to buzz around in thin air in one of those little things?"

"Those carriers are as big as mountains themselves. Do you have some kind of navy background I don't know about? We had a plan."

"Of all people, Colt. Wasn't LeMay one of your heroes, or did you have a brain dump in that pool?" His reverence about what he'd seen was gone.

After a high-altitude reconnaissance in a Black Widow and then a phased troop buildup into Astelaan's surrounding valleys—shuttled in on flitters to stage as rapidly as possible—we'd make a difficult movement through the mountains for our ground assault. All to be done without the reliance on any tool that their ray-killer could disrupt. And all the while we worked together to craft the operation, the Yellow deception continued.

"Loose lips sink ships, Mister O-and-I. You'll get over it once I give you the grand tour."

Sophena Pah smirked. "The Acelyx flew into the bedchambers of children who lied to their parents, and consumed them whole. Our flying predators are not myth, and will do no less." She didn't specify which naughty children she wanted to punish.

I had to play like I hadn't known about their secret project. "You didn't slap these together in the last couple of weeks. When were you planning on using them to invade Mihdradahl, Tourmaline?"

Her sparkler ignited in bright sparks. "Take care, Thulian! If you let slip that name again, alliance or no, I will see you silenced permanently."

Bryant was a tepid mediator. "Now, now, Sophie, we're all friends here. Geeze, Colt, you're getting what you want."

"These were your idea, weren't they, Bryant?"

He smiled. "I told you the Yellows appreciated my knowledge. The Acelyx project was a way to keep us neck and neck with you in the arms race, Colt. All part of my plan for a deterrence, not a first strike against you guys. We were close to letting you know what we had when the whole White thing exploded. Now you know."

The flitters with the Amazons peeled off to land on the deck while Bryant guided us into an internal hanger. "Don't worry, Colt. You're still ahead of us in most lethal tech. But we're allies now. After we cement this friendship by wiping out the Whites for you, we can pull back from this cold war. Sunny days are ahead for both of our kingdoms. C'mon. I promised you the nickel tour."

Sophena Pah steamed off as he led me down companionways and corridors that separated cavernous compartments and holds filled with thousands of troops and all the basic facilities for their transport. They had fizzle guns, and their own version of a slug thrower, and plenty of pointed, sharp, stabby things.

"Here's what I wanted you to see."

While not exactly a carbon copy given our atmosphere, anyone would recognize the bulbous bodies and fins sprouting from the tapered tails for what they were.

"They're not JDAMs, but they're not dumb, either."

He paused at a rack and pointed to the stone in the nose of a nearby bomb. "We have actual smart ones that will take live guidance to the target. These not-so-smart ones follow the energy spikes of the detonations on the target. I don't have a Karlo to translate the physics of the gobbledygook magic of the ray science for me, but their tech works, doesn't it? And so do these bad boys. Heck, we're floating on it."

There were hundreds of the bombs. If there were more magazines elsewhere, it meant that between two ships, there were enough bombs to cover every square meter of Astelaan.

"You and I'll do an SR-71 from the Black Widow to nail down Astelaan's location, then we'll lead an Acelyx back from so high up, the Whites won't even know we're there. Then we turn their valley into a parking lot. When we're satisfied, we drop, the troops mop up, and the treasure hunt starts."

It wasn't a terrible plan. "We don't know that they can't detect us overhead, or what the effective range is of their ray-killer."

"Which is why the *Justice of Heaven* is taking the first run. We'll follow up with the *Wrath*."

"Which one's this?"

"The *Wrath*, of course. C'mon. You're berthing in the command deck near us. We're not worried about you having free run, Colt. After all, we're on the same side again. And be a little nicer to Sophena Pah, huh? It's gonna be a long trip. Don't forget—next to me, she's your best friend." He took an uncomfortably close step into bad breath range.

"And the future supreme magnate."

✳ ✳ ✳

It was a long and painful journey together, but after almost a week, the white peaks of the Sharpa reflected starlight like rows of tiny, sharp teeth. The command deck was in the superstructure that resembled the face of an angry sphinx, the bridge windows tucked beneath the ridged brow of the massive head.

Bryant was right about one thing. Navigation was one of our biggest hindrances. By night, we were no different from the sailors of Oceania, steering by the stars. By day, it was old-fashioned dead reckoning. The Area 51 team hadn't yet cracked the White ship's nav system, but Karlo had done a high altitude recon of the route to the Sharpa, keeping well away from the polar mountain range as he mapped out the route over the desolate eastern range of the Korund, the plains beyond, and the start of the sloped palisades of ice and snow that protected the Whites.

Amazons stood watch at all the ports around the command deck, and a pair flanked Sophena Pah wherever she went. We'd had no interaction since the first day, so the opportunity for me to give an inch to Bryant's plea to make nice with her hadn't happened. I'd spent most of my time on the bridge, spotting landmarks and correcting our course. When the quartermaster and captain had a question, an Amazon fetched me from my rack, silently gesturing for me follow. If they were going to try kill me, it wouldn't be until after I showed them the way to the lair of the Whites' secrets.

Bryant's overconfidence was inspiring—it inspired me with the strong possibility that this could be a shitshow. I knew my limitations.

Just as I knew Bryant didn't. He was an able small unit tactician, but neither of us were a Chester Nimitz or a Chuck Horner—Navy, Air Force, whatever the right strategic paradigm was for what we were doing. But I was also a little jealous. Had we built something like this first, I may have used it on him. But somewhere between the idea and the execution there would have been a lot of learning before we tried something as large scale.

Not Bryant. This was the shake-down cruise of all shake-down cruises—straight into war against an enemy we didn't know very much about, trying out tactics and equipment together in the worst kind of acid test.

War.

"You and me, Colt. Time to make history."

I eased my way to the latex-coated woman. The Amazons raised palms to halt my approach. She looked up from the glowing scroll of the map board she bent over in a hip-thrusted pose and spared me a glance.

"Sophena Pah. This would not have been possible without your leadership. Talis Darmon and I are indebted to you. You have our respect and eternal gratitude." I gave her my best salute and held it.

Rather than the brusque dismissal or even haughty wave I expected, she returned my salute with one of her own, one extended fist covered by a palm.

"It is auspicious that the two Thulians who have brought so many new ways of warfare to us now lead the way. Good hunting."

I did an about-face and joined Bryant at the exit.

"That was classy, Ben. It may not seem like a big deal, but it was, trust me." He called me Ben. Apparently, kissing his girlfriend's bulbous posterior made me his buddy. "Ready to bring the shock and awe?"

"That's how we hope it all goes down."

"The psych profile you gave us sounds like they're primed for it, just like Saddam was. I was just a young troop for Desert Storm, but that's who they remind me of. They think they're invulnerable. Shit, they think they're gods. Even after you smacked them around in their own living room, their egos won't let them stay cowed. And just like Saddam, I'm positive when the heat came off those turkeys, they got brave again once they were left alone. It's easy to pump yourself up that you're the biggest and baddest when there's no one punching you in the nose on the reg to remind you differently. But since it was just three of you who took their lunch money, they think if someone's coming for them, it'll be more of the same. So now, we put the smackdown on them."

He flashed me a big grin.

"Then we take their shit. You fly us, Colt. I don't want to miss a second of this."

26

"Bingo. That's it."

The football-shaped bowl was a dozen klicks wide and twice as long. The distinct peak at the head of the valley split into three caps. It was the first thing I saw when we spilled out of the underground tunnel system with our hostages. It marked the border above the lush valley floor and the nightscape of the hidden city, damn near as good a landmark as if it'd been a trio of blinking radio towers. Viewing the terrain from overhead like a map, it all exactly matched what I remembered of my ground view perspective and what I'd burned into memory as we put the valley in the rearview mirror of our escape.

"You sure, Colt? I know what you said, but there oughta be *some* kinda indicator there's a tropical city down there. It's just another rock and snow covered buncha nothing."

"It's cloaked, Bryant. Like something out of *Star Trek*."

He rolled his eyes at my analogy. "Then run us back to the *Justice* so I can hail them." He held up an MBITR. "I only have three of these left. Their science can levitate a battleship. We breathe because a sect of nutballs make our air from those pipe organ lookin' factories. We have ray guns. But the comms are barely better than two tin cans joined by a string. You need to let Karlo set us up with the wristlet tech for ourselves. We get that, and a nav system better than dead reckoning, and we can explore the rest of Vistara. You aware how they don't even know who or what else is on the rest of the planet?"

The two carriers were a few minutes away, at the same altitude as us—thirty thousand feet, where jet liners flew back in the day.

"*Justice*, this is Bryant, prepare to follow us in."

A scratchy squelch I hadn't heard in a very long time broke, and a voice came over the tiny speaker.

"Acknowledged. The *Justice of Heaven* brings the will of the supreme magnate." The captain continued with more of her praises and dedications. Bryant turned the volume down.

"It's tiresome, all the ass-kissing flower-talk they do, afraid that the dragon lady's spies are listening and gonna have their arms ripped out by the Guardians. There're gonna to be a lot of changes when Sophena Pah takes over. Her eyes are open about the delusions they suffer under. One of the first is getting rid of this bullshit about the head honcho being some kind of god. I mean, they make fun of the Reds and their whole thing about the underworld. The Tarns? The Yellows think they're demons. Them, they just plain want exterminated. But, the deification of a ruler, that's number one out the window. She's going to be a real reformer. That kind of modernization will win over a lot of the upper caste, too, not just the proles. Eidolon Sah says it's a lock."

It was a crawling pace to lead the *Justice* back over the valley of the Whites. Between frequent radio checks, Bryant's nervous talkativeness was a curious peek into what he and Sophena Pah envisioned.

"The Guardians are going down in the first wave. Any of them not killed in the assault are getting the axe on the way back. I've seen how they're made—err, hatched. They grow them in a lab. Mess with the embryos in the egg. It's diabolical, Colt. If it wasn't for them, someone would've toppled the old girl long ago. Sophie's got her core of supporters ready. The Yellow Roamak are fed up with things, too."

I just nodded, content to let him dish.

"Just so you know, nothing's going down with our regime change at home until after we drop you off safe and sound back in Shansara. But when we take these two Acelyx-class beasts back across the Furrow, our first stop's over the inner citadel. The sharp knife cuts the quickest, and once we cut the head off the dragon lady, things will fall in to place pretty damn quickly, all right. These cats love to be told what to do by someone with power. And our move will demonstrate who has that power."

He was convincing. Maybe I had it wrong. "Why're you spilling the beans on all this to me?"

"It's a new era between you and me—*and*—between Yellows and Reds. It's the only way, if we're going to make this place somewhere better than the garbage pile we inherited when we got dumped here. It'll never be like home, and maybe that's a good thing. We can make Vistara how Earth shoulda been. And we're this close to pulling it all off." He made the tiny gesture with the pads of his thumb and index finger almost touching. "I screwed up putting so much faith in the Mydreen. The Harridans—that was just bad luck. But, I shouldn't have made an enemy out of you."

I wanted to believe he wasn't full of it—at least about regretting our personal history. Everything else, he was a five-pound bag stuffed with ten pounds of the stuff from a bull's hind end. "Past the next peaks is the rim around the Astelaan Valley."

Bryant grinned. "It's go time." He keyed the radio. "*Justice*, bear on the triple peak at the top of the valley. We'll lead you in, just off your starboard bow. Start your bomb run at will."

The captain responded with more prose about the coming some-thing-something falling blessings of her majesty, and he turned the volume down. I kept us on course, but rolled slightly so we could both see out my side. Something much larger than the bombs I'd seen were dropping from the carrier.

"There go the smart bombs. They'll blanket a good spread around the valley, then the real bombardment will start. You'll be impressed. Things worked like a charm, and we tested the hell out of them. I've got the stick. Take a look."

The falling objects weren't very clear under NODs, and they fell away so rapidly, I never got a good look at one. "Those things didn't look very aero."

"Don't need to be. Stone power vectoring. Once the drivers get them over their selected target, they just fly their bomb on a course straight down."

"Say what?"

"I told you the bombs were guided, I just didn't say how. The kamikaze thing was their idea, by the way. The pilots are sealed into the cabins with all the oxygen they're ever going to need for a three-minute ride down."

Faster than I could say, "That's the craziest thing I've ever heard," the lights blinked off in the cabin and I was hit by the feeling of stepping into an elevator shaft without a car waiting. We pitched down and began dropping like a stone. Arrows and bullets always fall point down, even on Mars. But our tiny wings and the thin air wouldn't keep us from staying that way.

Our part in the physics demonstration did provide us with a full-on view of the results of the kamikaze hits. The guided explosions lit up like birthday candles across the sheet cake below us. In the span of a second—one that was the longest year of my life—the power was back. The safety mode righted us and we hung still.

Bryant and I competed for who could out-Dave Dave in the expletive contest.

I was first to recover from the seizure of profanities. "They *do* have a ray-killer for ADA!" Call me Captain Obvious.

"The *Justice*!" Bryant gasped. We both knew what had happened. Too late for them, the Whites had hit us with the ray-killing weapon, but not before the human flown bombs impacted and disrupted the effect. The question was, did we take their guns out permanently, or could they hit us again?

Bryant was on the radio to hail the ship, with no response. I pushed us into hyperdrive and we shot away. I made a tight bank to come around—too tight, I realized, as I became lightheaded—and was forced to let out of the turn and throttle back at the same time.

"Nice goin', Top Gun! That's a high-G maneuver, dummy. Why'd I think you could fly better than me?"

"Thought you hated movie references, Bryant."

"SHUT UP, COLT! Where's the *Justice*?"

I flipped up my NODs. Astelaan was fully exposed. Not only had the kamikazes taken down the ray-killer, the camouflage concealing the entire valley was crippled. The snow ringing the ridges around the limit of the shield's roof now reflected the escaping lights of the city. The buildings, the greenery, the forests, and cultivated fields—all stood out in the chaotic checkerboard of incendiary fires. And above the enormous valley, the massive *Justice* dropped.

I held my breath, bracing for the inevitable crash.

"It looks like the *Justice* is slowing," Bryant said.

It did slow, and I breathed again. It assumed a gradual hover to hang a few thousand feet above the newly revealed Shangri-La. One populated by soul-sucking, metallic-skinned Nazis.

Bryant had the radio to his mouth. "*Justice*, regain altitude and continue your bombing. Respond."

A new voice returned. "We are regaining control. Damage is severe. The captain is dead."

"Get the ship to safety. I'm calling the *Wrath* in for her run." Bryant brought his wristlet up, and the cloud appeared with Sophena Pah.

"Bring the *Wrath* and start your run. The *Justice* is disabled. The first bombs knocked out their air defense, but they may be able to re-arm themselves. Hurry while the first strikes still have enough signature for the bombs to guide on."

"Understood," Sophena Pah said calmly.

I spoke loud enough for her to hear me. "We'll guide you in, but it's lit up like a road flare down there. Your captain and the bombardiers should have no problem identifying the target."

She frowned away my jargon. "Is the *Justice* clear?" she asked.

"Sophena Pah," Bryant took her attention from me. "The time for commitment is on us. If the *Justice* has not moved off, the bombing must proceed. The ray-killer is beyond our ability to overcome. We win, or we die."

Sophena Pah made a sickly smile. "Have no fear, Brandon Bryant. Today we win everything."

✳ ✳ ✳

The *Justice* was off the target, gaining altitude and banking slowly away.

"This should go a little smoother," Bryant said.

I put us into the same roll again and slowed. I've seen a lot of incredible things in my short life. Had experiences beyond imagination. But below us was something I'd never, ever seen. I'd never taken part in such total warfare. Just like the films of B-52 strikes, rolling destruction paved the valley. If this is what it was like to be in the Air Force, I'd had those guys wrong for a very long time.

This is what it meant to wield the power of a god.

The *Justice* was in the pattern again and started a run from the base of the valley just as the *Wrath* completed hers. When it was finished, what remained below made even Bryant wax philosophic.

"I've never felt pity before," he said with awe. Then he sniggered and brightened. "Pity I didn't convince the dragon lady to let me build these sooner. Just kidding, Ben. I think it's clear for us to take a low-level pass for a BDA. Whaddaya say? Swoop down and let's get a close look at how we did."

He was on his wristlet to Sophena Pah and also on the radio, narrating the bomb damage assessment to both command decks.

"Munitions effect excellent. There are very few structures left standing. There are secondary effects throughout. Especially around the rim of the valley where low-level discharges of stored energy are still bleeding off. I'm guessing they come from the network of the mechanism that shielded the valley. I don't rate the effects as a danger to any landing aircraft. Little to no ground activity. Highest confidence that the valley has been rendered incapable of providing resistance to our ground forces. Anything to add, Colt?"

"We haven't touched the subterranean levels. There are miles of them, and we only saw a small portion of their ant farm." I had us on a racetrack over the face of the mountain that I knew for certain contained Farnest and the laboratory where they'd tortured Talis Darmon. The bombing hadn't touched the network of paths or the many levels of tunnels leading into the complex.

"That's what we have troops for." He returned to direct the ships. "Launch the ground attack."

"Should we put down and guide them in?" I asked. "I'm the only one who's been in there."

Bryant laughed.

"You've never learned to delegate, Colt. Or is that you want to be the first one in to get some payback? No. We're going to stay out of it. Let the troops have their fun. There'll be plenty of time to get our feet wet. Hey, Colt!"

I turned to see his big grin. He twirled his finger.

"Who's Warlord now?"

27

FLITTERS DESCENDED IN WAVES, DISPERSING YELLOW SOLDIERS IN heavy cloaks. Snow blowing across the valley did nothing to quench the flames.

"The Yellows have never experienced this kinda cold," Bryant said. "But look at those Guardians. Still dressed like it's a day at the beach. Maybe we'll let the scientist bring them back in a new mod someday. They are impressive."

Vanguards of Amazons dashed up the trails and into the warrens of tunnels ahead of the troops, massed together like lemmings as they tried to keep pace with the Guardians. This went on for hours, until I wondered if there could be a nook or cranny of the underground mountain complex left unfilled by the horde.

The cloud opened above Bryant's wrist. "Are you ready to march with me to the scene of our victory, Brandon Bryant?" Sophena Pah was in her favorite pose, hands on hips, a flowing cape open to reveal and even accentuate her skintight uniform.

"I am. Empress."

She put a finger to her lips and winked.

"You two are pretty lackadaisical about using the wristlet lately," I observed.

"The ship captains and officers are with us. Letting them see the wristlets in action is part of the wow factor to let them know we're holding the best hand. Let's do it, Colt. I'm anxious to see what's in there."

She was flanked by her pair of Amazons, who marched with her and Bryant into the largest passage into the mountain. Troops lined the rocky walls at stiff attention. I trailed the procession at a distance, my presence more or less ignored by the soldiers, who as soon as the head honchos were out of sight, went back to doing what privates did in all such situations.

Bitch like it was their true calling.

"Hurry up and wait," one mumbled as I passed. "All this way, just to freeze our asses off in some cave."

"Don't complain. Yesterday we thought we'd be dead by this time."

"If she's here, it means the fighting's over. I go home with all my parts and pieces intact, and I'll still get a chance at some loot."

"The best stuff's probably already gone."

Another trooper laughed as he stamped feet. "Finders ain't always keepers. It's a long ride back. Any choice bits are all just a dice throw away from landing in my satchel."

Through the maze we went. A green-uniformed officer with his shoulders covered in rows of sunburst insignia saluted Sophena Pah and offered to lead us forward. We walked around the bodies of many mutilated Whites. I examined one lying next to the body of a badly singed Amazon, her rigor mortis grip still clenched around a limb that had the ragged look of having been torn from its previous owner.

Bryant had dropped back to see what I was doing. "You can tell the Guardians got to them first. They've got a thing about tearing off arms. Kinda their signature move."

In what I recognized as the tunnel leading to the laboratory, a portal was blasted from the stonework, the charred remnants of Yellow soldiers nearby.

"P for plenty is the only charge calculation they know," Bryant continued. "I tried to help them out, but they've got their own way of doing things. Effective, but it does eat up troops. Fortunately, that's one thing Annameria isn't short of."

The tanks bubbling dark fluids and the slabs were just as I remembered them. On his knees, bound, and surrounded by soldiers, was the

Guarantor—in the same place where the boys and I had found him hiding, waiting to defend his territory like a gold miner on a claim. Sophena Pah inspected the surroundings, saw me enter with Bryant, and hailed us. "Is this the one you described? Their chief scientist?"

The Guarantor had none of the resilient disdain he'd shown me on my first visit here. He shivered in the chill air and his eyes remained fixed on the ground. The Amazons had done a good job identifying the HVT I'd described.

"That's him."

Sophena Pah pointed to the general. "Take him yourself to a cell in the *Wrath*. Then send down the technicians. They can begin here. Everything gets taken. Remind them that the dance of remorse awaits anyone who is careless in their task and damages even a single item. Leave nothing behind."

The general saluted and a detail snatched the Guarantor to his feet. He stumbled, his legs probably numbed in paralysis after being held kneeling for so long. Before he was carried off, his eyes met mine, and they cleared in recognition. "You are a crueler beast than any we could have created." His feet dragged along the ground as they hauled him away.

"You've got a fan," Bryant chuckled.

Sophena Pah smirked. "Do you know the route to the reception hall you described? I wish to see it myself."

I took over. Troops halted, prying gems out of the floors and walls, and assumed attention as we passed, then returned to their looting. Strewn about the great hall were as many Whites as our three-man assault had killed. Which is to say, a freight car full. Every door and portal had been breached. Through one of them, the silver river of a branch of the Blix was visible. On the dock, soldiers dipped their fingers in and out of the mercurial fluid.

"Where does this lead?" she asked me.

"It was on our list of things to investigate. It takes a course through the Sharpa like the one we traveled, but Lashura said it went east. The way they talked about it, there must be another kingdom they drew pilgrims from. I never learned more."

Her eyebrows raised. "It is as you described. Mihdradahl was not alone in feeding their deception. What people lay at the end of its strange waters may be a question best posed to the aedile memorian. It is surprising what she sometimes comes up with." She shot me a look to let me know that she knew I had a confederate on what would be *her* council.

I'd find a way to do something about that. Sister Wavecrest wouldn't be staying in Aetheria.

The Guardians and Yellow troops had laid to waste everyone, and destroyed everything less technical than a stick of furniture. We spent hours trudging deeper into parts of Astelaan I'd only suspected must be here.

The library was an orchard like our own, the same wilting crystal willows, dangling gems of untold knowledge. Behind the wreck of the work to peel open its seal was a rotunda, the floor littered with shards of mirrored glass.

"I've seen these hocus-pocus History Channel mirrors," Bryant said. "Entertaining for a little while. No loss here."

One of them had a special place of honor in the room, different from the others, but in as many pieces as the rest. It made me wonder.

Enclaves of luxurious redoubts beneath the mountains housed more communities. Deepest in the caverns were the greatest treasures—vast farms, water stores, and other infrastructure to support their closed kingdom. And in them all, the bodies of slaughtered Whites. Only some of them had been armed. I never saw the body of a child, nor did we discover a hatchery. Perhaps there were only adults in Astelaan— immortal, conceited, and soon to be extinct. So far, the Guarantor was the last one alive. But there was another yet to be found.

"Look on my works, ye mighty, and despair," Bryant said as he passed me a bottle. We'd been at it for hours. "But unlike Ozymandias, the works of this kingdom aren't turning to dust. They're moving south."

"I didn't know you were into poetry, Bryant."

"There's a lot you don't know about me, Colt."

An officer ran up to Bryant and saluted. "Sophena Pah summons."

"What it is?"

"She has found their regent."

It reminded me of the Spectral Hall, vaulted high by grand arches. A pair of thrones fit for a king and queen occupied a dais. Lashura was on the floor beneath them, bound as the Guarantor had been.

"Ah, Benjamin Colt." Sophena Pah gestured me close. "She will not speak. This White appears little different from the others, but since she was found here, the Guardians exercised restraint and bound her for later examination. Is this their queen?"

The dazzling room glimmered in the same gentle patterns that had bathed us on the long train ride to the gates of Farnest. It was not so cold, deep in the bowls of Astelaan, but the White queen trembled as if the icy winds of the Sharpa had reached her.

"Hello again, Lashura."

No tears spoiled her smooth, leaden face, but her eyes swelled like a dam holding them back.

"I knew this day would come. Many on the council of the supreme debated me daily. Had there been any but me who had witnessed your murderous rage, they would not have refused to believe there was such wrath or guile hidden within our children. Some argued that it was only because you were Thulians that we had no dominance over you. If we struck you with all our might, the Reds would once again return to their natural order. We had only to kill you to accomplish this.

"But it was your cruelty and the deviousness of your queen that made me fearful for my people. I cautioned them not to anger you further. Because if we tried and failed, you would erase us from memory as you promised. Was this your true intent all along—to bide your time? To see our extinction at the vengeful hands of an army so grand we could never win against you?"

"Always, Lashura. You sealed your fate the moment Zan-Sha took Talis Darmon."

She shook her head. "My brother Zan-Sha would have committed us to your destruction. My mighty king would have succeeded in crushing you. And we would have lived until the death of the sun itself. But he fell to your treachery, and us with him."

Now the tears rained.

"Some things are destined to be, Lashura."

Her sobs stopped, and she glared through her tears.

"I know yours, Warlord."

"My what?"

She raged at me. "Your destiny, you vain, stupid ball of clay!"

My intuition about the one mirror, smashed, but different than the others was correct. "What did you see in the mists of time, Lashura?"

Some of the bluster went out of her. "How would you know of the mists of time? There are but three on all of Vistara!"

"I know the mists are unreliable. They never show a perfect future. That for a fool, they only feed foolish delusions."

Sophena Pah stepped close. "What do you two speak of?"

Without acknowledging her, Lashura continued. "How little you know, Thulian. We are the exalted of Vistara, yet we are lesser than those who sowed us, as you are lesser than we. We cannot match their greatness nor wield the gifts of their knowledge as they did. What hope of such do mere animals have?"

Refusing to be ignored, Sophena Pah grasped Lashura by the chin, forcing her to break her locked gaze with me. "What riddles do you speak, woman?"

Lashura tore her face away to find mine. "On my return from your dungeon, I looked into the mists. And each time, I saw the same. Your face. Our end. When your war machine cast its shadow over us, it was almost a relief. But I took comfort in what I saw of your end, Warlord!"

She spat at me, then took stock of the Amazons and the many soldiers.

"What becomes of me now? Am I to be a pet for your pleasure?"

"Not up to me, Lashura. You'll be joining the Guarantor." I knelt to her level. I might never see her again.

"What happens to the souls you stole?"

"Ahhh!" She drew out. I'd pleased her.

"Your queen is still tortured by this question! I told her I did not know, so many times and so convincingly, each and every time she questioned me in my cell. It will be my greatest joy to hold the answer within. Peel the skin from the Guarantor and I both, we will never tell. Let her be forever—"

A fizzle gun buzzed and Lashura's eyes melted within their sockets.

Sophena Pah's pistol was pressed to the back of Lashura's head, the only way for the weak weapon to have such an effect. For a moment, I thought I was next. She holstered it and shrugged.

"I don't keep pets."

Talis Darmon answered immediately. My message was simple.

"It's done."

"The Whites have been dealt with?"

I nodded. "They have."

"Lashura?"

"She's dead. Everything's been laid to waste."

"Was there more to learn about—"

A knock came on my cabin and I extinguished the cloud without further word.

It was Bryant, all smiles. "Last day before we pull out. I got the call. Let's go look at this together."

The holds were all but packed to the last with the wealth of Astelaan. Flitters laden with the valuable, the mundane, and the mysterious made a constant conveyance from the devastation below up to the hovering giants.

As we flew, the air froze the rims of our hoods and the breath in our lungs. We landed and followed a patrol up the snowy peaks to examine the steep valley perimeter. Soldiers scooped snow away to reveal what they'd found.

As the men worked, the officer said, "Our orders were to bring to your attention anything that stood out. I thought this qualified. This is the first we found not destroyed by our barrage. They have odd rites for burial of their dead. But the bodies do not have likeness of the White enemy, at least, what's left of them."

The soldiers pried back a lid, revealing what had once been a person. A trunk. A skull, the cranium partly removed. Tubes and wires and contraptions wove in and out of the remains.

Bryant nestled close to me so only I could hear him above the howling wind. "It's worse than you described. They deserved everything we gave them, Colt."

The officer pointed around the rim of the valley bowl. "There was a continuous line of them. It is a puzzlement. But who knows why inferior peoples do what they do?"

✻ ✻ ✻

The quartermaster conferred with me about our reverse course, then I excused myself to retreat to my cabin. I let Dave know we were on our way back, and he gave me a simple thumbs-up. It was understood that our communications had to be brief. There was no question I was under surveillance, even if it was nothing more sophisticated than a midget with a decipher stuffed into the walls, transcribing everything I said for Sophena Pah to pour over later. It was the second day of the journey back when a Guardian woke me up, pointing into the corridor and signing forcefully for me to exit.

On the bridge were Bryant and Sophena Pah, gazing out of the massive face, the living eyes of the behemoth, contemplating what next would be worthy of destruction. Bryant smiled and waved me over, so warmly that it further eroded at my suspicious feelings toward him.

The Whites were done. He and Sophena Pah were on to their next conquest to rule the Yellow kingdom. They had holds full of treasures and technologies just waiting to be exploited. What could they truly gain by expending further efforts to bring us down?

"Colt! I was just on my way down to the hold to check out some of the loot. We tried out that paralyzing ray. Pretty effective. Most of the other stuff we can't figure out yet. Maybe you'll have some ideas."

I took the casual walk with him.

"If I haven't said it, Bryant, I'm grateful. You came through. This was masterful. Turned out a thousand times better than if we'd had to take it all on foot, one hill after another. This was your victory, Chief."

I followed him through the narrow hatch into the hold. Massive arms tackled me from both sides, pinned me, and lifted me off my feet.

I'd fooled myself that it wasn't coming. And now I was caught in the bear trap with no escape.

I couldn't even gnaw off my arms.

"What? Can't play superman if your feet aren't on the ground? You could maybe pull it off on Tarns, but you know from firsthand experience you can't beat a gang of Guardians, don't ya? You just barely beat one of them."

"What gives, Bryant?"

"I respect you too much to drag it out, Colt." He waved away the statement as he laughed. "Well, I respect you just enough, maybe."

The Amazons levitated me ahead. I struggled, but my most violent twisting didn't cause them to miss a step. We were headed for the exterior hull. All the while, Bryant rambled.

"I'm finally on track to setting things right. You gotta pay. Every death we suffered was your fault, Colt. Mike shoulda listened to me and never brought your ass to the team."

He was the same Bryant who'd taunted me in the dungeons below Maleska Mal.

"That's a lotta spilled milk, Bryant."

"So it is." He slammed a fist into my gut. He telegraphed it, and I collapsed into it so I didn't take the full force of the blow meant to fracture my spleen, but it packed enough to knock the wind out of me. "But it's still gotta be cleaned up."

He grabbed a handful of my hair.

"It's entirely *your* fault the team fell apart. *My* team. But, except for Mikey and Chuck, the rest of the team I wasn't really so tight with. Not really. Buncha children. I ever tell you how nuts you all made me with your constant gibberish? All those freakin' movie quotes and video games. I tried to make you passel of pumped up adolescents act like grownups, but Mike and the captain always pulled me back. Told me I needed to be more chill about things. That I needed to adapt to the team dynamic, not try and change it to suit me."

I got my breath back. "I should've stuck with my gut feeling that all the stuff you told me about a way forward together was bullshit. What about your coup?"

"Not BS. That's going down. I just didn't mention that on our way back to Aetheria, we'll be giving your buddies in the Korund some payback. I'll personally be sending some love to your squeeze's kingdom. I really, really kinda meant what I was telling you about us finding a new way. Sophena Pah even agreed it could work out. But ultimately, she said she'd back whatever I wanted to do."

He made an exaggerated wink. "When you've got a good woman behind you, anything seems possible, doesn't it?"

"So, you decided Mars really isn't big enough for the both of us?"

"Right in one, Colt. The *Justice* is headed to Califex, and we're cruising straight for Shansara."

The exterior door opened and cold air rushed in. We'd lowered our altitude enough to be level with the peaks in the distance.

"Thin air, but we won't be here long." He thumbed toward the door and the Amazons floated me over. They spun and lowered me with my back to the open door, my heels dancing over nothing past the edge of the frame.

"Been thinking about this for a long time, Colt. Trying to come up with just the right words for the occasion. I know you and your buddies think you're so slick with all your shit-talking. Bet you don't have anything smart-ass to say now, do you?"

My heart pounded, and I maybe peed a little. There was no way out of this.

"Guess not, Bryant."

He peeled the wristlet off me. "These come in handy. Who knows if there'll be any salvageable once we bomb Shansara flat. We may find something better in our haul. It's going to be fun to find out. But waste not, want not, and all that."

I tried with all my might to break their hold, but the Amazons constricted their grips until I felt my biceps tearing from the bone. Bryant moved in front of me and cocked back a fist.

"Well, Colt, the simplest sayings are the best, and there's none I know better than this… Fuck you."

He caught me square between the eyes and the vices crushing my arms released. A cold, weightlessness wrapped me and I passed out, succumbing to the freedom of the last freefall I would ever take.

28

MY NOSE WAS NOT ONLY BROKEN, IT WAS BURIED. I BLEW OUT A BLOODY sand-snot mix from skewed nostrils and hacked warm blood before I pushed to roll onto my back. I felt like a stretched rubber band at the end of its elastic life span. The ground was cold, but it wasn't the biting cold the air at altitude had been. I'd landed in a wide plain between high, snowless peaks on all sides.

I laid my head back and gave thanks.

Thanks that I hadn't been searched. Thanks that this was almost over and I'd be alive to see it. Thanks that Bryant was the predictable piece of shit I knew him to be. Mostly, I gave thanks to Karlo and Cynar.

The marvelous antigravity harness I wore next to my skin had become the most maddeningly uncomfortable undergarment I'd ever worn.

I might never take it off.

I'd wanted to take a clandestine dive out of the ship *before* I became a victim of some skullduggery, but I'd hesitated. In the Tears of Oceania, I'd seen the part of myself I was ashamed of. And it made me want to be better. For her, for our child, for our world. I'd let myself believe that there was a possibility that Bryant didn't have to die. I'd been foolish, but it made me proud. I've done terrible things, but in the final analysis, my choice was to preserve what I held dear, not to feed a selfish need for power or revenge.

What happened next was wholly on him.

I dug into my boot to find the hidden wristlet. The cloud came to life and there was Dave, Doug, and Karlo. They were on the deck of a transport in flight.

"For shit's sake!" Dave exploded. I knew I looked a mess.

"I'm fine. Are we ready?"

"More than," Karlo said.

"They're headed for Califex, too," I told them. "Is Khraal Kahlees set?"

Doug said, "Everyone's set. Hang tight, I'll send a Widow to get you. You'll be back in time to see the show."

"Stay on mission! Keep those Widows on patrol to guide the intercepts onto those battleships."

"Roger," Dave said. "You gonna be alright for a while?"

"I'll be fine as long as I know you're all on the job. Finish this."

"We'll be in touch," Dave said. The three greatest warriors alive snapped to attention and fired off a salute before the cloud vanished. Sometimes, the moment called for solemn discipline.

And there was nothing more solemn than the moment before the executioner's disciplined hands swung the ax to carry out the sentence.

I jammed my hands deep into my pockets and took inventory. This was the northernmost of the Korund. No snow, but the winds were whipping and icy cold. The sun was on my right and past its zenith. Everything ached. I was in no hurry to get an early start on climbing the rising slopes in the distance, so I discarded ideas about bounding and trudged in the general direction of south. Some superman. I wiped myself off as best I could—which wasn't very good at all with only blood-tinged saliva for a solvent for my filth—and brought my wristlet up.

She gasped in the cloud.

"Oh, Benjamin Colt! What has happened?"

I laughed, and it hurt. "It's all okay, sweetheart. I know I look rough, but I feel great."

"This will make you feel even better then, husband."

She beckoned Beraal into the cloud. Nestled in all four of her loving arms was our egg.

"She returned from Califex with Douglas Knoblock yesterday. We have only to await your return and our family is finally reunited. We will never be parted again, husband."

"It seems my promises to you about that are always idle ones, wife."

Her eyes softened in the knowing way of a forgiving goddess. "I do not see it as such. Each time given, you mean it with all sincerity. It is only because your love is so great that you ever part from me. Always to fulfill your duty, encumbered by the burden of the great purpose you carry for us all. How soon will the enemy be met?"

"It won't be long. The task forces moved to their forward positions the day we departed for Astelaan. They're going to be busy, but we'll know how it went before the sun sets on Mihdradahl."

Beraal gurgled joyfully between her tusks. "I must return this child to the creche. I leave you to speak with your wife, dear brother. Come home quickly."

Apache whined and pushed into the scene between them.

"Oof. Clumsy toddler," Beraal scolded. "I left you in the outer chamber. He heard your voice. Truly, he minds only you, Benjamin Colt."

"Be a good boy, Apache. Do as you're told. Papa'll be home soon."

His stubby tail wagged as Beraal took his collar in a lower hand and hauled him away.

Talis Darmon sniffled. "You do look a fright, Benjamin Colt. Are you safe? Must you hurry off?"

I gave a look around. It was as barren as the solitary moon that once hung over me on a planet I could barely picture anymore. "There's nothing I have to rush off to do."

She wiped her eyes. "It has been so long since we've spoken. I try to forget the dark days of my illness, but our short time together after my restoration was too brief. I worried frightfully that we might not see more days in which I might have the opportunity to further heal the lingering pains you suffered on my account."

"You've already healed all my hurts. And we're going to have an endless number of days together. All the time there is and more."

"I've done a great deal of thinking. I've made some very sweeping decisions about not just our future, but that of the kingdom."

"What?"

"I prefer to speak about it when we are again reunited. Suffice it to say, I am not content to return to the same manner of conduct as has always been. I want something more. For our family, and for Mihdradahl."

"Whatever your will, I'll see it done, my queen."

She smiled brightly. "You always do."

I tried to lighten things. "She looks much, much bigger. It almost seems like Beraal's arms were getting tired."

She giggled. "She is too tiny a thing for that to be so. That is the first you've agreed our child is a girl. Are you no longer holding hope for a son?"

"I just know better than to doubt your intuition. You are a sorceress, after all."

She beamed, then her face grew heavy. "Benjamin Colt, I am firm in my conscience no matter what, but I must ask. Did you learn anything about the simulacra before—the end?"

I gave her a sad smile. "No. I asked Lashura before *her* end. She was sick and twisted to her last. I don't believe she knew." I also didn't believe a word she said about my end.

Mostly.

Talis Darmon wilted slightly and shook her head. "Husband, this was a maneuvering not even Machiavelli could have imagined, much less orchestrated. I am glad for the destruction of the Whites' simulacra and whatever it may have contained. Souls. False constructs. Something we may never know.

"But by manipulating the Yellows to be the means of our solution, you have spared the stain of blood on my own hands and from bearing all guilt for the destruction of whatever the underworld was. Mine is a rationalization. I know this. But it is one I have embraced. What guilt I do carry for my part in this act, I can bear."

It was everything I'd longed to hear.

"I don't know what the simulacra really was, wife. It wasn't the underworld. And I don't believe anyone's soul was there."

She lowered herself to the floor. I thought she'd collapsed. But it was with perfection and control that she flowed up again, pausing at half lift to leave her arms spread wide as she slowly raised her beautiful face to me.

"I only know that I am filled with your grace, and in awe that you weaved such an intricate tool for justice. And that you did it all for me."

The sun was touching the tops of the peaks when my wristlet buzzed.

"It's your turn for a dust off, brah. Hold tight."

Shivering, I said, "Report, General."

"Splash two. We intercepted the ship headed for Shansara at about twenty thousand feet. There was nothing to it. We held the beam on it all the way down. She dropped like a stone. Picture the *Hindenburg* going down, only about a thousand times bigger. It came apart like a dropped Lego model. What stayed intact after impact was that way for only a few seconds before the secondary explosions. Looked like a damn nuke. The biggest tire fire you've ever seen. We might have another problem, though. If it doesn't burn out, it might eat up the last of our oh-two."

Dave showed all his teeth with his Cheshire cat grin. "Just kidding. I mean to say, it's been obliterated, brah. One hundred percent certainty no one survived."

"What about the ship headed for the Korund?"

Dave's eyebrows shot up. "Interesting, that. Karlo said it was cruising a few hundred feet off the ground when they intercepted it. It went down hard, but didn't break up too badly. There were a lot of survivors. Were. The crews made runs over the scene and chopped everything up. Tarns, you know? Then they cleared the whole ship. No prisoners, Ben."

"Double-K," I said it as the answer to the how and why.

"You got it, brah. I guess the Tarns have a thing for the Yellows as bad as whatever it is the Yellows have for the Tarns. Anyway, there's going to be salvage from that one."

"Then I want everything out of it we can get. For now, I want every bomb we can recover. They had plenty held back to use on us. I want to be reorganized ASAP and moving for Aetheria. It's time to settle their hash once and for all."

Karlo swooped over in a Black Widow not long after. Wrapped in a fur and with an amber stone warming my lap, I made him fly us to the site of the *Justice*. It was dark, but by the light of the twins, the hulk stood out like its own mountain. Korundi and Red troops swarmed the scene.

"No idea why that Acelyx was flying so low, Ben. I almost wonder if they were lost, skirting the southern chain of the Korund to find Califex."

"If the skipper had lived, the board of review would've made him do the dance of remorse. Kinder this way."

I hailed Khraal Kahlees below.

"You had good hunting, clansman. That's quite a kill."

"You look like you fought a gazraal and lost, Warlord. Come, and I will show you the prize."

"No time. Will the Korundi join us for the assault on Aetheria?"

"It would be impossible to keep the Korundi from this cause, even had Chieftain Parkus Laan not committed fully our support to Mihdradahl. Our enmity for the Yellows is deep and fierce. Meting such complete punishment for their brazen attempt to harm us in our homeland has only ignited the ancient lust for all Yellow blood."

"It's not revenge we're after. It's a regime change. We're going to decapitate them. And we're going to permanently take away their aggressive abilities. We hit the inner citadel with everything. Once we've destroyed that, the rules of land warfare will apply. If you want your commission back as general of the Mihdra forces, there's no negotiation about that."

"As you wish, Warlord. It will be so. Discipline is our bond."

"We'll have time for a full op order later. Good to have you back, General."

By the time we were nearing the site of the *Wrath*, the sky was getting lighter. From a hundred miles away, black smoke still hung over the crash as a grave marker. There were no fires, but the ground around the destruction was singed for a square mile or more. It wasn't quite as complete as Dave had made it sound. There were many, many large sections, not intact, but clumped into the debris of spars and girder works. The superstructure of the huge head was folded like it had been caved in with a giant baseball bat, but was otherwise recognizable.

I raised Dave on the ground.

"Not for a second do I think anyone made it out of there, but I want it gone over with tweezers. If there's a piece of Bryant and his girlfriend left to make a positive ID on, I want it. The holds were packed with stuff from Astelaan. Something survived."

"Got it, Ben."

"But it'll wait. Nothing down there's going anywhere. Meet us at home. Double-K's in. As soon as we can, we're headed back over the Furrow."

✳ ✳ ✳

"You're not going," Doug said.

Before I could dismiss him, Dave joined in to shut me down. "Fact. You're not going."

"I want her out of there, safe and sound, and I know where she is."

Doug groaned. "Why is it you think you're the only one capable of doing stuff? *I'll* be the one taking the rescue team in before the air campaign kicks off. Not a purple hair on her head will be outta place when I return. The ladies have been there, and Jodal Jark and Sarkan

Sell can come with me. I'll have everyone I need to get her out. You just keep the zoomies from dropping any bombs on us."

I opened my mouth to counter, but got cut off again.

"Brah, you stay airborne and run C-and-C. Double-K or I will holler if we get into some kinda situation that *only a Warlord* can manage." He made jazz hands to emphasize the point. "Got it?"

I knew Talis Darmon had given them an earful, just like she'd done to me.

Sometimes, even a Warlord has to bend.

I compromised. I flew the Widow with the modified weapons pods. They were crude, and ruined the sleek profile, but the next generation would no doubt be more elegant. Cynar and Karlo worked together in the back and guided the first bombs onto the supreme magnate's palace from so high, for all anyone in Aetheria knew, it could have been an asteroid that hit them.

"Did the Yellows truly throw away lives to do such a simple thing?" Cynar asked, still amazed at the revelations about their kamikazes.

The palace grounds, the opulent quarters, and the inner citadel were burning. The campaign to end the constant threat from the walled empire of Annameria was underway.

We took out the port and the centers of their security forces. K-max and minigun fire from conventional flitters worked precisely from altitudes above what the Yellows could defend against. Others dropped dumb bombs, the inability to guide them precisely not a necessity from the lower altitudes.

"Sierra Whiskey is clear, Ben," Karlo reported. "The whole team made it out and are on a tender, loading her into a Widow bound for Shansara. Doug says she's not happy about it."

Talis Darmon would be there to welcome Sister Wavecrest when they landed. If anyone could help her see the necessity for it all, she could. Whether I'd ever have Sister Wavecrest's understanding or trust again, only time would tell. But she'd be alive and free to hate me if she chose to.

We were still far above Aetheria. Airborne command and control was worse than being on the ground. My stomach was in knots as I waited for the progress reports to come in. Dave and Double-K were running the ground assault into Aetheria. Dave had just landed with the first of the airmobile assaults into the inner citadel, while Khraal Kahlees landed troops in the outer rings to seize the park and stadium to begin flooding the city with Green and Red troops.

Compared to the invasion of Pyreenia, it had been relatively easy. It wasn't bloodless for us, though. There'd been tough street-by-street fighting. We took losses in several air-to-air battles, and our makeshift bombers and ground support flitters were still running harassment and delaying missions to keep ground forces from nearing for a relief.

By daylight's awakening, we held Aetheria.

I escorted Eidolon Sah myself onto the ruined grounds of the despot's capital. The psyops campaign was underway as scrolls were dropped by the hundreds across Annameria to declare the reign of the supreme magnate over, and announce the ascendence of a new regime—one that promised an end to tyranny.

As a potential leader in exile, Eidolon Sah wouldn't have been my first choice for a replacement to cobble together a new government for Annameria, but Talis Darmon thought he was our best bet. We stood by the rubble of what had been the palace.

"Eidolon Sah, we'll keep Red troops in the city and the Korundi battalions in the outer bounds until the security situation is settled, but we're not staying. It's on you to make it work."

"I understand, Warlord. The queen was most clear that would be the case."

Dave had a green-uniformed Annamese in tow. The army troops had largely gone to ground once the fighting started, then surrendered to our troops in droves. The woman accompanying Dave was the highest ranking officer we'd located.

"We're finding a lot of these. Show him, Colonel." The Yellow officer hefted the discarded black uniform of a Yellow Roamak.

Eidolon Sah waved it away. "They will all be captured. They cannot hide. The people will gain courage and reveal them. The loyalty of the remaining army is mostly secured. It is as I assured your queen. I know best how to gain the cooperation of my people. The commanders of forces in the other domains of the kingdom will be only too glad to join in a new government—with my promises of ascendancy and position in the new order."

The colonel gave a crisp bow of agreeable obedience. The former first consort raised an eyebrow to me as if to say, *See what I mean?*

"As you have suspected, Warlord, dissension and the conspiracies to topple her have ever been alive, though deeply concealed. With the fear of the Yellow Roamak and the Guardians of Heaven removed, the winds of change will blow steadily. There will be brief gales, but they will calm. And with the threat of the return of Red forces to bolster my claim, I will establish a new Annameria."

Talis Darmon and I had no illusions that he was about to institute a truly benevolent rule.

"Just remember, Eidolon Sah. We can do the same to you if you turn into another Supreme Magnate."

"*That* is something your queen also made abundantly clear. I will establish the title of Most Benevolent Protector."

I left the new ruler of Annameria with his people, and Dave and I marched off. The grandeur that had been the inner citadel was nothing more than a series of bomb craters. The antiquities borough remained, as did the rest of Aetheria. Most importantly, the three atmosphere works stood tall.

I nodded to one of the Easter Island heads. "I hope the next time I visit, all these Big Brother statues will be gone. They still give me the creeps." The faces seemed to know their days were numbered.

"Once I put this place in the rearview, they can do whatever they want, brah. Tranya Olan and I have plans that have nothing to do with revisiting this clown show. Besides, it'll be a hundred years before they get up the gumption to screw with us again."

"We might live to see it, Davey-Dave."

"True dat. Say, there's nothing for you to do around here. The queen's sending an ambassador and a diplomatic mission to help advise Eidolon Sah. Karlo and Cynar are getting ready to head back. Why don't you hightail it with them? I'd say you've earned a break. "

Tonight, I'd sleep next to my wife in our own bed, the egg with my child close by, Apache's midnight farts polluting the air of the home I longed for.

"Bro, for once, I don't have an argument to the contrary."

29

I FLEW, TALIS DARMON NEXT TO ME. SISTER WAVECREST AND MOTHER Oceansong rode in the back of the Widow, oblivious to the world around them. The two women hadn't released hands since the moment of their reunion. Mother Oceansong's fury at our sudden appearance on her doorstep melted into tears at the sight of her sister. Not even they knew how long it had been since they'd last seen each other. It got very smoky for me, too.

I'm like that. I didn't even try to hide it.

"We're there, if you want to come look," I said over my shoulder. "I thought you might want to see it from above before we put down."

Not by much, but the waters filling the Furrow had grown since we'd been here last. It was far from an ocean, but who knew? Maybe someday it would be.

Talis Darmon and I stayed back as the two walked arm in arm to the shore. They knelt together and touched the surface, caressing the waters, their different shades of their unique purple auras growing together to spread across the lake.

"Do you see, husband? Do you see as I do what once must have been?"

Through the glow, the waters came alive. Gentle swells appeared. Schooling fishes roiled the surface, a gentle breeze carried the scent of salty caramel, and boats with magnificent sails glided on the horizon. The fantasy remained for a minute, then faded away as their combined energies receded.

Hand in hand, they returned.

Mother Oceansong placed hers over her heart. "My sister tells me that you know my crime against your mothers. I am so very sorry for all that I did. Can you forgive me?"

Talis Darmon burst into tears and embraced her. "Had there been another way, the choices and acts of our dynasties would not have been necessary. None are without blame. None are without fault. And none of us are beyond redemption or forgiveness."

Sister Wavecrest slipped her arms around both of their shoulders. "There is no undoing history. All we can do is seize the opportunity to forge the present to our wills."

Mother Oceansong laughed tearfully. "You always were the wisest among us, sister. Though if Talis Darmon someday achieves our decrepitude, I believe she will outdo you."

"What's next, ladies?" I said. "Where to?"

Sister Wavecrest had her answer ready. "I will remain in Shelasa with my sister. When we can further beg your assistance, I would like us to travel to the Tears of Oceania."

My breath seized and I stammered, "You're not, you're not—going to join them? Are you?" I didn't want to imagine a Vistara without them.

Mother Wavecrest again placed her hands over her heart. "You touch me deeply, Benjamin Colt. No, Warlord, guardian of Vistara, worthiest inheritor to our great son, Jawn Kurz. We will not leave to join our sisters. There is work to be done in this world. And it is only we who can do it. Never did I think when I tested your queen or tempted you to reveal weakness that someday it would lead to such joy."

Sister Wavecrest raised her arms high. "The cruel reminder that is the Furrow of the Creator's Hand may again be the Amethyst Sea. I see it as it was. The lifeblood of all Oceania. A paradise of plenty, inspiring all who see her shores."

Before we left them at the shrine of Mother Wavecrest's ancient cove, I asked her, "You once told me you could never leave here."

With an arm around her sister's waist, she smiled. The storms I'd always sensed from her as ready to build to hurricane gusts were placidly absent. "And it was once true. The pain of dry and desolate Vistara was too great to bear in any place save this prison of my own making. But with my sister at my side, there is nothing I cannot do, no place I cannot be without feeling hope instead of helplessness."

Sister Wavecrest hugged me. "We will touch our sisters in the Tears of Oceania and visit Aetheria. There are other shrines and sacred places that may yet exist. And we have time to find them all. Together."

"You will see us again, Benjamin Colt," Mother Oceansong yelled as she waved goodbye. "You need not worry."

Sister Wavecrest did the same. "Farewell for now, Queen Talis Darmon. You have made Vistara a better world in which to raise your child. And because of you both, she will inherit a Vistara primed for splendor."

I set our course, too overwhelmed to even speak about all that had happened.

"Husband, do you think Sister Wavecrest foresees a daughter for us? She said, '*She* will grow up.' She!"

I kissed her hand.

"I would never second-guess the greatest physician who ever lived."

✹ ✹ ✹

"Benjamin Colt, come see! Our child comes! Hurry!"

I snapped awake and rushed into the nursery. The creche was open and Talis Darmon bent deeply over it. The egg shook and tiny cracks raced each other across its curved surface. First one piece fell, then another.

Barbed tentacles shot out and splayed the shell away. Green eyes opened, and a maw of jagged teeth screeched before bellowing, "ANSO-KYLON LIVES."

I screamed as I sat upright.

Talis Darmon startled awake with a gasp. I rushed to the nursery. The egg was fine. I laid a hand on it and hers was there a moment behind to join mine. It was not the tiny thing I remembered when I first tried to imagine the child inside. As it grew, it had darkened into crimson freckled with purple, and so warm beneath my hand, it seemed almost hot to my touch. It had changed. I wondered if I had, too.

"She is asleep. Is everything alright?"

I lowered the cover and led her out. It wasn't until the door was closed that my absurd sense of humor made it clear that I hadn't changed at all. Trying to suppress the laughter made the deep muscles of my viscera ache where Bryant had landed his blow.

"Are you quite well, husband? You made my heart seize, thinking assassins or the Mydreen hordes had fallen upon us."

Splinting my abdomen as I convulsed didn't help, because the body-wide stretch I'd gotten from the sudden stop above the floor of the Korund made everything hurt as I tried to suppress my laugher. There was nothing to do but give in and let it all out as I fell back on the bed.

"You'll wake the baby," she said, trying to shush me. Apache had just settled down when my guffaw brought his head off the floor to find me. He made an annoyed exhale before collapsing again. The worst of it was out of my system. I told my wife about my dream.

"There is nothing funny about such an awful dream! Ugh. I wish you had not told me. I will not be able to remove such an image." Then she giggled. "No wonder you leaped from our bed as though it were on fire. What nonsense lives in that head of yours, Benjamin Colt."

"You're right, baby," I said as I put my arms around her. "You can send the boy to Vistara, but you can never get the slasher movie ending out of the boy."

Long ago I'd learned that a wristlet request for a private meeting with any first shield was never a good thing. Zaylin Twee's serious face so early in the morning meant trouble. I tried to put myself in her position and act cheerful, so I wasn't cause for the poor woman to learn to hate her job.

"It can't wait for the council meeting in a few hours?"

"The news I have is for yours and the queen's ears only."

"I figured as much. Come to our quarters as soon as you can, then."

Talis Darmon sighed. "I prefer not to sprout worries about that which might not even exist, but my attempt falters. Have Thorian sparkle dust cartels murdered the city council? Have tribes of Vermeel Tarn been spotted in the Furrow? What possible calamity could warrant her to be so guarded?"

We found out.

"The priests in Clymaira and in Thoria have been murdered in the same manner as were those in Shansara."

Talis Darmon straightened in her chair. "When did this occur?"

"Clymaira, two weeks ago. Thoria, last week. My judgment was that in the midst of all else occurring, there was nothing that required your immediate attention until I could be sure."

"Kleeve Hartus's work?" I asked.

Zaylin Twee nodded. "He was in Pyreenia. My Guards took notice of him, though he was quite cautious about his activities there. He was seen with many followers of Desudun Cahlair, dressed in their garb, seemingly in their fold before the surveillance lost track of him. I surmise he countered their efforts and traveled to Clymaira and then on to Thoria."

"Where is he now?" Talis Darmon asked.

"It is unknown. All the Guard are alerted for his appearance here or elsewhere, but I think it likely he has returned to Pyreenia. I have obeyed your orders to leave him unmolested, Queen. Have I correctly done your will as first shield, or do you rightly have censure for my inaction?"

Talis Darmon paced, leaving Zaylin Twee and I both in limbo. She sat again.

"I have no remonstration for you, Zaylin Twee. I am sorry for what you have had to endure in this matter."

"Is he to be brought to account for these crimes?"

"No. I think it has run its course."

I was unsettled. "You're not afraid there's some other target he may choose to exercise his demons on?"

"I am not. He will never be the man we once knew, but if he has found the followers of Desudun Cahlair, then I think there is a possibility he may learn peace."

"From serial killer to monk? I don't know, Talis Darmon. It seems a bit of a stretch. Once a fanatic, always a fanatic." She hadn't seen what the first shield and I had of his handiwork.

Zaylin Twee was hesitant, but broke our reverie. "Queen, was this your plan all along? To mold him into the means of your revenge?"

"Whatever you may think of me, Zaylin Twee, I have not the power to do such. But yes, I hoped to create the conditions for him to take action against the priesthood. They were conspirators with those who preyed upon us. And they deserved punishment. As did he. And I think he will punish himself for a very long time. And that is sufficient for my justice. If he does not act out again, I will consider the matter concluded. And you, Zaylin Twee? Are you able to come to peace with this?"

Her chin quivered, but she remained silent.

Talis Darmon coaxed gently. "It is not your queen and your Warlord to whom you now speak. Unburden yourself, child."

Zaylin Twee relaxed. "His sense of duty and rectitude manifested in him like a hero of myth. He was worthy of love. So kind. I once dreamed of a long life together in the service of the Guard we both loved. Now all that remains is the Guard. If I have your confidence, it is there I desire to remain."

"It shall be so, First Shield."

When we were alone again, I relaxed. "Thank you for being so kind to her, Talis Darmon."

"For all she has done for us, inadequate as may be, she deserves every comfort I can give her."

"The priesthood may be quaking in their boots, but it isn't entirely gone, is it?" I didn't know. It was a small and secretive sect. "Are you hoping they'll reform the faith, or is the Pyreenian faith one you want to spread?"

"It is not for me to choose. Freedom will decide. Come. To council, and then we travel. If there is success, then all else will fall into place."

Karlo flew, Cynar with him in the right seat. I dozed on and off as Talis Darmon read scroll after scroll. Deceleration and a pitch down woke me. Maleska Mal was below us. At the atmosphere works, Tyreen Sorrell waited.

"It has been tested, Queen Talis Darmon, but it is most appropriate that it be you that fully awakens the works."

He led us into the mystery of the ancient atmosphere works, to a panel with many stones and glowing gems, and pointed to the largest of them, a dimly lit multifaceted green stone.

"Please, do the honors."

She waved a hand across it and a deep, soothing light glowed.

"No chance this thing's going to have a meltdown?" I whispered to Cynar, who scoffed.

"Pessimist. I have overseen the labors of Tyreen Sorrell. He is a boob, but if so, then I am as much of one. The atmosphere works of Filestra are restored."

One of the air wizards spoke while monitoring a larger console. "The flux of all rays has settled to constancy." Another spoke from his station. "Output continues to rise and should reach maximum—now."

Tyreen Sorrell clucked. "It is well. If it please you, shall we observe from outside, Queen?"

We craned our necks up the maze of tubes and pipes to the very tips of the towers. A white mist spilled from them to form a hazy cloud over the works. It grew wider and wider. I took a deep breath.

"Am I just imagining it, or does the air seem thicker?"

Karlo took several deep breaths as well. "It's not your imagination, Ben. It's finally happened."

Talis Darmon thanked the Air Wizard Supreme, who bowed deeply and took his leave for the bowels of the factory.

"What is next, Karlo Columbo? The works of Shansara?"

"Yes, ma'am. Now that Tyreen Sorrell has the process, he thinks it will only take a month or so to have that one working again. The next may proceed even faster."

"Is there enough Element X to repair them all?" I asked.

"Yes, Ben. Baby Blue's come through and we've made enough for a hundred atmosphere plants. Tyreen Sorrell's already working on plans to rebuild the one in Califex and then as many more as can be built."

Talis Darmon savored a deep breath. "It is almost unbelievable. The long crisis of Vistara's inevitable suffocation is all but over. Our world breathes and lives again."

Cynar humphed. "The task will be a lengthy one. With a growing atmosphere, waters, a plan to return vegetation to the surface of Mihdradahl, it is possible that in a thousand years, Vistara will green and the works become unnecessary to sustain it all."

"Good. Then we can get the Blue Fairy back to working on other things."

Karlo gave me a head tilt and lifted both eyebrows, the same way my dad did when I'd do something futile like put bigger rims or lighted running boards on my pickup truck. It was a junker, doomed for the scrap heap, but I kept it looking stylish until the end.

"Baby Blue's dead, Ben. It ran out of star juice making Element X. It was worth the price."

"Oh no!" I said. "There was so much more we wanted to do!"

"Like what?" he puzzled. "What could we need from it that we can't possibly make ourselves?"

I struggled for an example. "Huh, I kinda wish we had iPads and phones again. Maybe a game console or two. Not to mention night vision, and optics, and all the stuff to really outfit our army and make them peerless."

"I think we're past that, Ben."

He had me there.

I shrugged. "The Blue Fairy saved us a hundred times over. But if she's on empty, then we can be thankful her magic lasted as long it did."

"There is much yet to be discovered, Benjamin Colt," Cynar said. "Ours is a world of wondrous things."

Flying home again, Talis Darmon threw herself into work. She wrote furiously between trances of staring into space—what she visualized constructing I didn't know—before she returned to press a stylus to a lighted scroll, lining through sentences and composing new ones.

"Whatcha working on?" I asked during a particularly long pause.

"Your Thulian language is quite inelegant, husband. Will you not use your Mihdra? It has become very refined and lends you dignity."

"I'll always be a hillbilly at heart, sweetie."

"I am composing an address to the kingdom. It is overdue that all my subjects hear from the mouth of their regent the wonderful things that have transpired. I have been anticipating the successful restoration of the air works, and now that it has come to pass, I can share that joyful news as well. I mean for this to mark the blossoming of the new age. It is with that news given that I shall then deliver my proclamation for Mihdradahl's future."

Doug and Dave were on the landing deck next to their own Black Widow, unloading containers from the back. I strolled over to see what they were doing.

"Yo, Ben-dog. We were about to check in. How'd things go?"

I gave a thumbs-up. "We're cooking with gas. The factory's cranking full bore."

Dave wiped his hand over his brow and mocked flinging away worried sweat. "That's a relief. Not that I didn't think Karlo and Cynar couldn't pull it off."

The two mentioned walked up just then. "David Masamuni has never doubted my brilliance, Benjamin Colt. You should take to the example of your friend, oaf."

Talis Darmon appeared out of the bird and was handing off a stack of scrolls to her attendants and moving to join us.

Doug gritted teeth. "Huh, maybe this isn't the best place to do this, Davey-Dave."

"What?" I said.

"We found what you wanted, brah."

Talis Darmon was there, demanding to know what was being talking about.

Dave nudged Doug in the ribs to come out with it.

"It's Bryant and Tourmaline. Their bodies were found on the command deck of the *Wrath*," Doug said. "It's not pretty."

"Thank you for your consideration, Douglas Knoblock, but there is little I have not witnessed in this war. I will see as well."

They obeyed and opened both containers. There wasn't much, but what there was, left me with no doubt it was them. The patch of scalp with silver hair atop a halved skull without a face. A woman's partial trunk, charred and vacuum packed in a shrink wrap of black latex.

I remembered Khraal Kahlees's words on the day his blood oath was fulfilled, and I used them.

"No revenge is ever perfect. A warrior takes what is offered."

It would have been more satisfying to have had a more direct hand in their end, but you get what you get.

Talis Darmon waved them to close the containers. "Thank you. It is another reason for gladness today, no cause for sorrow." She touched my arm.

"Take time to be with your friends. I have work to do."

Cynar solemnly took his leave. "I must return to other investigations, as well." He talked to himself as he walked away. "Hehehe. Gravity is the ultimate force in the universe."

The four of us just stood around for a while, staring at the two containers. Doug pulled out a pouch and put some dried leaves in his mouth, then spat. "I know you're not supposed to speak ill of the dead, but he was an asshole. He didn't get half of what was coming to him. And she woulda kept making trouble for us like it was her full-time job."

"It's done. We can bury and forget them," Karlo said.

Dave made one of his usual shrugs that could mean almost anything. He was glad. He was mad. He was tired. He was geared up to lay hate. You just never knew.

"I'm hungry. We deserve a luau. We can deal with this later. They ain't going anywhere."

As we walked off, it was Dave who brought it up first.

"Wuz next? I mean, what's our big mission? To be honest, Ben, if it's just gonna be a life in garrison, I don't really feel like being a big kahuna in the army anymore. If Double-K wants it, more power to him. We've got guys like Tolan Garth and Pen Segus who can step up. I'm not saying I wanna quit today, but, just so you know, the time's coming for me, brah."

I understood. "How about you, Dougie?"

"Never thought I'd be bitching about there being more fighting than waiting, but we *have* been at a very long run of nuttin' but the boogaloo. I'm looking forward to some chill time with the girls. I won't leave you high and dry, but eventually, it'll be same-same for me, broman. I'm not cut out for a peace time staff job… I'm sure something'll come along. Maybe the Guard's hiring?"

"YOU! A cop, brah?"

"Who better? Takes one to know one."

"Karlo?"

He'd left the life of a full-time action guy for his dream job, and I didn't expect to hear anything different. He threw his palms up with finality.

"Satisfied where I am, Ben. What we're recovering from the wrecks is going to need careful examination, and we still haven't cracked everything about the White ship in Area 51. Uhhh, about that. There's something I should tell you. You know the nav system and the global map?"

"What about it? You got it turned into a GPS for us yet?"

He stopped in his tracks, squeezed his eyes, his neck disappearing as he scrunched his thick traps up. "I kinda… lost it. All of it. I was removing the core of the system to transfer it to the lab, and, I dunno—I think I did something out of sequence. It just puked out. I can't recover it."

Vistara's secrets were what kept her spinning on her axis. The status quo had been maintained.

I busted out laughing. Pretty soon, I was on the ground, tears rolling down my face as I tried to catch my breath. Doug and Dave were laughing, too, though maybe not for the same reason.

Karlo'd had enough.

"Hey, screw you guys. I was working twenty-four seven to get that ray-killer up and running, in addition to the five hundred other things everyone dumps on me to pull outta my rear. I'm a human being, too."

Doug had his hands on his knees. "That's what we're laughing about, bro. It's the most normal, regular, human-type thing you've ever done."

Dave gave Karlo a light punch on the shoulder. "Shaka, brah."

"C'mere!" Doug grabbed Karlo in a big bear hug and lifted him off the ground. "God, I love you, man. It's just good to know that sometimes, you fat finger shit like the rest of us."

He dropped Karlo, who laughed as he pushed the big man off him and gave one of his reserved grins. "What can I say? I live to serve. Even if it's only to give you all hernias laughing at my expense."

"Tell me you at least got a picture of it, dude?" Doug asked.

"It's always part of the process that I take pics of everything. It's not much, but it's better than nothing."

"Brah! There were some crazy-looking places on that globe. Heck, if we got the time and the tools, maybe we go exploring? We're the only SF group on Vistara. Think of it! Worldwide mobile training team, boys."

They all looked to me.

"Well, I wasn't going to say anything just yet, but Talis Darmon's in the early stages of something. It might turn into a gig for us. It's going to take a while to develop."

"She got a mission for us?" Doug asked.

"More than that. There's a shake-up coming. And when it does, we might have to get out of town before they tar and feather us."

30

"Our enemies are vanquished. Mihdradahl returns to the wealth of abundance. The advances we have developed will soon proliferate to all parts of the kingdom, and the obstacles that have long separated the islands of our realm will be reduced to as much dust as the deserts between us."

The Spectral Hall was filled, as were the grounds of the palace.

"With the return of our life-sustaining air, we herald the great task of restoring other necessities. The commission to reestablish Filestra represents another part of Mihdradahl's rebirth."

The written text of her planned remarks had already been disseminated throughout the kingdom, and her speech seemed merely a recitation of the same. My palpitations started, like they so frequently did whenever my anxiety could find no other outlet. She paused before making the revelation she saved for the live address.

"But in the rejuvenation of this land, as vital as they may be to our destiny, it is not enough that we rejoice in the merely tangible necessities and worldly comforts to come. We must also cultivate a means to our spiritual rebirth. And it must begin with me.

"I will step down from the throne."

Low murmurs permeated the crowd.

"And never again from this seat will a monarch rule over Mihdradahl."

Amazement and uncertainty joined together into a rumble that filled the sparkling crystal sanctuary.

Karlo had been a great help. As with most things, he was a re-pository for the history that led to the words captured in the tattered pamphlet I'd given Talis Darmon. Plus, he'd also had a complete one, in much better shape than the one I had—truly, the only record of the products of an enlightenment that had shaped a country that no longer existed.

Many nights we'd talked, pondered, and struggled to help her build a framework for what she envisioned. She continued her address, fore-shadowing for the kingdom what was to come. Mists over a mirror that weren't yet clear enough to serve as a model for a portrait to be painted by the brushes of many more artists.

"All Mihdra must feel equal in voice and have a personal stake in a future we work to build together. The egg of a new and just form of governance will not have one set of parents nor hatch by predictable and timely gestation. But I am determined its conception must be now. To that end, it is my royal decree that the investigation into a new and enlightened means of fostering, protecting, and guaranteeing the pros-perity of all our peoples be commenced. Perrin Halser, step forward."

There was some theater here. The head of production wasn't placed in the same position I'd been the day she called me forward. I recalled my day on this floor, the jolt of the electric chair that had been her call to become Warlord. Karlo threw all confidence behind the choice, and Perrin Halser had been the first to take part in our think tank once we'd gotten the inklings of how to move ahead. He might not have looked like Ben Franklin, but he had all the qualities of a Renaissance man.

"Do you accept this commission?"

"I do, Queen Talis Darmon."

If anyone could manage the human lab experiment to dilute the bluster of the aristocratic council with the solvent of reason stored in the combined wisdoms of the many guilds and other repositories of brilliance in the kingdom, he was the man for the job.

And when there were obstacles, the queen would still be there as regent. Her Warlord by her side.

"I soon embark on a royal visit to every corner of Mihdradahl, so that all may receive my personal dispensation for this great work to begin.

"Banished is our fate to be that of a broken land, held together only by our common struggle to breathe, to avoid starvation, and fight off our subjugation at the hands of an enemy. We can be much more. A land free of fear, with true prosperity for all.

"Our best days lie ahead of us. Long live Mihdradahl. Long live her people. Long live our freedom.

I had my part. I doubted they'd be the last words I'd ever speak on her behalf, but if they were, I meant them to be good ones.

"Long live Queen Talis Darmon Sylah, mother of the future. The last regent of Mihdradahl."

✻ ✻ ✻

Of course it wasn't going smoothly! Nothing about Vistara is like a fairy tale.

These months since she dropped her bombshell of a speech were as painful as any skirmish I'd ever fought. More so because, like chopping off the head of the hydra, whatever conflict Talis Darmon resolved was replaced by two more. If we were getting any closer to her being able to step down, it didn't seem like it.

Karlo was philosophical about my gripes as our small group strolled the shipyard grounds. "We knew it wasn't going to be easy, Ben. By any accounting, it took a decade to ratify the US Constitution. Before that, a provisional government was running the colonies for an even longer period than that. Even after a war to throw off one king, a lot of people just wanted to appoint an American one. And that was in a country pretty dang close to being of one mind about things. Mihdradahl wasn't even thinking about a new form of government when she sprang this on them."

"I know, I know," I groaned.

Dave stopped in his tracks. "Brah, it's gonna to be a friggin' mess. You know what I learned from school? Democracy's the *worst* form of government—right after all the others. I think we were doing just fine with Talis Darmon."

Khraal Kahlees and Doug were in their own world as they contemplated the construction rising above the desert shipyard.

"We will still need cavalry, Douglas Knoblock. Arkall are without peer in their ability to strike fear into an enemy."

"Straight up, Double-K. A squadron or two of mounted cavalry, a couple of companies of light troops and armored reconnaissance vehicles, an air wing—we'll be an independent combat team."

Cynar scoffed. "It is for the purpose of discovery and diplomacy that the ship is designed, not a crude conveyance for dimwitted savages bent on conquest or piracy."

Cynar had been the one to bring the idea to us. When he saw the Aceylx-class ships, he'd said that if he'd been given the task, he would've designed something more elegant and efficient. And here it was. Though half the size of the surviving *Justice*, the materials salvaged from it were taking shape into something sleek and beautiful, yet massive enough to project a gravitas about its builders.

To me, the *Hope of Vistara*'s many decks sporting gun stations and flitter ports combined with the artistic lines of her hull to say, "We come in peace. Or else."

Talis Darmon wouldn't be abandoning her throne to go exploring anytime soon. Not until the new charter was hammered out by Perrin Halser's commission. She'd sworn to the participants she would be patient, but tempered that promise with the reminder that if needs be—if the commission dawdled too long in hopes this would blow over and things would stay the way they were—she could use her power to decree the structure for a new participatory government.

But that was a last resort. Instead, she dangled a carrot in front of the aristocrats of the council; they'd all be important voices in this new form of government as they'd all remain in the upper house of legislators.

And if her regency wasn't enough of a proverbial stick—ready to clout them on the nose for dragging their feet—then I was.

Warlord was a title I held in perpetuity, as was the power that went with it. The honorific hadn't been simply bestowed on me. It had been conferred by the supernatural guardian who first held the office, across a gulf of time wider than ancient Oceania. Not to mention, it couldn't be denied by even the most petulant of the aristocrats that I'd saved Mihdradahl's bacon a few times over, more or less.

As protector of Mihdradahl, I could use my powers to intervene in any matter endangering the kingdom, including internal politics. So, the elites agreed—existential problems would always need a solution greater than the threat. The hoity-toity never took a shine to me as one of their own. Even though I was married to their queen.

But it was nice to know that when push came to shove, they all knew who to turn to when the feces hit the blades of the oscillator.

And when the day finally came, Talis Darmon wouldn't surrender her title as queen, just her regency. Eventually. But when a charter was agreed on and Mihdradahl rose with it, the *Hope of Vistara* would rise as well, with Talis Darmon on her prow to lead us as ambassador. We could begin the task to discover what mysteries lay beyond our own shallow horizons. Vistara was a big world. It was our goal to make it smaller.

My wrist lit up. It was Beraal.

"Brother, come quickly. The time is at hand!"

We'd all been on edge for days that the moment was almost upon us. I'd sworn to not be more than minutes from home, and flying outside the city to the shipyard had been stretching my oath to the limit.

"Yikes! I'm on the way. C'mon, boy. Time to go!"

Apache was trying to dig a vereen out of a hole. Only his rear pair of legs and tail were visible. For all his mighty efforts, he'd never once snagged a rat from its warren. But like me, he knew that the only sure-fire way to fail was to quit. I'd eaten vereen. They weren't savory. But then again, I wasn't a gadron. They might taste as sweet as candy to Apache. We were out of MRE chili mac—and would be forever—so the eight-legged rats might just be the next best thing. He ignored my pleas to come, digging even deeper.

"I'll get him home, Ben-dog," Doug said. "You better fly, dude."

I only hoped Apache's stubborn persistence would pay off for him as sweetly as mine had. For everyone that kept getting up no matter how many times they were knocked down, I wished for them all even a fraction of the full heart my hopeful endurance had brought me.

Double-K raised sky hands and shooed me. "Be swift, clansman. I know little, but I know what human women demand of their mates. You best be gone. Go welcome your new warrior!"

Karlo and Dave slapped me on the back to boost my bound into the flitter, and I peeled away. I pushed the air car full out to reach the palace. I weaved and pitched between spires and beneath floating paths. Heads turned and hands shielded brows to see who dared bring back such commotion above the seat of a kingdom trying to rid itself of the memory of such strife.

Someday there'd be floating stoplights, billboards, traffic jams, and transit cops, and what I was doing now would get me arrested. And I'd tell my grandkids what it was like, back when Shansara was a hick town in the middle of a desert. Not the one they knew. The garden paradise of sprawling suburbs, the public lakes crowded with rowboats, parasols shading lovers from the sun as they floated the lazy day away, streets crowded by tourists and their cameras.

I wasn't even a dad just yet, and here I was daydreaming about grandchildren.

I burst through our bedroom and into the nursery where Talis Darmon and Beraal crowded over the open creche. I squeezed between them and we locked arms around each other's waists to watch the miracle. The egg vibrated, twisted, and the fine cracks in the porcelain grew. The shell parted and fell away, and the bluest eyes I'd ever seen met mine.

Suddenly, I knew the reason I'd been born.

My name is Deacon Benjamin Colt.

And there is only one Warlord of Mars.

ABOUT THE AUTHOR

DOC SPEARS IS A VETERAN OF THE UNITED STATES ARMY AND WORKS AS a consultant and trainer in the defense industry. Writing has been the worst vice he's found yet and doubts he'll be able to stop even with help, which he refuses to seek. When not offending the sensibilities of all decent peoples everywhere, he can be found with Nick Cole and Jason Anspach plotting to infiltrate all realms of sci-fiction.

To be notified about Doc's upcoming books, including the sequel to this title, visit www.WarGateBooks.com

"

www.ingramcontent.com/pod-product-compliance
Lightning Source LLC
Chambersburg PA
CBHW020530020726
47494CB00006B/1702